“With appeal to both young adult and adult audiences, this charming, inviting LGBTQ+ fantasy novel is set on the shores of a magical realm and tells a very human story about love, sacrifice, and self-discovery.”

— *Foreword Reviews*

“A delightfully queer and genderqueer romance set in an inventive fantasy world, *The Quicksand Theatre Company* has slow-burn yearning, magical bargains, joyful performance, and all kinds of drama. I loved it.”

— **Felicia Davin**
author of *The Scandalous Letters of V and J*

“A cozy delight wrapped up in a warm hug of a book! *The Quicksand Theatre Company* will sweep you into the found family you didn't know you needed.”

— **Jasmine Kuliasha**
author of *The Midnight Pack*

“*The Quicksand Theatre Company* is a book for this age, complete with election fraud, unbreakable contracts, and deadly prejudice. It explores ordinary people doing extraordinary, hard things that completely disrupt their lives. And it is the best love story I have read in a long while. The story, the characters, the romance, and the writing—just beautiful.”

— **Bianca M. Schwarz**
author of *The Innkeeper's Daughter*

“Seamlessly blends a unique magic system, complex family dynamics, a poignant romance, the everyday chaos of a traveling theatre company, and wonderful queer characters. The result is a story that's as vibrant as it is compelling.”

— **Jamie Deacon**
author of *The Music of Unexpected Things* and
the *Boys on the Brink* series

2026

Content Warnings:

Abduction, anxiety, betrayal, grief, family deaths (in past), imprisonment/ confinement, injuries, mental and physical damage caused by magic, murder, sexual content (consensual), suicidal ideation.

Cover Design: Coral Black
Map design: Annie O'Quinn

Published by Central Avenue, an imprint of Central Avenue Marketing Ltd.
centralavenuepublishing.com

Printed in United States of America

1. FICTION/Fairy Tales 2. FICTION/LGBTQ+

THE QUICKSAND THEATRE COMPANY

978-1-77168-442-2 (pbk)
978-1-77168-443-9 (ebk)

1 3 5 7 9 10 8 6 4 2

For the whistleblowers, the comedians, and the lovers.
The world needs all of you very much.

EIDOLONIA
Highway
Forest
Mountains
Town
Desert
Sea
Bridge
Fae Realm
Serpentshore
Port Baleia
Città del Tesoro
KAGAMI LAGOON
KIKENNA BAY
Kagami
Amizade Bridge
PUNTA ROSA
Bahía Rosa
PITCHSTONE MOUNTAIN
Delta Esmeralda
Sevinee
Amanecer
Dasdemir
Amaris Town
Miryoku

PRONUNCIATION NOTE

Eidolonia's humans come, ancestrally, from a wide variety of countries, a mix that is reflected in personal names and geographic names. Names derived from non-English languages are pronounced more or less in that language's fashion.

The letter combination "ch" in Italian is pronounced like English "k"—thus "Delvecchio" = "del-VEK-ee-oh." And in Italian, "c" followed by "e" or "i" is pronounced like English "ch"—thus "Città" = "chee-TAH" (stress on second syllable), and "Marcello" = "mar-CHELL-o." Otherwise, Italian consonants are similar to English's, and Italian vowels are pronounced nearly the same as Spanish vowels. "Vai" rhymes with "my."

"Javier" should be pronounced in more or less the Spanish way, with an English "h" sound for the "j."

The Chinese sound transliterated as "x" doesn't have an exact match in English, but "sh" is closest. "Xian" is roughly "shyen," one syllable.

Names native to Eidolonia, such as names of fae, follow a more phonetically transparent pattern, from the English-spelling point of view. Your best guess at how to pronounce "Melu Ros" or "Nalibak" is probably pretty close to the way I've been saying them. None of us humans are pronouncing the fae tongue correctly anyway.

This page is part of the Eidolonian Intranet: protected by fae spells and certified Unhackable Crosswater by Eidolonian witches. Welcome!

Eidolonia

Eidolonia is an island country in the north Pacific Ocean, consisting of one large main landmass and more than one hundred smaller islands. Only about one-sixth of this area is inhabited by humans, nearly all of it along the main island's coast, the rest being fae territory.

The country has no close neighbors, lying roughly equidistant from Hawaii, the Aleutian Islands, and Japan. Its climate is temperate. Eidolonia is a constitutional monarchy, with a royal family as well as a prime minister and other democratically elected officials.

Eidolonia was entirely fae territory until the early 1700s, when the fae allowed a few sailors from various countries to find the island. They permitted a limited number of additional human immigrants over ensuing years, making deals to allow human settlements, which gradually grew to encompass the entire coastline. Eidolonia is undetectable to outsiders (crosswaters) due to concealment spells maintained by the fae, and humans who leave the island will not remember it, with false memories taking its place, unless they carry a memory charm, enspelled by witches and fae, that preserves their knowledge of the country.

An estimated two-thirds of Eidolonian humans have some fae ancestry due to intermixing. Approximately half of humans on Eidolonia, regardless of ancestry, are born with witch abilities, being matter-witches (able to manipulate inanimate matter), exo-witches (able to manipulate other living things), or endo-witches (able to manipulate their own forms). The magical powers of the fae, in nearly all cases, are stronger than those of witches.

The verge, the border between fae and human territory, underwent select alterations in 2020 to revert certain parcels of land to the fae but otherwise has not changed since its previous adjustment in 1799. Since then, occasional crime between fae and humans has still occurred, but at a low rate. Entering fae territory, however, remains significantly dangerous for humans.

Fair Feasters

Fair feasters are a type of fae who feed on the energy, emotions, and blood of mortal creatures. Their name comes from the human term "fair folk," an antiquated euphemism for fae in general. Fair feasters are unusual among fae in that they do not belong to any of the four elements, and also in that they are able to lie. To lure victims, they frequently wear an attractive glamour, though their true appearance is pale and corpselike. They abhor sunlight and other bright light, fire, the flowers of St. John's wort, and crowds, preferring to stay in darkness with no more than one other companion at a time. Though these conditions make it reasonably easy for humans to avoid or ward off fair feasters, these fae are still considered one of the most dangerous types in Eidolonia.

THE QUICKSAND THEATRE COMPANY

CHAPTER 1

VAI

I had my bag packed by the time Kwal's footsteps came down the corridor. Night had fallen, but I hadn't turned on a light. I sat on my bed, chilled and scared, wearing my shoes and coat, the zipped-up bag on my lap.

Kwal appeared in my doorway. "Vai," he said, soft and heavy.

I gave him a vague nod in greeting.

Kwal glanced around the dim room, then set himself to glowing, the pale green of bioluminescent fungi. He was a hob, a type of earth faery, stout and bulbous and four feet tall, and as familiar to me as my closest relatives. Dressed in his usual wrinkle-free sleeveless black kimono, the glow radiating from his bare arms and feet and head, he regarded me gravely.

"I'm sorry to put you in this position," I said.

"I understand why you did it. I even approve. But I'm bound to fulfill the deal."

I hugged the bag tighter. "Have you been to them all?"

Soft taps filled the silence, accelerating into a patter: raindrops hitting my windows. "I have, yes."

"So." I knew the next step, but I felt weak, immobile.

"You'd better go." Kwal sounded sorrowful. "Your mother will be home in twenty minutes, maybe sooner."

I roused my strength and stood, slinging the bag over my shoulder.

"Is there anything more you'd like to bring?" Kwal asked.

"Just this. I want to travel light."

Travel. Was that the word for what I'd be doing? I supposed so, if things went according to plan. My insides spiraled in anxiety as if I were falling.

"Where will you go?" Kwal asked as we walked down the corridor.

I tried not to look at each room we passed, each plant, each staircase, each framed picture, and not think about how it was the last time I'd see them in a year or more. Possibly the last time I would ever be in this house.

"I asked someone about a job," I said. "It would take me other places, around the island."

"Will you let me know when you're settled? I can't help you—I'm bound to that condition. But I would wish to know you're well."

"I will." We crossed the shining stone tiles of the foyer, and he opened the front door for me. The smell of rain on fallen leaves swept in. Bare branches, silhouetted against the twilight, raked the sky in a cold wind.

It was early November; Lord Festival was wrapping up. Any traveling festival performers would be moving on from our city tomorrow morning.

"Where you're going," Kwal said as I opened an umbrella, "is it somewhere you'll be safe?"

The lights lining our front walk gleamed in reflection on the wet pavers, beckoning me outward, like the foot-level aisle lights in a theatre.

"I'm not sure," I said. "But it's somewhere I wouldn't have the courage to go, if it weren't for this."

~

The caravans of the Quicksand Theatre Company stood in a ring on packed dirt and grass in Merrilo Park. Their windows made rectangles of light gleaming through the rain. Beats of music trailed from some. I counted thirteen vehicles in total, the biggest being two buses, the rest being trucks and caravans.

"Go to the one you'd most want to stay in and start asking there," the person had said two nights ago, when I'd asked about jobs. They'd been standing near the stage in the park, giving swift orders to performers going on and off, so I assumed them to be someone of authority in the troupe.

A few people hung around, sharing joints, laughing, wrapping their scarves tighter against the drizzle. They looked like fans, hopeful and nervous, not like folk who lived with the company. I ignored them and trudged along until reaching the caravan labeled LEONIDAS THE OBSTREPEROUS in winding yellow capitals.

The one you'd most want to stay in.

I studied it, umbrella held over me, rain dripping from its tips.

This might be a celebrity crush. I acknowledged that. A thrill did kick through me whenever Leonidas, bowing from stage, swept his black-lined eyes across the audience and—I could have sworn—gave each of us our own personal smile as a thank-you gift. But he didn't know who I was, and I didn't truly know who he was. That fact stood at the center of my focus. Besides, he probably didn't count as a celebrity. Most Eidolonians were familiar with the Quicksand Theatre Company, but fewer could tell you the names of any performers in it.

What I mainly wanted was to understand. This feeling that came alive in me when he performed—every jubilant laugh, every despairing collapse to his knees, every salacious line—what was it? Why him more than other performers? How did he do it? What was it like to be him, and live in this thirty-foot-long teal-and-yellow vintage mobile home, and tour the country ceaselessly with the troupe?

These were questions I would never have had the courage to set out and explore with my family's eyes still on me. But as of tonight, under Kwal's spell, my family members didn't know I existed and wouldn't remember for another year. I needed somewhere else to be, something to do. So here I was, with my packed bag and a fluttering, undefined yearning in my heart.

I knocked on the lime-green door. If Leonidas had no use for me, which was entirely likely, I'd try one other caravan. Whichever looked friendliest. If that failed too, I'd catch the late train to Port Baleia, or Bahía Rosa. Or even pay a taxi to take me, despite the exorbitant cost of such a long ride. I just wanted to be far enough from Tesoro to avoid most of the fallout from the scandal.

No one answered. I knocked again. Raindrops ran steadily down the painted letters.

I should try another caravan. Or give up and take the train—no one in the theatre troupe was expecting me, nor did they need me. My feet, however, would not budge. *Please,* I thought with all my might toward the green door.

When no one answered my third knock, I waited ten more seconds, then set my hand on the door latch. I sensed spells on the vehicle—mainly against malicious fae or other harm-doers, but nothing I couldn't get past. A tiny push of magic was all it took. The latch opened. I folded my umbrella and stepped up into the caravan.

The interior was quiet, with only a Turkish lamp on, hanging from the ceiling at the front end, throwing a soft glow through its glass mosaic. I shut the door and turned slowly in a circle, taking in the crammed-tight chaos of gilt, velvet, colors, and small compartments. The tiny kitchen was in the front, just behind the driver's seat. Flanking the central and only corridor, where I stood, were a couple of additional seats, jammed between cupboards and cabinets. The bathroom had a garish sunflower mural painted on its open door, and when I poked my head in, I found it smaller than any I had ever seen, a broom closet with water pipes. Past that were more cupboards and another seat. And across the caravan's back end hung a purple velvet curtain, probably concealing a bed. It was the likeliest place for Leonidas to be, if he was here.

I didn't dare approach it. "Hello?" I said, not very loudly.

Still no answer.

The rain rattled louder against the metal roof. My soul recoiled at the thought of going back out into that. Leonidas couldn't blame me for waiting until the worst of the storm passed. He probably wasn't even here. It was almost ten o'clock, but theatre people were often out late. Or so I'd heard. I would do no harm; I'd just sit quietly.

A skinny alcove by the door seemed to be a coat closet. I set my wet shoes there, beside a pair of mid-calf black leather boots with multiple sets of buckles. Above them hung a long black coat with more silver buttons than was practical, its silky red lining worn to shreds in spots. Coat and boots both held a lived-in type of wearing. I could see the shape of Leonidas's calves and forearms in the warp of the materials.

Still wearing my damp overcoat, I took one of the seats farther from the purple curtain and set my bag down. Warmth seeped pleasantly into my chilled socks. Leonidas apparently had heated floors. Settling back to wait, I took a deep breath and caught a hint of powdery cosmetics and the dusty-wood scent of theatres. It reminded me of my mother, a sensation both comforting and poignant.

The windows had teal curtains with gold tassels, drawn back, though I couldn't see much in the rainy night. Someone with light-colored hair strode past outside. A moment later, the driver's door opened and shut, sending a thump through my side of the vehicle. Heart pounding, I leaned forward to look up the corridor.

The driver was visible in profile under the dome light as they leaned to check something on the dashboard. It was the light-haired person, with pale skin and almost invisible eyebrows. Not Leonidas.

I opened my mouth, then shut it. If the person looked back and saw me, I'd speak up. If not, I was allowed to just sit here, ride to the next city. That was the rule I decided on.

The driver faced forward again. The dome light switched off. The engine started up with a grumbling roar, making the caravan vibrate.

When I leaned back into my seat, I couldn't see the driver's rearview mirror, so they couldn't see me. I glanced toward what I assumed to be Leonidas's alcove, but he didn't emerge from his curtain. Perhaps he was riding with someone else. How should I know?

I was trembling. Somehow I had gone from loyal family member to whistleblower to stowaway, in less than twelve hours. I'd become something bizarrely unlike my usual self. I really should alert the driver to my presence.

But. Going out into the cold rain. Trudging to a hotel not even a twenty-minute drive from my house. Or dragging myself to the train station and finding a hotel in a different city, at an even later hour, all the while wondering wistfully what might have happened if I'd stayed with the Quicksand Theatre Company, my only appealing escape plan—my one selfish goal, after having sacrificed so much of my life for the greater good.

I peeled off my damp coat and draped it around my front like a blanket. If stealing this ride made me outlandish, well, it had already been a day of outlandish things for me anyway.

We bumped forward over the grass, wheeling in an arc. The tires thumped onto pavement, and with a bass growl, we picked up speed.

Dark road curving, climbing. A couple of other caravans trundling along behind us, aglow with lights. Flashes of manicured landscaping and gated driveways. Then a half-minute of a view that made my heart ache: the skyline of Città del Tesoro, my hometown, glowing at the base of the hills, Art Deco buildings lit in warm whites, pale yellows, and watery blues.

Before I could locate our house on Argento Hill, roadside trees swept into my field of vision, and the city was gone. After a slope down, we joined the Great Eidolonian Highway. Since I was on the vehicle's left side, and outside my window was the sea rather than hills, we had to be going south. That matched what I had looked up—Quicksand's next performance was on Punta Rosa.

It was no use wondering *Did I do the right thing?*, because it was done, right or not. Instead I tried to acclimate to my separation from my family. Though I was thirty-one, I had lived in my parents' house until tonight—mainly because the house was so large that it'd be a waste of space not to. I'd had several rooms to myself, adjoining the garden, and could easily go a whole day without seeing anyone.

The house had often felt vast and lonely. I had set up folding screens around my desk, and around my bed, for coziness. Maybe that had been part of what drew me to the idea of a caravan. I wanted to tuck myself into a small space, drive it around the country, change the view outside my windows.

Tonight, having snuck into exactly such a caravan, the nomadic life struck me as unsettling. My family consumed my mind. My older sister, Daphne, in her downtown apartment. My mother at home with Kwal and perhaps a visiting friend to comfort her. My father and uncle almost certainly out on bail but warned not to leave the city as they awaited trial. All of them in a firestorm of stress. None remembering who I was nor knowing I had been the one who struck the match.

And I had fled to the sparkly junk drawer that was the caravan of Leonidas of the Quicksand Theatre Company. Without, so far, his knowledge.

I didn't know what he and the driver would do when they discovered me. I didn't know if the troupe would have any use for me. And I wasn't allowed to know the details of the devastation I had left behind in my family.

I resigned myself to, first, probably not getting any sleep tonight, and second, not knowing much about anything I was doing anymore, for the next year, starting now.

CHAPTER 2

VAI

"They're not a friend of yours?"

"I've never seen this person before. I would've asked you before allowing someone to stay."

"Then where'd they come from?"

Sleep had not only arrived despite my expectations, but had crushed me under its weight. I struggled to open my eyelids, and finally succeeded.

Daylight. The caravan was parked. Two people were peering at me. One, the pale driver. The other, Leonidas.

At the moment he didn't resemble the gleaming, colorful person I had admired on stage. He wore no makeup, morning scruff darkened his jaw, his black hair was a chaotic nest, and he had on plaid shorts and a gray sweatshirt with the sleeves ripped off. He lolled on the seat across from me, arms folded, cell phone in one hand.

"Hi!" he said with a theatrical type of brightness. "Who the hell are you?"

"I'm—I'm sorry." I shoved upright from the slump I'd fallen into, cringing at the crick in my neck. "My name is Vai Delvecchio. I go by 'they.' I...didn't mean to fall asleep."

"Leo, Wayshaw." Leonidas—Leo?—pointed respectively to himself, then to the slim, pale person. "He, she. Fantastic to meet you. You're in my caravan because?"

"I knocked," I promised. "Last night, in Tesoro. No one answered, so I came in, but then...it started driving away." I was trembling. This was not how I had envisioned introducing myself to Leonidas.

The driver, Wayshaw, looked calmly at Leo. "You didn't hear them knock?"

"I took one of Ayda's sleep-like-the-dead herbs. I wasn't going to hear a damn thing till morning. *You* didn't hear them?"

"I must have been outside, readying the caravan to leave."

"So you just sat there silently, getting a free ride to Punta Rosa," Leo said to me.

With a meek nod, I patted back my hair, some of which had stuck to my cheek overnight. "That wasn't my plan. I was going to ask if I could work for the troupe. For free. Or rather, in exchange for lodging in the caravan. If there's room."

He tilted his head toward the coat closet. "And why would a person with Magnanni shoes and what appears to be a genuine fucking Prada raincoat"—his glance flicked to my coat—"want to live in this rattletrap?"

I curled my hand self-consciously around my coat collar. It had folded back as I slept, displaying the label.

They might as well know. They'd hear soon enough anyway, if they paid any attention to the news. "I found out some of my family members were aiding a politician in illegal activities, and I blew the whistle on them," I said. "So I need a new job. Preferably outside of Tesoro."

Leo's expression went blank. "Which politician?"

"Walda Portnoff. Parliamentary representative for the greater Tesoro area."

"You're helping bring down Walda Portnoff?"

"It...appears so."

Leo swiped a finger along his scruffy jaw. "Huh. May she crash hard, swiftly, and in flames. Okay. You can stay for the day and see what you think. Audition when you're ready."

"No, no." My arm twitched, sending the coat slithering down my shins. "I don't want to act. I'm...not a comedian, I'd be no good. I'm a matter-witch. I can do backstage work, keep things secure, or clean, or repaired."

Leo glanced at Wayshaw, who shrugged. She was probably a faery in human form, to judge from the symmetrical face, pearly-smooth skin, and webbing between her fingers. "Troupe can always use that," she remarked.

"Matter-witch," Leo said. "*That's* how you got in."

"Security is one of my specialties," I admitted.

"All right. Whatever. Splendid." Leo rose and reached to a compartment above his seat. A twist of a handle, and the door folded down to reveal a flower-patterned mattress. A loft bed. "Yours for the time being if you want it."

I looked at Wayshaw. "It isn't yours?"

She looked mildly puzzled. "I'm fae. I don't sleep."

"Wayshaw dives into the nocturnal waters while the rest of us slumber," Leo informed me. "Nor does she share my bed, for we are just friends."

"I'm not the slightest bit interested," Wayshaw agreed.

"So no one's used this in a while." Leo waved to the bunk.

I decided not to ask any further questions. They were being more generous than I had any right to expect. "Thank you. That will do fine."

Leo thumbed at his phone screen. "I took a picture of you while you were asleep and sent it around to the company to see if anyone recognized you. They didn't, but a few people said you're hot, and they'll take you if I don't want you. So. You already have options."

Wayshaw left to return to the ocean. Leo showered, put on his long black coat and boots, and told me, "If you're planning to steal the caravan, be warned it's a beast to drive. Good luck!" He went out as well.

I tottered into the kitchen for a drink of water and looked out the nearest window. Punta Rosa may have been mostly a scrub-covered piece of rock sticking into the sea, but any ocean vista is a stirring sight, and this point was particularly dramatic. Whitecaps crashed against the shore. Sea stacks dotted the ocean, foam ruffling white against their bases. Cliffs marched away, vanishing in the mist. Against this backdrop, Leo stalked like a Brontëan hero, coat flapping amid brown salt-grass. He descended below a line of boulders, and I lost sight of him.

The kitchen, meanwhile, was less inspiring. Tiny sink, stove, fridge, cupboards, all in need of cleaning, with counter space so minuscule it seemed impossible to prepare any significant quantity of food. People lived like this?

I caught that thought, labeled it snobbery or perhaps elitism, and reminded myself I didn't get to invade someone's home and then judge everything in it.

I took stock of the kitchen supplies. The corner cupboard didn't have much food, nor did the fridge. I might as well take the initiative and be a generous guest—or volunteer worker, whichever I was—by buying breakfast.

From my phone's map I learned we were in Nopal Park, and the nearby town, Bahía Rosa, had an online grocery that could deliver here. My order arrived within half an hour, carried by a sylph. By then I had taken a five-minute shower in a stall so tiny it felt like being squeezed inside a wet sock, shaved to keep my face smooth, expelled water from my hair with magic, and put on a touch of plum eyeliner. Although Leo had not asked me to clean anything, he hadn't forbidden it either, so I gave a touch of magic to the discolored toilet bowl, soap-spotted sink, and smudgy mirror.

I hadn't packed many clothes. The blue-gray cashmere sweater I'd worn yesterday was my favorite, so I cleaned it with a skimming of magic and put it back on, along with yesterday's gray jeans.

I made tea, a dish of sliced Asian pears, and a pot of sweetened congee with chopped peanuts. Jammed into the kitchen window frame was a card with a composite of the faces of what looked to be everyone in the troupe, each making an absurd expression. I plucked it out. The inside was covered with signatures. A lot of *Happy birthday, Leo!* and similar messages. One said *35! You'll have to impart to me some of your ancient wisdom. xoxo, Fred.*

I put the card back. Assuming this birthday was recent, Leonidas was four years older than me. He also seemed to go by "Leo" to everybody. Perhaps "Leonidas" was just for playbills and the sides of caravans.

As I ladled congee into a bowl, he returned. I swallowed hard enough to feel a click in my throat. After leaving his boots and coat in the closet, he came into the kitchen, blowing on his knuckles to warm them.

I lifted the tin of Mao Jian. "Tea?"

He squinted at it. "Hmm. Not enough caffeine. I'll make coffee."

Having found a near-empty bag of dark-roast beans in the pantry, I had forecast this possibility and put coffee in my grocery order too. I held out the new bag.

Leo took it, unrolled the top, and sniffed. The furrow left his forehead. He hummed a note in interest. The kitchen table was a slab sticking out from the wall with two chairs under it. I took my tea and congee there to give him room at the stove to brew coffee. He did so, his movements precise. Now that he was properly awake and put together, I could see I hadn't been mistaken about his attractiveness. I couldn't decide which feature I liked best: his eyes, bold and striking even without eyeliner, or his full and mobile mouth.

With his mug, he sat opposite me. His legs were long, like mine, and as he swung them under the table our knees knocked together. Sipping coffee, bundled in an oversized red-and-black-striped sweater, he watched me as if I was auditioning. Which I supposed I was, in a sense.

"Vai," he said, elongating the word as if trying out its taste.

"Leo," I said in return.

His mouth quirked up in amusement. He plucked out a pear slice from the dish and ate it. "You're very quiet, compared to most who sneak into our caravans."

"I am quiet generally."

"You really just wanted to get out of Tesoro."

"I did."

"Then…you're not looking for a hookup? I'm not, either. Just figured we should establish that."

I shook my head swiftly. Celebrity crush notwithstanding, seducing him had not been my goal. "No. I'm just…curious about the troupe."

"And now that you've seen how unsophisticated it is"—he took another pear slice and waved it in a circle to refer to the caravan or possibly the whole troupe—"are you planning on hopping off in Bahía Rosa?"

"You seem to have heated floors. That's at least somewhat sophisticated."

He snorted a laugh and ate the pear.

"But," I added, "I'll get off in Bahía Rosa if you prefer. Feel free to have some congee."

Leo studied me. "Why Quicksand? Why my caravan?"

I set my spoon down as I assembled my answer. "I've seen Quicksand perform every time you've come to Tesoro for the last seven years. I always find you one of the most interesting actors. I rarely perform at all, except with festival groups, like everyone, and it seems incredibly brave to me. At your performance last Tuesday, someone I was with said, 'The likes of you and I could never be like that, could we.' And that's when I knew. This is where I would go, when I reported my family."

Leo leaned back, cradling his mug. "You wanted to prove that person wrong."

"He doesn't know where I am, so not that, really." Although in my own heart, yes, that. "But I wanted to learn what it's like. To travel with you all. Work on performances."

He hummed in acceptance, squinted out the window, and downed the rest of his coffee. Then he got up and scooped congee into a bowl. He grabbed cinnamon out of a drawer, scattered some in, and stirred it. Wandering past the table, he ate a bite.

Since he seemed about to leave without another word, I said, "Leo."

He turned expectantly, sucking on the spoon.

"Why didn't you kick me out when you found me?" I asked.

He ate another spoonful. "You don't look particularly dangerous. If anything, you looked like you needed protecting. But mainly, I detest Walda Portnoff, so if you're getting her arrested, I approve of you."

"Fair. Thank you."

"Your story's intriguing," he added. "Not that I know much of it." He looked me in the eyes, and I could hear the unspoken word: *Yet*.

I lowered my gaze. "It's all still unfolding. I'm sure everyone will hear eventually."

"This congee is actually *good*. I don't even like congee usually. Did you use magic on it?"

"Only a little, to ensure the right texture. I like things to be done correctly."

"Stay a while if you want. Use your skills to make things more correct around here." With a nod, he spooned more congee into his mouth and walked off with his bowl.

When Wayshaw returned, she inspected the pantry, then the fridge. "You obtained groceries?"

I rinsed the pot in the sink. "I took the liberty, yes."

"These foods look healthful. Best of luck in getting Leo to eat them."

"He did eat some congee and said he liked it."

"I did eat it and liked it!" Leo shouted from the other end of the caravan.

We ignored him.

"Were you swimming?" I guessed. Not because she was wet—she did not appear to be—but because swimming seemed a likely activity for a water faery at the ocean.

"Yes. Visiting some of my folk."

"Which do you belong to?" When a faery took human form, you couldn't always tell what they might be in their original state. Wayshaw looked like a person with neat, short sand-colored hair and an immaculate gray suit.

"I'm of the merfolk," she said. "And your people?"

"We're from Tesoro. If you mean my ancestors, the largest portions in my mix are Italian and Chinese. One great-grandparent was an air faery."

That ancestor had been the inspiration for the name of our family business, Airtight Spells. A name that was probably all over the news today.

My stomach whirled as if I had stepped off a high-dive. I hadn't dared look online yet, but it was time. With a flick of magic I expelled the water from the damp dishtowel into the sink and murmured that I was going for a walk.

Leo was leaning against a cupboard, tapping at his phone. As I put on my coat and shoes, he slid his glance to me. Veiled, unreadable. Perhaps looking me up online. Finding my family in the news.

Couldn't blame him. I was about to do the same. I nodded to him and went out.

CHAPTER 3

LEO

Did I run a search on Vai's name and the word "whistleblower" in Tesoro's local news, two minutes after leaving this stranger alone in my caravan? Of course. Who wouldn't wonder at such an apparition?

This Vai. With forlorn rosebud lips and sleek bobbed hair and a designer wardrobe. Why did they choose my caravan as an escape pod, and what did they intend to do at Quicksand? My news search couldn't answer that, but it did back up their story.

Airtight Spells Owners Arrested. A man and his brother—Marcello and Giovanni Delvecchio—were charged with bribery and money laundering, having allegedly aided Member of Parliament Walda Portnoff in committing electoral fraud and the covering up thereof.

The charges didn't surprise me. Politicians and rich businesspeople were always miring themselves in shit like that. But I felt a pang for Vai, who seemed honestly shaken.

The article went on to report that Airtight Spells had operated for over thirty years with a pristine reputation till now. They were matter-witches specializing in document security: making things unreadable to anyone except the client. Good deal if you were paranoid about your personal info—or if you were committing crimes.

Stupid, the things people will do for money. There are so many better reasons to do stupid things.

The article said a whistleblower—name withheld per protection law, but presumably Vai—had discovered the contents of Portnoff's documents and reported them to the authorities.

Being the innocent in a rich family who had fucked up and landed themselves in handcuffs: was that better or worse than being the fuckup in a well-behaved middle-class family, like me? Hard to say.

I did know, however, that I abominated Walda Portnoff. Execrated her. She was a member of the unctuously named Humanist Party, which stood, supposedly, for the protection of innocent humans. But Portnoff called fae "glowing lumps of slime" who should be sent back to "the volcanic crevices they slithered out of."

She had called ordinary witches, who made up half the human populace, "toxic dangers, disasters waiting to happen." As a witch myself, I was a disaster who was constantly already happening, thank you very much, but I wouldn't slap that label on my magical friends.

And regarding the fae territory encompassing the entire interior of the island, Portnoff was in favor of pushing back the verge to gain more land for humans. Which was not just stupid but apocalyptic.

I had solid reasons to resent certain of the fae. But this rhetoric was psychotic. To hear the Humanist Party tell it, Eidolonian humans had been languishing in oubliettes, getting whipped by fae and witches, for the last three hundred years, rather than essentially flourishing and mixing with our fae friends just fine.

Lately, scads of Humanist Party members had been arrested. But since their crimes were often concealed via artful magic (oh, the hypocrisy), it was taking the law a while to ferret all of them out. So if Vai Delvecchio was a voluntary instrument in Portnoff's downfall, then Vai was welcome in my caravan.

Having verified that, I put down my phone, lifted my sweater, and examined my newest tattoo, stinging as it healed under its enchanted clear bandage. A chain of stars, points touching, meandered from the red footbridge on my shoulder to the inkwell-and-quill above my hipbone, linking them up. Another step in my plan to save myself. And if this and the other tricks in my bag didn't work…

Well, at least my friends would see I had tried.

VAI

Kwal's spell affected only my parents, sister, and uncle. Everyone else still knew who I was. Therefore my phone had accumulated a storm of text messages—innocent clients, a neighbor, a friend from college, a cousin—all asking some form of *What's going on, Vai?*

As I trudged down the beach, I copied and pasted the same wording to each: I myself was not being charged, but otherwise I shouldn't talk about it yet, and Kwal could answer anything business related. I ignored their responses—frustration from the clients, consolation from everyone else—and checked in with Kwal.

I have a safe place to stay for now, I texted. *Are the lawyers and investigators dealing with everyone who's asking the family about me?*

Yes, Kwal answered after a few minutes. *They know about the spell. Where possible, I'm answering people's messages to your family myself to explain it. I expect word will get out soon and they will cease to bother you or ask after you.*

I pictured texts piling up on my sister's phone, and our parents' and uncle's, asking *Was Vai the whistleblower?* And my family members' minds failing to latch on to the question, sliding away, moving to the next of their concerns. Not even wondering what my name meant.

I thanked Kwal, braced myself, then went online and found the article. My chest squeezed tight as I read it, hunched on a driftwood log. Dad and Uncle Joe were out on bail, and their lawyer was not issuing comments at this time. June Xian (Mom) and Daphne Xian (my sister), though they had never been employed at Airtight, had agreed to be questioned under a truth spell and were found to have no knowledge of the illegal activity.

I released a breath of relief. I hadn't been sure.

Walda Portnoff, meanwhile, had been arrested. So at least I had accomplished my central goal.

I dared look at the comments on the article for half a minute.

The first: *Shocking. Such a respected family.*

Second: *Politics in this country has gotten disgusting. Now even the Delvecchios are sullying themselves. It's enough to make me want to move out of this province.*

Third: *I went to school with Daphne and her sibling. She was always sweet. I assume it's the sib who was the whistleblower. Talk about a rule follower. Ice chips wouldn't melt in that kid's mouth.*

I shut the browser and took careful breaths of ocean wind until I no longer felt like I might throw up. Then I walked down the beach until I could only see the troupe's vehicles as tiny blocks of faraway color. By the time I came back, my cheeks and fingers felt raw with the November wind.

Pausing outside Leo's caravan, I touched the exterior. The yellow paint was rough with texture: dried St. John's wort flowers, hundreds of them encased in the pigment. It was common sense on Eidolonia to carry the flower, dried or fresh, if walking alone at night. They repelled fair feasters. There had been a couple of deaths recently, people found lifeless next to the verge, drained of energy and also some of their blood, in the telltale manner of a fair feaster attack. If you stayed in cities, among lights and crowds, you weren't in danger of falling prey to them. But I supposed caravan owners, who often parked overnight in dark, rural locations like this one, would have incentive to ward them off.

I knocked on the caravan's door.

Leo let me in. "Vai Delvecchio," he said. "Nice walk?"

I nodded. In the wake of that article, I didn't feel up to further discussion.

"Matter-witches always have plenty to do around the troupe," he added after a few seconds of silence. "I can show you around, get you started with a task or two."

It was much kinder than interrogating me. And since I couldn't very well answer, *I'd rather just lie in your caravan and stare at the wall for a while if that's all right,* I nodded. "Thank you."

More people were out of their caravans now that it was midday. Some sat on the steps of their vehicles, sipping from mugs, while others rehearsed lines or assembled what I assumed to be set pieces. Leo sauntered down the row with me, rattling off names. Some I recognized from Quicksand's programs, but he listed too many for my tired memory to retain this morning.

Costume department was a bus festooned with rhinestones. Props and scenery was a box truck decorated with a pink-and-black geometric pattern. Lighting and effects was a bus painted with green sea serpents, and apparently was also the abode of the actor Shelini Saru—one of the names I recognized—and her fire-faery lover.

"Ideal to have a fire faery to help with lights and explosions, if you can get one," Leo remarked.

"How many people are in the troupe?" I asked.

"Twenty-five at the moment. Eighteen humans, six fae. Handful of others, here and there, who join sometimes for a season, then hop off again."

"How many of the humans are witches?"

Leo tallied on his fingers, his gaze flicking down the crescent of caravans. "Ten. Exo-witches like me are overrepresented. There are five of us. Only three matter-witches, though, so you'll be valuable. For the whole day or two you can put up with us."

"Surely it's a matter of how long you can put up with *me*."

"Ha. It would take effort on your part to be more insufferable than the average person here. You'll see."

"Then I'll start by asking the costume manager for tasks. When do you have dinner? I'll cook something."

"Oh, you don't have to," he said. "I usually just heat up a pack of ramen."

I gazed at him for several seconds. *Don't judge,* I reminded myself again. Nonetheless, my mouth stepped ahead of me and said, "I will cook something better than a pack of ramen."

Leo burst into laughter and swung his long coat so the hem swatted me. "The disdain! Your face! All right then, seven o'clock, how's that?"

Leo introduced me to Mathilde, the costume monarch, then left with some others to prepare the venue in Bahía Rosa. Mathilde was about my mother's age but otherwise different from her in nearly every aspect: stout instead of willowy, hair messy and purple instead of arranged in a silver chignon, flannel shirt and work jeans instead of Chanel.

Mathilde dumped a pile of mud-splattered costumes into my arms and requested that I clean them. I recognized the clothes from the performance in the park a few nights earlier. Sitting on a padded bench in her bus, I expelled the mud, sweat, and grime from the first five costumes, then brought them to her.

She lifted her head from the lime-green dress whose stitches she was letting out and held one of the costumes into the light. "Nice. Full dry-clean. Didn't even fade the colors."

"Preservation was one of my tasks at my previous job."

"Do the whole stack if you have the energy. Then hang 'em on the end of that rack, would you?"

As I got to work de-mudding a gown in marigold shades of red and yellow, I asked, "Is the venue outdoors here too?"

"Nope." She tapped her fingertips along the dress's edge, creating a new hem without a needle. A matter-witch, then, like me. "We get a theatre here, thank gods. In frickin' November, it's much better than performing in rain and mud."

Recalling the performers who had done handsprings down the center aisle—thus the costumes with mud on the arms as well as the legs—I asked Mathilde how many could do gymnastics. "Just four," she said. "Kornelia, Fred, Xiu, Maki. Everyone associates Quicksand with the tumblers, but most of us can't do that shit and would rather not break our wrists trying."

Since she'd said "us," I asked whether everyone performed, even the people—like her—who specialized in backstage tasks.

"Oh sure. At least sometimes. They always need extras. We get roped in."

I wondered how long I could avoid being put on stage. Maybe someday I'd be interested, but my bravery was absolutely tapped for this month.

I grew tired pouring energy into the costumes. They were larger than the documents I'd usually worked with at Airtight, and there were lots. Eventually Mathilde noticed me yawning and sent me off to rest. I returned to Leo's caravan, found it unlocked but empty, and climbed up to my bunk. There I discovered that the loft bed seemed sized for a child, or possibly a gnome. As I'm six feet tall, I had to draw up my knees in order to fit my legs, and when lying on my back, that brought them almost in contact with the vehicle's ceiling. Which was painted shiny gold. In part despair and part amusement, I turned onto my side, knees bent. It was comfortable enough, and I was exhausted enough, to fall asleep that way.

I dozed for forty-five minutes, having set a timer on my phone to awaken me. Any longer than that and I would damage my ability to sleep tonight.

By six o'clock it was getting dark and the rain was tapping again on the caravan's roof. Gusts of wind made the vehicle shudder. I got to work cooking a risotto. It was an easy dish, not actually much more complex than a pack of ramen, but healthier and tastier. The smell of the saffron, white wine, and mushrooms made my heart ache. Daphne and Uncle Joe teased each other in my memory, joking about which of them cooked Italian food better.

My appetite waned. Nonetheless, I opened a loaf of bread and put together a side salad of greens with sliced fennel bulb and orange. I was shaking up the vinaigrette when Leo got back. Wayshaw hopped in after him and flicked the rain off both of them with a shimmer of magic.

"Holy shit, Vai," Leo said, shucking his coat. "It smells amazing in here." He came into the small kitchen, wafting the alluring smell of someone who's had cold wind blowing through their hair. He grabbed a slice of bread, dipped it in the dish of olive oil and balsamic I had made, and moaned in pleasure as he chewed it. "I'm starving. This is ambrosial."

Gratified, I handed Wayshaw a plate, though I wasn't sure how we would all fit at the one tiny table. It didn't matter; the two of them could eat first.

She said, "I'm interested only in the salad, thank you," and calmly served herself some. After declining the dressing, she took the plate and sat in the seat under the Turkish lamp. She opened a book on the seat's arm and began munching undressed salad while she read.

Returning my attention to the kitchen table, I found Leo sitting there, gazing at the votive candle burning in a pink glass holder. I had discovered the candle in a drawer, along with a lighter. He blinked at me, his forehead wrinkled. "This is all really nice. You don't have to do this every night, okay? You *can't,* actually."

"It's not that much," I said, confused.

He laughed. "Pack of ramen, remember? We have performances most nights. This time Thursday, we'll be at the theatre in Bahía Rosa getting makeup on and won't be back here till like eleven."

"Then we can have dinner at eleven. Or before the show." I set out plates and silverware.

Leo spooned risotto onto his plate. "I'm just saying, save your energy for helping the troupe, not for making me dinner."

"It's dinner for all three of us, and it's just cooking." I sat and handed him one of the faded cloth napkins I'd found in the drawer.

Leo already had his mouth stuffed with risotto. "This is *so good,*" he mumbled around it.

After dinner I got ready for bed, climbed into my bunk, and tucked myself under the sheet and blanket Leo had given me. My eyelids felt heavy. Even in a new space and with my knees bent, I could tell I would sleep better tonight.

I was already drifting when I heard the rustle of someone passing, then a pause. Leo said softly, "Thanks for cooking today."

"You're welcome," I whispered, rolling over, but he had already shut himself into the bathroom and was turning on the water.

I nuzzled my nose into the pillowcase, wrapped the blanket around myself, and collapsed into sleep.

CHAPTER 4

LEO

There was a text from Ayda waiting when I got out of the shower.

I still can't forgive you.

I settled onto the padded trunk next to my bed. Wayshaw had gone out to spend the night dolphining through the waves with her folk. Everything in the caravan was dark except for the Turkish lamp I kept on as a nightlight, and the low lights from the rest of the troupe's vehicles filtering around the edges of my curtains.

At least you're talking to me again, I typed back. *That was a harsh week of ghosting, friend.*

Serves you right, she said.

A minute passed. I got fidgety, fearing this was all she would say.

I'm sorry I didn't consult you first, I finally added. *But you wouldn't have let me do it.*

OF COURSE I WOULDN'T. Why do you think I'm upset.

It'll be okay, I wrote. *I'm collecting a bag of tricks. Also I have an idea with my tattoos: I'm getting them linked up with extra designs so a protection spell can be put into them all at once. Like a shield around my whole body. Well not my face. Probably won't tattoo that. Or I could actually, with invisible ink.*

Ayda took another minute to answer. *You know you cannot count on any of that. And even if you can… Fuck, Leo. Think what a horrible year it'll be.*

I don't know, couldn't be worse than performing during summer season when everyone smells like a bag of sweaty crotch.

She had no response to my hilarious imagery.

You can't be flippant forever, she eventually said.

I've gotten through hard things before, I wrote. *Anyway, you'll send me chantagrams, right? We made Nalibak agree to that part, so you'd better.*

Of course. Gods. Stop making me cry.

I'm sorry. I meant to help. I'm giving this to you and Javier as a gift. Which I know sounds ghastly but can you also accept how it makes your lives better?

I'm trying. But this was so so stupid Leo.

What in our 20 years together as BFFs led you to expect smart decisions from me?

I got a *Ha* again. Then she asked about the troupe's upcoming performances, and we chatted about that, and about Javier. We ended up saying goodnight on civil terms—an enormous comfort. But now I couldn't sleep.

At 3:00 a.m., I got up and tiptoed past Vai to the kitchen for a drink of water. I slumped into a kitchen chair, leaned my forehead on the windowpane, and stared toward the ocean.

After some time, a wraith wafted into view: Vai, reflected in the glass, wearing white T-shirt and drapey yoga pants.

"Are you all right?" they asked.

I tipped my empty glass back and forth on the table. "Just pondering rash decisions I've made. As one does at this hour."

Vai padded closer, arms folded. "I suppose one does."

Vai's dramatic break from their family shifted back into my thoughts. Something like that would give a person sleepless nights for sure.

"I won't ask you for details," I said, the words emerging without my having sanctioned them. Insomnia could do that to me. "I just have one question."

Vai watched me, looking vulnerable in the simple T-shirt, eyeliner washed off, hair tucked behind their ears.

"If anyone comes looking for you," I said, "should I tell them you're not here and I've never heard of you?"

"Oh. I don't think it'll be a problem. The investigators and the prosecutor have my number. And my family…won't be reaching out. If you mean anyone else, coming for me out of revenge…" Vai tucked their lower lip into their teeth in thought. "I don't think anyone involved is *that* horrible."

"But in case they are, then yes, I'll check with you before giving out information. And I'll ask the whole troupe to do the same."

Vai released a sigh. "If anyone gives you trouble, I'll leave. I promise."

I swatted the idea away with a flutter of my fingers. "No trouble. We get weirdos approaching us all the time. I'm just asking your preferences."

"It isn't fair of me to put you in danger."

Given what I'd brought down on myself with Nalibak, I actually laughed a bit. "I assure you, you're not the biggest source of danger in my life."

Vai nodded, though didn't look convinced. "You're all right, then? I bought some herbal teas. If you don't feel well…"

"I don't need anything. Thanks. I'll go back to bed if you will, okay?" I put down the glass and stood.

"Okay." A smile graced their lips. A pretty sight, turning the fashion mannequin into a darling human for a moment.

"Why are you so sure your family won't reach out?" I asked before Vai could turn away. "I know, I know, I said I wouldn't ask anything else. I just. You know what, never mind, forget I asked. Go to bed, it's okay."

Looking thoughtful, Vai stood up straighter. "We have this good friend, Kwal, an earth faery—a hob. He's worked with our family since I was a child. He takes care of lots of things for us, personal and business, and we've always made sure he's set up comfortably in the human realm. Part of the guarantee that Airtight offers is backed up by a deal we made with him. If any of us break confidentiality in our clients' contracts, Kwal will enact a spell that makes it so the rest of the family does not—cannot—know or remember the offending party for one year."

"Oh." The word slipped out as a sigh. "So…they don't know you're the whistleblower?"

"They don't even know who I am. And won't, for another year. My parents, my uncle, my sister."

The reasons behind Vai's night flight from Tesoro became clearer. "Total banishment. That's brutal."

"I knew the deal. I did it anyway." Vai's mouth twisted wryly. "Rash decisions one has made."

"Has this deal been enacted before? Anyone else ever triggered it and gotten…" I twirled my finger. "Nullified for a year?"

"No. This is the first time."

While I searched my brain for some appropriate theatrical quotation in praise of immense integrity, Vai murmured goodnight and returned to bed. And, since I had promised to, I did the same.

VAI

In the middle of the next day, during lunch break at the theatre in Bahía Rosa, I received a text.

Oh Vai, I can't imagine how hard this is for you. I've been to see Daphne. She's shaken of course, but strong and gracious and going about her day. I thought you'd want to know she's doing all right.

The message was from Charles Christopher, the friend of Daphne's who had commiserated to me that "the likes of you and I could never be like that" when we were watching the troupe. His fawning, lowly demeanor sometimes annoyed me, though I could not point to anything precisely he had done wrong. I felt guilty whenever I caught myself thinking less of him, because he was not only Daphne's friend but a crosswater, an immigrant from the U.S., and I didn't wish to be a nationalistic snob.

His message today was a relief. I did want to hear about Daphne.

Thank you, I texted back. *I miss her. I'm sorry to have caused trouble.*

Hey, you didn't cause it, you just found out about it, he said. *You're an honest person, I admire that.*

I know you've gotten along well with my father and Uncle Joe, I added. *I expect it's a shock for you too.*

Daphne had been the one to bring Charles to Eidolonia. She'd met him in America ten years ago, when she'd taken a sabbatical, rented a car, and gone exploring deep into the continent. She'd decided he needed rescuing from his depressing small town, and he had enthusiastically agreed. My family welcomed him with warmth. My parents and uncle delighted in his awe at the magical country he hadn't known existed, and they took pleasure in helping establish him as a citizen. I had been more reserved in my interactions with Charles, as I tended to be with everyone. Still, he had expressed appreciation for me, calling me "so calm and relaxing to be around."

A shock for sure, he answered. *But your family's always been good to me, and anyway as an outsider I'm probably not getting the nuances of the politics! I still view you all as friends and don't want to burn any bridges.*

That's kind of you, I said.

Are you still in town? We could meet up for coffee if you want to talk.

I'm not in Tesoro anymore, no. I hesitated, tempted to tell him I had landed myself a bunk in the home of the beautiful and cantankerous Leonidas. But I only said, *I found a place to stay for now. I expect I'll be moving around a fair amount for the next year.*

OK. Let me know when you're back in Tesoro. My door's always open. He added a heart emoji.

I thanked him again and picked up my pasta salad. I was having lunch in the theatre's lobby, as there was no eating allowed in the house or onstage. The lobby had faded carpet, old wooden benches, and a ticket window trimmed with shabby gold paint.

The house door stood open, so I wandered over and studied the backdrop from a distance. Between festivals, the troupe often put on comedic plays. Here and in a few more towns, they would be performing *Peter Pan Goes Wrong*. My job today was the backdrop: pink striped wallpaper for the Darling children's nursery. I'd gotten three-quarters of it up.

As I assessed the wallpaper, Leo and Fred, an attractive endo-witch, walked out on stage, carrying a bunk bed frame, and set it under the backdrop's window. Both were in costume, Fred as Peter Pan, and Leo as his shadow in all-black bodysuit.

As I watched, munching pasta, someone fit Fred into a flying harness, trailing overhead wires. Then Fred spoke his lines, and Leo shadowed him, sometimes smacking Fred in the head as he mirrored Fred's arm gestures. Fred lurched into the air via the wires, toppled halfway over, and flailed to a perch on the windowsill. Leo, unwired, scrambled up the bunk bed to the sill—the shadow trying to keep up. When Fred flew back to the floor, Leo windmilled his arms and fell backward from the window. My heart jumped in alarm—but of course every ungainly step of their performance was intentional, and a second later, he popped up grinning to give a thumbs-up to the director in the front row.

The director, Genevieve, was in their sixties, and was the person I had spoken to in the park in Tesoro, who'd told me to pick the caravan I'd most want to live in.

"Good!" they called. "Let's run it again."

I finished my lunch that way, watching rehearsal from the back of the house. Not until I had returned to the stage, carrying the last sections of wallpaper, did I realize I had gone nearly half an hour without thinking of my family.

CHAPTER 5

VAI

Over the next week, news about Airtight Spells dwindled. The law, it seemed, moved slowly after its dramatic start. I busied my nervous hands by helping the troupe.

In Leo's caravan, I restored the spells that held his possessions crammed together in the closets. When he finally noticed I was too tall to fit on my bunk, he laughingly berated me for putting up with it in silence, then sanctioned me to slice open the cupboard wall at one end and open it into a shelf that expanded the bunk's length. I extended the mattress, too, reshaping and affixing old materials from Mathilde's stash of fabrics. I promised to repair the wall before I left the troupe's service. Leo swore he did not care and wouldn't notice if it stayed that way forever.

On opening night of *Peter Pan Goes Wrong*, he said, "Oh, hey. You can antishine my makeup and fix it in place, right? Then pull it off me afterward? And make my tats invisible for a few hours? Sweet, I don't have to wait in line for Korn or the others to do it. I call dibs on you."

So I entered the whirlwind of backstage with him and pressed myself up against the powder-dusted counter, trying not to be in anyone's way, while he applied his stage makeup in the mirror lights. When he was finished, he turned to me, smelling of foundation and tangerine deodorant. I traced my fingers over his face—not quite touching the makeup, just near enough to infuse it with a spell to keep it matte for the next three hours. I ran my pinky softly along the sweep of his long eyes to smooth his eyeliner, too, then did the same to his brows and lips.

I felt a little shaky. I was used to enspelling inert materials lying on desks, not matter clinging to people's faces. And this was the face of the one person in Eidolonia who flustered me the most.

My rattled state must have shown, because Leo's smile turned anxious. "Is this okay?" he asked. "You don't have to. Really."

I thought of Daphne, her hands on patient after patient every day, treating sicknesses and injuries. I also thought of someone else getting to be up close to Leo's face when it could have been me.

I nodded, reassembling my features into a smile. "It's no trouble. I promise."

During performances, I assisted backstage. The production involved a great deal of intentionally broken set pieces that I helped reset with spells afterward, plus I stayed on hand for any unintentional costume or prop damage. For the rest of the time, I was free to watch and grin, while the house rang with laughter.

Then, in the middle of smiling, I would remember what I had done to my family. I didn't deserve to enjoy myself. This was banishment, not vacation.

After each performance I pulled Leo's makeup off with a sweep of magic, collecting it into a glob in a paper towel. Sometimes, during such sessions, he rested his eyes on me, studying me. Other times his gaze drifted to the side, lips sealed shut.

I thought of his closed purple curtains and distracted moods. His three a.m. insomnia, brooding in the kitchen over rash decisions. Something was troubling Leonidas the Obstreperous, and I had no idea what. I didn't even know his real name.

One evening, which the troupe had off—a resting day—I cooked dinner for us again. After eating, Leo propped his chin on his hand and examined me. It was a much warmer gaze than the way he had looked at me that first morning, not quite two weeks ago.

"How are you finding it?" he asked. "Our inglorious troupe life."

"Different from my previous job. Not as quiet." He laughed, and I added, "Also, here, the things I change or fix get used right away, rather than being put into storage. And they contribute to making people laugh."

Leo hit his palm against the table. "Exactly. We're a bunch of asses, but we improve moods."

"Plus it's artistic expression. That makes it more satisfying."

He scraped a crust of bread around the inside of his soup bowl. "What I do is too ridiculous to be glorified by that phrase."

"Not at all. It counts."

Leo ate his crust. "I've seen you laugh at the shows. But some nights you don't. Have you been hearing from home? Any news?"

"No. I just…think about them, sometimes."

"What are they like? Your family."

"My father and uncle are proud. Passionate, funny. My mother is…steady, calm. Cold, some people say, but they're wrong. She isn't, she has passion. You can tell by how she plays. She's a pianist."

"Oh, for real? As her profession?"

I nodded. "For an orchestra, and other events. And my older sister…I think she's the one I miss the most."

Leo made a hum of sympathy, and I rushed on before he could press for details.

"What about your family?" I asked. "Where are you from?"

"Me? That isn't interesting. How much older is your sister? What does she do?"

I gazed at him, trying not to look accusatory. "Why would it be more interesting if we spoke only of me?"

He laughed, leaning back. His voice dropped into an eerie likeness of Hannibal Lecter's. "Quid pro quo, Clarice?"

"Yes. I've heard you're from Tesoro too. Is that true?"

"Oh, who said that? It's sort of true. I moved there when I was six, so."

"And before that?"

"The Southwest Peninsula. My parents were from there." He gazed at the votive candle flickering in its little glass.

I registered the past tense. "You don't have them anymore?"

"They died in an accident, and I got shuttled to Tesoro to live with my aunt and uncle and cousin." He drew in a brisk breath as if shutting a door. "So. Your sister."

My chest ached at what he had gone through, at merely six years old. "Daphne is three years older than me," I said gently. "She's an exo-witch, a healer. The kindest person I know."

"Will you go to her first, when your year is up?"

I nodded, straightening my silverware across my bread plate. "A year. It seems long."

"It does." His tone was somber.

I decided I was allowed one more question. "Is Leonidas your real name?"

He grinned, crinkling his nose. "Noooo. My parents wouldn't have picked anything so grand. Just Leo. Not even short for anything. L-E-O, right there on my birth certificate."

"Surname 'Obstreperous'?"

He rolled his eyes. "Takahashi. Leo Takahashi. Excruciatingly pedestrian, right? You see why I took a stage name."

I thought both names suited him beautifully. Like two different roles. Rather than try to articulate that, I stacked our plates and mentioned I'd bought salted caramel ice cream, which, as expected, made his eyes light up, and he demanded I bring it to the table immediately.

LEO

Vai did not hop off in Bahía Rosa but instead stayed on with us when we continued south to Sevinee. That pleased me. I had made it my new hobby, trying to cheer up Vai, make them feel appreciated. It was in any case more enjoyable than ruminating over my own problems.

Nalibak was following the troupe. To name one such problem.

I'd heard rumors of fair feasters sighted on the outskirts of Bahía Rosa, but none of us had seen any. Then one evening in Sevinee, I was coming home with a bag of groceries, and as I walked past the woods bordering our troupe's parking area, a pale form congealed out of the fog.

"Friend." The voice rippled through the air like a rustle of dead leaves.

I glanced around, ensuring no one else was near, then walked to him and stopped several feet away. "I can't stop you from stalking me. But this is as close as we come, for now."

Nalibak wore the glamour I'd seen most often on him, looking like a K-pop star, with chiseled cheekbones, spiky purple-black hair, sleeveless tee, and studded belt. Even knowing his appearance was fake, and even knowing it had lured Ayda to him when she was thirteen, I preferred the illusion over his true form, which I had seen on occasion. Picture something sharp-toothed, dead, and leathery that's still moving and speaking.

Nalibak crinkled his nose and drew back a step. "Rude. Distrustful."

I patted my jacket pocket, which held dried St. John's wort. "Necessary precaution. I won't have them on me when it's time."

"It would not save you if you tried." He sounded reasonable. "I would find an accomplice, a weasel faery, say, who would rip the flowers from you."

"Listen," I said, "the deal is with me alone. Stay the fuck away from everyone else in this troupe, as well as every human who comes to see us. Do you understand?"

"You cannot ask for this condition. But I savor the taste of your fear."

"I'll be much better company if you abide by it. Otherwise I'll sulk and be the most boring houseguest ever. Or lair-guest. Do you even have a lair when you're gliding around the country? How does that work?"

I played it flippant, but he was right about the fear. My hands trembled in a way they hardly ever did anymore onstage.

"I can make a lair," he said in the sing-song tone he sometimes adopted, "anywhere I go, with fluffy birds' wings, and teeth licked clean, and curtains of stories and fir needles, all lovely and dark under the rocks."

"Not the absolute creepiest thing you've ever said, but a contender. Are we clear on staying the fuck away from everyone?"

"My stubborn dandelion, I will hunger. I must eat."

"You can eat deer," I reminded him. "Mountain cats. Eagles. All the things fair feasters sucked the life out of before humans arrived on the island. We've talked about this."

Years ago, in the cockiness of youth, I had demanded to know why he, or any fae, ate at all. They surely didn't need to, as they were essentially immortal and could tap straight into the energies of nature. Nalibak had said, "Ah, but we love to eat. All of nature consumes each other. If we do not, hunger will make us quite, quite mad." Given Nalibak was already the maddest hatter anyone had ever met, I had agreed I didn't want to see what "quite, quite mad" looked like on him.

Now, at this reminder of eating, his eyes glimmered with an odd sheen that would have sent any wise human stumbling backward and running for their life. "You remain interesting," he said. "The taste of that, it feeds me, a little."

"Great. Are we done?"

"I always know where you are, and if you try to escape, it will be someone else who comes with me. Ayda or another."

"It'll be me. Now fuck right off, please."

His face gleamed in a rapt smile. The next second, nothing was there but the shadows of trees.

I gulped down cold air, whirling in a complete circle to make sure he was gone. Finally I wiped the sweat off my forehead and turned toward the caravan.

The door opened before I reached it, spilling light toward me. Vai stood there, a silhouette in oversized designer white shirt and slim-cut jeans.

"Vai, hey." I lifted the bag. "Got the food."

"Why were you talking to a fair feaster?" Vai demanded.

Ah. Shit.

"Don't worry," I cajoled as I squeezed past with the groceries. "I always carry St. John's wort at night. Don't you? Doesn't everyone with half a brain?"

Vai stood in the kitchen doorway as I began putting the food away. "People with half a brain don't have conversations with them."

"How could you tell he was a fair feaster, just from the window? Your eyes must be amazing." My mind shuffled details at top speed, deciding what to reveal and what to hold back.

"It was how he moved." Vai sounded unnerved. "I wasn't sure. I asked Wayshaw, and she said yes, it was a fair feaster."

"And I can't lie," Wayshaw added mildly. "Unlike fair feasters." She stood behind Vai, looking over their shoulder.

Crouching to fit a yogurt container into the fridge, I glanced in annoyance at her. Sevinee was farther inland than many towns, so Wayshaw hadn't bothered to trek down to the ocean to spend the night. Instead she was apparently staying here to supply truths to Vai.

"What *else* did you say?" I asked.

"That Nalibak is someone you've known for years," Wayshaw replied. "That's all."

"Which doesn't make sense," Vai said. "Fair feasters aren't people's friends. They aren't 'someone you know.'"

"Vai, how prejudiced of you. How many have you ever talked to?"

This levity got me nowhere. Vai employed a silent stare while I put away the noodles and lemons.

Finally the grocery bag was empty. I folded it up. "All right, yes. He's dangerous. Nonetheless, it's true, Nalibak and I have known each other for many years. But he and I are not friends. Just…people who know each other."

"I'm confused," Vai said, clearly and softly. "And I'm concerned. Two people have *died* in the past year. After a long time of no fair feaster attacks."

I picked up the bag of wine gums I'd bought. "Come." I nodded toward the other end of the caravan. "Let's talk. With these, because I need a blood sugar boost after that."

Vai looked dubiously at the candies but stepped out of the way.

"I assume this conversation is better for two than three," Wayshaw said. "I'll go out." She slipped out the door into the fog.

At the corridor's end, I pushed my bedcurtains to the sides to make room for us to sit on the mattress. My bed took up the end of the caravan, bigger than Vai's dinky overhead bunk—which I felt guilty about, and I had offered to swap, but Vai had refused.

The bedspread was purple, like the curtains, and there was a window over the bed, though most of the time I kept its blinds shut. I switched on a wall-mounted lantern above us, then ripped open the wine gums and shoved a tangerine one in my mouth. I tilted the bag toward Vai.

They took a blackcurrant one, bit into it, then looked at me, waiting.

I cleared my throat. "My best friend from high school, Ayda. She was enchanted by Nalibak when she was thirteen. He lured her in, wearing that same K-pop glamour you saw tonight."

"That's awful," Vai said. "Did she survive?"

"Yep. Still with us. She's half fae, which makes her more resistant. Her dad's a bear faery. Nice guy. It's funny, Ayda's small and really no more hairy than you or me. You'd never guess she's part bear." I poked through the wine gums and selected a pineapple one. "She only stayed in Nalibak's lair one night the first time. Her dad tracked her down. He and some healers got her healthy again. Except she ended up with some effects they couldn't eradicate. One is that…she needs to consume blood."

Vai stopped chewing the wine gum.

"Not much!" I added. "Not human. Or, doesn't *have* to be human. And she eats other food too. It's just, ever since then, her body needs some blood to stay healthy. So, we've found ways to get her that. Blood banks will sell it to you, did you know?"

"We?" Vai asked.

"I've helped when I could. I met her in school when we were fourteen. Kids were making fun of her, being ostracizing dicks. You know how kids are. I thought she was cool. I got in fights on her behalf."

"Compassionate," Vai said. "If violent."

"I was a dick in my way too. Anyway—some of Nalibak's enthrallment stuck with her. She ended up being drawn back to him a few times over the next couple years. Got her enchantment damage re-upped, and…it was a whole thing."

"Horrible."

"Yeah." I scratched the back of my head. "The real issue is she made a deal with him. Under enthrallment, one of those nights. She agreed to spend a year with him in the future. Entertain him, let him feed on her energy, all that stuff fair feasters like. Without killing her—she did specify that bit."

Vai looked alarmed. "But she's still…"

"She's fine! She's good. Because, see, what I did a few months ago was I went to Nalibak and arranged to switch her deal to me instead."

Vai shot to their feet. "You—when? What will—"

"Hey, hey." I grasped their clean white sleeve and tugged down gently. "Sit. It's okay."

Vai sat again but insisted, "A fair feaster can lie. Deals guarantee nothing with them."

"Ah, we know. This is why I had Ayda's dad come along to broker the deal. Who's going to break their word if a ginormous bear faery is going to drag them into the horrid, nasty sunshine and pummel them for it?"

"But what'll happen to you?"

I lowered my eyes. The entire truth was known only to Ayda's father and Wayshaw—and lately Ayda, who was horrified. I could not horrify Vai like that, nor anyone else, until absolutely necessary. Vai would surely tire of Quicksand and be long gone from the troupe before the day came, anyway.

"Like you saw," I said. "He gets to stalk me instead of her. I consent to let him get sort of close, and I entertain him with nonsense. I also did insist on keeping the clause where he doesn't kill me."

Vai's tension seemed to ease, but only a bit. "This continues for the rest of your life?"

"No, no. A year, is all." I offered the wine gums again.

Vai selected a piece. "I can't see how that would be satisfying enough for a fair feaster. And it's still dangerous for you."

"I'm providing novelty, which he craves. As to the danger, I'm not only carrying St. John's wort, I've also got lots of other protective charms. I'm aiming to be safe, I promise."

This was all true. But my optimism was nowhere near as steady as I made it sound.

Because here was the part I didn't say: my year of thralldom technically hadn't begun yet. It would start on Ayda's thirty-fifth birthday, which was May twenty-seventh, about six months from now.

And the entirety of it would take place in the fae realm, in Nalibak's lair.

I smiled serenely at my caravan-mate while those conditions screamed in silence in my head.

"It's selfless of you." Vai rubbed their fingers together, likely sticky from candy. "Drawing the danger to yourself. Giving your friend that peace of mind."

"That was the hope, but of course she's mad as hell that I did it." I laughed, as if learning of my deal-switch hadn't agonized her. "Anyway, you're more selfless than me—you did the right thing for justice, even though it meant getting banished."

Always turn the spotlight onto someone else when you can't bear to talk about yourself anymore. High up there on Leo's rules of life.

Vai grimaced. "I *was* being selfish, though. If I didn't report it once I found out, I could've ended up in legal trouble too. I was saving myself."

"Nonsense. You found out all those voters got defrauded, and you spoke up. If it was *your* vote, you'd want someone to take action."

"It probably was my vote, given I live in Portnoff's district," Vai said dryly. "But yes. I did think of all the people it affected. It added up to a good enough reason to banish myself." They scooped up two more wine gums. "Or so it seemed at the time. I don't know yet if I'll say, in another ten years, that it was worth it."

"It absolutely was," I said. "Besides, you wouldn't be here if you hadn't reported on Airtight. I'd never have met you. That obviously would've been a tragedy."

Vai met my gaze, head tilted, hair falling in a drape around one cheekbone. "A tragedy," they agreed.

I didn't look away. My heart picked up speed.

I wasn't flirting. Just—appreciating a friend. Like people do. But the line between those things could occasionally be blurry, couldn't it?

CHAPTER 6

LEO

As if to round out the week's drama, my brother Javier texted me a few days later. *You're in Sevinee awhile right?*

Yes, why? I answered.

No reply until around lunchtime. Then: *Ayda and I are here too. Come meet us.* He attached the address of a café near the train station. Before I could ask why they were in Sevinee, he added, *Ditch work if you have to. Just get here.*

I wasn't alarmed yet. Javier was always brusque. Still, uneasiness crawled up my throat.

For real, wtf? I typed back. But I did have some spare time—I was out to get lunch, not far from the station, and afternoon rehearsal didn't start for a couple of hours. I added, *Be there in a few.*

The café was buzzing with voices, the air thick with the smell of toasted sandwiches and espresso. Ayda and Javier held down a corner table. Ayda waved to me. Javier glowered.

Ayda wore a green paisley top, stretchy orange trousers, and chunky boots, her dark hair in a half-up do. She stood and hugged me.

"Hey," I murmured into the manic waves of her hair. "What are you doing here?"

She held up a splayed hand. I could see nervousness in the diameter of her eyes. "Do not kill me, okay?"

"What the fuck, Ayda?" I asked, mystified.

Javier stood too, his eyebrows and mouth in scowl mode. "Gods damn it, Leo." I could have sworn he wasn't just casually irritated as per usual, but distressed.

A terrible suspicion dawned on me. I snapped my gaze back to Ayda. "Did you—"

Now she had both hands splayed in front of her. "I told him."

"You total *moron*," Javier said to me.

"Ayda," I protested. "What exactly did you tell him?"

"Everything," Javier said. "You're going to spend a year in the fae realm with Nalibak, starting on Ayda's birthday, because you're a fucking idiot with a martyr complex."

"Oh, so, everything," I conceded.

"I'm sorry," Ayda said. "But it wasn't fair to keep it from him."

Javier stalked toward me. "Do I get a hug, too, or what?"

He gave me what could only be called an angry hug, then we all sat, and the two of them examined me—Javier with hands fisted beside his silverware, Ayda looking like someone waiting under a desk for a bomb to explode.

She had looked like that on her worst mental health days when we'd been teens. Hating her spell damage and how it made other people view her. Dreading the next time Nalibak would appear and lure her into the shadows. Scared. Traumatized.

I softened the muscles of my face, which had gone into defensive tension. "Well, cat's out of the bag," I said.

Ayda picked up her insulated green water bottle and sipped from it. She always chose opaque bottles, to hide the color of the blood she had to drink. Another reminder of why I was doing this.

"When did you tell him?" I asked.

"Two days ago," Ayda said.

"And why?"

Javier answered, "Because what does it say about the state of our relationship if we can't tell each other the most important things? Especially about my own brother."

Ayda waved her fingers toward him in agreement. "He deserved to know why I was distracted and upset."

"But I didn't want anyone else to know yet," I protested. "It's my problem. I took it on."

"If one of us were about to go through something like this," Javier countered, "wouldn't you want to know about it?"

"Yes," I said. "So I could help you by switching the deal onto myself and making it unchangeable. As evidenced by what I *did* do when it was about to happen to one of you."

Javier just sputtered.

"And you caught the train down here on your day off just to confront me in person?" I added.

"We're discussing. Not confronting," he said. "And it's not *that* long a ride."

"No one else knows?" I checked. "You two, Ayda's parents, and Wayshaw. That's it, are we sure?"

"We're sure," Javier said. "I'm insulted you didn't tell me, though."

I fidgeted. "I was going to. When the time got closer."

"Bullshit. You would have texted me sixty seconds before getting abducted. Emailed five minutes before, if you were being really considerate."

Given I had in fact been planning a written approach, the guilt pinched me harder. "Well, see, knowing about it is just making you unhappy."

"We did try to find out if the deal could be changed again," Ayda said. "I went over it and over it with my dad. But it sounds like you specifically made sure we couldn't."

"Right, because I knew that's what you'd try. Look, I'll go through with the year, get it over with, then you're free for life. We're *all* free."

"Explain the deal again," Javier said. "Tell me exactly what you agreed to."

I exhaled. "At least let me order coffee and an éclair first."

Once we had our food, I picked apart my pastry and, under the cover of the patrons talking around us, succinctly explained all the conditions I had insisted upon:

Nalibak would not kill me. We could not exact that promise from any other forces in the fae realm, however.

The length of my captivity was to be one year as measured on the human side, not the fae side.

Melu Ros, Ayda's father, got to track us down once every three months, as measured on the human side, to check on me and bring supplies.

Nalibak was to cease harassment of everyone close to Ayda or me, effective for the full term of not only our lives but our loved ones' lives.

This deal could not be changed again. It was now untransferable.

"And you really think Nalibak's going to abide by all this?" Javier said.

"If he doesn't," Ayda said, in the tired tone of someone who has already gone over this, "my dad will wallop him. In the full sun. Regularly and often."

I nodded toward her, sipping my coffee.

"But—okay," Javier said. "*Nalibak* gets to lie. Why can't we? Why do we have to comply with the lame-ass deal?"

"Because," Ayda said, same tone as before, "if we don't, he'll keep harassing us as long as we live. Me, you, Leo, people we love. We can't stop him from stalking us, and it's horrible to live that way. Trust me. It's how I've lived from age thirteen till just lately."

Javier and I were silent a few beats in acknowledgment of that.

"At least this way," I added, "we'll be through with him forever after I serve out the year."

"But how do you know?" Javier said. "He can lie!"

"See earlier clause about Melu Ros walloping him if he reneges," I said.

Javier frowned at his mug. "Then I don't see why Melu Ros can't start walloping him *now* and just avoid this whole thing."

"Because my dad is fae," Ayda said. "Fae don't think like us, and they're fanatical about deals. I made a deal with Nalibak back when, and now Leo owns that deal, so we have to do it. That's that. According to them."

Javier turned his gaze toward the rainy street. "Fine. I'm allowed to hate it, though."

Ayda put a hand on his leg.

He cleared his throat and sat up. "So, next order of business. How to keep your stupid ass alive for the year."

"Like I haven't been researching that," I retorted.

"We're both going to send you things," Ayda told me. "No arguing. All the best materials we can get."

"You don't have to," I mumbled. "But thank you."

"*Obviously* we have to." Javier set his phone on the table and opened a notes app. "Our train back to Tesoro leaves in an hour. Let's see what we can think of till then."

VAI

Orphaned in his childhood and shunted to the other end of the country to live with relatives. Then making a deal, in the middle of a successful career, to draw a fair feaster's attention to him. Those were at least two valid reasons for Leo to feel haunted in the wee hours of the night. But it didn't seem like enough. Surely there were further troubles that accounted for the somberness that wrapped around him from time to time.

But everyone had their secrets. I couldn't expect him to open the wardrobes of his mind and pull out every tattered item to show me. Not when I wasn't doing the same. There was such a thing as oversharing, and I always tried to avoid it.

Then, near the end of the month, I got news from home.

We were still in Sevinee. Our show had ended half an hour ago. I was leaning on a wall in the wings, staring at the texts from Kwal, when Leo wandered up in his coat, boots, and a purple cashmere scarf. I had whisked the makeup off his face, then caught up on my messages while he changed clothes.

"Hey, you good?" He sounded anxious. I must have looked more agitated than I realized.

I put my phone in my coat pocket. "Airtight Spells is going out of business. Not really a surprise. It'll involve restitution to lots of clients, though, so…my family has to sell the house."

"Like, the one you lived in?"

I nodded. "I knew it might happen."

Leo leaned his shoulder on the wall beside me. "What about all your stuff?"

"Kwal already put it in storage for me. My car is in a neighbor's garage. Still…this makes it all feel very final, what I've done."

"What you did for *good reason*," he said. "You weren't in the wrong."

I looked at him, then out across the stage. "You don't know that."

He waited a few seconds, then said, "All right." And stayed, giving me space to speak.

"Technically," I said, my mouth dry, "I broke the law when I read those documents. I didn't know what was in them beforehand, but I suspected. The amounts of our contracts with Portnoff were too high, way above our usual. And she'd said all those disturbing things in the news, that sounded—to me—like she might use illegal means to get what she wanted."

Leo's voice hardened. "Disturbing is a diplomatic word for it."

"Well. After an article came out where she said, 'The people want my agenda, they voted for me,' I got a bit panicky, knowing we had expensive contracts with her, documents in our storage, ones I myself had enspelled. Usually, I never read them. Total confidentiality is the agreement. No one knows the contents but the client. Our job is only to seal them."

"So you would've been innocent if you didn't open them," Leo said. "You didn't know what they were."

"Probably. But there were things I'd overheard my uncle and father say. My sister and I already knew they leaned toward the Humanist Party, which appalled us, but everyone's got relatives like that. We still loved and trusted them."

I resettled my shoulder blades against the stone wall, breathing the dusty scent of the theatre. "I started obsessing. I can get like that when something worries me. So I went into the storage room, got down the envelopes, and unlocked my own spell. And found out that not only had Portnoff arranged to falsify thousands of votes, but my father and uncle were assisting her. Their names were in it—they had personally used their magic to help change election results. They weren't innocents who were swindled, they were collaborators."

"And using you to cover it up." Leo sounded fierce, as if he might have punched Uncle Joe or my dad if they were here. A gratifying, if absurd, idea.

"Yes. My spells are stronger and longer-lasting than theirs—they've always said my magic was perfectly suited for the job. But they knew I wouldn't have helped alter the ballots, so they didn't tell me. Instead they used me to hide the evidence. That…hurt. So I turned them in. I got legal immunity for my breach of contract, in exchange for reporting the crimes."

"Vai…" Leo stepped in front of me and took my wrists, near my hips, loosely caging me against the wall. "I'm sorry. Families can fucking suck. And this does not change my stance one bit: You. Did. The. Right. Thing."

It was stupid, really, that such a simple sequence of words could make the bridge of my nose tingle with the threat of tears. I wasn't a crier, never had been. Life was just weakening me lately. "Thank you," I said. I swiveled my hands and caught his wrists too.

He smiled. Half his face was in shadow from the curtain hanging near us. His clean-scrubbed cheek gleamed in the backstage lights. He smelled like fresh moisturizer and aged leather.

This was what I had wanted, I realized. When longing to get into Quicksand and station myself near Leonidas, my deep-down desire had been to talk alone with him, tell him my problems, and have him take my side. If he were holding my hands (or wrists, close enough) while he declared his allegiance to me, that would just be a bonus. All that was left on my fantasy list regarding Leo was to have him confide equally in me.

And maybe to kiss him. Or more. But the fantasies got unwise and complicated at that point and were best left in the unrealized realm.

I drew a breath, looking away. Leo let go of my hands.

"Just one more show here?" I asked, though I knew the schedule.

"Yep." We set off toward the stage door. "Then down to Amanecer, and we have to start rehearsing the Fire Festival sketches *while* we're doing *Peter Pan* in both Amanecer and Dasdemir." He rubbed his eye. "Going to be a busy December. If you bail on us by the end of it, I'll understand."

"Where would I go? My house is being sold," I said, deadpan.

He laughed, opening the door. "You want beignets? Sevinee has a good beignet place. Let's go."

The next day I received a text from Charles Christopher. We were back at the theatre, and I read it while waiting for Leo to finish applying his makeup.

Hey Vai—I'm so sorry about the house. Daphne's sad too even though she moved out long ago. She had her childhood there and all. Anyway, please let me know if there's anything I can do to help.

I thanked Charles, turned down his offer to help, and agreed again to the notion of meeting up for coffee when I was next in Tesoro. At the moment, having been reminded that my actions were tarnishing Daphne's childhood memories, I felt no inclination to follow through on his invitation.

As I put my phone away, Leo caught my eye in the mirror. "Whoa. What's that scowl?"

"Just someone back home. Texting condolences about my house."

Leo applied the last swipe of color to his lips, smacked them, and spun to sit on the counter. "In Tesoro? Who? Let's gossip. I might know them."

Stepping close until his knees bumped my hips, I started enspelling his makeup. "His name's Charles. He's a crosswater, from America."

"Ha! I do know him. How many 'Charles the crosswater from America's could there be?"

"The fae are picky about who they let in," Kornelia remarked, beside us. She was one of the tumblers as well as an actor, some ten years younger than me.

I nodded. "The committee's hard to get a pass from." I remembered Charles bemoaning he had gotten only the barest majority, four of the seven fae representatives voting to allow him to stay. It wasn't uncommon, Daphne and I had assured him. The fae had denied entrance to loads of people.

"How do you know him?" I asked Leo.

"I think through Ayda? I don't know him well, I just remember I've met him. What did he say to piss you off?"

"He was offering to help move my possessions into storage. It's not important." I smoothed his brows. "I'm over it." Which I was, now. Leo's friendly interest had already wiped out the sting of Charles's message. "Anyway, he provides updates about Daphne, which I appreciate."

"I think I've met Daphne too," Leo mused. "Suppose I must've heard your family's names often enough around Tesoro."

I glanced along the mirrors, toward Kornelia and the others, but they didn't so much as blink. They had all learned who I was by now, to judge from occasional casual inquiries, but all of them had been remarkably incurious about the family scandal. Instead they tended to ask me theatre-oriented questions: How long would I stay with Quicksand? Would I be able to help next weekend with costumes? What was my opinion, as a longtime patron, on Quicksand doing another musical?

"Daphne's had thousands of patients by now," I commented to Leo. "Chances are you know someone who knows her."

"I already do. Duh." He bumped my leg with his knee and grinned, his face dazzlingly pretty in its makeup.

"So you do." I finished blending his lipstick, then let my finger rest on his lower lip for a second before pulling back, thrilled and shaky at my own boldness.

When I glanced down the mirrors again, several perceptive eyes darted away from us. Dreary political scandals may not have interested the Quicksand troupe much, but *this* behavior did.

CHAPTER 7

LEO

When someone's sole reason for being close to your face is to help with your makeup, it is not the done thing to hook your arm around their neck, latch your legs around their hips, and slide your tongue into their mouth as thanks for their assistance.

And I did not do so! But out of nowhere, I wanted to. Sweet Spirit, how I wanted to.

Welcome to *Leo Has Bad Ideas*, a one-act play by a dumbass.

I wouldn't make a move, of course. As I'd be getting abducted into the fae realm in six months, best plan was to avoid having any lovers I'd get attached to—or who, unlikely though the scenario was, might get attached to me.

So I pushed that temptation away and instead shot a text to Ayda to ask her how she knew Charles the crosswater and whether she also knew Daphne. Then I put down my phone and channeled my focus into the play.

She had sent me an answer by curtain call.

"Vai." I bounded through the milling troupe, careening into people's shoulders, and caught Vai's sleeve. "Your sister was one of Ayda's healers. Now Ayda supplies herbs to her sometimes."

Vai's eyebrows drew together. "Herbs?"

"Ayda's an herbalist. Owns a shop on Cherry Boulevard in Tesoro. Okay, she says…" I read the text aloud. *"Of course, I do business with Daphne all the time. Started as one of my healers, buys herbs from me these days. I met Charles through her. I don't really know him but he's a friend of hers. Remember, we ran into them together at Caffe San Marco once? It was back when you were just starting with Quicksand."* I looked up at Vai. "I'm barely remembering this. That would've been like eight years ago."

"That's possible. It was about ten years ago Daphne met him in the U.S. and brought him here."

I stopped in the middle of thumbing a response to Ayda. "Your sister sponsored him?"

One side of Vai's mouth hooked upward. "She felt sorry for him. Thought he would be happier somewhere other than the small town where he lived. And he...was in love with her and thought they had a future together."

"I take it that part did not pan out."

"No. She's never felt that way about him."

"Well, getting Eidolonian citizenship is a pretty good consolation prize." I went back to my text response. *I kind of remember! Or at least I remember meeting one of your healers in the café and I sorta remember someone was with her. Guess that was him.*

I didn't recall what we had talked about. All I remembered was being tight-chested with worry because I was joining a traveling theatre troupe and would therefore be away from Ayda for months at a time, and I fervently hoped Daphne or anyone else taking care of Ayda would do the job well in my absence.

Vai and I ducked into the makeup room and wedged ourselves into a spot, me with butt on counter, Vai standing before me. They began pulling off my makeup, fingertips brushing my face.

Ayda's next message came in. *Why do you ask about Charles and Daphne?*

"Why do you ask about them, she says." I looked into Vai's eyes. They were a deep brown, almost black, even in the bright mirror lights. "Can I tell her who you are?"

Vai flicked a blob of makeup into a paper towel. "Sure. Just ask her not to tell anyone, please. I'm enjoying living in an undisclosed location."

"Gotcha." Holding my face still for Vai to keep working on, I typed back, *WELL, don't tell anyone, not even Javier, but Daphne's sibling Vai is staying in my caravan and working for the troupe at the moment. They're super cool.*

A half-minute later, I laughed at her answer. "She says, *Oooh, lucky you. That's a good-looking family.*"

Vai smiled, lashes lowering as they balled up the paper towel. "Daphne's much prettier than me."

"My dear," I said, "I have no wish to insult your sister, but I simply don't see how that's possible."

A rosy hue tinted Vai's face, and they flicked me a glance.

Fine. So perhaps I would flirt a *little*.

VAI

The first evening after the Sevinee shows, we drove south to Amanecer. Wayshaw parked our caravan near a row of palms by the waterfront. When I got out, a soft breeze touched my face, less brutally cold than it had been in the north.

Leo leaped out the door, thudded onto the grass, and punched his fists up to stretch. "Ahhh. Amanecer. Quicksand started here, did you know? Back in the eighties. Little comedy troupe who specialized in 'quickest ever' versions of historic events."

"Which you still do," I said.

"We do. They performed by the beach, thus the 'sand' part." He bumped his shoulder against mine. "Let's get takeout, then watch TV till we fall asleep."

We bought cartons of food from a Chilean restaurant and sat at a picnic table, sharing our dinner with three other troupe members, who had brought Vietnamese food to share. Six floating torch-size flames surrounded the table, for light and warmth. They'd been provided by Uwila, a fada—a type of fire faery—who belonged to the troupe. She sat beside me in the form I usually saw her in: a plump woman with gleaming waves of orange hair, and eyes like the blue heart of a flame. No matter the weather, she always wore a sleeveless magenta dress and bare feet, and smelled like a tropical flower.

Over dinner, she and I discussed the fire and explosion effects she provided for *Peter Pan Goes Wrong*. Wayshaw, being a water faery, often stood by to help keep those under control.

After chatting with the others, Leo searched through his phone, then set it on the table to show me a picture. "This is Ayda and Javier. He's technically my cousin, but we've always said 'brother.' They've been together a year."

Their faces filled the frame. Ayda was beaming, dark hair in a cloud around her head. Javier had stylishly disarrayed short hair and a face that was gentle despite the frown crease between his eyebrows.

"They look happy," I said.

"That's Javi's idea of smiling. Such a doofus."

I searched my photos too, then showed him one. "This is my mother playing at a winter solstice party. And that's my sister, standing by the piano."

"Their gowns are gorgeous. The whole *place* is gorgeous. What venue was this?"

My tongue stuck for a second. "It's our house. Well. It was."

"*This* was your house? With—pillars, and balconies, and stained glass..."

I shouldn't have chosen that photo. Only now did I sense, with painful clarity, how pretentious my family had been. "It was good for events," I said. "Ridiculous for everyday living."

"How many bedrooms?" he asked.

The others at the table heard the question and glanced at me.

"Nine," I confessed.

Leo lifted astounded eyes to me, and the rest emitted a chorus of impressed sounds.

"Fuck, Vai. How are you even dealing with my decrepit caravan? With living in essentially *one room*, with two other people? Well, one and a half. Wayshaw's not there half the time."

"It's an adjustment," I conceded, which made all of them laugh. "But the nine-room house can't roll around the country. That's the trade-off."

"You're adamantly finding the bright side there. It's polite of you." Leo gathered up our food boxes. "Come on. TV time. I'm ready to veg."

LEO

On a December day, a year before I met Vai, the happy news reached me: Ayda and Javier were dating.

I was in Dasdemir, lounging naked in my bed with a young man named Otto, who was snoozing against my shoulder. Reading Ayda's text, I smiled and thumbed with careful non-jostling motions: *OMG FINALLY. The chemistry between you two when I visited—I was gonna be devastated if nothing came of it. I'm so happy for you buttheads.*

Thank you, she said. *I'm shocked how happy I am myself. Also freaked out.*

Why? He knows your deal already.

Yeah, he knows about the blood diet and enchantment damage. But there's always more. And it's scary to imagine how someone will feel when they learn everything.

Though her "everything" in its specifics was surely different from my own everything, the statement resonated with me. *I get that. But I know your everything, and I love you,* I wrote. *He will too.*

Do you really know though? A second later she added: *Does anyone really, for anyone?*

Look how good things are. You two didn't even use to get along, and now you're mutually enamored. Miracles happen. Don't fret, yeah?

That's true, she said. *I'll try. Get back to your honey!*

I kissed Otto's head, savoring the buzz of his clipped hair against my lips.

By April, what a different scene I had crash-landed in. Sitting on the ground under a rehearsal tent near Port Baleia, I stared at the rain battering the mud on the other side of our invisible magical weather barrier. Ayda had just texted: *I'm looking forward to seeing you next month! How's Otto? Is he ever going to meet us?*

Not likely, I answered, and sent her a screenshot of the last texts Otto and I had exchanged, a day earlier.

I would love to have you move into the caravan, I had texted. *Travel with me. I love you and miss you, and I want you around all the time, if you're ready for that.*

To which there was a four-hour delay—even though my message got marked "read" right away—then Otto answered: *You are the sweetest, but I can't. We were always just casual, I thought. Meeting up when you were in town, sending messages for fun.*

I do enjoy fun, but this is a genuine offer. No answer for a few minutes. I added: *Which I guess you're turning down.*

Another hour's delay. Then he said, *I guess so, I mean I can't just abandon my life here. It was a good time though.*

After another span of silence, I typed, with leaden fingers, *Then I guess this arrangement probably won't work anymore.*

Otto answered promptly enough this time. *I understand. Fun while it lasted.* And he added a heart emoji. End of final act. Curtain down.

Oh Leo no!! Ayda texted. *That fucking gremlin.*

Thanks. I'm okay, I said. While slumped alone in a corner and staring at the rain.

You are so worthy of love. He didn't see that, but I do, and so do lots of other people, she wrote.

I lifted my gaze to the tent ceiling, blinking to hold in the tears. How did she always slice straight to the tenderest part of the hurt and know the right thing to say? Even if it wasn't something I could believe.

Over the next couple of weeks my troupe-mates offered their versions of consolation, none of which lifted the despondency off my shoulders. Everyone was better at relationships than me. Even Ayda and Javier, who had sniped at each other throughout high school and thus were the two people I'd have said were least likely to get together, had fallen in love. My unlovability seemed an intrinsic, incurable trait.

Quicksand rolled back around to Tesoro. I went to see Ayda first, because she insisted we meet up. I assumed she wanted to give me a lecture to boost my self-confidence, and though I doubted she'd be able to change my attitude, I went dutifully to her apartment.

She let me in, hugged me, then broke into tears. "Leo, I'm so fucked. I don't know what to do."

All my own problems vanished. We sat on the floor in front of her kitchen sink, her head on her knees, my hand stroking her back, while she spilled the story.

"I agreed to a deal with Nalibak, back when I was fifteen. One I never told you about. I agreed to spend a whole year with him. But I was scared, so I pushed it ahead to when I turned thirty-five. That seemed like centuries in the future."

I went cold from my center outward. Nalibak had shown up from time to time over the years, though not for a while now—I thought. Going back to him had never, as far as I knew, been part of the deal.

"Wait," I said. "You were under his enchantment when you agreed to this? Then it doesn't count."

She gave me a despairing look, brown-black curls tumbling every which way. "When has being enchanted ever 'not counted' to the fae?"

"But—"

"Believe me, my dad has been working on him for years, trying to call the deal off. Nalibak is whimsical as fuck. But no. This one he's hanging on to." She thudded her head on her knees again.

The kitchen faucet dripped in the silence. "You never told me."

"I didn't tell anyone except Dad. Not even Mom, till lately. I'm sorry. I've been hoping the fucker would forget, or let me out of it, or we'd figure out a solution."

"No, I mean—you don't have to be sorry for not telling me." I pulled her into a hug. "It's just awful you were living with this without any support."

"It's one year and one month till my thirty-fifth birthday. And now I'm with Javier, and I'm actually, truly happy, and in a year we might still be going strong, and…he doesn't know. What am I supposed to do?"

At that moment I decided. It was exactly as simple as if she'd shown me a wounded puppy she couldn't take care of. I would take this charge into my own lap, no question.

I owed Javier and Ayda, for the ways I'd complicated their lives, and the ways they'd taken care of me. Given my record of failed relationships, I felt no particular wish to keep soldiering on through the human realm, not if spending a year in the fae realm would help people I loved.

Never mind that spending a year in the fae realm was something a human rarely survived. I'd cope with that detail later.

"Don't tell Javier yet," I said. "I've got fae friends in the troupe. Let me talk to them, and to your dad, and see if we can change this deal."

"We've tried. Nalibak won't let go of it."

"Maybe he'll alter it, though. Wayshaw might have ideas. Let me try, all right?"

I got in touch with Melu Ros, Ayda's dad. He lived part-time in the human realm and had a cell phone via which he could be contacted while on this side of the verge. (On the fae side of the verge you couldn't get a signal, as a general rule.) Melu Ros was a burly guy in human form, and even huger and more intimidating, not to mention furrier, in bear-fae form. But he had a gentle disposition—unless anyone was threatening his daughter—and also a beautiful baritone voice. The main activities he undertook in the human realm were visiting his mortal loved ones and singing with musicians.

One such performer was Ayda's mom. Alondra Quijano had been living with other musicians in a polygamous arrangement whose membership changed every so often. They had invited Melu Ros to join them. Via one such occasion, Alondra became pregnant, and Ayda was the half-fae result.

Despite Melu Ros's time with Ayda being sporadic as she grew up, the bond between father and kid was deep and affectionate. He was as keen as I was to find a solution, so when I contacted him, he promptly went to track down Nalibak.

It took a while, given the bending of time between the fae and human realms. But on a humid night in August, Melu Ros finally brought Nalibak to the verge to speak with me. Nalibak liked my offer. Melu Ros did not, but he allowed me to make it. It saved his daughter, after all. He witnessed and oversaw the transference of the deal to me, including the clauses I insisted upon.

Nalibak slithered away satisfied. I requested that Melu Ros not tell Ayda. I would tell her myself, next time I was in Tesoro.

That date arrived in October. When I finally broke the news, she yelled, wept, despaired. Shoved me with both palms. Told me this was horrible; she couldn't even be grateful.

Tough, I told her. It's unchangeable. Please enjoy your newly unfettered life, because that's what I purchased for you.

She threw me out and ghosted me for a week. During which time one Vai Delvecchio trudged up to Merrilo Park, broke into my caravan, and, before long, became an unexpectedly charming new reason for me to wake up every morning.

As a theatre professional, I recognized a tragedy when I saw one. But I could not ask to be recast in a new role. So I did the only thing I could: I vowed my performance would make my friends and family understand they were loved. Make them smile, even. Because tragedies be damned.

CHAPTER 8

VAI

One evening in Amanecer, when it was our turn to go through the theatre house after the show and pick up trash, Leo asked out of nowhere, "What did you first see me in? Do you remember?"

"Sketches. The usual festival things. They were funny, so I kept coming back whenever Quicksand was in town." I left out the part where I had thought, even at my first glimpse, *That Leonidas the Obstreperous is bewitchingly cute.* "Then one year," I added, "you did *Much Ado About Nothing.*"

Leo slumped over with a groan, letting his trash bag hit the floor with a plastic rustle. "Ohhh. You saw that?"

"You were Claudio. And you were wonderful."

"I was new. I took myself too seriously. It's a comedy, for Lady's sake."

"It still involves dramatic moments."

"I chewed the scenery." He picked up a scrap of paper and stuffed it into the bag.

"You did not chew the scenery. When Claudio believes Hero's betrayed him, and then when he believes she's dead, he *should* seem anguished. Which you did. I had goose bumps."

I had teared up, in fact. Leo's grief-racked cries had stabbed into my chest. It was gripping, seeing a funny, clever actor transform into a human ripped apart by emotional pain.

Leo crossed the aisle to the next row. "That's kind of you. But Vai, here's the thing." He turned and looked into my eyes as if this next piece of information was deeply important to understand. "Being good at drama is easier than being good at comedy. Comedy is the *hardest.*"

"So you're saying what impressed me is something that should not have impressed me."

"Well—no, you can like whatever you like. I'm honored! But it's also true about drama versus comedy."

"I believe you," I said. "And I would like to see you in drama again, because I enjoyed it."

"Not you too. Has Catarina been asking you? Genevieve? Who?"

"Asking what?"

"Some of them are pushing for us to do a 'real show.' Still with comedy, but also with drama. Like *Much Ado*. To show we're capable of 'serious acting' or some bullshit."

"If they ask me," I said, "I will tell them I'd love to see it."

"You are awful."

We arrived in Dasdemir in time for Fire Festival, which would start a few days before winter solstice. On our first afternoon there, a resting day, I received a phone call from one of the lawfolk to whom I had reported Airtight Spells. She wanted to give me an update and, I presume, check that I hadn't disappeared from the island. The update, like the case, was dreary. There were still mountains of evidence to acquire and sift through, dozens of people to find and question. The charges against Walda Portnoff, while a separate case, were connected with the Delvecchio case, so that complicated matters. My father and uncle were cooperating, though "not happy, naturally," in the lawperson's words. The trial date still hadn't been set and would likely be months away. I repeated my promise to testify.

Also, she added—"just to prepare you"—I should keep in mind that while the press's initial interest in the case had subsided, it would likely flare up again at the time of the trial. I could be in the news, along with the rest of my family.

I shut my eyes. I said I understood. We wished each other a happy Fire Festival.

Feeling sick, I pleaded off making dinner and got into my bunk. Though I'd intended to nap, mainly I just lay there, my gaze moving around the caravan, miserably attempting to think about theatre-related topics and failing.

Leo and Wayshaw ate leftovers. Then Wayshaw went out for the night, and Leo appeared at my bedside with his laptop.

"You're awake?" he said. "Okay, good, I need your help. Could you tell me which of these lines are funniest? I'm trying to improve the festival sketches."

Though nothing seemed hilarious to me that evening, each of his lines was certainly ridiculous, and I did end up smiling. The distraction eased me back toward feeling well enough to get out of bed and make herbal tea.

Leo padded in while the kettle was heating and looked at me with large, concerned eyes. "I'm not saying I'm awesome at it, but if you tell me where it hurts, and if you want…" He held up his palms. "I could exo it for you?"

He often used his healing magic on troupe members, to fix twisted ankles or headaches, or infuse their bodies with energy or calm. For whatever reason, it hadn't crossed my mind to ask him to use it on me, tonight or at any other point. I usually didn't think of asking Daphne either, not for something emotional anyway, and she was a healer by profession.

I was about to turn down the offer, but he rushed in with: "You use your magic to help me all the time. It's rude of me not to reciprocate. Can I?"

I know you prefer to give and not receive, Daphne reminded me, in a memory from years ago, *but receiving can be as much of a kindness as giving. It's a way of appreciating people.*

The kettle reached a boil. I poured the water over the tea infuser. "It's… nausea and fatigue. Headache too. Brought on by anxiety."

"Ah. I know that feeling. So—should I—"

The rose petals in the tea leached their purplish color into the water. "All right. Thank you."

He had me sit in a kitchen chair and stood beside me, then he set one hand on my back and the other on my chest. His long fingers held me like a harness, a sensation that was already soothing even before he started using magic.

"Let's try a dose of 'everything's cool and serene,'" he said. "Technical biochemical term."

Then the sweetest calm flowed through me, starting in my rib cage between his hands and radiating up into my head, down through my gut, and along every limb. Knots in my muscles melted away. My headache evaporated. The sourness in my stomach vanished into blessed neutrality. I slumped in my chair in relief, and his hands spread wider to hold me upright.

He chuckled. "Better?"

"Much." My neck felt like a drooping flower stem. I let my head loll to the side to rest on his chest. His sweater was soft against my temple.

He kept infusing me with serenity, his chest rising and falling steadily against my head. I could have fallen asleep this way.

Then he took a breath, gave me a pat with both hands, and stepped back. "Whew! Warmed me up." Fanning his sweater against his body, he dropped into the chair opposite mine.

I smiled, drowsy and content. "Magic use does that."

"So..." He winced. "Was it a change of plans that brought it on? You took a call outside earlier, and then...if you have to alter your schedule and leave soon, it's fine. Just let me know, okay?"

"No new plans. It's only that eventually I'll have to face my family, and a judge and jury. Possibly journalists. The call brought it all back." I sipped the tea, tasting rose and spearmint.

"Ah, makes sense. But. I'm glad. That you aren't leaving soon."

"Thank you for the healing. Seems you're talented in more ways than the theatrical."

Leo reclined in his chair, stretching his legs to collide with mine. "That's halfway to a good pickup line right there."

LEO

"Best part of being in the troupe," I remarked to Vai as we strolled through historic downtown Dasdemir. "Traveling to magnificent cities. Surrounding ourselves with gorgeous sights." I waved my gloved hand at the twinkling lights wreathing every tree. It was a few nights after winter solstice, and the city was decked out for Fire Festival.

Vai looked up at the stained-glass windows of a temple. "I haven't been to the capital in ages." They had borrowed a hat from Mathilde's costume stash, a fleece beret in pale lilac that looked uber-stylish on their chic head, though it would have looked like a literal macaron on mine.

"You should really be on the stage," I said.

Vai gave me a tolerant smile. "I told you the first day. I'm not looking to perform."

"It doesn't have to be a speaking part. You could just be a beautiful set piece."

"I haven't noticed a lot of need for actors who merely stand there looking beautiful."

"It happens. I'll let you know."

We reached a plaza with a fountain in it, magically converted for the festival to spray fire instead of water. Multicolored flames danced. Sparks arched. At the safety rope surrounding it, couples held hands and kids shrieked in excitement, faces aglow. People took selfies.

I was fishing out my phone to do the same with Vai when they said abruptly:

"If my family doesn't want me back, once they remember me, do you think I could stay on with Quicksand? Would the troupe allow that?"

Vai's spine was rigid, hands deep in the Prada coat pockets. They stared at the fire fountain.

"Are you kidding? Of course. Everyone likes you. You're so steady and reliable, and you're not a pain in the ass at all, ever. We'll take you as long as you're offering."

Vai's shoulders softened. "That first night, I thought I just needed to get out of Tesoro, and I was curious about Quicksand. But maybe, subconsciously, I was setting up a backup plan for my whole future. In case this was it, with my family. Which it could be."

They sounded so forlorn, and the topic of being ejected from one's family tore so deeply at my own issues, that something tender and unnameable blossomed inside me. "I'm going to hug you, okay?" I said. "Step away if you'd rather not."

Vai and I had never hugged yet. Which, in a theatre environment, was unusual to the point of being extraordinary. Still, I wasn't sure they'd consent.

Vai flickered a smile toward me and drew their hands out of their pockets, as if to prepare. It was one of the only times I'd ever seen them look awkward, and it was adorable.

I launched at them—gently—and enfolded them in a side hug. The fuzz of the lilac beret brushed my nose, along with the ridge of Vai's ear, cool in the winter night. They hooked their arm around my back and, sighing, leaned their temple on my head.

"You've probably figured this out," I said, "but everyone in the troupe was originally running away from something, or closing the chapter on a part of their life. You sort of have to, if you're joining a traveling theatre company. You fit in fine, is what I'm saying."

Vai melted closer, their arm tightening. "Thank you."

And, oh. Those feelings I'd thought unnameable—they had a name after all. One of the most common names in the world, one of the darlings of playwrights.

Oh, dear.

I squeezed Vai, then let go. Lifting my phone, I steered them around to face the screen. "Selfie with the fountain. Say 'Happy Fire Festival.'"

CHAPTER 9

VAI

I carried around a lot of habitual social ice, I realized, because in Leo's arms I felt it melt and break. More surprising still, it didn't refreeze afterward.

Toward the end of the year, a short-statured, gray-haired performer named Darius strolled up as I was prying open a can of paint. As I understood it, he and Genevieve shared most of the troupe's administrative duties. "Just sent you an email," he told me. "Fill out your direct deposit info. We're going to start paying you as of January. Do not even bother arguing. First, it isn't that huge a salary. Second, we get arts funding and we might as well use it. Third, you're working hard and you should be paid. We're clear? Excellent! Good talk. You're fabulous." He sauntered away without my having uttered a word.

Having that proof of the troupe's faith in me helped too. And they provided me plenty of work to distract me from my family troubles. The city of Dasdemir gave Quicksand more bookings than anywhere else on the island. During December and early January, we performed as many as six days a week, sometimes twice a day.

During performances, Leo often slumped to sit beside me in his offstage minutes.

"Keep me awake," he said on one such day, his head on my shoulder. "Tell me something interesting."

"In medieval times, narwhal tusks were passed off as unicorn horns and sold to wealthy Europeans," I said.

He snorted. "I meant something about you. Like, did you ever get in trouble at school? No, not you. You never did."

I hesitated. Warmth stained my face. "Once in high school, I was caught in a room I wasn't supposed to be in."

Leo lifted his head to look at me. "The library, after hours?" he said in a dramatic whisper.

I smiled. "An empty classroom, during lunch. I used my magic to get in, which the teacher didn't appreciate. Even though we weren't going to steal or vandalize anything."

"We? Who was with you?"

I focused on a stack of stage furniture. "My boyfriend and I were just looking for somewhere private for a few minutes."

Leo gasped in delight. "Oh gods, tell me you weren't caught naked."

"No, but...it was clear what we were there for. And the teacher was not keen for it to happen against her classroom walls."

"Against the wall!" Leo was a bit too loud, considering we were backstage during a performance. He earned a hiss from Wayshaw, who was stage-managing nearby.

I wrapped an arm around Leo's head to cover his mouth.

He pulled down my fingers and whispered, "I love that. It's—oops. I'm on." Leo smacked a kiss on my palm and dashed to the stage.

After the show, while I pulled off his makeup, he asked, "What was your high school boyfriend's name?"

"Diego."

"How long were you together?"

"A little under a year."

"Why'd you break up?"

I tapped the top of Leo's head to make him look down so I could get the makeup out of his hairline. "We had different interests. It got boring. The usual."

"What kind of interests," he began, but I interrupted:

"When did you first have a significant other?"

"Are you asking when I first had sex?" Once again he projected his voice too well.

"No one is asking that, Leo," Kornelia said from the opposite row of mirrors, over the room's laughter.

I clarified, "I meant the first person you dated in a committed way."

He brought his volume back down. "Well. Same answer, same person. High school girlfriend. *We* were never caught being inappropriate on school grounds."

"Hm. I would've thought you the adventurous type."

"I just said we weren't *caught*." He gave a double-lift of his eyebrows. "Same with my college boyfriend. The campus buildings we christened..." His gaze floated into a dreamy distance.

I threw away a ball of paper towels. "What ever became of him?"

"Who knows. I think he became an engineer of some kind."

"And the latest?" I began removing the makeup from his neck.

"Last spring. Long-distance. I was attached, he wasn't." He shrugged. "It's funny. I was shattered at the time, but I'm realizing I haven't even thought of him in months. Since...hmm, early November or so." He met my eyes with an electric zing of a smile.

Early November. When I had arrived.

"Good." I swiped the neckline of his shirt, pulling makeup from it.

"And you?" His voice was low.

I spun the unused paper towels back onto their roll. "Three years since a real relationship. Just a few disappointing dates in the interim."

"How dare they disappoint you. I'll send them a very stern letter." Leo's threat was interrupted by a yawn. He hopped off the counter and collapsed upright against me, arm over my shoulder, face smushed against my chest. "I am going to sleep for eleven hours tonight."

Without dislodging him, I snagged his coat off a wall hook. "Good plan."

Over the next few weeks we exchanged further questions, leading us into debates about films, agreement about music, comparison of family festival traditions, and fantasies about what we'd wear to an awards show. Me: a black-and-pale-pink suit in traditional Eidolonian tatters style—shirt, vest, knee breeches, and long coat, with fluttery tattered silk hems. I had coveted it since seeing a celebrity wear it in a photo shoot. Leo: "Easy. Jessica Rabbit gown in dark purple. Hair dyed to match."

More often than not, I went to bed in a good mood and slept well.

Then Nalibak came back.

It was the middle of January. We were performing at an open-air venue in Delta Esmeralda, on the southern bay. Uwila the fire faery, with the cooperation of witches and local fae, provided floating flames around the amphitheater for warmth.

"We hope you linger after the show," Wayshaw announced to the audience before the last sketch. "We have a treat for you. Here in the south, winters get chilly, but one thing you don't often get is...?"

The audience members, by now attuned to the comedic mood, shouted suggestions ranging from "polar bears" to raunchy things best not put into print. But a few hit on the right answer.

"Snow." Wayshaw extended a webbed hand toward the audience. "Thank you. We've made a deal with your local air fae for some snowfall after tonight's show. We hope the entertainment has been sufficient recompense, or they might simply dump slush on us and leave." She waved to the back of the amphitheater.

From where Leo and I were, backstage and peeking out, we could only see the air fae as an ethereal line of blue figures—probably sylphs—perched on the outer wall. They waved back. A gust of cold wind rolled across the audience and into the stage, sweeping past us, eliciting shrieks and cheers.

"Stay after for more," Wayshaw said. "Now, our final sketch..."

Leo shivered and looked over his shoulder. The backstage area, though under a cover, was open to the air, and the amphitheater's grounds rambled out to meld with forests and fields. Lanterns marked paths. Benches sat half-hidden in winter-blooming shrubs. A few fans clustered under a tree, talking and watching the actors. Nothing unusual.

"What?" I asked Leo.

He opened my coat lapel and nodded upon seeing the sprig of dried St. John's wort I had affixed to the lining. "Making sure," he said.

I glanced again at the woods. This was our first outdoor venue in several weeks, and we hadn't discussed fair feasters for some time. I had nearly forgotten.

"And you?" I eyed his costume, a suit he had worn in the previous sketch.

He opened the jacket to show the yellow-tipped stem in his shirt pocket. Then he frowned toward the three fans. "Hope everyone's carrying some."

"Fair feasters don't like crowds," I reminded him. "There are plenty of people here."

"I'm going to look around. See you after curtain call." He strode off toward the fans.

After the show, I helped the others collect props and tidy the stage. The audience trickled out, chattering and looking toward the night sky. Leo and Kornelia talked with fans. The back garden was filling with people, who cheered as snow began drifting down.

I carried out an armload of props, set them in a rolling supply bin, and wandered into the garden, lifting my face. Tiny frozen flakes brushed my cheeks and eyebrows. I hadn't seen snow in years—not since the last time I'd gone skiing with Daphne and other friends on a slope near Tesoro. Then, as now, the snow had been fae-made and bargained for. Eidolonia rarely got snow otherwise, down on the coastal lands where humans lived.

I did not wander off on my own. A hundred other people were in view, twirling in the snow, and I was merely a few strides from the back of the amphitheater. But I must still have been isolated enough that a fair feaster felt comfortable approaching.

"You desire him." The voice was thready and cold.

I whirled. Nalibak stood a few paces away, between a bin and the wall of a storage shed. He wore his pop-star glamour, looking underdressed for the snow in his sleeveless T-shirt. Not that the shirt actually existed, and not that the cold could harm him.

I stumbled backward, fumbling for my phone.

"He desires you," Nalibak added.

"Leave." I didn't sound as commanding as I hoped. "Leave everyone here alone."

"I sense it on you both." His gaze was riveted to me. "Smell it on you. Such passion. What will you do when the two of you are separated?"

My hand was shaking. I tried to pull my focus together, get my phone light on so I could amplify it with magic. I accomplished none of those things in the few seconds before Leo bolted in and spread his arms in front of me, as if to take a bullet for me.

"Leave them the *fuck* alone," Leo told Nalibak.

Nalibak flickered his pale tongue in the air. "I could take you both. Entertain me, entertain each other. One to rest while the other dances. Twice as much flavor."

"Your deal is with me. Do not even fucking speak to them."

Nalibak's mouth widened in rapture. The snow thickened, the winter wind whistling. A short sprint away, people exclaimed in delight, oblivious to the fair feaster in the shadows.

"Rich musk," Nalibak said. "Ripe fruit."

I clicked my phone light on and poured my magic into the device so it blazed five times brighter than usual.

Nalibak cringed as the beam hit him, his glamour melting into a skeletal face for a second. He flung himself back, crashing into the shed wall, shielding his face. Then he managed one last glance at us, eyes glimmering. "Delectable," he purred.

"Get out!" Leo roared. He grabbed a rock from the ground and flung it.

The rock smacked against the wall, through a dissolving shadow. No one was there.

A blue figure streaked in, trailing sprays of snowflakes—one of the air fae, probably noticing the bright light. They swooped toward the wall where Nalibak had been, then turned in midair to look at us. "We'll ensure the fair feaster is gone," they said in a voice like a bracing winter wind. "We do not welcome such in our lands."

Leo nodded, panting.

"Thank you," I said.

The sylph took off in a whirlwind of snow.

Leo and I spun to face each other.

"I'm all right, are you—"

"Yes, I'm okay, are you okay?" Leo put his hands on my face, my neck. Even with his makeup on, he had become visibly pale.

I caught his hands, holding them against my collar. "I'm all right. We have the St. John's wort. He can't get near us."

Leo's hands slid loose. He staggered toward the stage. "Fuck. Oh gods."

He desires you. I tried not to believe it. Fair feasters could lie. Except—*You desire him.* That had not been a lie. Perhaps Nalibak had been trying to rattle me, picking the most effective words to do so, lies or not.

Leo dropped into one of the chairs backstage that had been shoved into a row. He had picked a spot where an overhead light cast its beam, as if instinctively staying out of the dark. He bowed his head and took deep breaths.

I sat beside him. "We're all right," I repeated. I set a hand on his back. "It's only a year. Right?"

He blinked at me. "What?"

"The deal with him. It's only a year? Some of it must already be past. It'll be over eventually."

He shut his eyes and turned his face downward again. "I suppose."

"Are you stressed because he approached me? I promise, I'm okay."

So I said, though I was still trembling. I had never come so close to a fair feaster in all my life, nor spoken with one, let alone had one threaten to take me and *taste* me. But I was clearly suffering less anxiety than Leo, so I offered what assurance I could.

He rested his face on the heels of his hands. "He's got to leave other people alone. There's only so much I can do."

"We sent him away." I stroked circles on his back. "We can handle this."

"Oh, Vai." The words sounded broken. I could feel clammy sweat through the fabric of his costume.

"I wish I could do your kind of magic," I said. "To calm you. Should I find someone who can, or…"

"No. Just. Give me a minute. Don't leave, please."

I nodded. Then, deciding we had come far enough that I didn't need to ask first, I wrapped my arms around him and pulled him against my chest.

He toppled into the hug, curling inward. We stayed like that for several minutes, my heart simultaneously breaking in lamentation of how little I could do to help, and brimming with gratitude that he was letting me hold him.

Catarina strode in from outdoors, caught sight of us, and hurried over. She was an actor around sixty years old, with a throaty voice, light blue eyes, and a shrewd gaze. "Leo, love?" She set a hand on his shoulder. "Do you need help?"

He grunted and didn't move.

"Anxiety attack," I offered.

"Poor darling. I'm familiar with those." She straightened up. "Shall I get you some water?"

"No, but thank you, Catarina," Leo said, his face still hidden. "I'll be okay."

Her gaze took in my arms holding him, then my face—I don't know whether I looked fiercely protective or nakedly terrified—and she gave me a gentle smile. "I am confident you will be, yes." She kissed her fingertips, tapped them on Leo's head, and left us.

A minute later, Wayshaw swept in. "The air fae told me about Nalibak," she said. "They've chased him off, far into the fae realm. You'll be left alone the rest of the night, and likely a long while yet."

Leo peeked up. "Thanks, Wayshaw."

"I'll see about further protection for you. For the future."

Leo cleared his throat and pulled upright, withdrawing from my arms. "Good idea. We'll discuss later."

Wayshaw examined him, silver-green eyes aloof. "The caravan should be safe. I'll check before you get there, though." She stalked away.

"It is safe," I assured Leo. "I check the security spells on it every day. And the flowers are still there, in the paint."

"I trust you. Best security witch at Airtight Spells."

I smiled and tipped my chin toward the front exit. "Shall we go home?"

CHAPTER 10

LEO

Home. Vai could have no idea how sweetly it touched my ears to hear them call the caravan that. No one else ever had, except me. Wayshaw traveled in it, but "home" to her was the ocean.

If I can live through my year with Nalibak, I thought to whichever kind-hearted gods were listening, *and reach some future where home means nothing more than the caravan and Vai and me, I swear I'll be the best-behaved and most grateful person in the whole Pacific.*

And—this part was vital—*please make Nalibak leave Vai and everyone else alone until then.*

Vai now counted as someone close to me. But the clause under which Nalibak would leave my loved ones alone wouldn't begin until my year of servitude started. How was I supposed to rest easy until then?

Our deal was one of the worst deals in Eidolonian history. But it was also the only one on the table.

Resentment blazed away the worst of my anxiety, leaving me in a twitchy, glum mood. In the caravan, I showered off my glaze of sweat. Vai made a small meal—wild rice, salad, herbal tea, and a few wine gums for dessert. I didn't say much, except to thank them. Repeatedly. They'd been so kind, holding me during my freakout, despite not knowing why I was so shaken. Making sure I was all right. Not even asking questions.

I checked the social media feeds of Javier and Ayda and everyone else I followed, reassuring myself they were alive via their updates about weekend plans and haircuts. Ayda had messaged me, asking how the audience liked a new sketch. I answered, *Went great, think we'll do it again!*

I would not tell her Nalibak was pestering me. She didn't need to know.

I put away my phone, stretched out on the corridor floor, and stared at the chips of colored light thrown onto the ceiling by the Turkish lamp.

After washing our dinner dishes, Vai walked over to examine me from six feet above. "Are you well?"

"Sure. It's just, when you live in such a small space, it's good sometimes to lie on the floor. You see things from a new angle."

Vai allowed this wisdom with a nod and got down to lie beside me, hands folded on their chest. The corridor was so narrow that we only just fit. We considered the ceiling together.

"Why is it painted gold?" Vai asked.

"Why would it *not* be painted gold?"

"Well argued."

"If you're going to leave home and join a traveling band of performers, you might as well go all in. Purple velvet, gold ceilings, the works. I've done a lot of improvement here, Vai. You should've seen the caravan when I first bought it. Beige, beige, and more beige."

Vai traced a finger along a cabinet, cleaning away dirt. "Were you running away from your family too?"

"Kind of." My gaze hooked on the sunflowers in the bathroom door mural, climbing from one leaf to another. "They weren't going to miss me. I was a problem."

"Being orphaned doesn't make you a problem."

"It wasn't just that. I was constantly arguing with teachers. Getting into fights. Being a flake, forgetting things."

"They made you feel that way?"

I turned my head to find Vai looking at me. "Not always. Javier and I did fight a lot, but we were also close. Still are. That's what siblings are like."

"And your aunt and uncle?"

I returned my focus to the kaleidoscope of lamplight. "My uncle lets us each choose our path, doesn't step in much. My aunt...has definite ideas about things. I did not usually align with those ideas. We butted heads a lot."

"I expect they still love you."

"I don't know." The admission only hurt a little, given all the years I'd spent getting used to it. "I never got the impression I was really one of their kids. Javier and I called each other siblings from the start, and my uncle sometimes calls me his kid. But with my aunt, I'm the nephew. Her son's cousin. Who causes problems."

"They never had you call them 'Mom' and 'Dad'?"

My gaze followed a winding line of purple diamonds of light. "Nope."

Vai shifted their arm to nestle against mine. "I'm sorry. That's a terrible way to treat a child."

"It's fine. I'd feel weird calling them that. And I really *was* a problem." I turned to look Vai in the eyes. "In one of my fights with Javier when we were teenagers—over a video game—I broke his nose. I used my powers to make him punch himself in the face."

Vai's eyes widened.

"Yeah," I said. "Blood everywhere. Screaming. Naturally I tried to heal him, but I wasn't very good at that yet, so they still had to take him to the hospital."

"All right, but—"

"Javier isn't a witch. Neither is my uncle. My aunt's an endo-witch, but that was all the magic in the household till I came along. So I was adding literal injury to insult."

"They can't hold that against you," Vai said. "No one chooses the magic they're born with."

"True, but also, I fucked up Javi's love life. The girl he dated in high school was this snotty person who'd been my nemesis for years. I was the biggest goblin anytime she came over, Vai. It was like I couldn't control my mouth. Real reason was, I didn't think she was good enough for him. I *wanted* to drive her away. But when it worked, when she was like, 'Screw this, not worth it,' and broke up with him—well."

"You felt bad," Vai guessed.

"Yeah. And the worst?" I looked away, focusing on the corner of Vai's bunk. "I burned down their beach house."

"What?" I had finally startled Vai.

"Accidentally! But still. Reckless negligence." I laced my fingers together across my chest. "When Javier and I were in college, Luis and Yubara bought a property at the shore. They'd been saving up for like ten years. Took another whole year fixing it up. It needed new *everything*. Finally it was almost done, and one day someone was scheduled to come out and do some final spells and repairs, but my aunt and uncle couldn't be there. Crazy work week. They asked if Javier or I could meet the repair witch. I said, sure! I'll do it. Nice opportunity to get away from my roommates, spend some time at the beach."

"Generous of you," Vai said.

"Well." I folded my arms over my eyes. "The repair witch would be coming first thing in the morning, so I decided to go out there the night before. Make an overnight of it. Then that evening while I was puttering around there alone, Melu Ros called. Ayda's dad. She was missing again. I took off, back to Tesoro, to help look for her. I'd get back to the beach house in the morning in time to meet the repair guy—I hadn't forgotten. While I did that, Melu Ros went into the fae realm, because we were pretty sure Nalibak had enticed her again. It had happened twice before."

"Is that where she was?"

"Yeah. He did find her, and got her back. It was only one night on the fae-realm side, but three weeks on our side. Three weeks where I didn't know if she was okay. And in the meantime..." I cringed, under cover of my arms. "While I was combing Tesoro for her, I didn't forget the repair witch appointment, but I did forget I had started a fire in the fireplace, out at the beach house. And left it unattended."

I heard Vai's inhale. "Oh."

"I got a middle-of-the-night call from Yubara, screaming that *she* had just gotten a call informing her their vacation property was on fire, and *what is going on, Leo?* By the time I got back out there, my aunt and uncle were there, and the place was gutted. Still standing, but...now it once again needed new everything."

Vai was silent for a bit. "It's not even *easy* to burn down a house. Everything's made with fireproofing spells. If it's done to code."

"Correct." I brought my arms down and turned my head toward Vai. "Two fun facts. One, the repair witch who was coming out in the morning? He was going to finalize the safety spells. Including the fireproofing. Two—the way I started the fire? I couldn't find matches—place wasn't fully supplied yet—but I did have, in my backpack, a couple of kindling sticks that one of my roommates, a matter-witch, was working on as a project. When you activated them, which you could do without matches or other fire, they'd start burning and wouldn't go out for like four hours, even with water pouring all over them. You know, as a camping supply idea."

Vai winced. "Ah."

"Unsurprisingly, her idea was later deemed to have safety issues, and her prof advised she not make any more of them, under probable penalty of law. So, my using it, then leaving without even thinking…that was reckless."

"You were panicking," Vai said. "It was an emergency. Your friend had been kidnapped."

"Well. My aunt and uncle were furious I'd put 'that blood-drinker person' over my own family. None of my apologies were enough. So that was kind of the end. I stopped going to see them for a long time. Dropped out of college not long after. They didn't reach out—except Javier, though at first just to rant at me about how I was throwing my life away by dropping a business-degree program and taking a lobby-assistant job at Jin Troia Hall."

Vai's eyebrows lifted. "Your first job in theatre?"

"Mm," I confirmed. "First paying job, anyway. Which obviously I don't regret, as I love theatre about eight thousand times more than I could ever love business. Soon I finagled my way into a tiny speaking part, then a slightly larger speaking part, and on up, till one year Quicksand swung into town and I auditioned and got in. But, well, none of that has ever particularly impressed my family."

Vai allowed the respectful pause that such a pathetic story required. "And Javier and Ayda are a couple now."

"Yeah! Miraculously. They never used to get along. But in the last couple years, they ran into each other again and started talking. And fell in love. They're so good for each other, Vai. It's incredible how much happier they both are."

"So you feel you have to sacrifice yourself," Vai said. "To ensure Nalibak doesn't disrupt it for them."

"Not 'sacrifice.' More like…repay my family, after messing things up so many times. I can do that. I *should* do it."

"Nalibak's attentions are not something anyone 'should' have to put up with."

"Agreed. But Ayda ended up with this shitty deal, and it has to be served out, so. Anyway. Enough about me! Gods. New topic. Narwhals maybe?" I shook out my tension with a shudder from shoulders to toes.

Vai shifted to lie on their front, propped up on their elbows. "You aren't being fair to yourself if you view it only as you having caused trouble to them. They've hurt you too."

"You're a sweetheart, but I promise, I'm a pain in the ass. You'll see it before long."

They sighed as if already beginning to find me a pain in the ass. "Drama would be cathartic, I think."

"You mean as opposed to comedy?"

"Yes." While I groaned in protest, Vai continued, "I believe you about comedy being harder. I *am* impressed by your comedic skills. But I like you best when you're being real. Like this." They brushed a finger against the side of my neck.

It sent a euphoric shiver through me. I tried not to show it.

"And drama," they concluded, "is more real."

I ran a knuckle along their jaw, lightly enough to be playful, though I reveled in the intimate scratch of their stubble. "What about this. I'll agree to do a drama when it next comes up with the troupe—which it's bound to, because we're planning the coming season soon—if you agree to appear on stage."

Vai bowed their head with an exhalation. "No lines. No nudity. And no singing unless as part of a chorus."

"Standing there like a beautiful tree," I promised. "You get the far better end of this deal, you realize. Your side's easy. Mine involves an entire role, with lines and emotions and everything."

"Then it would be cowardly of me not to agree."

There. Distractions. Things to look forward to. That was how I'd been tricking my brain to keep bowling ahead with life all these years, and it was clearly the only way forward now.

CHAPTER 11

VAI

We meandered up the Southwest Peninsula. Winter fog swathed agricultural fields and timberlands, clearing now and then to reveal a cobalt ocean with golden-sand beaches. The troupe performed in laid-back small towns, then alongside the canals of Kagami, the lagoon city. Selkies and fish fae, in part-human form, rested their forearms on boardwalks, their lower bodies in the brackish water, and bantered with the humans who strolled past.

In Kagami, the troupe created a special extended sketch called "Eidovision"—like Eurovision, but with each act representing a region in Eidolonia, parodying its stereotypes. The songs were covers backed with downloaded tracks, but the singing would be live. As I worked on scenery and costumes near the rehearsal space, I discovered that not only did Shelini, Fred, and Genevieve have excellent voices, but so did Leo. After he had delivered a pitch-perfect version of a Port Baleia pop star's latest hit, all of us burst into applause.

"Leo, why don't you sing more often?" Shelini chastised. "You're incredible."

Laughing, he waved his hands back and forth. "Nooo. I'm really not. I'm just doing an impression."

But he went on to "just do impressions" of several more songs, all equally stunning, even if supposedly only in the service of satire.

A couple of days later, they had chosen the final songs—Leo would be singing two of the ten—and were piecing together production details. The rehearsal space was a large open-sided tent in a park. Chilly lagoon air drifted in, but Uwila's floating flames kept us comfortable. I was sitting on a mat with a row of shoes and leggings, turning them all bubblegum pink. My foot tapped to the beat of the act they were working on, a country-western song from Punta Rosa, which Fred was belting out.

Leo and a few others tried dances to go with it. "Wait, maybe like—" Leo demonstrated a step, holding another performer's hands. "How does it go?"

"Don't ask me." She laughed. "I'm a tumbler, not a ballroom dancer."

I spoke up. "Are you trying to do a two-step or a swing?"

"Good question," Leo said. "Uh. Swing? Maybe?"

"Lindy Hop? East Coast swing?" I asked. "Which kind?"

Leo stopped and sent me a shrewd gaze. "Vai, do you know how to dance?"

"I've taken classes. I perform in group dances for festivals when I have time." Those festival dances, in truth, tended to be the highlights of my year, and there had even been a time in my early twenties when I'd considered a career in dance. But my magic was so ideally suited for the family business, I had ended up doing that instead.

Or had been talked into the family business instead, rather, by my father.

Leo set his hands on his hips, staring at me. "All this time and you never said? Get over here. Show me how to two-step. Or East Coast swing or whatever."

I set aside the shoes and got up. "Hand on my shoulder," I told him. I tried not to notice the warmth of his grasp or the sparkle in his eyes. I aligned my posture upright and began teaching him the two-step.

I did not get any more costumes colored that afternoon. Leo asked to learn one dance after another, and I didn't make the vaguest attempt to escape. Each song required a different style—swing; street dance; modern dance with ballet influence; the Coconata, a party dance tinged with flamenco that had swept the nation in the aughts.

Breathless and warm despite the February weather, I taught Leo spins, then the basics of krumping. Pulled his back against me to demonstrate fancy moves you could add to the two-step. Let him dip me in a swing. We kept colliding, messing up, laughing. He braced me to keep me from falling, arms steady around my torso.

Finally Kornelia turned off the music and started giving notes. Leo listened, his arm around my shoulders, his side snug against mine. As the others voiced feedback, Leo swept his finger up the side of my neck until his knuckle nudged my ear. Casually, like he didn't realize he was doing it. I slid my hand around his back to land on his hipbone. My fingers found a sliver of bare skin, between his shirt and trousers, and settled there. We stood like that, dutifully paying attention to Kornelia.

I took deep breaths to cool down, thankful for the confining denim of my jeans. My body was already threatening to get too excited. I could smell his skin, deodorant, hair, breath—all things I was familiar with from being close to him in makeup rooms and the caravan. But now I also knew the weight and fluidity of his body, how he felt grabbing me, leaning into me, moving with me. Dance peeled off several layers of distance, bringing you and your partner into intimacy. I knew that, should have guarded against it.

Maybe there was no guarding against him, though, the way I felt. Maybe I didn't want to resist.

That night in my bunk, I let my mind wander, fantasizing about ways we could touch if we were alone, if we dropped the pretense of rehearsal. As a quiet person, I had learned to be quiet at this, too, stroking, sweating, reveling in the erotic world behind my closed eyelids. Was Leo, behind his velvet curtains, doing the same, muffling his gasps so no sound reached me? Had he ever done this while thinking of me, these last few months?

Naturally the next day I would go on pretending. I was not going to act on these feelings, and neither, I expected, would Leo. Because he was a professional, and for him, intimacy was just part of his daily job, not something that shook his foundations.

LEO

My heart was enmeshed now. I couldn't even be upset about it. Vai looked too beautiful, glowing in the misty winter sun, arching and twirling in grace. Hauling me close and maneuvering my body parts where they needed to go. All of said body parts, plus a few others not yet touched by Vai, were sending me strongly worded memos that they were enraptured too.

This had been an inevitable consequence of inviting them to dance. I had known that even at the time, but I did it anyway. Vai seemed to enjoy it, too, so no harm done, except to my own levels of yearning.

"Be one of our backup dancers," I said the next day as we walked to the rehearsal tent.

Vai blinked at me. "In Eidovision?"

"You've danced for festivals before. It's no different."

"Well. If there's time, with my other tasks…"

"There is. We'll make sure there is."

Ultimately, Vai was slated to dance in three of the ten acts. We debuted the performance a few days later at an open-air theatre in Kagami. Vai appeared backstage in their first costume—which was for the country-western song, and thus was a red cowboy hat and boots, fringed leather vest over a white tank, and denim short-shorts. I tried not to stare at the fantastic things this ensemble was doing for Vai's legs, and instead focused on their face. Even under their makeup, I detected a pale sheen.

I approached and showed my palms. "Hey. May I?"

It took them a moment to understood, then they nodded. "Thank you."

I laid my hands on their chest, on the white fabric, and beamed calm into their body. "This is cheating, technically," I said. "Stage nerves are part of the tradition. But we hauled you into this on short notice, so it isn't fair."

Vai exhaled, color returning to their face. "Silly," they murmured. "I shouldn't be nervous. The acts are only a couple minutes each."

"Plus this is all in the service of comedy, so even if you mess up, it doesn't matter. No one cares. Okay—places!"

To nobody's surprise, Vai was flawless. By their second act they were standing confident in their next costume, flashing me a grin, laughing at something Genevieve said.

After curtain call, I hugged them. "You were amazing. What do you think? Going to do it again?"

Wearing a healthy flush now, Vai shook back their sweaty hair and nodded. "I could."

"Good! Because we want to do at least four more performances of this sketch, and otherwise we'd have to find someone else."

The next morning, over breakfast, Vai propped their chin on their knuckles and looked at me sidelong, smiling. They said nothing.

Two could play at this game. I returned their gaze, holding my mug under my chin, breathing coffee steam.

Vai broke first. "I've performed on stage," they said. "Now you have to do a drama."

I lowered my lips to the rim of the mug. "Ah. Yes. Deals are deals. I'll do my best."

Then after Vai went out for some solitary seaside yoga, I hauled a box from my closet and, panic rising within me like a swift tide, took out each item. Enchanted dried galangal roots so I could drink fae-realm water without being enspelled. The velvet-over-iron choker to repel fae from my neck, along with iron chains for self-defense. Chantagrams of videos, and an ebook reader packed with plays and novels, so I wouldn't run out of stories with which to entertain Nalibak. The magic-enhanced charger to keep my tech going, since in the dark I couldn't use a solar charger. Glass spheres and penlights that would light up as needed and not go out for years. Whisper-thin silk garments with enchantments to keep you warm even in chilly conditions, and witch-created nonperishable food that would keep you alive for days per bite. Packets of magic herbs from Ayda, with instructions on their medical use.

Some of these I had bought. Ayda had mailed others, and Wayshaw had obtained some as well. I now had all my tattoos linked up, the last pieces added a few weeks ago—slim vines around my torso and along my limbs, connecting foot ink to hip ink, and wrist ink to shoulder ink. One protection spell could go into all of them at once.

None of it guaranteed safety, though, nor even survival. Fair feasters weren't the only dangers in the Eidolonian wilderness. Any reasonable person would say it was a forfeit of my life to stay there a full year, in conditions I didn't know much about except that Nalibak lived in a "lair" and would keep me in it.

Ayda had said it was cold, dark, and damp. And sometimes she saw beautiful, alluring things, but those were probably hallucinations. That was all she remembered from her few visits there, which had only been a night or two each.

While I was there, Ayda's father would track me down once a quarter, deliver messages and human-realm food, and make sure Nalibak was holding up his end of the deal and refraining from killing me. But it would be months between such visits, and meanwhile everyone I loved would be moving on with their lives.

It was also possible I wouldn't come back.

One night in the fae realm could equal weeks in the human realm. But it did sometimes happen the other way around. I could languish in the fae realm for ten years, from my point of view, while only a year passed out here. If it went that way, my chances of surviving shrank to a sliver.

I shoved everything back in the closet, banged the door shut, and took deep breaths.

The obvious conclusion was to do everything I could to make my loved ones happy in the time I had left. There. See? I had already been putting my attention where it should be.

Ayda's thirty-fifth birthday, the day I'd be taken, was May twenty-seventh. I had more than four months left. If I spent it worrying, rather than relishing my freedom, I knew I'd despise myself later, when locked away somewhere dark and damp and cold.

CHAPTER 12

VAI

Even after our stint of Eidovision performances ended, and I went back to working in props, costumes, and scenery, Leo kept suggesting we practice dances. Given he seemed to enjoy it as much as I did, I obliged.

That was how the rest of February passed. Tango lessons in dewy parks, with foghorn notes floating in from the sea. Cooking together and bantering. Makeup on, makeup off. Sets built, sets dismantled. Movie nights with the troupe, TV nights with just us two. I had begun to love my life.

One day in early March, in a routine search on my family's name, I found an article that stopped my feet on the trail where I was walking. Kikenna Bay lapped against the stones in cold musical chatter as I took in the words.

My mother and father were divorcing. It was only one paragraph. Dad and Uncle Joe, it reminded readers, had recently been charged with fraud, and Airtight had closed its doors. The implication was unstated but detectable: the legal troubles had strained the marriage to collapse.

As panic spread in my chest, I got onto social media and checked my mother's account—nothing new for several months—then Daphne's.

My sister had put up photos the night before. My mother had played a Rachmaninoff concerto at a charity gala, which Daphne had attended. They looked resplendent in silk cheongsams, Daphne's in ruby red and Mom's in midnight blue. They were hugging in one picture, smiling at the camera in another, and speaking together in a few candid shots, their expressions emotional and heartfelt, as if they alone understood what the other was going through.

I had caused them this trouble. And I was unknown to them and had to live without them. I didn't know which part was worse.

I wasn't far from the caravans but couldn't face anyone yet. I sat on a rock and stared at the bay in a blur, tears spilling down my cheeks.

I didn't even know Leo was near until a step crunched in the gravel, then he swung down to sit beside me. He made a soft noise of concern and brushed a knuckle against my wet face. I wordlessly showed him the article.

"Ah," he said. "Shit. I'm sorry." Then he handed my phone back and hugged me around the waist.

I loved him. It was a calm realization, dropping into our silence like a flower petal. I wasn't going to speak of it—not today, anyway—but the knowledge shored me up. I could love new people, and whether or not they loved me back, they could show me kindness, and I could have a new life in their orbit.

After I had wiped my face and calmed down, he insisted we go out to lunch. Catarina was just stepping out of her caravan, and he invited her along.

This may have been shrewd thinking on his part or mere luck. Over the next few weeks she quickly became one of my favorite people to talk to. Older than me, wise and compassionate, she comforted me in a way that reminded me of my mother and sister, though Catarina was funnier than either. In addition, she was a crosswater, having immigrated from Canada some twenty years ago, so she related to the poignancy of being isolated from one's family.

"I've been doing theatre since I was a teenager," she told me while we carried props into a venue one afternoon. "When I came here and saw theatre with *magic*? Paradise. I could never live anywhere else. Thank goodness the fae agreed."

"I expect in your case their vote was unanimous," I said.

"I'm sure I just got an unusually amenable bunch."

"Who brought you?" I asked.

"Darius." She nodded toward him, across the parking area. "When I was thirty-nine, he came to Montreal and saw a show I was in. He stayed after to talk, and we hit it off. At the end of summer he told me there was a place he *had* to take me—did I trust him? Thank the gods I said yes. We even spoke of becoming spouses, long ago, but luckily we were sensible enough not to ruin it by doing that."

I set the box of props against a wall. "Did you ever direct?"

"I have, though it's been a couple years. At Quicksand we take turns. Whoever's interested."

"You should direct the next play. Make it a drama, and cast Leo in a juicy role."

She gave me a conspiratorial smile. "I'm several steps ahead of you. I have *plans*."

We inched up the west coast. The days grew longer and greener, the coming of spring outpacing us. There were two things I looked forward to in March: first, discovering which dramatic role Leo would play, to fulfill our agreement. That would apparently be decided near the end of the month. Second: the spring equinox, during Water Festival.

While many places in the world held the tradition of kissing at the stroke of midnight on New Year's Eve, Eidolonians kissed at the astronomical moment of the spring equinox. It was a way of saying goodbye to winter and welcoming the new life of spring.

The actors kissed on stage all the time without it meaning anything except entertainment. After everything I'd been through, and would go through later this year, surely it wasn't asking too much of the gods to grant me one equinox kiss from the person I was in love with.

My body, of course, surged with adrenaline sweat and other hormones whenever I thought of it, letting me know that from its point of view such a kiss would by no means be a small matter. But that didn't have to be anyone's problem except mine.

LEO

One afternoon while Vai was fitting me for a costume in Mathilde's bus, it occurred to me to ask the annual question everyone asks in early March: "What time is the equinox this year, anyhow?" I got out my phone to check.

Vai didn't answer, letting out the hem of the trousers I wore.

I groaned after finding the information. "Four thirty-two a.m.? Seriously? Is there a worse time of day than 4:32 a.m.?"

"It is not the most convenient," Vai said.

"So if we want to see the fireworks, we either have to stay up way too late or get up way too early. Or skip the whole thing."

"Or," Vai said, affixing stitches with taps of their fingers, "we go to sleep, set an alarm for, say, four fifteen, enjoy the fireworks, then go back to bed."

I put my phone away. "As ever, Vai, you are impeccably practical. Oh! You know what? We should camp out."

They looked at me. "At night? Outdoors?"

"That is how camping out is usually done, yes. Oh, you're thinking of fair feasters. We'd take precautions. St. John's wort. Spells and iron. Besides, other people would probably join us, so we'd be a crowd, and Nalibak wouldn't get close."

My tone became uncertain by the end. I had already begun to rethink the idea. But gods damn it, Nalibak didn't get to ruin the few remaining festivals I had left. If I wanted to camp out with my friends, then I would.

Vai resumed work on the hem. "True, one would usually prefer to have other people around on the equinox."

I swear to the powers that be, not until that moment did my scattered brain remember the main feature of the spring equinox, the one that wasn't fireworks or theatrical obligations. The kiss.

A different type of pyrotechnics exploded within my chest.

"Yeah!" I said. "Let's do it."

By which I meant *I want you there so that you are the one who kisses me at 4:32 a.m., of all stupid times but I'll take it, so please agree to my plan.* That was assuming Vai had any interest in kissing me, or kissing anyone at all. Whatever they wanted was fine. I simply needed to place myself nearby, in case.

Come the evening of the equinox, we stood on a hillside overlooking Port Baleia and the sea, setting up a large tent in a blustery wind. We had finished our evening performances in the city. Only a handful of others wanted to sleep in the tent, the rest opting to come out of their caravans at the equinox hour, so our small group made campfire popcorn, s'mores, and decaf, then retired around midnight. Vai laid their air mattress down next to mine.

Uwila created flames that were dim but hot, and Vai added an insulation spell to the tent, so even though we kept the front wall open—the better to see stars and fireworks—the wind didn't batter us, and we stayed comfortable. Near us, Uwila, Kornelia, and Shelini held a quiet conversation, one of the lengthy philosophical discussions they sometimes got into.

I couldn't shake thoughts of Nalibak, who could be a few yards away this very moment, salivating to prey upon us. Even if he tried, he couldn't reach us. Protective spells encircled the tent, like those protecting the caravans. We were just as safe here as in our vehicles. But only by pulling my gaze away from the ominous proscenium of the open tent front and latching it onto Vai was I able to relax. They looked adorable, eyes shut, mouth relaxed, hand drawn up under the pillow.

In the caravan, I rarely saw Vai asleep, except when I crept past their bunk to get to the bathroom. Here, I was close enough to stroke their cheek, or roll over and hug them, though I didn't move. Imagining it, however, must have soothed me into slumber, because then a mellow meditation-gong sound was chiming, and Vai picked up the phone and stopped it.

"Four fifteen," they informed me.

I produced a groan in response.

The others got up, blankets around their shoulders. "Coming, Vai, Leo?" Korn called.

"In a bit," I mumbled. "Or not."

Vai sipped from a thermos, then offered it to me. "Mint tea. No caffeine."

Mint. Because when you might soon kiss someone, it's polite to rinse your mouth first. Who was Vai planning to kiss?

I dragged myself up and took the thermos. The tea was cool and minty. I swished it around my teeth before swallowing, then handed it back to Vai with thanks.

Our friends emerged from their caravans and joined Korn and the others, a few paces downhill. They formed a huddle, watching Port Baleia's festival lights sparkle below.

"Going to join them?" I asked Vai, super casual.

"I'm all right here. You can go, of course."

I pretended to consider it. "Nah. I'm cozy here. You know what we should do, though." I got up and dragged my mattress, blankets and all, to just outside the tent, and sat back down on it. "Better view."

Rather than drag their own mattress out, as I'd expected, Vai simply walked over and plunked down next to me on mine.

I was wide awake now. My heart was doing twice its normal speed.

We were near one of Uwila's dim violet flames, so the air wasn't cold. I settled back on my elbows. Vai did the same. A green firework shot up from the city and burst into the numeral 60, in calligraphic script. It began changing with the countdown: 59, 58, 57…

Cheers arose from Port Baleia. Noisemakers rattled. Everyone started chanting the seconds at the last ten—everyone other than Vai and me. We sat motionless, watching the numbers sparkle.

"Three, two, one—HAPPY SPRING!" The cheers swelled to a cacophony. An array of fireworks exploded, splashing colored light across our hill.

Vai and I looked at each other, smiling.

"Happy spring," I squeaked, and leaned toward them.

"Happy spring." They moved closer.

We balanced on our elbows. Our lips touched, a swift but silky collision, mint-flavored and much too brief.

If there was anything I'd learned from rehearsals, it was that you got to do a thing over again if you knew you could do it better.

"Awkward angle," I said. "Here. Maybe..." I let myself fall onto my back, on the mattress, and waited to see what Vai would do.

Politely ignore me and look up at the fireworks? Lean down for a perfunctory kiss and *then* pull back to watch the fireworks? Those seemed the likeliest options.

I was wrong on both. Vai *pounced*.

Their torso slanted across mine, forearms framing my shoulders. They took my face in both hands and kissed me like they had no intention of stopping anytime in the next half hour.

I hardly need to say I was up for it. Though I laughed in surprise for a second, against Vai's mouth, this was not a comedy kiss, a caricature of passion. Vai kissed like a lover from a drama.

So I shifted to sincerity too. My pretenses fell away, and I kissed Vai with all the upwelling feelings they had sparked in me these past five months. Admiration. Friendship. Fondness. Desire.

Love.

I wound my arms around their back, sliding a hand up into their sleek hair. Tilting my face for a deeper fit, I kissed Vai like I was drinking them in, reveling in soft lips and lean muscles and the weight of their body on me. Fireworks whistled and burst, light flaring through my closed eyelids.

"Bravo, Vai!" Fred yelled from a distance. "That's how it's done!"

"Shut *up*," Kornelia snarled, softer but still audible.

Vai withdrew, gave me a modest smile, then turned to wave to the group down the hill. I tottered up onto my elbows. Grinning, Korn and Fred waved back, Fred adding a double thumbs-up before Korn whacked him on the arm.

I felt blissfully weightless. Failing to think of some socially acceptable way to say *Well, I'm completely hard now, how about you?*, I said instead, "Full marks.

I don't think I've ever had a hotter equinox kiss."

"I feel one should do things well if one's going to do them at all." Vai sounded calm and proper. But they caught my gaze, breathing through parted lips in a way that appeared flustered.

We said nothing else about it. Commented on the fireworks a few times. Laughed at Uwila picking Fred up and flying him into the air, while Fred screamed ecstatically. The noise and lights died down. The wind drifted to our hill, smelling of pyrotechnic smoke. We all shambled back to bed.

With my mattress next to Vai's again, I shut my eyes—as Vai had already done—but instead of sleeping, I replayed and triple-underlined every detail of the kiss so I wouldn't forget it.

Vai probably had little romantic interest in me. They wanted to kiss *someone*, and I was just the least stressful candidate around. No problem, I was happy to be that. And they'd poured such passion into the kiss because, like me, they probably felt a bit starved for intimacy. Unless they'd been quite discreet, they hadn't been with anyone since joining Quicksand. And unlike me, Vai probably hadn't adopted a "no lovers" guideline for this year, so they might be feeling the craving more strongly.

Lovely thing about festivals like this one was that the kisses—like kisses for performances—didn't count as violations of such guidelines.

My eyes snapped open as I remembered the one remaining festival left before my deadline. Lady Festival, in early May. In which *people had no-strings-attached sex* on Rose Night, if they wanted.

Well, shit. Now I definitely wouldn't be able to sleep.

VAI

I did not sleep a wink the rest of the night, though I lay with my eyes shut and my breathing slow. Never had I felt more euphoric while experiencing total insomnia.

I was in love. That half-minute of kissing had been heaven. And Leo had given it full marks. The rest of my year in exile was looking like a holiday dipped in chocolate and gold leaf.

CHAPTER 13

VAI

A couple of days after Water Festival wrapped up, Leo attended a troupe planning meeting. I stayed in the caravan, since he had told me reluctantly, "Everyone says you're welcome to come. It's just, these can go on awhile and get kind of stupid. And I know your schedule could get crazy later in the year, so the autumn season might be undecided for you..."

I took that to mean I would not be the best fit for the meeting, and I agreed. Five months of living among them had been a theatrical education beyond any I'd ever had, but it held no candles at all to the other troupe members' experience. I used the afternoon to replenish our groceries and read one of the plays in Leo's collection.

I had begun cooking mattar paneer and rice for dinner when Leo wandered in, looking dazed. "Hi," he said in my approximate direction. He peeled off his coat and shoes at half the normal speed.

I set the wooden spoon down. "What's wrong? Did Nalibak show up?"

"Huh? No, nothing like that. We've, uh..." Taking the seat beneath the lamp, he absently scratched his ear. "Decided to put on *Moulin Rouge*. As the drama. It counts as a drama, right?"

Joy bloomed through me. "It absolutely does."

Then I had to drag a kitchen chair over to him and sit down too. Images bombarded me: Leo sleek and dandy in 1900-era top hat and tails, or, even more perspiration-inducing, ruffled petticoats and fishnet stockings.

"Catarina's directing," he added.

"Wonderful, I hoped she would. Has it been cast?"

"Um..." He cleared his throat. "Everyone thought it would be a good vehicle for Shelini's voice, because she's amazing."

"Agreed."

"But she wants to play Christian, since she likes his songs better. So for Satine, they said? Everyone looked at each other and then...then a lot of them were looking at me?" Leo blinked at me, as if he couldn't quite focus.

My jaw went slack. It was perfect. Sublime. It would run my heart through a shredder, every rehearsal and performance, and I would love every second of it. "And?"

"Well. Using my actor negotiation skills, I said, 'I would require a dress that was sequined purple. With hair dyed to match.'"

"The Jessica Rabbit gown."

Leo lifted his fingers in acknowledgment. "They said sure. So, yeah. I'm going to be Satine."

"I love this," I said, quietly fervent.

He met my gaze. "It'll do? As a dramatic role? I want you to be satisfied."

"I will be. Everyone who sees it will be."

His mouth stretched into a cautious smile.

I moved forward, landing on my knees, and grabbed his hands. "I'm more excited about this than I've been about anything in ages."

Leo laughed—finally. He whipped my hands back and forth. "Oh my gods! What am I doing?" Looking down, he slid a thumb back and forth across my skin. "Jessica Rabbit gown," he said, as if reciting a mantra.

"I will personally ensure every sequin is perfect. And I'll color your hair myself."

"Of course. I still have dibs on you." A smile lit his face, and he poked my shoulder. "And guess what. This show needs an ensemble. People who can dance, and also just stand there looking pretty. So I repeat, *guess what*, Vai."

The words knocked me back to sit on my heels. But I answered, "I'm willing. If Catarina wants."

"She does. She told me to ask you. There, *now* I feel better. We'll be in it together."

So perhaps it would also be me in ruffled petticoats and fishnet stockings. The things we do for love.

LEO

I did have to pause and ask myself: what in the name of the seven powers that be was I thinking, taking on the role of a doomed person working in a theatre, who cannot be with her beloved, and who in fact dies at the end? To the degree I had thought it through, I figured it could be cathartic—the way Vai kept claiming drama was supposed to be. Also, I wasn't the one who had picked *Moulin Rouge*, and even if I hadn't been Satine, I would still have been involved in the story and its sadness.

But on a practical level, the best thing about playing the lead was that it would keep me extremely busy. I wouldn't have much time to think about what came after. I might not even have time to think about Vai, and maybe that was good and maybe not, but I would at least enjoy having Vai in the show alongside me.

There was one underhanded thing I didn't like. I had discouraged Vai from coming to the planning meeting because, in that meeting, I had to inform everyone I wouldn't be available for shows from the last week of May onward.

"I have family and friend obligations I've been putting off, and it'll be time for me to tackle them," I had explained, to the puzzled faces of the two dozen friends who had given me something to do with my aimless life these past eight years. A lump rose in my throat. "It'll be a full year. I don't really want to do it, but… Could you please, all of you, promise me—don't mention this to Vai? I haven't told them yet. I'll do it in my own time. They…count on me. The situation's unique there."

The others nodded and were silent except for some sad murmurs of agreement.

I was such a dishonest shit.

Vai *would* find out, and from my own lips, before I left. But I couldn't bear to deliver a half-truth to their face in the meantime. Somehow that would feel worse than doing the same to everyone else in the troupe combined. Besides, the minute Vai found out where I was *really* going, they would try to fix the problem—save me; or worse, come with me. There was no saving me with this deal, and absolutely no putting any of my friends in danger. Ergo, I would delay.

Given the manic schedule involved with *Moulin Rouge*, though, Vai would likely not suspect anything for a while. There was *loads* to do. A whirlwind essentially arrived and yanked us all up inside it. Quicksand had never, in all my years with them, put on a show this big. Possibly never in the troupe's history. We had to hire extra musicians. We began song and dance rehearsals at once, to get everyone's vocal cords and can-can muscles into shape. We started building the set, which had to be movable, because we'd be running performances in three cities.

Aside from me as Satine, and Shelini as Christian, the cast encompassed basically everyone. Genevieve, rotund and powerfully voiced, was to don a mustache and be Harold Zidler. Fred was embracing his debonair, evil side as the Duke. Darius, with his haunting baritone, would be Toulouse-Lautrec. And, as promised, Vai won an ensemble spot as one of the dancers. After seeing them tango me around our parking areas, Catarina had declared we absolutely needed Vai on that stage.

As the cast gathered for our first costume-planning session, I asked Vai, "When you snuck into my caravan last November, did you ever imagine we were going to be courtesans together?"

Vai laughed. Their eyes shone in the spring sun. "I did not."

I took their chin between finger and thumb. "And I didn't imagine I'd ever see you this happy."

I loved Vai. I had known I loved them since our first hug, at that Dasdemir fire fountain, but now I was getting in so deep that it was going to cause me grief. I didn't care. I walked straight into that blinding light anyway, because soon I would have more than enough of darkness.

VAI

Leo stepped out from behind the dressing curtain in Mathilde's bus wearing a black-and-silver corset with a skirt of sparkly fringe that barely made it past his hips, with elbow-length black satin gloves, fishnet stockings, and garters. The sight knocked me dizzy.

"I should go grocery shopping in this," he remarked.

Mathilde assessed him. "Make the tattoos invisible. Shave everything, if you're willing. Limbs, pits, chest."

"Vai's good with hair," Leo said. "You could do that, right? Magic it all off? If you're up for it."

I gripped the door frame of Mathilde's bus to steady myself. "Mm-hm," I said. "I can."

"You both looked up for it on the equinox," Mathilde added, nonchalant.

Leo gasped, laughing. "Voyeur!" he accused her.

She took hold of a lock of his hair and examined it. "Could dye this while you're at it. Unless you prefer a wig?"

"Dye," he said, standing in splendid dishabille with hands on his corset-accentuated hips. "For my existing hair. Purple extensions for the rest."

Hair on living creatures—along with nails or feathers—was the universal recipient for witches' magic. Not alive itself, yet belonging to a living body, hair defied clear categories and responded to both exo-witch and matter-witch spells, and endo-witch spells too, as long as the hair was still attached to the endo-witch's own body. I had magically dyed, removed, or trimmed the hair of dozens of acquaintances. I sent them silent heartfelt thanks now for all the practice.

Our opening night was to be in Serpentshore, at the northern tip of the island, on the twenty-first of April. All performers, as soon as possible, were to get accustomed to rehearsing in costume. Therefore I soon found myself sitting with Leo in a sunny park on the northwest shore, facing the task of magically pulling hairs off his body.

Hills rolled away above us, and the sapphire sea crashed below. Pink phlox and white-and-orange narcissus grew between clumps of heather. The air smelled mossy and wild. Like a nymph in the middle of it sat Leo, wearing nothing but palm-leaf-patterned briefs and the black silk robe from his Satine wardrobe.

My task involved placing my hands on him, latching my magic onto all the hairs within reach of the spell—usually those I was touching plus those in a surrounding few centimeters—and coaxing them out of their follicles. I started at his ankles. Leo was blessed with a generous coating of body hair, which I found quite attractive, though admittedly, by now nearly all his features struck me as attractive. So I was also palpitatingly curious to see how he'd look after being magically waxed.

He wiggled his feet in my grasp. "This is going to take all your energy. Look how hairy I am. I'll revive you if you pass out."

I pulled out the first batch gently. Little black hairs fell from my palms into the grass. "Hairs are small. They don't take much energy."

"Have you ever depilated anyone before?" he asked in the sultry voice he'd been working on for Satine.

"I have. Including myself." I lifted one of my elbows to indicate my smooth arm, visible in my tank top. I had already prepared my own skin for my courtesan role.

"I love that tattoo, by the way," he added, in his regular voice. "It's super cute."

I glanced at the ink near my shoulder: a lavender treble clef with a blue winged faery curled up above it. "It's in honor of my mother's music. And my air fae ancestor." I nodded at the tattoos sprawling across Leo's body. "We'll have plenty to render invisible on you, for performances."

I had seen most of his ink, but rarely all at once like this: a happy collection of artistic symbols, Eidolonian landmarks, flowering jasmine vines, stars, and more.

He sat back on his hands. I did his shins. Calves. Knees. Lower thighs. I moved beside him to do his upper thighs, because kneeling between his open legs when he was barely dressed was going to be too much for me. My fingertips were almost touching the edge of his briefs, and my thumbs hovered one swipe away from the interesting shapes the fabric contained. The skin of his inner thighs was silky-soft. He looked relaxed and pensive, his gaze near his feet.

Was he thinking the same as I was? How we had never touched this way before, and how it would be pleasurable to go further?

I drew out the hairs, scattered them, and sat back on my heels. "Legs done."

He ran a bare foot up the opposite leg. "Ha. I feel like a Barbie." He tugged an arm out of the robe and offered it to me. I started on his wrist.

Evidently his mind was not running along the same pleasure lines as mine, because after a minute he said, "I'm having trouble with the genuine emotion. Catarina's right, isn't she."

I shifted closer to access the back of his arm. "You're vamping wonderfully. And you're quite funny in the comedic scenes."

He was already pulling off his first song, "The Sparkling Diamond," with ravishing allure, snapping his hips to flick us ensemble members with his corset skirt, or dragging a gloved hand across our chests. And his comedy skills got full rein in the scene where Satine thinks Christian is there for sex, and Christian thinks he's there to read poetry.

"But when I need to be falling in love," he said, "or heartbroken, or abused…"

"In some scenes you do seem to be resisting. Not letting yourself get swept up in the moment."

"See. This is the trouble with drama. In comedy you're—tap dancing. It's a technical skill. Timing and rhythm. You have to stay in control. But drama is like, 'Now let go and lose yourself in a mess of emotions. Get swept away.'"

"I thought comedy was harder?" I said, innocently.

"Don't make me kick you with my dolphin-smooth leg."

Smiling, I searched his arm for any hairs I'd missed. "What do you think is holding you back?"

"I suppose...the part where it's ugly. Uncomfortable."

"For you or the audience?"

"Both. I don't want to be a mess and make it awkward. And even if I do it right and make them cry, part of me feels like that's cheap. Manipulative."

"They come to the theatre to feel things. It's an honor to make people cry."

"I know. Of course. I just...feel like I'm not that kind of actor, I guess."

I moved to his other side. He slid the robe off his shoulders and pulled his arm free for me to work on. "You did it when you were Claudio," I said.

"I was younger then. Fearless. In your twenties you can be like, 'Yeah, death, come get me!', throw yourself into a tragic scene, and laugh about it five minutes later. Then you get older and..." He didn't elaborate.

"Then we're not just playing anymore, with the serious issues."

"Right," he said. "We are not. And I don't want to open the door to those and then realize I can't handle it, and drown in it. In front of everyone."

I drew the hairs out of his forearm. "I think Satine fears that too."

Leo cocked his head, frowning.

"The theme of the play," I tried to explain, "is freedom, beauty, truth, and love. Right? Well, she has beauty, but she dies because she doesn't have, or can't learn to accept, enough of the other three."

Leo blinked at me. "She dies of *tuberculosis*, Vai."

"In literal terms, yes. But the tragedy is that she could not get free, be open with the truth, and embrace the love she found, before she dies."

His gaze slid to the flowers bobbing in the wind. "Huh."

"If it helps, try thinking of that. What it'd be like to feel that way."

Leo stared at the sea. When I lifted his elbow to reach his underarm, he tucked his arm over his head without a glance at me. Not until I had rendered both underarms smooth, plus his chest and jaw, did he speak again.

"It's true we have beauty." His voice was soft. "Look at all this." He lifted his chin toward the seascape, then took my hand and ran his thumb over my palm, which felt hot and tender from the magic I'd been channeling through it. "Look at all this."

"Everyone who sees this show will fall in love with you." I hardly had enough breath for the words. They felt too bold.

Yet he heard me and lifted his face, his eyes vulnerable. "And just like Satine, I won't believe I deserve it."

"You do," I said, as simply as I could, and sat up taller as if to prove my confidence. "Take that feeling into rehearsal and see."

CHAPTER 14

LEO

I didn't regret taking on Ayda's deal. Truly I didn't. In my teenage years, every time Aunt Yubara's remarks had cut me too deeply, it was Ayda's place I escaped to. Her mom's caravan was tiny, disorderly, comfy, and full of music and snacks, as well as musicians who were unfailingly good-humored and took Ayda's magical affliction in stride. She couldn't have known how much it meant to me, having a home that embraced me when my own felt like it excluded me. Yubara and I couldn't stop insulting each other, Uncle Luis stayed out of it, and Javier just scowled.

But I had not known Vai when I shouldered Ayda's deal. I didn't know I'd soon have a caravan-mate who would spill sweet, soothing light into my nocturnal life and improve my existence immeasurably just by being near.

I didn't know I'd be in love.

Take that feeling into rehearsal, Vai said. Show that. They couldn't have known the emotions they were inviting me to unleash. But if this was what it took to step up my performance, I would try.

We had settled in the town of Serpentshore and started rehearsing in our venue—a century-old theater with a seating capacity of eight hundred. A few hours after my depilation job at Vai's hands, we would be running the entire play. Catarina had previously said I was coming across as coy in the love scenes, rather than sincerely enamored; and that in the breakup and death scenes, I was too composed.

This time I took a while, pacing in my stockings and heeled boots, to put myself in Satine's mindset. My life overlaid onto hers. Falling in love when I wasn't free to do so. Choosing to savor each moment with my beloved, even under the shadow of my doom. Honoring my deal with my tormentor, despite loathing his existence.

I gazed across the stage at Vai—breathtaking in strapless corset, ruffled skirt, and black mascara—and I dove into those floodwaters of emotions and started swimming for my life.

I melted close against Shelini as we kissed. I let my fearful revulsion show when Fred loomed over me. I felt beset by phantoms as we moved through the increasingly tragic scenes, despair wringing my voice until I worried the emotions were knocking me off key. My face contorted of its own volition as I broke Christian's heart, and I thought for sure Catarina was going to tell me afterward not to look so absurd. In the death scene, in Shelini's arms, my voice choked on the sadness of our final lines, before I fell limp and let my wet eyes close. Six of the ensemble members, including Vai, lifted me and carried me offstage as Shelini huddled in grief. I took everyone's echoing silence as proof that I had delivered an excruciating performance.

But then the lights went down, and my friends set me on the floor gently. And they were…sniffling. Crying?

"You were fantastic," Genevieve whispered to me.

"Made me cry," a dancer added, his voice broken.

Stunned, I looked to Vai. In the dim blue light, their eyes shone. They beamed at me and dabbed away their tears.

When it was time for notes, Catarina gave us a long, radiant smile. "Shelini, Leo—*yes*. Oh my Lord! The emotion is there. I think it rolled out of this theatre and the whole town felt it. Now—I marked a few places where the lines got garbled in all that *wonderful* emotion, so let us note those spots and think about enunciating."

That evening, Vai and I walked to the seashore. Wayshaw raced ahead, onto a small pier with two lanterns on its end, one red and one green. She vaulted the wooden railing and morphed into her merfolk form as she dove into the waves and disappeared.

Vai nodded toward the sea. "How did you meet Wayshaw? I asked her once, and she just said, 'I met Leo when he was unhappy, then we met again when *I* was unhappy, and he invited me to join the troupe.' I didn't press for details."

"It's a bit of a long story. I can do it in 'quickest ever' form. Although…" I rubbed my chin. "I can't think of a way to make *all* of it funny."

At the end of the pier, I rested my elbows on the railing. "First, some background. My parents. They grew and sold weed—typical for the Southwest Peninsula. My mom was a witch and tinkered with blends for magical effects. My dad was not a witch but did like weed a lot. They both loved windsurfing and rock climbing and flying air surreys. You see where this is going, right?"

Vai said nothing. I pressed my fingertip against a nailhead in the railing and went on. "One day Mom was trying a new strain that apparently impaired judgment more than usual. She decided to go windsurfing. During a high-wave warning, with a storm coming in."

"Leo," Vai said. As if to tell me I didn't have to elaborate.

"She…her body…was found that night. Dad lost his mind. I barely even remember this, I swear." What I remembered was a sheet of blackout terror over all my senses, and crying nonstop because I didn't understand, and then later because I did begin to understand. But, as stated, no way to make that funny. "He took an air surrey out by himself," I said, "in the middle of the night, in the storm, to scream at the fae to bring her back."

Vai leaned against my side. "I'm sorry."

"Again, you can guess how that ended. Okay! So that's the background—"

"You were six?"

I looked down and poked the nail harder. "Yep. And I got sent to Tesoro, to live with my cousin's family—"

"Didn't you have grandparents?"

"Vai." I smiled gently. "You're holding up the comedy. Yes, I had—I *have*—grandparents. The ones on my dad's side live in Port Baleia in a splendiferous apartment, and have pet birds and zero interest in comedic theatre. My mother's folks lived in Miryoku, but they split up. My grandma moved crosswater, with a memory charm, and lives with an expat community in Costa Rica. She mails me about once a year with a picture of some rainforest snake she got to hold. My grandfather, from whom apparently my mom got her sense of personal safety, wandered across the verge a few years after my parents died and, in his turn, died of enchantment damage. But apparently he was an earth faery's lover for a few days before that, so I like to think he at least went out feeling okay."

Vai took my hand, lifting it off the nail. "I've never seen you smoke," they said after a moment. "You don't seem to drink much either."

"Tried all that, in my twenties. Sensed the potential of it becoming a problem, so I stopped. The one good decision I ever made. Other than joining Quicksand—and letting you stay in the caravan, of course." I grinned.

They did not smile back. "I don't know what to say. I doubt you can make anything funny after that."

"Challenge accepted! So—the scene. Ancona Beach, a blustery March night. Seventeen-year-old Leo has totally skipped out on doing laundry like he's supposed to, and has taken the bus from Tesoro to the coast because he has a very important, very emo mission." I leaped onto the bottom rail and splayed a hand across my heart. "Spirits of the obsidian ocean, of the amaranthine deep, I summon thee! You took my parents! And now my girlfriend has broken up with me, and my aunt and uncle are fascists who make me do laundry, and I'm gonna stand here on a rock with waves splattering me and declaim the entirety of Poe's 'Annabel Lee.' I beseech you to either drag me into the briny abyss and end my misery, or appear and make my life fun again!"

The sides of Vai's mouth tilted up. "Amaranthine?"

"I didn't know what it meant. It means 'purplish,' or also 'undying,' neither of which are quite the word for the ocean depths, but it sounded good." I cleared my throat and flung both arms up. "'It was many and many a year ago / In a kingdom by the sea, / That a maiden there lived whom you may know / By the name of Annabel Lee.' I'll spare you the rest. It's tragic, it's melodramatic, it's not even all that apt because it's my parents who died in the sea, not my ex-girlfriend—*she* is alive and well—but! At the end of the poem, this head pops up in the surf." I screamed and leaped backward onto the pier boards.

Grinning, Vai caught my elbow. "Wayshaw?"

"She climbed out and introduced herself. Of course her name isn't 'Wayshaw,' it's this long sequence of sounds like a wave crashing, but the start of it is something like 'Wayshaw.' She told me she appreciated the poem, then asked why I was risking my life in a storm. We talked awhile. When someone tells you they've been alive a hundred and ten years, it does give a seventeen-year-old some perspective."

"And you stayed in touch?"

"Sporadically. When I was at the beach, I'd yell her name, and sometimes she'd be near and some faery would fetch her. Finally one year, I was a brand-new Quicksand actor, I was at Ancona Beach again and shouted for her, and…" I shrugged. "She was feeling low. Her closest friend had returned to the elements after a long life. I told her if she needed a change of scene, she could travel with us. Which she's been doing ever since."

"I'm glad she took you up on it," Vai said. "Not least of all because she's a much less scary driver than you."

"Rude," I said. "So that's the story. Funny?"

"Admittedly it's a *little* funny to imagine you declaiming Poe into a storm."

"Right? That shit's hilarious."

"Please tell me you wore black eyeliner."

"As if you have to ask."

Smiling, Vai gave me a once-over. "We need to do your hair. The extensions and the purple. Tomorrow?"

My attention rushed a different direction, one I was happy to follow.

Vai's heated hands on my skin, in the wildflower meadow. Their long legs encased in fishnets. Their kiss on spring equinox. How familiar they were with me, even right this second, shoulder and hip touching mine, mouthwatering imported perfume swirling from their collar to my nose in the sea breeze.

I'd had several erotic dreams about Vai by now. Daydreams too. There was one where Vai climbed into my bed, shushed me, and pinned me down. One where they pulled me into a deserted classroom, undid their jeans, and pushed me to my knees. One where we were wearing corsets and snogging in a makeup room surrounded by the troupe, and I opened my legs on the counter for them—who cared if everyone could see. And so on. My imagination had been revving its engines.

Rose Night, in Lady Festival, was three weeks away. When you could have sex in an arrangement understood to be casual, as a celebration to honor the Lady. Though I doubted Vai was in love with me, I guessed from their glances and touches that I might have a chance at a yes that night.

I released my breath, jittery but relieved at how much there was to do, how much yet to enjoy, before I lost control of my life.

"Absolutely," I answered—regarding Vai's offer to do my hair. "Tomorrow."

VAI

Leo sat in a folding chair in the sun while I added purple extensions to his hair, fastening each strand with a glimmer of magic.

"How are you feeling about going back to Tesoro?" he asked.

I applied magic to a section of his roots, watching purple spread into the black. "Nervous. Someone's bound to recognize me, even with my alias."

In the play's program I was Lu Colette—a generic first name, and a surname taken from the Belle Époque theatre performer and writer. I'd initially had no objection to being listed as Vai Delvecchio, as my family still wouldn't recognize me or my name until November. But then I remembered the journalists and decided I could do without a handful of new articles exposing where Vai Delvecchio had been all this time.

"No one could have cared that much where I was," I added, "or someone would've already tracked me down and run the story. But I might as well not hand it to them on a plate."

"Agreed. So you're not going to tell anyone you're in town?"

"I don't plan to. Although…I might try to see Daphne. From a distance." I sighed. "No, that's stalking. I shouldn't."

"I don't think it'd be stalking. You wouldn't be creepy. If I were you, I couldn't resist trying either."

"Are you going to see your family?" I asked.

"Yeah. I'll have to." Then, as if realizing the statement sounded odd, he amended, "I want to."

"A bit fraught, then, Tesoro. For us both."

"Good word. Fraught."

"It's not till the end of the month, though. And Lady Festival will keep us busy for the first two Tesoro weekends."

"Lady Festival," he agreed.

His reflective tone spun my thoughts in a giddier direction. Rose Night had been on my mind, to a greater or lesser degree, ever since our scorching equinox kiss. I had to plan my approach. But not right this minute, with my hands buried in his warm hair.

Leo shifted, adjusting position, and the strands spilled out of my grasp.

I gathered them back up and tugged downward. "Stay still."

"Did you just pull my hair to make me hold still?" Amusement danced in his voice.

"Apologies. *Please* hold still."

"Let me say that a different way." Leo cleared his throat, then said in his husky Satine voice, "Did you just pull my hair to make me hold still?"

Sparks burst deep within me and swirled out through all my flesh. I sighed, hoping it sounded long-suffering rather than turned on. "Am I pulling in a way that's uncomfortable? I don't want to hurt you."

"No," he said, in his own voice once more, and reached up to pat one of my hands. He tipped his head back to peek at me, brown eyes gleaming in the sun. "Your touch is always the most pleasant of anyone's."

Then, while I stood stunned, he folded his arms and settled back to allow me to continue.

CHAPTER 15

LEO

Somehow or other, we pulled off all our Tech Week tasks. The Quicksand Theatre Company skidded, stumbled, wept, and can-canned our way to opening night.

"I've never been right here before," I whispered to Vai, five minutes before curtain. "The lead of a tragedy, about to open."

We were both powdered, spangled, corseted, and bare-shouldered. The backstage blue lights were mellow as moonlight. Our fellow actors glittered in the shadows around us, waiting. The air felt electric with tension.

Vai twined their hand into mine. "You've been on stage a thousand times. This is just one more."

I was superstitious enough—like nearly every actor—neither to say anything too optimistic nor too pessimistic. An example of the latter being *As the lead, if I bomb, the whole show bombs*. Instead I clutched Vai's hand, looking up through the rigging. "One more," I echoed.

The audience's babble flowed through the closed curtain.

"I gather Quicksand doesn't often get a full house?" Vai asked.

"No, it's been a while. Do *not* go and peek through the curtain, that's super bad luck."

Twenty minutes earlier, in the green room, Catarina had delivered to us the blessed words: "Friends, we have sold out all seats. We have a full house." No pressure or anything!

At that moment I'd had the twisted thought, *At least I'll get to run away and hide in the fae realm for a year, if I choke onstage*. Which was a horrible thing to think. But dark humor had airlifted me out of multiple freakouts in my life, and it did the trick this time too.

"Places." Wayshaw, our stage manager, spoke the word in a whisper that carried across backstage.

Vai was in the opening number; I was not. They kissed my cheek, then squeezed my hand and strode away.

The house lights darkened. The audience hushed. The spotlight snapped on with a click. Genevieve's voice boomed out a welcome to the Moulin Rouge, and the first song burst through the theatre as the curtain swept open. I and the others offstage could only see certain pieces of the action without the audience seeing us. But the glimpses of kicking legs, swirling skirts, and splayed hands in satin gloves, and the sounds of the harmonies and the audience's cheers, lit me up with rapture.

Vai! You're doing it!

Soon I was climbing into the silver swing and being lifted into the air for my entrance. Our matter-witches and fae had enspelled the swing so it floated without wires, and Uwila controlled it from the wings with flicks of magic. Before I was lowered into the audience's sight, I had an overhead view of the whole spectacle.

A dozen artistically mismatched chandeliers hung just below me. The scarlet windmill with lights on its sails turned placidly at stage right. The papier-mâché elephant with spangled headdress guarded stage left. Genevieve in tux and mustache held up their cane triumphantly while Vai and the other dancers, in a rainbow of colors, struck poses around them. Shelini and the two other Bohemians, charmingly scruffy, awaited my entrance, looking up.

Then the hush. The darkening to one spotlight, into which Uwila lowered me, in a flurry of silver confetti. I took a steady breath and sang my first word.

No opening night is perfect. Or at least not any that I've ever heard of. Shelini and I stepped on each other's lines for a moment in the poetry-reading banter. A violin screeched an off-key note in "El Tango de Roxanne." One of the glowing green absinthe goblets malfunctioned and came back on when it was supposed to be off. But at curtain call, when the audience shot to their feet in a standing ovation, I realized with astonishment that, on the whole, we had done just fine.

Everyone tumbled into the post-show chaos of hugs. Catarina wriggled through and presented me with a bouquet of purple-black roses, giving another to Shelini. My ears were so bombarded with the tumult that I couldn't have reported what anyone said.

At last I turned, and there was Vai, in iridescent green corset and ruffled petticoats. I set the roses into their arms, then hugged them from the side, careful not to squash the blooms. "Thank you for hoodwinking me out of my comfort zone," I said in their ear.

Their free arm held me snug around the waist. "If you think you haven't brought me a little out of my own," they said, "you're mistaken."

I laughed. "Come on, professional theatrical dancer. Let's go sign programs."

VAI

Professional theatrical dancer. I rotated that title in my head like a jewel over the next several days. Not a newly won jewel, even, but one unearthed from a box of childhood mementoes and which proved to still have luster once dusted off. It was exhilarating and exhausting, coming into such a role at age thirty-one, rusty at dancing, but I clung to it. Lately I even shrugged and said "Probably" when people asked if I'd want to perform in another Quicksand show.

Whenever I said it within Leo's hearing, he beamed, the grin stretching far enough to crinkle his eyes, and looped an arm around me.

Another benefit of being a dancer was the personal bodily care Leo provided. The exo-witches of the troupe, after each show or rehearsal, made the rounds to ease sore muscles, sprained joints, mashed toes, or other pains. Without our ever having voiced an agreement about it, Leo always attended to me first before moving to others. Given how deeply I desired him, having his hands on me was becoming a test of my fortitude, but no prize in the world could have induced me to swap a different healer for him.

Such thoughts were unprofessional. Leo had not made it weird any of the times I had removed the hair from his body or turned his tattoos flesh-tone, so I could not make it weird when he healed me. Where would a theatre company be if everyone took advantage of all the physical intimacy?

Not that such behavior didn't happen. Our props manager sometimes emerged early in the morning from Mathilde's bus. Fred was constantly immersed in some whirlwind romance. The main reason I didn't have to fear Shelini and Leo developing feelings for each other was that, for one thing, Shelini was involved with Uwila, the fire faery. And for another, in a makeup-room conversation, Shelini told me she almost never experienced romantic feelings for others. "Lust, sure," she said cheerfully. It made Uwila an excellent match for her. Fadas, Uwila's folk, were famed for their generous and insatiable sexuality.

Leo had not been involved with anyone since I'd joined the troupe. Except me, if you counted caravan-sharing, a considerable amount of trust, and one head-spinning equinox kiss. Now Rose Night was approaching fast.

There was a week and a half between opening night and Rose Night, and in that time, we finished our shows in Serpentshore, dismantled the sets, took a resting day, then packed the caravans and drove southeast. To Città del Tesoro, where both my family and Leo's lived.

We were silent while Wayshaw drove us there—me in the seat beneath my folded-up bunk, Leo across from me. He squinted out at the spring landscape, his knuckles on his lips. Finally, as we climbed the road to Merrilo Park, he set his hands in his lap and gave me a bright smile. "So. How much stress are *you* experiencing about being here?"

"Why do you feel stress about Tesoro?" I asked. "Because of your family?"

"Oh-ho. Not even going to answer the question this time before quid-pro-quo'ing me."

I just gazed patiently at him.

He caved. "Yes, of course it's my family. And anyone who knew me when I was young." He picked at his seat cushion. "It's my first 'serious' role in ages, so that's extra pressure, plus I always fall into old patterns when I see them, which I hate, so." He flapped his hands as if shaking something disgusting off them. "It's fine, it's nothing, I do this every time. How are you?"

Unease had been fluttering like a moth inside me. In the park, people in sundresses walked designer dogs and played drone soccer. A party was underway, laughter and cocktails beneath a tent of silver-and-white lace, decorated with what had to be a thousand lira worth of pale blue flowers. Had my hometown always been this…chichi? Had *I* been that way?

"Stressed," I admitted. "I'll likely be recognized. People will try to talk to me—journalists, or just acquaintances. It'll shatter my peace."

"I will *not* let that happen." Leo's voice had taken on a knife edge. "Anyone comes knocking here, *I* will answer the door, and they'll suffer my wrath."

"That will at least be entertaining."

Wayshaw swung us into our parking spot, the same expanse of grass and gravel where the troupe had been stationed last November. When I had broken into this caravan, and stammered to Leo the next morning that I definitely did not wish to hook up with him. Now here I was, a handful of days from Rose Night, plotting how to accomplish exactly that. If my stomach was in knots lately, my family scandal only accounted for half the reason.

"At least we'll be too busy today to get ourselves into trouble," Leo remarked as the engine shut off. He stretched. "Ready to check out Jin Troia?"

Tesoro had several opulent theatres, and I'd been in them all at some point, usually for my mother's piano concerts. Jin Troia Hall, named after the eighteenth-century playwright, was my favorite, and I'd been thrilled to learn Quicksand had booked it for *Moulin Rouge*. As Leo and I entered the theatre, along with Catarina and a few others, I looked up and smiled. Gold ceiling. Unlike the one in Leo's caravan, however, this ceiling was textured in medallions, rosettes, and geometrics, all centered around a painting of dragons in a night sky, which in turn surrounded a chandelier. The theatre had been built in 1901 and held twelve hundred seats spread over three levels—orchestra, mezzanine, balcony, and six boxes.

As Leo and the others spread out, conversing about which set pieces would go where, I threaded a path to third row center and sank into a seat.

Leo, having climbed on stage, walked to the edge and peered at me, shielding his eyes from the lights. "Come see backstage. It has *eighteen* dressing rooms. I get my very own."

"I'll come soon. I'm taking a minute. Every time I've been in this place before, I've sat out here. Whereas this trip, I'll only be up there."

He rocked back on his heels, looking utterly at home on the elegant stage despite his faded coat and sneakers. "You live on the other side of the looking glass now."

I nodded, deciding I was all right with that, and rose to explore backstage with him.

LEO

I slept, barely. Urgent thoughts chased each other around in my head.

I opened my eyes. It was still dark. Was it after midnight yet? I drew my phone out. 2:13, April 27.

The twenty-seventh. The twenty-seventh.

I tried the usual calming reminders about how much else still had to happen before May 27—the number of performances left; Lady Festival, including Rose Night; two dozen breakfasts and other meals with Vai. But 2:13 a.m., after maybe two hours of restless sleep, is not a time when rational thoughts help.

I curled on my side, freezing. I grew too hot, pushed the covers off, and lay on my back like a starfish. Thoughts crescendoed, details becoming gigantic-font important.

How to tell Vai? How to tell everyone else? What was I forgetting to pack? What snide things would my aunt say? What was Vai going to think? Where was Nalibak? Would he lurk nearby every night for the final week, ready to grab me when the time came? Should I tell Vai I was in love with them before I disappeared?

My stomach was twisting, cramping. Sweat beaded on my face. I shouldn't writhe around and wake Vai up. I tried to lie still.

The windows were lightening with the dawn by the time it became clear I was going to throw up.

Couldn't wake up Vai, I still thought, and crept as quietly as I could to the outside door—because they'd hear me if I used the bathroom, a mere few feet from their bed. I succeeded in opening the door, getting out, and closing it with minimal sound, then rushed several steps away before falling to my knees in the grass, retching and spitting.

The door clicked again behind me, along with the squeak of someone's weight on the step. I was still spitting and wiping my mouth when Vai sank into a crouch beside me, hand settling on my back.

"What's wrong?" they said. "Are you ill, did you catch something?"

"Just…anxiety." Shaking, my eyes streaming, I sagged back on my knees and glanced at them. They looked sleep-rumpled and terrified. So much for not disturbing them.

They stroked my back. "Why are you out here?"

"Fresh air?" I tried, with a weak smile.

Vai looked dubious. It was a cloudy morning with chilly dew drenching the grass, soaking my legs and the hem of my shorts. My shaking had morphed from the trembling of nausea to the shivers of coldness.

"Was trying not to wake you," I admitted.

"I'd rather help. Do you..."

Vai's sentence trailed off as someone appeared across the expanse of grass. Wayshaw, returning from the ocean. She stopped near us and took in the scene.

"You feel unwell," she informed me.

"No shit," I said, though in a kindly way.

"Do you want to get back in the caravan?" Vai asked.

"I can enspell you so you feel calmer," Wayshaw said.

"I can make ginger tea," Vai said, almost defiantly, which made me smile a little.

"You can both take turns at caring for pitiful, disgusting Leo," I promised.

After I'd splashed water on my face and rinsed my mouth, I got back into bed and accepted a mug of mint-ginger tea from Vai. Wayshaw set her fingers on my stomach and radiated a soothing sensation through me, banishing the nausea. I thanked them both.

Vai sat on the edge of my bed. "Is it your family? You don't have to see them, you know."

"It's not just that." I blew on the tea, rippling the surface. "It was one of those nights where I got all up in my head, and little things blew up into huge things, and...really, I'm better now."

"Our schedule today is fairly open," Wayshaw said, standing near my cabinets. "Nothing you need to do until tonight's pickup rehearsal."

"Not till seven," Vai added. "So you can go back to sleep if you like."

I nodded. "What were you going to do today?"

Their gaze flickered away. "I can't really see my family. But..."

"You might be able to meet up with someone who knows them," I guessed.

"Maybe. But—if you're sick, I'll stay."

"No no no. I'm fine. I'll be right as raindrops on roses. If going out today will settle any of your worries, then do that."

Vai's thumbs batted each other. "I might. For a bit." They lifted their gaze to Wayshaw. "You'll stay?"

"If he wishes," Wayshaw said.

I met Wayshaw's eye and gave her a nod. I couldn't unload on Vai about Nalibak, but I could on Wayshaw, and I needed to.

It took a bit more coaxing, but Vai soon showered, dressed, and went out, after exhorting me again to sleep. When it was just us two, Wayshaw relaxed into the nearest seat and asked, "You're upset because of Nalibak?"

Sitting with my knees drawn up, I rubbed my eyes. "One month. That's all I have. Today's the twenty-seventh. One month from today, Nalibak takes me."

"Why is one month significant?"

"Because now there's only one of each date number until that day. I get one more twenty-eighth, one more twenty-ninth, et cetera. That's it. I don't have surplus days for each number anymore. I don't know, it's how my mind works."

"I don't understand."

"I'm not saying it's logical. But it's how I see the calendar, and I…spiraled."

"The calendar numbers are arbitrary human fictions. Are they not?"

"Panic attacks don't make sense, by definition. But the numbers mean the day is getting closer. That part is a fact."

"It is." Wayshaw sounded somber. "I dread it too."

In the window behind her, the sunshine illuminated the park greenery, too cheerful for the question I was about to ask. "Is there any way to send him out of this life?"

"You've asked before. The answer hasn't changed."

"I know, fae don't die, they regenerate. But what about when they're pressured into regenerating? Because him leaving this life and starting over in a new form would solve a lot of my problems."

"I don't think it's ever been proven that anyone has pressured another into it."

"Sure it has. They get bested by an enemy, or decide life's gotten intolerable for one reason or another, and they decide now is a good time to return to the elements."

"But how would you make him decide that?" Wayshaw asked.

I pressed my temple against my knee. "Fair feasters hate the sun. It's torture for them. What if we captured him in iron chains and dragged him out where he wouldn't be able to avoid the sunlight when dawn came? How long has a fair feaster ever willingly endured that?"

I felt sick again by the time I finished speaking. Wayshaw's grave gaze didn't help. "How long are you willing to act as his jailer and torturer? Is perhaps the question."

I shut my eyes. "Fuck. I couldn't. Even knowing what he's done to Ayda. I'm not that person."

"Besides," Wayshaw added, "it would be difficult to hold him captive that way. He would fight and likely break free. And then what?"

"Yeah. Then what. Fine, it can't be done. I just had to ask one more time. Make sure I'm really out of options."

"Remember, Nalibak has no reason to wish *you* dead. He has reason to keep you alive. You're his entertainment."

"True. Though we might as well acknowledge he's going to be *my* jailer and torturer. And once the year is up, he'll no longer have reason to keep me alive."

Wayshaw was silent. Outside, Genevieve called a friendly hello to someone. A dog barked.

"Shall we review the items you've collected?" Wayshaw said. "Would that reassure you?"

I rolled my head on my knee, looking toward the closet. "Yeah. Let's."

CHAPTER 16

VAI

My insides were churning. They would have been anyway, on a day when I was venturing out to try to glimpse my sister without her knowledge, but Leo's sickness had shoved my anxiety over the top. As I walked through Tesoro, I prayed he'd recover swiftly.

Partly for reasons of disguise, and partly because it had become habit to borrow clothes from Mathilde's costume stash, today I was dressed in green sneakers, loose jeans with a studded black belt, an off-white hoodie, and large sunglasses. All were items that would have been unlike me in my years as Security Specialist Vai Delvecchio of Airtight Spells. My hair was now long enough that I had gathered it into a ponytail, and I had changed its color to a dark honey-blond—a style and shade I hadn't sported since age fifteen.

Getting from Merrilo Park to the east-downtown district required a bus ride of some forty-five minutes, ample time for me to doubt the wisdom of this outing. By the time I got off near Daphne's clinic, I had made a deal with myself. I wouldn't go into the building. I would only sit on a bench in the front courtyard. It was a public place. That was allowed. And I would linger only one hour—her lunch break was to start soon. If she didn't come out, I wouldn't see her. End of story.

The courtyard was ringed with trees and benches. Kids drew with chalk on the paving bricks across from me while their guardians chatted. I sat on a bench, my insides doing flips. I doubted I could have felt more on edge if I'd been planning to rob the place at gunpoint.

If Daphne didn't show, would I try seeing my mother? That was harder. I wouldn't know where to find her. Her work and rehearsal hours were less regular than Daphne's and could take her to a number of different venues. The likeliest place she'd be was home, but now her home was a new address that I didn't know. Kwal was forbidden by the terms of the deal from telling me, and I hadn't sought the information elsewhere.

As for my father and uncle, I wasn't sure where they were staying either, but I had no desire to see them. Nor my grandparents: of the three still living, one had declining mental faculties and was in assisted living, and the other two had objectionable politics. None of them had contacted me all these months, and I felt no wish to speak to them now.

I shouldn't even be here. This was a flat-out creepy idea. I got up at two minutes before the clinic's lunch hour and checked the bus schedule on my phone.

"Vai?" someone said.

Jolting in a full-body startle, I looked up. I realized a second too late that this reaction gave me away.

It was Charles Christopher. He beamed, dimples forming in his cheeks. "Oh my god! It *is* you."

Before I knew what was happening, he wrapped his arms around me, making a groaning noise of commiseration. He was shorter than me by half a foot, and I could smell the coconut aroma of his hair products.

"Hi," I said helplessly.

He stepped back. "Wow! You look so different. You and your family always look cool, but you look, like, street-cool now. I love your hair. I'm not making sense, oh my god." He laughed. "How long have you been in town?"

I shot a shaky glance at the front of the building. "I'm not staying long. I didn't really tell anyone."

"Oh. Still working somewhere else?"

"Yes." I wasn't ready to tell him about Quicksand. I wasn't ready for anything happening at the moment. I wished Leo were here. He would have jumped in with an improvised, hilarious story to explain our presence, and would've carried it off without a hitch. "Tesoro was a stop I had to make for work," I added.

Charles's gaze moved to the clinic. "Just wanted to see Daphne?" His eyes were large with sympathy. They were dark-lashed and blue and always looked a bit wet, as if perpetually welling with tears.

"I thought I might try, but...it's not smart. I was about to leave."

"No, hey, don't." He shoved his hands into the pockets of his khaki shorts. "I, uh...come by here at lunch once in a while. To see if she wants to grab a bite. I mean, she's really busy, so it's a long shot, but..." He froze, his gaze on the building. "There she is."

I pivoted. Daphne was strolling out, in a flower-patterned shirt and black capris. She had likely just taken her hair down from a twist, as it coiled loose over one shoulder, the same near-black brown as my natural shade. Across her chest hung a canvas messenger bag with moon artwork. I'd given it to her, years ago, as a birthday present.

She noticed us and called, "Hello."

To Charles. Not to me, surely. She wouldn't have been so calm if she recognized me.

"Hi." Charles waved.

My heart was galloping. "I'll go," I mumbled, with seconds to spare.

"Stay," he said softly. "It's fine."

My feet wouldn't move. I had to know what would happen.

She approached. "Hi, Charles. Beautiful day."

"Yes! Thought I'd swing by and see if you wanted lunch, but maybe you already have plans."

"I do," she said, with what sounded like genuine regret, though I suspected she was brushing him off nicely. Her gaze moved to me. "But maybe you have plans too? Hi, I'm Daphne." She held out her hand.

I shook it, buzzing with adrenaline. Would physical contact break the spell? Maybe she would gasp and say my name and embrace me?

Nothing.

"I'm Vai," I said quietly.

My name didn't unlock anything either. She just said, "Lovely to meet you. Friend of Charles?"

"Yes," Charles cut in. He'd been watching us, agitation contorting his eyebrows. "We ran into each other just now."

"Oh, are you from Tesoro?" she asked me.

I wasn't sure how to answer. "Yes," I finally said.

"Do you want to grab lunch with us?" Charles asked her.

"I wish I could," she said, "but I only have a few minutes, and I'm going to try to squeeze in a call. You two have fun catching up. It was good to meet you, Vai."

"You too," I murmured.

"See you later," Charles said.

We watched her walk out of the courtyard.

"God," he whispered. He turned to me, eyes wide. "I've lived here ten years, and I still can't believe what I'm seeing sometimes. The sheer power of magic."

I was trembling. I nodded.

Charles grasped my upper arm. "Are you okay? Do you want to walk? Get some coffee—or, no, green tea. That's your drink, right?"

In my haze I registered surprise that he remembered I preferred green tea to coffee. I wouldn't have been able to say what drink he liked. "Thank you, but...no. I need some time to think."

"Sure, of course." He released my arm and stuffed his hands into his pockets. "It breaks my heart what's happening to your family. I know what it's like, being away from your relatives and your home."

As a crosswater, he'd had to leave behind everyone he had known in America, able only to send occasional vague messages. The fae's island-shielding magic would ensure that while his friends or family knew him and could answer, none of them would be curious enough to ask pertinent questions or try to find him. As with Kwal's spell on me—although in a lighter touch—their interest would glide away.

Feeling more compassion for him than I had before, I met his gaze. "I suppose I only appreciate now how hard it's been for you."

"Aw, I wanted to live here. I chose it. I knew the price."

"As did I, with this spell. That doesn't mean it's easy."

"Ain't that the truth. Oh! By the way." He got out his phone and started swiping. "The Quicksand Theatre Company's in town again. Remember we saw them last fall? They're putting on *Moulin Rouge*."

This day was going to be the death of me. "Mm," I confirmed. "I've heard."

"The first performance is tomorrow, then it runs all weekend and the next couple weekends." He appeared to be reading from a webpage. Lifting an excited gaze to me, he asked, "Do you want to go?"

I let my lips part as I assembled the quasi-lie. "I'm afraid I won't be free."

"Oh." His face fell, then he boosted it back up with a smile. "Maybe a festival meet-up, then, just to get drinks?"

"I...won't really be in town long." Guilt shoved at me. Charles had been nothing but kind. "Although if it turns out I have time, I'll text you."

A minute more of small talk about how he had to get back to his job, which involved assisting with imported goods from America. ("The only thing I'm useful for. Haha, kidding!") Then he hugged me again and we parted.

I walked mindlessly, feeling as if I were standing still and my feet were scrolling the pavement like a treadmill, rotating the Earth beneath me. When I ended up at a city garden, I dropped onto a bench. Probably I'd been dreaming and the last six months with Quicksand hadn't happened, and now I'd been flung back into reality in Tesoro, crushed under the curse I'd brought on.

My phone buzzed. My heart eased to see Leo's name. Our friendship did exist, then.

We rarely needed to text each other, given we were in near-constant proximity, but in past weeks he had sent me some memes, and we'd sent each other pictures from shows.

How's your day going? Any luck? he had texted.

I wasn't yet able to put together the words to describe my encounter with Daphne. *It's been strange,* I typed back. *Still processing. How are you? I've been worried.*

I'm fine! Please don't worry. I hate when people worry about me. I slept a little and I'm doing much better.

That's good. Going out to see your family?

He answered, *Yep, off soon.*

I couldn't even find it in me to be jealous that he had loved ones who would recognize him. Leo deserved all the good things in life.

Have fun. We'll debrief this evening, I wrote.

Absolutely. xoxo

CHAPTER 17

LEO

It was true I had gotten a nap, though only because Wayshaw, at my request, hit me with a spell to make me fall asleep. She woke me at noon so I could shower and go out to visit my family.

I caught a bus to the park where I'd be meeting Javier, Aunt Yubara, and Uncle Luis. Taking walks had become my aunt and uncle's preferred social activity. Luis said he liked getting fresh air and exercise along with conversation. Yubara said she hated feeling trapped in a restaurant or living room if the visit became tedious. In this particular case, I agreed with her. Having the option of walking off down the beach if I couldn't stand their company did appeal.

I should have known how it would go when Aunt Yubara said, after giving me a limp hug, "Lord, only two hours since lunch and I'm already famished. That café's 'protein shake' must have been mostly water."

Red flag. Everyone knew Yubara was ten times ruder when she was hungry.

Nonetheless, the four of us set off through Bardini Park, following a paved seaside path beneath wind-twisted pines. For a while we stuck to safe topics, predominantly our jobs. Luis was the chief accountant for the grocery that Javier also worked for, and Yubara was in the island's silk industry, designing fashions for boutiques.

When they got around to me, I verified that yes, I was still putting on costumes and making an ass of myself for laughs.

"Don't you write scripts sometimes too?" Luis asked.

"For sketches, yeah. We all pitch in on writing those."

"He's singing and dancing for this role," Javier said. "He always could sing well. Just way too loud."

I smiled and elbowed him.

"I don't know how you've put up with living in that tiny box on wheels for so long," Yubara remarked.

I sauntered five more steps, counting each in my head. "It's tight quarters for sure. But getting to perform in some of the most beautiful venues in the country makes up for it."

"Didn't you add a roommate recently?" Javier asked.

"Yep. Vai. But they're super considerate, so close quarters are working fine." I imagined adding, "They're also incandescently hot," just to see if it flustered my relatives, but that would be too gossipy. My beloved Vai deserved better.

Javier and Ayda already had their tickets to see *Moulin Rouge* this weekend, and he asked about special effects and costumes. I waited for my aunt and uncle to sound even half as curious, but Luis just smiled blandly, watching seabirds wheeling over the water. Yubara squinted ahead, lips pinched, as if the sunshine personally offended her.

When the conversation turned to Ayda, my shoulders stiffened. Uncle Luis spoke highly of her shop and its array of healing plant materials. Aunt Yubara conceded she'd had good results with a tincture Ayda had made, which boosted skin health and elasticity. They managed to avoid speaking of Ayda's enchantment damage, her bear-fae dad, or her freewheeling musician mom. Still, the cutting remarks they—mostly Yubara—had made in the past about those features kept chiming in my head.

So when Yubara eventually said, "Now if only I could get her to wear some of my nice silks instead of those dingy hemp things she loves," I was ready and I pounced.

"There's always something," I said.

We were coming up to a scenic viewpoint. Yubara didn't break her stride. "Would you care to explain?"

"Leave it, Leo," Javier said.

"You can never just stick to saying nice things about people," I told her. "You always have to make it known how, exactly, they've displeased you."

"I believe in being honest," Yubara said. "Is honesty not a trait you admire? Well, no, I suppose it isn't particularly."

That stung, given my lack of transparency lately. "What good comes of being honest about things like that? No one's ever going to meet all your standards. You're constantly irritated because you expect perfection, and no human is perfect."

"Let's step out on the viewpoint!" Luis said brightly. "Oh, look at that big flock of pelicans."

"Yes, having raised you," Yubara retorted to me, "I'm quite familiar with expecting better and being disappointed."

I stared toward the ocean. How I wished I were Wayshaw and could dive into those cool depths and disappear.

"Let's take a picture," Javier practically snarled. "Okay? Everyone willing to be normal and pose for a picture at the viewpoint?"

We walked to the railing and arranged ourselves, our backs to the sea stack with an ancient gnarled oak growing from it. Javier stepped in front of us to take the picture, but a passerby offered to do it so Javier could be in the photo too. Javier thanked him, handed him the phone, and came to stand next to me at the end of the line of family members, only one of whom (Luis) was smiling.

"Everyone ready?" the stranger prompted, as if to ask whether the rest of us ever intended to smile.

I faked a smile. I didn't look to see if Javier and my aunt were doing the same.

"Okay! Couple more." The man moved to the right to try a different angle.

"I shouldn't have agreed to this. I knew how it would go," I said, giving my voice the same false brightness as my smile.

"Oh?" Yubara said. "You knew you would run your mouth off yet again? Funny, I had the same prediction about you."

"Would you both *stop*," Javier hissed.

"Here—I'll try from this side too," the friendly stranger said, and moved to the left.

"What do you want me to say?" I asked.

"Leo," Luis whispered.

"I want to hear," Yubara said, "that you're grateful we took you in when you had no one else, even though it was a tremendous amount of stress and expense for us. That you're sorry you kept making trouble, year after year, the whole time you grew up. That you see now how hard your presence made everything, and how stubborn you were about the most ridiculous things. That you are sorry for it all, and that you are finally going to be a responsible adult and start treating your family with respect and be there for them in the ways they need you to be."

I stood motionless, taking it in, waves of hot and cold washing through me.

The volunteer photographer had frozen in helplessness.

Javier began, "What about the ways he needs?"—which was a shock, and I should have stood there and let my brother go on defending me.

But my old habits had long since taken the reins. My rebellious, pigheaded self had to show off my short-term memorizing skills instead.

I drew a deep breath and said steadily, "I'm grateful you took me in when I had no one else, even though it was a tremendous amount of stress and expense for you. I'm sorry I kept making trouble, year after year, the whole time I grew up. I see now how hard my presence made everything, and how stubborn I was about the most ridiculous things. I'm sorry for it all, and I'm finally going to be a responsible adult and start treating my family with respect and be there for you in the ways you need me to be."

My relatives' open-mouthed surprise was gratifying. For a second.

"Happy?" Javier muttered to his mother.

Yubara looked away. "It would be more sincere if it had been his own words." She turned her face in my direction, though her glance skipped past me. "Apparently you write scripts all the time. Couldn't write a few simple lines for us?"

I swore under my breath and stalked forward to the stranger. Wide-eyed, he handed me the phone.

"Thanks." I took out the slim envelope that had been crinkling in my jacket pocket and pressed it into his hand. "Two tickets to *Moulin Rouge*, Friday night. Good seats. Enjoy."

I handed Javier his phone back, then stalked off alone.

The tickets had been for my aunt and uncle. They hadn't requested any, but if they had shown interest in the play, said anything at all about wanting to come see it, I was going to give them the envelope. Gladly.

But they hadn't. Not today, and not once since I had shared the news of being cast as Satine, a month ago.

One month more, and they'd be rid of me. Possibly forever. Maybe then they'd be at peace.

I quickened my steps to almost a run, clambering over rocks to get to the strip of sand along the shore, focusing on moving my muscles to keep from doing anything absurd like screaming or bursting into tears.

VAI

I was apparently not done tormenting myself, because now I stood in front of my old house. I had to see it in person.

I felt…affronted. I had resigned myself to losing the house. I didn't think it would bother me much, knowing I could no longer walk up to the door and enter. Yet it did hurt, a pinch in my chest, like being coldly rebuffed by someone I knew.

Also, they had painted it *orange*. A pale gelato shade, with trim in brick red and white. In my opinion, our original off-white and charcoal had suited it better.

"Is that Vai?"

I turned. Behind me stood one of the neighbors, Heddy Baluyot, her silver curls fluffing out from under her tropical-print bucket hat. She beamed. "It is you! I love the new hair."

I found myself being hugged by the second unexpected person today, but in her case, I was comfortable with it. "Hi, Heddy."

She squinted at the orange house. "Nice enough people. But I'm still not used to that color. Are you here to get your car? I'm keeping it in tip-top shape."

"Not yet. I'm sorry, it probably takes up your whole garage."

"Nonsense. I've been driving it once a week to keep the battery charged, and that's no hardship, let me tell you." She laughed. "Makes everyone envious."

"Thank you. I'll probably come back for it later this year, but…here, let me give you money for upkeep." I tugged my wallet from my pocket.

Heddy pushed it back toward me. "There's plenty left from what you gave me when you dropped it off. Don't you worry. Come over for some iced tea."

We went to her place, two houses down, and sat at a small metal table in the shade of her flowering crabapple tree. I confided in her about Quicksand, and she clapped her hands and lauded, "Perfect! You were always so graceful. So creative. That job with your dad stifled you, your mom and I could both see it."

Startled, I asked what she meant. And I learned that my mother, in curbside chats with Heddy, had expressed that sentiment as long as ten years ago, and a few times since. "She even said once, 'Vai should be a dancer. Something in the performing arts. They always light up when we go into theatres.'"

I sat back in the garden chair, swamped by gratitude at being seen by my mother long ago without realizing it, as well as grief that I couldn't speak to her for another six months, and disappointment that she hadn't spoken of such things to me. Or had she, and I had brushed away the topic and then buried it in my own memory?

Heddy spoke of other things—her two dogs, who lay under the table at our feet; other neighbors and how they were doing; her niece, a kung fu sifu and, recently, a good friend of Daphne's.

At around 4:00, my phone buzzed. Leo was texting me.

Hey love. You doing all right?

My heart melted at the "love."

"Friend at Quicksand," I explained to Heddy, and typed back, *Yes. Heading back soon. How about you?*

"You probably have to get going." Heddy set her glass on the table. "I'm going to come see that play of yours!"

I stood. "I'll get you tickets. No arguing. Text me with the day you want and how many."

"Aw, honey, that'd be wonderful."

I was on my way down the hill when Leo answered. *I'm just desponding on a beach, as is my wont. Going back to Merrilo soon.*

Is despond a verb? I asked.

Indeed it is.

Apologies. I should not have asked that of someone who declaimed Poe at the ocean on a stormy night while wearing black eyeliner.

Truly. You can trust me about moping-related vocabulary.

I reached the bus stop. *Is it your family making you despond?*

Of course. But you know what's good news? I get to see you in an hour.

I smiled. Then I spent a minute on a web search to make sure I got the Shakespeare quotation right before I altered it and typed it in.

Gallop apace, you fiery-footed bus.

Leo answered with a laughing emoji and followed it up with: *Come night, come Vai, come thou day in night.* And a heart.

One should not fall in love with actors who are fluent in Shakespeare. It can entirely derange you.

I typed, *Swoon,* with a heart of my own, and stepped forward to board the bus that had pulled up.

LEO

I rose from the salt-encrusted boulder I'd been sitting on, brushed dried seaweed off my butt, and wandered down the beach.

Javier texted a while later: *We're at the gelato place next to the park. Just get over here.*

Not in the mood. Sorry. Then I added, *Thanks for trying to defend me. I should've let you finish.*

You're welcome and yes you should have.

So, honest question, I typed. *If you know I'm right, why did you stay with them instead of following me?*

After a prolonged agitation of the three dots, Javier's answer appeared: *Because at the end of the day what I want is a family that's relatively peaceful and isn't blown to bits, and what YOU want is to die on the hill of what you think is "right" or "fair." Exhibit A: you saying "you know I'm right" in that text.*

Valid. I see your point, I said.

Our thread went silent. I caught a bus back to eastern Tesoro, then walked the rest of the way to Merrilo Park. I made sure my character mask was in place. Tonight I would be playing Calm Leo, who, after a disappointing but definitely not ugly or disastrous visit with his family, has returned to his troupe and, though tired, is pleased to see them.

When I entered the caravan, Vai's hair was damp from the shower, and they were putting on a fresh shirt. Although I saw plenty of that broad, smooth chest lately, what with all the corset costumes, my gaze swept across it, and I stowed away another fond memory to savor.

Vai, meanwhile, was examining my face, as a polite person should. "How did it go?"

I turned away to hang up my jacket. "Good to see Javi. My aunt and uncle are exactly who they've always been. How about you?" I glanced at them again, concerned. I had in fact noticed their face and the weary quality to it. "Where did you end up going?"

Fastening shirt buttons, Vai lowered their gaze. "Daphne's clinic. Once I got there, I was about to turn around and leave—it felt wrong. But then I ran into Charles."

"The crosswater?"

"Yeah. And while we were talking, Daphne came out. Said hello to us." Finished with the buttons, Vai's hands fell loose. "She didn't know me."

I winced. "Shit."

"We were introduced. She was perfectly friendly. Then she left to have lunch." Vai gave me an empty look. "That was that."

"Ah, Vai."

"Then I went to my old house, on a whim." Vai's eyebrows furrowed. "They've painted it orange."

"How dare they."

"I feel like today wasn't real somehow."

If only it hadn't been. I straightened Vai's collar, flicking a damp strand of honey-blond hair out of the way. Gods, I loved that color on Vai. "Well, we're about to get back to normal. I'll shower, we'll grab some food, then off to rehearsal."

All of which we did, though my mind was not entirely in the game. No one remarked on the lackluster quality of my performance. The company was too busy fixing technical stumbling blocks as we tried to fit the show into its new venue. My imagination, meanwhile, meandered through ruminations such as whether that was the last time I'd ever see my aunt and uncle, whether all the choices I'd made so far had been worth it, and what my life had amounted to in the end.

I found time to fret over Vai's unhappiness too. After rehearsal, I eased their sore dance muscles, then they began removing my makeup.

"Tell me a nice memory from your youth," I said. "Something you enjoyed."

Vai thought it over, plucking a paper towel. "Winter solstice night. Our house was done up with lights, and friends would come over. My mom would play piano, and we'd open the verandah doors so anyone on the street could hear. Daphne and I would go out on the verandah and wave to people walking by, and watch the fireworks over the city."

"That sounds beautiful. I wish I could've attended."

"I wish you could've too. What about you? A memory."

I stretched out one leg, rotating my ankle. "Driving around on summer nights with Javier, when we were teens. Through the city or out to the coast or wherever. In the old tan Camry we shared—my aunt called the color 'champagne,' but you and I both know, Vai, it was not champagne. We would just cruise with the windows open and watch the world roll by. Talking to each other about any random shit."

Vai swept the makeup from the sides of my neck. "I expect he misses those times too."

"Maybe. I bet he doesn't even remember."

Vai tossed the paper towels in the bin, then studied me. "Are you free tomorrow, midday?"

"Um, yes? Why?"

"There's somewhere I'll take you. If you want."

"A surprise? By all means. Surprise me, darling."

CHAPTER 18

VAI

I was relieved Leo slept in the next morning, rather than having another night of illness. I ate a quiet breakfast of tea and yogurt, and was slipping my shoes on when his head emerged from the bed curtains.

"Oh, where you going?" he mumbled. "Should I get dressed?"

"Not yet. I'm going to get something, then I'll be back. You can rest."

"Is this about my surprise? Vai?"

I just waggled my fingers goodbye and exited the caravan.

Puffy white clouds sailed through the sky. The air smelled of fresh leaves and flowers. My steps were light as I walked to the bus stop.

An hour later, in the driver's seat of my car, I ran my hands over the butter-smooth leather of the steering wheel. Heddy waved to me and called, "Have fun, honey!"

I waved back, then cruised away, convertible top down, warm wind ruffling my hair.

When I entered Leo's caravan, he was dressed in a black T-shirt and jeans, and was munching toast. He beamed at me. "Hey. Surprise time?"

"If you're ready. Put on your shoes." I considered his long purple hair, loose down his back. "Also tie up your hair."

"Oh, so we're skydiving," he said.

"How did you guess."

I had already fastened my hair into a ponytail. Leo wrapped his into a bun and put on sneakers. I led him to the parking lot near the caravans. When I unlocked the passenger door of my car, he stopped dead. It was gratifying to watch his eyes widen.

"Is this—your car?" he asked.

"A neighbor's looking after it for me. I'm borrowing it back for the day." I opened the door. "Would you like a ride?"

"*Yes*, I'd like a ride—but I need to—to take all this in first." He prowled around the exterior, bending to peer at its details. "Vai. Holy fuck. Is this a Mercedes-Benz?"

"It is."

"An actual fucking Mercedes-Benz?"

"My uncle managed to import three of them, decades ago. Our family kept this one. Eventually it became mine."

"What year was it made?" Leo ran a finger along the hood.

"Nineteen seventy-nine."

"Ohhh, hello, beautiful. Tell me all the sexy car details, Vai. Give them to me."

"It's a 450SL, 4.5-liter V8 engine. Kept in shape over the years by several matter-witches, including me."

"Mmm," he groaned. At the driver's side, he leaned over the open top to look in. "Soft top?"

"Yes." I nodded to where it folded in.

"This color…" He stroked the car's side. "It's like a dewy, precious leaf."

"Its official name is Silver Green Metallic. I've looked it up when doing touch-ups."

"You've been the owner of a gorgeous 1979 Mercedes-Benz convertible all this time and, in your infinite modesty, you never once mentioned it."

"Was I supposed to?"

"*I'd* have name-dropped this beauty about twenty times a year if I had it stowed away somewhere."

I gestured to the passenger door, which I held open. "Would you like to get in?"

"Would I like to. What a question." Leo skirted the back end and slid into the car. He wriggled his shoulders into the seat, then beamed at me. "This is so much better than the tan Camry."

I shut the passenger door, leaned my elbows on top of it—the window was down—and smiled at him at eye level. "Where would you like to go?"

There was nowhere in particular he wanted to go. Or rather, there were a dozen random places. Down the street past the grocery where Javier and Luis worked. Around the park that adjoined their high school. Past the theatre that showed old movies. Up the steep hill leading to the water tower. Along Milano Avenue, the glitziest drag of downtown, skyscrapers with Art Deco facades looming on both sides, their shop windows full of thousand-lira shoes, jewelry, and perfumes.

We ended up at the southern stretch of Ancona Beach. I parked, and we wandered to a cove where a waist-high waterfall spilled from a creek onto the sand. Leo pointed to some far-off boulders and told me that was where he had done his Poe recitation and met Wayshaw.

"I like this part of the beach better, though," he added.

"It's lovely. I didn't even know this cove was here."

He turned to me, strands of purple hair fluttering in the breeze. "Thank you for this. I feel leagues better."

"Anytime we're in Tesoro and you'd like a ride, I'm happy to oblige."

"Deal." Then he flinched, muttered something about sand blowing into his face, and pivoted to the ocean. "Tesoro opening night," he said. "Are we ready?"

⁂

The show occupied our evening and the majority of the next two days. On Friday night I had the honor, and the stress, of getting to meet Leo's longtime best friend, Ayda, and his brother, Javier, who both came to the show. We all went to a bar afterward for dinner and drinks. Shelini, Uwila, and Catarina came along too.

Ayda had nothing of the victim about her despite her curse from Nalibak. She was no-nonsense and wry. I sat across from her, and we talked about the spells we used in our work. Javier seemed prickly and difficult to get a read on—but then, Leo had already told me that was his temperament. Even the brotherly taunts Javier directed at Leo sounded to me like they came from frustrated concern rather than actual contempt.

Leo asked me, after we said goodnight to the others, "Hope that wasn't too awful? They really liked you."

"I had fun. It was like being back in my own family, in happier times."

He gave me a side hug. "Good. That's what I hoped."

That moment of intimacy brought back the topic most on my mind lately.

Lady Festival would begin on the first of May, a date also known as Rose Night.

My heartbeat skittered through me, more erratic with each passing hour, even as I danced for an audience of hundreds, cleaned costumes, and assisted with the troupe's festival tasks.

Rose Night could be the start of a lifelong relationship. Or it could last one night. Or nothing would happen, as I might be rejected—sweetly, of course. I couldn't imagine Leo ever being rude about turning someone down on Rose Night. But I couldn't possibly relax, not knowing, not being allowed to ask, per festival tradition, until the day itself.

One of my recent tasks had been helping craft pink silk roses and attaching each to a black elastic bracelet, the troupe's gift to the masses. They contained no spells—it was illegal to put attraction charms on festival gifts, unless clearly labeled as such. My magic had only been employed to physically assemble the roses. There was now a box containing five hundred of them in the props truck, ready to distribute.

Four hundred and ninety-eight, rather. I had taken two.

The first of May finally arrived. I barely slept the night before.

No chance I was waiting until nightfall. I had to know first thing. In the morning, I showered and dressed before Leo got up. Then he awoke and washed too. When he emerged from the bathroom, barefoot in T-shirt and black trousers, toweling his face dry, I stepped forward. Butterflies swarmed inside me.

"Our street festival thing is at ten, right?" Leo said.

"Yes. We're to hand out flyers about the show. Also these." I showed him the rose bracelet on my wrist. My heart pounded in my ears.

"You made that? It's so pretty! That's one of the nicest pink roses I've ever seen. Are you going to wear it at the booth?"

"I don't think I'll wear one out in public this year, no."

He looked at me, eyes innocent. "No?"

"I was only going to wear it here. When it's just the two of us." It was hard to keep my voice level. My nerves were rattling me to pieces.

Leo's hands froze in place, still holding the towel near his neck. "Oh?" he said, barely a breath.

I took the other rose bracelet from my pocket and offered it. "If you're interested."

The tip of his tongue touched his lips. He set the towel on the seat beside him, his gaze lingering on the bracelet. Then he took it, slid it over his wrist, and lifted his eyes to mine.

"Maybe I'll just wear this here too," he said slowly. He turned the bracelet so the pink rose was on top, then extended his arm toward me.

A thousand times now I had touched his garments or skin or hair. It had become easy. Yet touching someone's pink rose on Rose Night carried such weight, it made me tremble to reach out and stroke the silk petals.

As soon as I did so, Leo's breath hitched. He gave me a stunned smile, then swiveled his hand and swiped his forefinger across my rose. I let out my breath in an astonished laugh.

"Really?" he said. "You're sure?"

"Completely."

He surged forward, tangling me in a hug. "Vai! I was hoping for this."

All of me was buzzing, glowing. "You were?" I let my hands glide around his back.

"Of course." He nuzzled my cheek.

And because it was so easy, perhaps even the correct thing to do when someone has just accepted your sexual proposition, I turned my head and brushed a kiss on his lips. He exhaled a laugh. A second later, his smile gave way to intense focus, a moment of electric silence.

Then he pushed me back against a closet door, sliding his hand into my hair, and kissed me, damp and deep, on the mouth.

Arousal burst to life in my belly, shooting sparks through me.

"I didn't mean," I said, "that we had to start immediately." Not that I stopped kissing him nor put any space between us.

"I know." He kissed my mouth, my cheek. "I'm merely showing you how happy I am. As a way of...formally accepting." He nipped my ear.

"Ah. How were you planning to approach me today? If I hadn't done it."

"Station myself near you and bat my eyelashes and hope you noticed?"

"Good thing one of us had an actual plan, then."

He melted against me in another kiss. I slipped my leg between his thighs. I was wearing lightweight clothes—a silk button-down shirt and flowy wide-legged trousers—and could feel that Leo was getting hard, and he could surely tell I was too.

He groaned against my neck. "We have to wait till tonight? After the show? That's like thirteen hours away. Gods, you smell so good."

I tipped my head back, and he took the hint and began kissing my neck. "There's no rule saying we have to wait," I pointed out.

"Hmm." He smoothed back my hair and framed my face with his hands. He was flushed, his voice sweetly earnest. "I do want to be with you tonight. I love the idea of looking forward to it all day. On the other hand…" He kissed me again, as if sampling a treat he couldn't resist. "On the other hand," he said, "rehearsing is good."

"Make sure we know what we're doing."

"Right. Make sure the two leads have chemistry." He pressed his forehead to mine, his cheeks rounding in a grin. "Though they did already have a really hot kiss on the equinox."

"I've wanted you for months." I strained against him, gripping his hips.

He slid his hand down my chest, taking his time to feel everything. "You're going to kill me here. Are you sure, though, for real? I would hate it *so much* if you regretted anything tomorrow."

I took his hand, drew it down between my legs, and held it there. We both skipped a breath. "I would regret it ten times more," I said, "if we did nothing."

"Huh." His hand flexed, caressing me. He kissed my jaw so slowly it felt like reverence. "That is precisely the conclusion I've reached regarding you."

I slumped back against the door, the teasing of his fingers unraveling me. My hands traveled the territory they'd never had permission to investigate before—the curve of his ass, the jut of his hipbones, the heat of his groin. Our lips slid and locked together again, our tongues entwining.

"Should we, um," he said. "Just a thought. Should we keep formally accepting this agreement somewhere more comfortable?"

I nodded. With a brilliant smile that beamed all over his face, he dragged me by the wrist to his bed. After a shove at the nearest purple curtain to get it out of the way, he bounced onto the mattress and stretched out on his back. I crawled onto him, slowing to get us arrayed. My chest on his. My legs between his thighs, which he had splayed open. My elbows planted outside his arms.

I kissed him, feeling his warmth up and down my front, pinned pliantly under me.

"Yeah," he said, a husky syllable spooling into my mouth directly from his. "This was a good idea." His hand grabbed my ass to hold me against him while he rolled his hips up.

Though my eyes felt heavy, ready to swoon shut, I drank in the sight of him close up, flushed with desire for me. For *me*. I had done this.

Even lying on him with both of us clearly aching to do more, I felt complete, happy to do nothing but bask in this hold. But doing nothing else soon became near impossible. We were grinding against each other, the motions of our tongues becoming overtly suggestive as we kissed.

"Fuck," he breathed into my neck. "What time is it?"

I pulled back to sit on my knees and checked my phone. "Nine-twenty. We should leave in about fifteen minutes."

"Right. Huh." Burrowing his hands into his hair, he groaned.

"Tonight, though." I tried to sound encouraging and only ended up sounding desperate.

"Okay, further thought." Leo fixed a businesslike look upon me, the gravity of which was undermined by the fact that he was lying on his back with his legs open, his hair in a purple tangle around his head. "You know how the first time with someone is, usually, not as good as the second or subsequent times? Because the first time is...awkward?"

"It does involve uncertainty," I admitted, liking where this seemed to be going.

"Uncertain, exactly. So...what if, here's my thought, what if we took care of the first time this morning—something easy that takes less than fifteen minutes—so we can relax and enjoy the rest of the day, then take our time with the second round tonight? That is, if you think twice in a day would work for you, which it absolutely would for me, judging from current levels of horniness, but—"

"Yes." I curled my fingers under the waistband of his trousers. "So—to leave in under fifteen minutes..."

Heat banked in Leo's eyes. His voice became clear and low. "Vai, would you be willing to unfasten your clothes and let me touch you?"

A delicious shudder ran through me. "If you will too."

He pulled off his shirt with a Satine-like shimmy. Things got silly and uncoordinated in our rush to undress each other, but in less than one of our precious minutes, I had unbuttoned my shirt and we had both pushed our underwear to our knees, and we arranged ourselves side by side, facing each other.

I closed my hand around him, swallowing, my heart in my throat. He grasped me in return, stealing my breath.

"Strange," he said. "I know how it feels to touch you, in so many ways. It's just these last bits I wasn't familiar with."

Those were essentially my exact thoughts, to the degree I had thoughts anymore. "From now on, we know," I said.

His beautiful mouth quirked up in a smile. "Happy Rose Night, Vai."

He leaned in to kiss me. Our strokes became rhythmic and determined. Kissing saved us from wasting too much time with conversation. We confined ourselves to the essentials—

"Like this?"

"Yes."

"Faster? Slower?"

"It's good, you're good."

"You first." Leo's whisper was hot against my ear. "For me, sweetheart, please."

As if the pace he was setting gave me any choice. I broke over the edge, gasping, trying even in that moment not to let any details slip past me. The smell of his damp hair. The silky-hard feel of him in my palm. His voice murmuring affectionate nonsense. Then I rolled him onto his back, tightening my grip, and within a few strokes he was arching his back and saying my name and spilling hot across my fingers.

We lay fused together, cozy and familiar, yet entirely transformed. My face was nestled in his neck. He bestowed a quiet kiss between my brows.

While I was formulating the best way to say *I love you*—a sentiment to be delivered tomorrow, not today, not on commitment-free Rose Night—Leo waggled his sticky fingers against my hip, making me twitch.

"I'm imagining," he said, "if we fell asleep like this and someone came looking for us."

"Awkward," I agreed. "I'll get a washcloth."

"We're going to be late," Leo said cheerfully as we rushed through cleaning up and putting ourselves back in order. "Worth it."

We tumbled outside and jogged toward the street fair. Rose garlands adorned the city, and pink roses made of fabric or paper sat free for the taking in baskets hanging from people's fenceposts.

Leo and I had left our pink roses in the caravan, our wrists bare, so no one else would proposition us. We were spoken for.

At the street fair we slowed, panting. People were setting up booths, selling wares.

"They may guess why we're late," I said. Though we had tamed our hair, Leo's lips were raspberry-hued, and his neck bore the mottled marks of having been extensively mouthed. Judging from a glance in the mirror before we'd left, I looked similar.

"So what if they do." Leo took my hand. "Know what? It wasn't even all that awkward."

CHAPTER 19

LEO

One day. One day was all I had as Vai's lover. But a skill I had honed was appreciating the time granted to me, and apparently I had mastered it, because I was *rapturous*.

Vai desired me. Enough to invite me—in the morning, no less!—to be their Rose Night partner, and certainly enough via ensuing events to convince me their desire was genuine. While I yearned for a much longer connection, my life right now could not accommodate that. Therefore I accepted this single-day relationship with gratitude. The pain of my concealed love just added a piquant twist of longing.

I lifted our joined hands as we neared Quicksand's street booth, which was festooned with Moulin Rouge–themed glitter and velvets. "How do you feel about public displays of affection?" I asked.

Vai slid me a glance that managed to be both shy and triumphant. "Let them see."

I leaned in to kiss them on the neck, under a warm sweep of honey-toned hair.

"I was going to ask why you two were late, but neeeever mind," Shelini chirped.

"About time," Fred hollered. "You could cut the pining with a chainsaw."

Genevieve, clutching a tablet for ticket sales, gave me a giddy grin and a thumbs-up. Catarina, in a folding chair at the booth counter, smiled tenderly at me and then at Vai, flicked her glance back to me with an assessing look, and turned again to face the street.

Uncomfortable. She had a way of divining one's soul too accurately.

As the morning tipped into afternoon, the bold flirtation increased among the citizenry. Some took a pink rose from our booth's basket. Others already wore one. At least three people strolled by topless with pink roses pasted on their nipples, and I spotted some of the inevitable college students wearing nothing but sandals and pink-rose-covered bikini bottoms.

Generally, anyone who didn't want to be in the midst of casual sexual offers steered clear of public spaces on the first of May. Those of asexual persuasion often held their own parties. Kornelia was attending one, for instance, hosted by a Tesoro friend.

Since we had a matinee performance, we had to dismantle the booth and leave the street fair by one-thirty.

"How often have you tried your luck with strangers on Rose Night?" I asked Vai as we walked to Jin Troia Hall.

"Not much. More often I've used Rose Night as an excuse to proposition a person I already had a crush on."

Our gazes snagged. We were strolling down Mille Colori Boulevard, under a row of Japanese snowbell trees. Their flowers wafted a rich, seductive scent. Vai pulled me into an alley, pressed me to the brick wall, and kissed me, open-mouthed. I twined my arms around their neck. Their hands roamed down to span my ass in a proprietary way that set me aflame.

"How the fuck," I panted against their lips, "am I supposed to perform a whole musical, when this is all I'm going to be thinking about?"

"We play sex workers in it. We'll be in the right mood."

"Ha." I tangled my hands in Vai's hair. "You're astoundingly hot in your costumes. I've been dying to touch you."

"I've envied Shelini. Getting to kiss you and hold you."

"All the times you put your hands on me to do my makeup or hair...do you know how distracting that's been?"

Vai's lips brushed mine. "All the times you put yours on me, to ease my muscles."

"Been a *long* session of foreplay, my love."

At Jin Troia Hall, we got into costume and makeup, then migrated to the wings. Vai drew up beside me, silent as a shadow, and then I had to stifle a yelp: their hand had stolen up the back of my silver skirt, and one finger stroked deep between my legs. I wore stockings and a pair of silky underwear, solidly made to hold up to stage usage, but believe you me, that caress still came through clearly. I clicked my teeth together to keep from making a sound. Lust sheared through me, washing out my pre-curtain nerves.

"Cheeky," I whispered.

Their finger slid up and down, teasing my tender places. "This is what I've wanted to do since I first saw you in this outfit."

"This specifically?" I tried to return the grope, but Vai's ass was currently covered by thick crinoline ruffles. I squeezed it through the layers. "Is that all?"

The tip of Vai's tongue traced my ear, making me shudder. "It's just the beginning."

"Who knew *you* were such a seducer? My prim and decorous Vai." I tried to bunch up their skirt to get under it, but it was too voluminous. I growled in impatience. "Later, when you're in just the corset and stockings, it's payback time for fondling."

"Duly warned." Vai kissed me on the lips. They had personally sealed our makeup. We could kiss without risking smears.

My complaint of distraction proved unfounded. Act like a person in love, indulging in caresses with her sweetheart, celebrating freedom, beauty, truth, and love even under the shadow of doom? Easy.

It was my best Satine performance ever. Not a note or step wrong, harmonies soaring until the chandelier crystals reverberated, tears breaking my voice when we could no longer outrun tragedy. The audience, already keyed up for romance thanks to Rose Night, leaped to their feet in applause at curtain call.

Vai embraced me after the curtain swept shut. "You've never been better."

I leaned on them, breathing their scent of powdery cosmetics and deodorant-sweetened sweat. "And to think, I wasted it on a Sunday matinee."

Between scenes, I had made good on my promise to fondle Vai in their most provocative costume: boots, fishnet stockings, and black corset bodysuit that was more straps than fabric. The moment had inspired prurient notions that had stuck with me for the rest of the show. "I suppose Mathilde would kill us if we wore costumes during Rose Night activities."

"What she doesn't know can't hurt her."

I laughed. "You would dare?"

"I'm the one who cleans and mends the costumes. I would ensure they were returned in perfect shape."

"Oh. Naturally. Well, that opens up ideas."

We signed programs with the rest of the cast at the stage door. Vai and I both regretfully told a number of flirtatious strangers that no, sorry, neither of us would be sporting pink roses in the streets tonight. Then we all flowed back into the ground-floor corridor.

"Get your things," I told Vai. "Come to my dressing room."

They picked up their bag from the dressing room they shared with three other dancers and followed me to one of the deluxe rooms reserved for leads. Vai had checked it out a couple of nights ago, at my invitation. Now, as they entered, they glanced around again. "It's bigger than the entire caravan."

"The bathroom alone is practically bigger than the entire caravan."

Vai set their bag on the makeup counter and looked at the bed, made up with a star-patterned duvet. "You even get a proper bed. Our dressing room just has a couch."

"Why do you suppose I invited you over?" I turned to present my back and lifted my hair out of the way.

Taking the hint, Vai unzipped my dress. "You'd like to stay here overnight instead of the caravan?"

"Thank you." I stepped out of the dress. "Thought it might be nice, for variety." I tugged my corset lacings loose. "What do you think?"

Vai scanned the ceiling beams, then my barely clothed form. They nodded.

"Excellent." I kissed them lightly. "But first, I must shower, as I am a mess, and then we must have dinner, because I am ravenous." I pulled their wrist. "Join me."

"One thing I've learned," they warned. "Shower sex is clumsy."

"Fully agree. Shower foreplay only. We did agree on dinner first."

We were able to stick to this agreement. As Vai had alluded to, the slippery wall tiles against one's bare butt, and the water spraying into one's nostrils, were not the most erotic features ever. But making out with Vai, naked and soap-slick in a shower actually big enough to fit us both, still unquestionably counted as a luxury.

Having stopped at the foreplay level, we dried, dressed, went out, and acquired rice bowls from a food truck. Rose Night revelers thronged the city. Sultry beats thumped from street bands and open apartment windows. The sunset was fading, and city lights were coming on, many of them pink, red, or purple in honor of the festival.

Vai and I settled on a grassy slope in Ninfea Park and watched a burlesque performance as we ate. "Imagine if you'd joined them for the year instead," I said.

"Yes. Would be awful if I'd ended up in a tawdry, revealing costume." They set their empty bowl on the grass and wrapped an arm around my waist. "I'm so glad I picked your caravan."

Love choked my throat. I leaned my head against Vai's. They were so kind to me, and we had so little time.

We strolled the path circling the park's pond, passing couples tangled on blankets. The water lilies had been enchanted to glow in soft colors. Luminescent pink bubbles the size of tennis balls floated through the air, staying just out of reach even though revelers, myself included, leaped up to try to grab them.

At the far end of the pond, Vai pressed me against a tree trunk, kissing me. I breathed the scent of their perfume and clean hair, mingled with water lilies and crushed grass.

"I never imagined us ending up here," I said. "Well, untrue. I *imagined* it, but…"

"Were you fantasizing, there in the caravan, a few feet away from me?"

"In the shower, mostly. Praying you wouldn't hear. Did you ever hear?" I felt a hot thrill, rather hoping they had.

"No. Did you ever hear me in bed? I was careful to be quiet."

I groaned. "No! Gods, that's so hot. Tell me what you want. I'm up for it."

"If I had your improv skills, I'd invent something outlandish, just to see if you'd agree."

"'Leo, I want to papier-mâché bits of tissue all over you, stuff candy in your mouth, then smack you with a stick.' There, I came up with it for you."

"Is that what you'd like? Should we go buy tissue paper?" They kissed me calmly, taking my hand. We stepped back onto the path.

"No, but thank you for being game. You were going to tell me what *you* want."

"When did you start liking me?" Vai asked. "I want to hear that."

"I *liked* you as soon as I learned why you were fleeing Tesoro. But you mean when did I start to desire you."

"Correct."

"One day, during *Peter Pan Goes Wrong,* when you were fixing my makeup, you touched my lips and let your finger stay there."

"I remember," Vai said. "I was...feeling bold."

"All of a sudden I had the urge to wrap my legs around you and kiss you."

"Mm. That would have been terrible," they remarked.

"Then—oh Lord, the dance lessons. It *tantalized* me, getting to cling to you and move with you like that."

"I knew I was in trouble then too."

We wandered back into the streets. "We've covered spring equinox," I said.

"And all the times we touched for *Moulin Rouge*." Vai's hand stole into my hair, fingers threading close to the scalp, and tugged lightly.

Arousal flashed through me. "Ah. You remember."

"So you did like it. You weren't just teasing."

"I liked it *and* I was teasing."

Ahead, the theatre's marquee sparkled bright, "JIN TROIA" outlined in white bulbs, and below that, a glowing red heart enclosing the words "MOULIN ROUGE!"

"Is the purple gown still your favorite?" Vai asked.

"It is. You tailored it perfectly. It's the dress of my dreams."

"Wear it for me tonight."

We paused to kiss at the next red light, again at the stage door, and again as soon as we were inside my dressing room. We turned on a light and lowered it to a gentle glow.

Vai undressed me, slipping buttons free and sliding zippers down, their mouth gliding over each revealed patch of flesh. Then they dressed me again, selecting the garments. Garter belt circling my waist and buckled around my thighs. Black fishnets clipped on. No corset this time—"Breathe free," they said, running a thumb over my nipples. No underwear. Last, the silky weight of the strapless purple gown.

I sat on the bed, my stocking-netted feet tucked up, the dress pooling around me, while Vai stripped naked and then put on the outfit of garters and stockings, with the corset bodysuit that snapped beneath the crotch. Going without boots, they walked over, pushed me back onto the bed, and straddled me.

I spread my hands around their muscled ass, two curves of bare flesh bordered by bodysuit straps. "You feel exactly as hot as I imagined, lying on top of me while wearing this."

Vai petted me from thigh to ribs and back again, flipping the sequins to run upward, then downward. "Making the sequins the reversible kind was wise of me. Feels sleek when I stroke you."

"You like stroking me?"

"Was that not evident?"

They applied their mouth to my exposed shoulders. Now that we had no particular time limit, we lay there for languorous ages, kissing, our hands wandering over and under each other's costumes. I unsnapped Vai's bodysuit to free them from their confinement. The high slit of my dress provided an avenue of access for Vai.

We had the small window open an inch, for air. It was high in the wall, a frosted-glass pane screened with a lightweight curtain. Downtown chatter trickled through. As the night grew late, thunder rolled and lightning flickered.

"Imagine all those outdoor-sex people scrambling for cover right now," I said.

"Hope everyone's all right." Vai looked toward the window, seeming genuinely concerned, as if they might halt proceedings to go out and rescue rain-sodden lovers.

I laughed, wrapping a leg around them to keep them from leaving, just in case. "It's cozy. Being in here with you during a spring storm."

Vai cupped my face and fitted their mouth across mine.

Rain fell, a white noise blanketing the city, punctuated with thunder. The smell of wet pavement wafted in. By around midnight we had gotten into a frenzy, having delayed culmination for quite some time.

"Come here," I breathed. I got on my knees on the floor, yards of sequined fabric slithering down with me, and arranged Vai to sit on the edge of the bed. Hands on their thighs, I parted their legs.

"Here." Vai reached for a pillow. "Kneel on this."

I shook my head. "I like it this way."

"With your knees hurting?"

I nodded, uncurling a smile and maintaining eye contact until I saw comprehension flare in their face. "Yeah," I said. "It's like that."

Vai slid a hand against my scalp at the back of my head, took a handful of my hair, and tightened their grip just enough to pull.

The thrill of being seen and welcomed made me shut my eyes. "Perfect," I murmured. I let Vai's grip guide me forward and took them into my mouth.

Their hand tightened in tandem with their quickening breaths. My jaw ached, and I loved it. My mouth kept ferociously at work. By the time Vai shook apart, my tormented knees and scalp had grown as hot as the rest of me.

Vai's fingers relaxed, smoothing my hair. I wiped my mouth, kissed the inside of their thigh, and smiled at them. They lifted me to the bed. Relief shot through my knees, acute enough to be a fresh pain.

Vai unzipped my gown and eased it off. "Get comfortable," they said.

I lay back, legs open. I still wore the garter belt and stockings, and could feel the imprint of fishnets on my knees and the tops of my feet.

Vai laid their hands on my shins. "Would you like all this off too?"

"Not yet. Leave them till after."

They stroked my hip with their thumb, below the tight-cutting line of the garter belt, then nuzzled the thatch of hair between my legs. "You've been so good. Lie back and relax."

I obeyed, not even shy about the whimper I made. Vai took me deep into their mouth, so warm and slick that my world went into whiteout, wrapped in the smell of rain. Their hands held me down by my open thighs even as I shuddered to pieces a minute or two later. Bliss floated around my consciousness like sparkling confetti.

And like those bits of tinsel in the show, it soon drifted to the ground and became a part of the past. Vai unclasped my garter belt, peeled it and the stockings off me, then crawled up to collapse beside me in a hug.

Rose Night and its events were officially behind us. Ahead, a slide into a dark tunnel. I folded inward, within Vai's embrace, my joy shriveling to a tiny pearl of love: indestructible, but useless against what faced me.

They took my shiver as a sign of cold and drew the blanket up. "Better?"

"Mm. Thank you."

I shifted, spooning my back against Vai.

"You are the most wonderful," they said, slurring in exhaustion. "I don't have the words. I wish I were a thesaurus, like you."

"I have too many words. They block my throat. I can't speak."

"That's pretty. Is it from a play? A poem?"

"I'm not sure. Maybe."

We lay silent. Vai's breathing shifted into the rhythm of sleep. The thunder receded. Someone sang love songs in Spanish, accompanied by mandolin, from a window high above. I slid in and out of a doze, mourning, grateful, peaceful, scared, paying my respects to everything the day had given me, and grieving that it was over.

CHAPTER 20

LEO

I blinked and it was dawn. Maybe I had slept after all, but not much, to judge from the grainy feel of my eyelids. Rain still plopped from the eaves outside. The street was quiet, aside from the occasional swoosh of a passing vehicle. The dressing room had grown cool.

Vai stretched, kissed my bare shoulder, then snugged the blanket over it. "Hello."

I turned onto my back to kiss their jaw, the piece of them most reachable at the moment. "Hello."

"After we shower, may I treat you to breakfast out?"

I lowered my brows in confusion. "You don't have to. Rose Night's over."

They gave me a concerned look. "Exactly how awful were your previous Rose Night partners?"

I snorted. "They weren't awful. Just—honestly, in most cases I didn't spend the whole night with them. But I already live with you, so it would've been weird not to. Or such was my reasoning."

"Well. The breakfast offer still stands. Think about it." Vai kissed me on the forehead, then got up to shower.

After I'd taken my turn cleaning up, and we had gotten dressed, Vai came and took my hands, where I stood near the door.

"This was the most amazing Rose Night I've ever had," they said.

I gave them a poignant smile. "It was for me too."

Still holding my hands, they looked down. "I'd like to do it again. Not for a festival. I'd like to date you properly."

My breath caught. Froze. Of all the things I wanted most in the universe and couldn't have—here it was, offered to me.

Except of course Vai didn't mean it. Or at least, wouldn't offer if they knew me better, knew my whole sad deal. Or if they themself weren't at a low point in their life, separated from their family, doing things their usual self would consider rash.

"But this was just Rose Night," I said in a small, careful voice.

"I know. But I…have feelings for you. You must have realized by now."

All my clever vocabulary dried up. I swallowed to jog my tongue into working again. "Oh, sweetheart. I—wish I could, but I can't. With my life. Right now."

Their fingers slipped out of mine. They stepped back, avoiding my eyes. "You aren't interested. I understand."

The scrape in their voice, their bowed posture—I had *hurt* Vai. The realization pierced me like a dart. "It's not that. I like you so much! You're too good for me."

"That's a ridiculous reason." Vai spoke quietly, but the words were cut sharp.

I staggered away a few steps. "I'm not going to do the Satine thing and pretend I don't care. I do care, I do want you. Obviously. But…"

While I sought the right thing to say, Vai filled in, "But not right now."

"Not right now," I echoed. Then, because I couldn't leave it at that, couldn't be quite this dishonest with someone I loved so much, I blurted out, "Look, I need to tell you, I'll be taking some time off from the troupe. After *Moulin Rouge* wraps, I'm not going to be here for a while."

Their eyes were blank with shock. "Where are you going?"

"It's something I agreed to, for my family and friends, before I met you, and now it's almost time, and…I can't be with anyone. For a while."

"How long?"

If I said "a year," Vai was smart enough to make the connection with my year-long deal with Nalibak. "A few seasons at least," I hedged.

"A few *seasons*? Why haven't you said?"

"Because—I'm the worst, that's why. I was going to tell you. Soon."

"You'll be here, in Tesoro? With your family?"

"I don't really know where I'll be. Everything's too uncertain."

"Why don't you know where you'll be? Even if it's a—a job where you move around, like this one…"

"It isn't exactly. There's a lot I don't know. But you can stay in the caravan, I was going to tell you. Wayshaw will still be there, so you don't have to worry about driving it or taking care of it. She can do all that."

Vai stared at me. "Wayshaw knows you'll be leaving? Does the rest of the troupe know too?"

I winced and paced farther away. "Yeah. I…recently told them. I was working out how to tell you—because you mean more to me, so I was putting it off and trying to find the right time, and…I'm sorry, I'm awful. Please, though, stay in the caravan. Make it yours, do whatever you like to it."

"I don't want to stay with the troupe, if you're not there."

I stopped pacing. "I thought you liked it. You've been doing fantastic, and everyone loves you—"

"I do like it. But I'd rather be with you."

I splayed my hands over my face. A bicycle bell pinged outside. People passed our window in conversation.

"You don't want to be with me," Vai finally said. "Never mind. You don't owe me details."

I do, though. I owe you so much more.

I looked at them, my eyes aching. "I *will* tell you more, soon."

Even now, I retained enough caution to resist spilling the whole story. Vai would panic if they knew, and there was nothing they could do to help me, so why make the next couple of weeks even worse for them?

They turned away, checking their phone, then slid it into their pocket. "Fine." An impersonal tone smoothed their voice. "I'd like things to be all right between us, whatever that takes."

"They are. They're completely all right." I shut up then, because how hypocritical did I sound?

Vai straightened their jacket. "I don't think I'm ready for breakfast after all. I'll go for a walk. Then head back to the caravan, rest a bit."

"You're…okay?" I asked.

Vai nodded. Their posture was stiff and formal, in a way I hadn't seen since the first month of our acquaintance. "See you later."

"See you," I said, but they were already in the corridor. The door shut behind them.

I closed my eyes.

There. It had happened, the thing I had known all along would happen. I had told Vai I was leaving, the illusion of my desirability had fallen from their eyes, and our lovely, close relationship was over. Vai would shake off their hurt within a few days, maybe even hours—no one had ever had trouble getting over me—and if I was lucky, we could remain on cordial terms for the time remaining to me.

Vai had always been out of my league, Nalibak deal or no. This was what happened in my relationships with everyone, because I was not constituted better.

It was in vain, then, to long for a world in which it didn't have to be this way, a parallel timeline in which I *was* better, and was free, and did deserve someone like Vai. Still, while I stood with my eyes squeezed shut, I let myself wish it for a few seconds, with all the love and loneliness in my being.

VAI

The thunder had ended, but it was still raining, and I had only brought a light jacket. I grew soaked as I walked away from Jin Troia Hall. My skin felt numb, either because the rain was cold for May, or because I was in shock.

I had no right to feel this wounded, as if he had punched the breath out of me. Leo hadn't wanted to hurt me, and his kind rejection of a relationship aligned with Rose Night traditions. I had always known he might decline. It was I who was out of line to expect more. He had given as much explanation as he was willing to, and he did not owe me access to his whole life. I simply had to accept that Leo would soon be leaving. And he had declined to keep me near him.

Leaving. For several seasons. To destinations unknown, or at least unshared. *What the fuck?*, I thought for the twentieth time in half an hour. *What the actual fuck?*

When I reached the caravan, I changed into dry clothes and brewed some green tea. Wayshaw wasn't around, which irked me. I wanted to demand an explanation from her as to why I'd been kept out of the loop about Leo *leaving for months*. Did they all think me a child, that I couldn't be trusted with such information without losing my mind in grief?

Are you not, then, acting like a child and losing your mind in grief?, I questioned myself, standing at a kitchen window and sipping my tea.

It was now eleven a.m.—a respectable time to contact people, even if they'd had a late night. I texted Catarina: *Good morning. If you're free, can we meet up?*

She answered, *Of course! I am lounging in tranquil solitude. Do come over.*

When I knocked at her caravan, she let me in, beaming. She wore a peach-colored chenille bathrobe and matcha-green slippers. Her face was free of makeup, and her blue eyes shone behind her glasses. Her caravan smelled sweet and toasty. "Sit," she invited. "I've just made cinnamon ginger scones."

I sat at her tiny table, not unlike the one in Leo's kitchen. But all of Catarina's furnishings were a marvel of economy and tidiness compared to Leo's. She set a plate with a warm scone in front of me, let me choose from her tea collection, and prepared a mug of the holy basil I had picked. We spoke of last night's rainstorm, and how thankful we were to have three resting days in a row.

Finally she sat opposite me and examined me over her Lapsang souchong.

"Did you do anything for Rose Night?" I asked.

"No. There were a few people who stopped by the booth yesterday that I might have said yes to. But I didn't see any of them later. I reminded myself I'm no good at casual sex anyway, especially the older I get, and gave myself a luxurious evening off."

I nodded, plucked a piece of candied ginger from the scone, and chewed it.

"And you?" she asked.

My sigh was long and ponderous.

"Ah," she said. "I did worry, when I saw you two together."

"It was wonderful. Everything I'd hoped. Except…I misunderstood. I thought it was the start of something, but he's going away. For a long time. After the show wraps." I looked at her in disbelief. "He said everyone else knows."

Catarina pursed her lips. "We all love Leo. But we could also throttle him at times. He did tell us, and requested we not tell you yet. He wanted to do it in his own time."

"Which was going to be when?"

"If I know Leo, he delayed it because he couldn't stand the thought of disappointing you. He wanted your life to be pleasant for as long as possible."

"So I could fall harder once he did tell me?" My voice broke. Averting my eyes, I slurped some tea.

"He wouldn't have wanted that either. The thing about Leo…" Catarina tapped her fingers on the table. "He will give anything he has, to anyone who needs it. Time, kindness, healing. A bed in his caravan. A yes on Rose Night. He cares deeply and generously. But he never thinks anyone truly cares about him in return. He doesn't plan for that."

I parted my lips to say something like *Then that's thoughtless of him*. But her assessment struck me as true when I checked it against our history. "He said he has to do something for his family."

"Giving to others again. I don't know what exactly this obligation is. I gather it isn't pleasant."

"I wanted to stay with him, whatever it was. He told me I couldn't." I crumbled the scone into pieces. "It's probably to do with someone else's problems, and he's not at liberty to say. I just…*thought* we were closer."

"There is no doubt in my mind that Leo has feelings for you," she said. "Whether he'll pull his head out of his nether crevice and rearrange his life to keep you, I can't predict. But you did not misunderstand about those feelings."

I nodded, blurry gaze fixed on my scone. "Thank you."

We drank our tea. Sun streamed through the breaking clouds.

"I found an idyllic little clearing in the woods about half a mile from here," Catarina said. "Would you like to go there with me and do qigong?"

"Yes," I said gravely. "I would."

When Leo and I ended up back in the caravan together, around dinnertime, he started with a tentative "How are you doing?" And, when I shut that down with a neutral "Fine," he moved on to what to eat for dinner. Errands he'd do tomorrow. Inquiries about my plans for the week.

I invented some plans on the spot, since it was harrowingly clear I had to get away from this charade. Leo might have had the acting chops it required, but I did not.

Charles texted me the next day. *Vai, isn't this you?? Your hair was this color when I saw you the other day. You're in Quicksand Theatre Company now??* He attached a publicity photo from the show: Genevieve in center stage as Zidler, me and five other courtesans posing around them.

Well. No point lying now.

I am, I said. *I apologize for not saying so. I wasn't sure I wanted people in Tesoro to know.*

Omg, this is the coolest! Don't worry, I get it about not saying anything. He added that now he would definitely have to come see the show, and I thanked him.

As we approached the weekend, I viewed the tasks ahead with agony. I couldn't stand inches from Leo anymore, sweeping my fingertips over his face, and not seize him around the head and either demand answers or smash a kiss onto his mouth. I couldn't present my body to him so he could treat my sore muscles with as chaste a touch as if he were a healer in a clinic. I didn't think I could even stay in the caravan anymore.

I entreated help from Catarina. She had it all arranged within hours.

From the clearing in the woods, where I had taken to spending time alone, I texted Leo.

For the rest of the show, Kornelia will be taking care of your makeup and wardrobe, and Darius will be healing my muscles. I'll also be moving into Catarina's caravan for the remainder of the month. It's best this way.

My heart thundered as I sent it. I was aiming to avert drama by imposing this distance, but the missive itself might cause drama. No escaping that.

The "read" notification came on. I made myself look up at the trees, barely breathing.

Finally his answer arrived. *I'll go along with whatever makes you comfortable. But I'm so sorry to have done anything to drive you away. I never wanted that.*

You acted fully within Rose Night traditions, I responded. *I'm the one complicating things.*

We are both complicated lately, he wrote. *I promise I'll explain more, before the month is out.*

Are things so uncertain that you can't explain now? I typed, with no little bitterness.

I realize it sounds insane, but yes, they are uncertain in many ways.

That stirred a whisper of hope in me. Did this uncertainty mean there was a chance we could be together during the next year?

I want you to be happy, he added then. *I support your choices. You're phenomenal and I know you'll be all right.*

Then you do not fucking understand anything, I wanted to type—but did not.

After a minute, I wrote, *I want you to be happy too. Even if I don't understand what you need.*

He answered with a heart emoji, and nothing else. And since I was the one announcing I was moving out, I left it at that too.

CHAPTER 21

VAI

That weekend's *Moulin Rouge* performances were like a bad dream. What had been a romantic, convivial experience had, without any outward changes, become delusive, tawdry, and tragic. Both those moods had been there all along in the play. I had just lived only in the "sparkling, giddy romance" side before, and now I dwelled entirely in the "she dies in the end" side.

Living in Catarina's caravan added to the strangeness. It was less cluttered, the colors neutral, the fold-out guest bed more comfortable, her company always soothing. But she was not who I was in love with. Now from afar I wondered how Leo was doing, and when I would next run into him. The distance felt wrong. It was also utterly unfair that this felt in every way like a breakup when we had never truly been a couple.

Each day might be the day he would explain his upcoming departure. Each day, he didn't. When we encountered each other, he would give me a smile that was almost a wince, and say, "Hey, how you doing?"

And I would say, "Fine, you?"

And he would say, "Good, yeah." And we would get on with our day.

We couldn't continue like this. The veneer would have to break. Even an explosion would be an improvement.

I'll be at Friday night's show! texted Charles on Thursday. *With friends.*

I did not care at all, but I texted back, *Thank you for supporting the troupe.*

Friday night was a nearly full house, as had been every performance. A triumph for the Quicksand Theatre Company, as the reviews were saying. A mere week ago, I would have overflowed with happiness to know the show was such a success. Now Leo and I were barely speaking and in different caravans, and he would soon be leaving, and the year ahead looked like an endless, dusty road.

After the show, I went to the stage door along with the rest. Behind a velvet rope, a crowd milled, taking pictures and collecting autographs. The thickest cluster was around Leo, Shelini, Fred, and Genevieve, but many friendly patrons spoke to us nameless backup dancers too.

While I signed someone's program with an illegible scrawl of my stage name, a voice said, "Hi, Vai."

It took me a moment to realize the name had come from the public's side of the rope. I lifted my head, handing the program absently back to the person who had requested it. They thanked me and stepped aside, opening up a space that revealed Charles.

Beside him was Daphne.

"Hello," I said. To her.

"We loved the show," she told me, in the impersonally friendly tone she would use for a stranger seated beside her on a bus.

"Made me cry like a baby," the woman next to her said. I recognized her as our neighbor Heddy's niece, the kung fu sifu. She had the defined deltoids to prove it, framed in a black tank-top dress, and she was grinning in a sunny manner.

"Daphne," Charles said, keeping a tentative gaze on me, "this is my friend Vai. I introduced you once."

"It's good to see you," Daphne said. "I'm so sorry, I have a clinic and I meet a hundred people a day. It's a constant issue."

So the spell made her unable to remember me even from one meeting to another. Fascinating. Good to know.

"And," Charles continued, "this is London. She's a journalist." He nodded to the shorter person beside him, a curly-haired woman with a lip ring.

"London," I repeated.

"I know." She laughed. "My parents were having a major Anglophile phase when they named me."

"No, it's nice. Easy to remember." I hardly knew what I was saying.

"And this is Hazuki," Charles concluded, gesturing to the sifu leaning her shoulder against Daphne's. I tracked that, and the fondness with which Daphne looked at her. *Too bad for you, Charles,* I thought, with some of the half-vindictive sympathy of a person who has just been romantically rejected themselves.

"Hi, Vai," Hazuki said. At her gentle tone, I realized that Kwal's spell didn't cover her and that she recognized me, even though we'd only been acquaintances.

"Hi, Hazuki," I said. "Thank you for coming."

A cosmetics-and-deodorant scent touched my nose, an intimately familiar combination that knocked me weak with longing. In my peripheral vision, a figure with purple hair stepped close.

"Charles, right?" Leo said. "I remember you." He sounded perky on the surface, with solid ice underlying it.

"Yes!" Charles beamed, clueless to the tone. "Gosh. I'm honored you remembered. You were magnificent tonight."

Leo waved the compliment away and focused on my sister. "I remember you too. Daphne, isn't it?" His voice was gentler now.

"I'm impressed," Daphne said. "Ayda's our mutual friend, I believe."

"She is. Was it Ayda who told you about the show?"

"No, it was Charles," she said. "He insisted we come. I'm so glad we did."

"Did he," Leo said. "Well, tell me how things are at your clinic."

They made small talk about their jobs. When Leo learned of London's career, he said with a hand on his heart, "A journalist! Oh gods. We beseech you, be kind in your review."

"No, no." Laughing, London waved her hands back and forth. "I'm here for pleasure. I'm not an arts reviewer. I cover local events and politics, and I'm not planning to bother anyone about those tonight either." Her gaze moved to me, and her smile softened.

Leo shot me a glance. Gauging whether I was all right.

I just nodded, with a dip of my chin toward London. So at least one journalist had already figured out I was here. On top of Daphne's presence and my problems with Leo, it became a bit much.

"I'll go back in," I murmured after another minute.

"Goodnight," Charles said. "I'll be in touch."

"Good to talk to you," my sister told me.

I walked into the theatre on unsteady legs. I looked back once, then paused. Leo had grasped Charles's sleeve and was leaning over the velvet rope to speak in his ear. Leo's face and posture were graceful, as befitted an actor conversing with an audience member. But Charles's face, as he listened, seemed to grow pale, though his smile stayed rigidly put. His three companions didn't notice—they were greeting Shelini.

Then, though other people were still coming forward for autographs, Leo turned and stalked into the theatre. He spotted me, caught my wrist, and drew me out of view.

"Are you okay?" he said. "That fucker. I swear."

I nodded. "I'm all right. Unprepared, that's all."

My phone buzzed. I fished it out. "Message from Charles," I mumbled. I read it to myself, then out loud. "*Vai, I'm so sorry if you're upset. I should've told you, but I didn't want to make you nervous before the show. My reasoning was that when the spell is over, Daphne would be sad if she hadn't seen you in the play.*" I twisted my mouth. "He does have a point."

Leo huffed. "Right. He wants to be the person she's grateful to."

Buzz. Another message from Charles. *Also please apologize to Leonidas for me. I didn't know he could be so scary, holy cow! You have a loyal friend there.*

I lifted my gaze to Leo. "He says to apologize to you, and that you're scary. What did you say to him?"

Leo snorted, looking away. "I told him...if he upset you, I'd have him banned from every theatrical venue in the country. A threat which I absolutely do not have the power to enact, but. Yeah."

"Thank you."

His gaze shifted down as he nodded. His lashes were coated with mascara, and he still wore the black dress of the final act, gorgeous collarbones exposed.

"Have your plans changed at all?" I dared ask.

"No. Unfortunately." He tipped his chin toward the door. "Say the word if he bothers you again." Then he paused and added, "I like your sister. She's lovely."

I nodded, aching at this barrier between me and all the people I loved.

Leo touched my arm, his hand warm, our flesh in contact for one second. Then he strode out to finish signing autographs.

LEO

Before our final weekend of Tesoro performances, I met up with Javier again. We chose a park near his grocery, where I could lie in the grass and look at the sky through the maple leaves. I was going to miss the daytime sky.

"I need to tell the troupe," I said. "I have to tell Vai."

"Yeah. Super clear you're into Vai. That one time we were at dinner, you glanced across the table at them about a thousand times." Javier picked up a slim fallen branch and started stripping it of leaves.

"Vai's too good for me. They'll realize it any second now."

"I hope you didn't bring me out here because you want me to say, 'No, Leo, you're so awesome, no one's too good for you.'"

"I'm not expecting that," I retorted. "Regardless, I have to tell them. Vai and everyone else. And...I don't want to. I'd rather just disappear. Leave letters explaining where I went, like you knew I would."

He tore leaves apart. The scent of maple wafted over me.

"It's your choice," he said. "You're the one going through the hard part. Why don't you want to tell them in person, anyhow?"

"It would seem like I'm making a grand announcement. It'd be tacky. I don't want to see the horror on their faces, the pity." Or, just as bad, the indifference. "I don't want them to feel obliged to perform a reaction for me. Does that make sense?"

Javier poked the stick into his palm. "Where are you going to be? On the twenty-seventh. When he comes to get you."

I averted my gaze to the sky again. "The troupe will be in Punta Rosa. So, somewhere along the verge near there, probably."

"Ayda and I could be there," he said, uncertainty making his voice waver.

"No. I don't want that to be...something you see." *The last memory you have of me,* I almost said. "Wayshaw will be there. I won't be alone."

Javier just glanced at me, annoyance and sadness battling on his tight face.

"It's what I want," I insisted.

He tossed the stick away. "Fine."

I watched the leaves flutter overhead. "So you think it's all right if I write letters, rather than telling everyone in person?"

"Everyone'll be upset no matter how they find out. It's your choice. I don't even know why you're asking me."

"Lack of other people to use as a sounding board on the issue."

He set his foot to rest against the side of mine. We glanced at each other, and before he looked away, I was sure the edges of his eyes were red. "Everyone just wants to help you, you know," he muttered.

My eyes filled with tears, but I smiled at the sky. "Thanks."

CHAPTER 22

LEO

When Vai left my caravan, they had apparently stuffed all the pleasure into their bag and walked off with it. The place no longer felt so much like a cozy traveling home as it did a shabby vehicle I happened to sleep in.

It was just as well they weren't here. My distress had become a constant condition that would have been obvious to anyone living with me. Only Wayshaw remained near, and if she noticed my neglecting to eat at times, she understood why and said nothing.

I hadn't seen Nalibak since that fae-gifted snowstorm at Delta Esmeralda in January. The days had been growing longer, giving him less darkness to roam around in, and I'd been around people a lot, what with the expanded cast and crew of *Moulin Rouge*. Likely there was also the time slip of the verge—for him, maybe that night in the snow was just last week. But his absence made me antsy. If he *had* by some miracle forgotten me and dropped our deal—or returned to the elements, if I were extraordinarily lucky—then I wanted to know, so I could stop living under his shadow.

If he was all set to come grab me later this month, on the other hand, then I wanted to know that too. I took to going out alone at night, on meandering walks in the dark. I had to be emitting such potent desolation that he couldn't resist approaching, if he still followed me.

On our last night in Tesoro, he answered my silent invitation.

I was wending my way through the trees in Merrilo Park, picking through ferns and ducking under branches with only a penlight to guide me.

"Friend." The voice was thin and hungry.

Adrenaline swept through me, but I didn't jolt, didn't turn. A chilly glow shaped like a figure stood in my peripheral vision.

"You're still around, then," I said.

"The time is oh so close. I have been asking, yes, learning the numbers of your human days."

I still had St. John's wort in my jacket. He couldn't grab me yet, not easily anyway. I nodded and continued wandering forward. "That answers that."

"Your grief. Your love and regret. What wound does this ooze from? It is delicious."

"Fuck you," I said, tired. "It's your fault I can't have a relationship."

"I? I am rarely near you. Likelier it is your fault."

For someone who enjoyed lying and deceiving, Nalibak had the irritating habit of saying things that were in fact true. I didn't answer. I kept wading through underbrush.

"When I take you to the lair," Nalibak said, "you will tell me the story of this relationship that has so mutilated your soul. Yes?"

"No. I will not be telling you that story."

I veered toward a footpath, emerged from the forest, and went straight to the nearest streetlight, where groups of other humans strolled in the night air. I'd left Nalibak behind. If he said anything further, I didn't hear.

We drove south to Punta Rosa for our last weekend of *Moulin Rouge*. Four more performances. That was all I had left as an actor, possibly for the rest of my life. I would perform stories for Nalibak, but I would be acting solo rather than collaborating with friends, and performing would no longer be a journey of delightful artistic expression but a grim means to stay alive. Was this why I had learned to act? All just for this?

Wayshaw parked the caravan in Nopal Park, as she had in November, on Vai's first night with us. Now the sky and ocean were a balmy blue, sea roses bloomed pale pink, and my laptop sat open on the kitchen table with fragments of a heartsore love declaration on its screen.

Wayshaw came in. "Still working on the letter?"

I laced my fingers into a net, rested my chin on them, and moved my head in a nod.

My letter to Vai was proving the hardest to write. The one to my aunt and uncle was polite and succinct. My brother and Ayda already knew where I was going, but I was writing them each a letter anyway to express my love, gratitude, and encouragement. My letter to the troupe, while full of affection and apology, involved no romantic angle and thus was straightforward enough. Vai, though…

"You're still not planning to tell Vai in person?" Wayshaw asked.

"It's better this way."

"What about the fact that Vai loves you?"

The tart-sweet impact of those words streaked through me like a bite of green apple. "They only loved an illusion of me. They'll get over it."

"And what of the fact that you love Vai?"

I closed my eyes. The apple, perhaps, was laced with a dangerous enchantment. "I've loved lots of people. That's how I am. Doesn't change anything."

"I'm sure I don't understand humans," Wayshaw said, "because that all sounds as if it could not possibly make sense."

For our shows in Bahía Rosa, my portrayal of Satine felt false, a pretty patch slapped on top of a heavy black coffin. It baffled me that the audience laughed and cheered, that none of the troupe demanded to know what was wrong with me. I couldn't have been that convincing. They were just seeing what they wished to see, as people do.

Four. Three. Two. Then one. One performance left. Five days after it, on Friday, the twenty-seventh of May, when the sun went down, I would be gone.

I tried to hold on to every moment. Silver confetti. Vai flexing with grace through dance moves. Glowing absinthe. Vai's lips painted crimson. The windmill blades twinkling. Vai's sleek hair shifting colors under the rainbow lights. My purple gown hugging my body. Vai's gaze trailing across it as they passed me backstage, as if remembering caressing it on Rose Night.

I took my final bows. My theatre mates and strangers from the audience stuffed my arms full of so many flowers I couldn't even make my hands meet around them. How heavy flowers could be, in that quantity. We dismantled the sets. The trickle of questions began.

"So you're leaving? Like, now?" Fred asked.

"Is today really your last day?" Korn asked.

"What can I take care of for you?" Catarina asked, quieter than the rest.

I handed her a bouquet of pink and white gerbera daisies. "Who. Not what. The one you're already taking care of. Please keep doing so."

"Always. But we could use some answers if we're to feel settled about you."

"Soon," I promised.

The night scintillated with stars and fireflies. The breeze smelled of wild roses and the sea. I sat on a bench, the caravans' lights shining in strings and rectangles off to my right. The waves glimmered blue with sea sparkle.

Surely *some* nights in the fae realm would be as pleasant as this, I tried to believe. Even in the company of a fair feaster.

A figure approached along the beach path and stopped near my bench, cradling one elbow. I couldn't see their features except as patches of shadow.

"When are you leaving?" Vai asked.

"Tomorrow."

The green spark of a firefly rose beside their knee, then winked out. "And the explanation you promised?"

"How does Friday sound?" My voice cracked a bit.

"A precise date. I'll take it." Some people would have said those words bitterly. Vai merely sounded tired.

"Vai," I said, before they could walk away.

They waited, in profile to me.

"I'm so sorry I've made you unhappy. It's the exact opposite of what I wanted."

The caravan lights traced Vai's lips in silhouette. "Those things we said—*you* said. They weren't the kinds of things people would say if it were 'just for Rose Night.' They meant more."

"I do feel all those things. I only thought...you wouldn't want to pursue it further. So it wouldn't matter what I said."

"It mattered," Vai said, two slow, weighted words.

I nodded, miserable. "I'm sorry. It's a terrible thing to not feel loved. I wanted you to feel as loved as you are."

"I did," they said. "For that one day. Then you ended it, and I haven't felt it since."

My breath caught in a half-sob. "Vai," I pleaded.

They completed their pivot and walked away.

❧

I didn't want that to be the last time I saw Vai. But the next morning, when I went around the caravans to find as many people as I could and say goodbye, Catarina told me Vai had gone out for the day, on some epic walk down the beach.

"They didn't feel up to facing this scene," she said, then hugged me. "You two will patch it up. I know you will."

I lied to all my troupe friends, one after the other. Yes, I'd keep in touch. Of course I'd see everyone again soon. Naturally I'd update them with my plans. Lies, lies, lies. Maybe it was my self-disgust that kept me from crying.

Wayshaw and I got into the caravan and drove off, waving from the windows. Once we were on the highway, swooping north toward Tesoro, I tried to compose a text to Vai.

I've left. I wish I could've hugged you goodbye. Maudlin. Delete.

I'm gone now. You can come back to the park. You won't have to avoid me anymore. Sulky. Delete.

Catarina said you were out on a long beach walk. Sounds fun! Anyway, I'm off. Sorry to have missed you. Have a great time! Fake as fuck. Delete.

I've been haunted by what you said last night. Every minute I've known you for the last five months, you've been loved. I've loved you since Fire Festival, at that fountain in Dasdemir. And I love you still.

Entirely too sincere. Delete.

So I said nothing. Vai didn't text me either.

But at least now I was beginning to know what to put in my letter.

VAI

The next few days were a fog, though I walked through sunshine and bright May colors. Leo was going to explain on Friday. Fine. I would wait.

No journalists contacted me. Charles had texted, amid a flood of further apologies, *London isn't going to write about you, btw. She says good journalists have great appreciation for whistleblowers, and she respects your privacy. Anyway the real story is Portnoff and all the stuff coming out about her.* I said nothing, and he added, *Also I didn't tell her who you were! She's just too good at her research, darn it. She apparently knew before the show.*

I answered, *That's all right. Please pass along my thanks to her.*

There. Evidence that I not only didn't matter enough to Leo, I didn't matter to the nation's news outlets either. A silver lining, I supposed.

I took apart set pieces for *Moulin Rouge*, for repurposing in future shows. Quicksand folk chatted around me as they helped, sometimes speculating about what Leo would be doing and why he was being so mysterious. I didn't say anything.

On Friday, agitation chewed through me as I cleaned costumes and waited for his message. I checked my texts and email ten times an hour. Then, a little after six in the evening, while I was alone in Catarina's caravan, sulkily chopping bok choy for dinner, I paused to check email and found a message. Not from Leo, but from Wayshaw.

Leo instructed me to send this attachment to you. He told me to send it tonight, after he's gone, but we did not make an official deal about that, so I do not have to obey him. I think you should have a chance to read it sooner, because in my opinion he is being a fool in how he's treating you.

We will be near the verge above Punta Rosa, where Garland Road dead-ends, until nightfall.

My breath was fluttering. I dropped into a chair and opened the attached document.

Dear Vai,

Your letter was the hardest to write. There's so much to say. But I'll try to cut to the heart of it. I owe you an explanation, and an apology.

The reason I have to be away for a year is because of the deal I made with Nalibak. What I told you about that deal was only partially accurate. It's true I'm to spend a year entertaining him, but the year hasn't started yet. It begins tonight, and it will take place entirely in his lair in the fae realm. He will take me there at nightfall, and after one year has passed in the human realm, he will release me.

Other details I told you were true. The deal was originally Ayda's, and I transferred it to myself, without her knowledge, a few months before I met you. She'd been through enough—so many years of her life mangled by this fair feaster. She and Javier are both finally happy, and I wanted to give them their freedom. They deserve it.

Melu Ros—Ayda's father, a bear faery—will check in on me once per season to bring me human-realm food and supplies, and to take me home at the end of the year. He will make Nalibak's life very unpleasant if Nalibak kills me. I also have a huge bag of charms to protect me, so I should be all right. It'll just be…an interesting year.

After I met you, of course, I began regretting this deal. Bitterly and intensely.

I would rather stay in the human realm with you, Vai. It hurts like fire, thinking of what could have been. You can't imagine how my heart broke when you offered a relationship and I couldn't accept.

I need to apologize to you. First, for not telling you the truth about this deal. There was nothing you could have done to change it—that's one of its conditions—and I didn't want you to know about it any longer than you had to, because life was already upsetting you enough.

Which brings us to the second thing I need to apologize for: hurting you, on Rose Night and after. Vai, you must not for a single second believe you're unloved. The truth is I do love you, so incredibly much. I can't express how deeply I desire you, how giddy I get when I'm near you, how constantly I think about you.

And because I want only good things to happen to you, I couldn't let you be in a relationship with me—someone who hasn't been honest and is about to be abducted into the fae realm for a year, the effects of which can't be predicted. You deserve a hundred times better. All I can do is tell you how sorry I am to have caused you pain.

You've given me the most wonderful memories to take with me. But I stole them unrightfully, at your expense. I don't ask you to forgive me. I don't think what I did is forgivable. I just beg you not to think that any of it was your fault. Please know you are amazing, I love you, many other people will also love you in the future, and it is only misfortune that tangled you up with me for a few months of your life. Do not be down on yourself for anything that happened. You are the honorable one here.

Please live your life and be content, for this year and beyond. If I do return, and if someday you decide you're willing to speak to me again, I will forever be glad to see you.

May all the powers and all the living things on Earth be kind to you, Vai. You light up this world every day, just by being who you are.

Love, Leo

I had leaped to my feet by the end without realizing it. Hyperventilating, I sprinted out the door.

Sunset, this time of year, was around 8:00 p.m. I had less than ninety minutes. Garland Road's dead end was some five miles away, and uphill. Even if I ran, I might not make it.

I skidded to a stop, spun, and raced back to the caravans, yelling Uwila's name, making everyone in my path halt and stare in astonishment at the quiet Vai Delvecchio losing their shit so completely.

CHAPTER 23

LEO

The setting sun turned the sky into a sheet of gold behind the fae forest. I drank it in, even though staring at it was starting to cause me temporary blindness. It might be the last time I saw the sun for a year.

I hadn't cried during my final visits with Ayda and Javier, these last few days. I let myself sob all the way back, on the drive from Tesoro to this hilltop above Punta Rosa. Now I was done. I wasn't going to cry anymore. My composure was an eggshell-thin but solid crust, and within that dignity I would walk on my own two feet into Nalibak's lair.

Ayda and Javier also hadn't cried, though each, at some point, wore valiantly bright smiles and shimmering eyes. They wanted me to believe that *they* believed I would survive. I'm not sure any of us believed it.

Except Ayda's mom. She had hugged me a full twenty seconds, murmuring, "Thank you, thank you, thank you," then looked me in the eyes and said, "This journey will be *transformative* for you. A spiritual path, the mystical experience of your *life*. I know this. I've seen it."

"Have you?"

She nodded seriously. "Yesterday. During a psilocybin trip. Those little fungi have never lied to me, Leo."

I'd take that prediction with a grain of mushroom salt, but at least it made me smile.

I pivoted to face the ocean—daytime vistas of any sort were going to be in short supply for me soon—and spotted a dark blob against the horizon. I squinted. A large bird, rising from the coast? An air surrey? It flew toward me and resolved into a faery, with someone on their back, hanging on for dear life.

Uwila. Carrying Vai.

My mouth dropped open. My eggshell cracked under a flood of emotion.

A few paces from me, Uwila landed on her feet with a light bounce. Vai leaped off and captured me in a suffocating hug.

Everything would have been fine if I had been left alone. But this I could not handle. I shattered into silent sobs, pressing my face to their collar. Vai was shaking, damp with sweat.

"You weren't supposed to find me," I choked out.

"Wayshaw sent me your letter early and told me where you were."

I grimaced at Wayshaw, who stood off to our right. "You asshole," I said.

"I'm not sorry," she answered, aloof as ever.

Vai stepped back, holding my shoulders. They looked pale, their eyes ravaged. "How do we stop this?"

"We don't. If I escape, he takes someone else. I'm not having that."

"We negotiate, then. Change the deal."

"I made it unchangeable."

"Then I go with you."

"No. In five months, your family will remember you again. You need to be here."

"They can wait," Vai said, but the answer came after a pause, their gaze slipping aside.

"You're staying here, where you're safe. Please don't argue." I laid my palm on Vai's cheek, sending a soothing flow of magic into them.

They closed their eyes, accepting the spell, but their face didn't relax. Uwila moved to stand beside Wayshaw. The two of them watched in sorrow, eyes aglow in sunset tones.

"I'm glad you're here," I said to Vai. "Now I can tell you in person: thank you for making these last months so much better than they would've been for me otherwise."

Vai flinched backward. "I didn't know they were your 'last months.' It's fucking unfair." Tears slipped down their face. "You let me fall in love with you, and you never..." They swallowed.

"I love you. I do. But I know you'll get over me, which is how it should be. And don't worry, okay? I'm really going to try to come back in one piece."

"Do I look like I will 'get over you' and 'not worry'?"

It's an honor to make people cry, Vai had said, a couple of short months ago. Such bullshit.

I gently wiped the tears off their cheeks. "Please. I don't want you to suffer, that's the last thing I want."

The light dimmed. I turned to look west. Behind the forest, a layer of clouds had swallowed the sun. A few minutes more and it would be gone.

The wind picked up. The meadow grass rippled. How tall and tangled the fae-realm trees were, how wildly beautiful and impenetrably dark.

Vai grabbed my wrist, shoved up the cuff of my coat, and splayed their hand on my arm. Magic poured into my tattoo, strong enough to spark pins and needles all the way to my shoulder, then along the ink lines to my chest, my other arm, my back, hips, and legs.

I swayed. "Whoa."

"That protection spell wasn't strong enough." Sweat beaded on their brow. "You should've come to me."

"Thank you. I'm bringing charms too—this is full of supplies to keep me safe." With my foot, I indicated my backpack, in the grass.

As soon as Vai finished enspelling all my ink, they knelt and spread their hands on my pack, casting magic on that too.

"Thank you," I repeated.

They rose to their feet, wobbling. They'd surely thrown tons of energy into those spells. Eyes wild, they stared toward the fading light in the west, then back at me. "What charms are you bringing? What else can I enspell?"

Since they seemed about to dive into my pack and start pulling things out, I caught their shoulders. "Everything's set," I said. "It's all right."

"No it isn't. I can't let you go in there, not without—"

"Vai, listen, okay? Please? Don't be unhappy. Don't wait for me. Be free. That's the best thing in the world, to be free."

"*You* listen. This..." Their eyes caught something behind me and flared.

I turned, my insides shrinking in dread.

In the shade of the nearest tree, against the backdrop of dark forest, stood a gray-white figure staring at us, motionless and with mouth open in a hungry smile.

Uwila snarled a tight sound, like a lighter clicking a flame to life. Wayshaw murmured something to her—probably telling her to stand down and not conjure fire against the fair feaster.

Vai moved in front of me, as if to shield me. "He takes us both," Vai snapped.

I wrapped my arms around Vai from behind and leaned my head against theirs. "No," I murmured.

Twilight colors pooled in the shadows. The sun was gone, below the horizon.

"Two, yes, I'll take two if this is the feast you offer." Nalibak's voice was near all of a sudden.

Vai startled in my arms. The fair feaster now stood almost within arm's reach.

Nalibak's glamour still resembled a generic K-pop star more than anything else, but he had altered it a little—hair bobbed, a loose white button-down rather than a sleeveless tee, slim brown belt in place of the studded one. He had chosen to look more like Vai, I realized, nauseated.

He examined Vai. "Though this one must discard the putrid sunshine flowers they carry." At least Nalibak's voice, gestures, and facial expressions were nothing like Vai's. Thank the gods.

"This one isn't coming," I said.

Vai pressed back against me. "It's both of us or neither."

I hugged them close. "I'm sorry. I love you."

"You're not going without me," they insisted, turning their head. "I'm..." A foggy, confused look overtook their face. Their eyes fluttered shut, and their body slumped limp in my arms.

I lowered them to the grass, tears coursing down my cheeks, my heart drumming from the sleep spell I had just poured into them. "I'm sorry." I kissed Vai's forehead. Then, sniffling, I grabbed my backpack and stood.

Uwila and Wayshaw watched somberly. "We'll do everything we can for you," Wayshaw said.

"Start here." I nodded toward Vai. "Please."

I swept a last glance across the wide-open human world. Then I followed Nalibak through the meadow, and we crossed the verge in a crackle of static.

CHAPTER 24

VAI

I was very foolish in those first days.

When I awoke, I was on Leo's bed in the caravan, alone except for Wayshaw, who sat nearby, reading. My phone said it was 10:45 p.m., and I had a heap of text messages from troupe folk. None of whom, I verified in a quick scan, was Leo.

I stared at Wayshaw, who stared back, her eyes as indifferent as the tides.

"Where did they go?" I demanded.

"Nalibak moves his lair about, so it's hard to say."

"You knew he was leaving all this time, and you never told me."

"It was what Leo asked. By the end, I didn't like that restriction."

"If you really wanted to help me, you would've told me sooner. All you gave me was five minutes with him." My voice shook with rage.

"It didn't occur to me until then. I apologize."

I turned away, my hand crushing a fistful of bedspread.

"Even if you'd known sooner," Wayshaw added, "you couldn't have done anything."

I didn't answer. I flicked through my messages.

Kornelia: *WHAT THE FUCK. Vai, are you okay? I'm here if you need to talk.*

Shelini: *I'm so mad at Leo right now. Uwila told me what happened at the verge. We're here for whatever you need, all right?*

Fred: *Vaaaaiiiiii, nooooooo. I'm so sorry. Let's cry over ice cream together soon, sweetie, ok?*

Mathilde: *Well that's some messed-up news. If work helps you get through stuff, come see me. Or if you just want to come sit and be quiet that's ok too. I get that.*

Catarina: *Oh darling. I would say "Tell me what you need," but I expect you don't even know how to answer that. Please do me the honor of letting me look after you until you're feeling steadier.*

I pushed aside the window curtain. The other troupe vehicles formed a string down the beach parking lot. Wayshaw had evidently deposited me in the caravan and driven us back to Punta Rosa. As if we would both just resume our jobs now, get back to work.

Madness clawed at my throat, tempting me to roar aloud or rip apart a pillow. I stayed silent, burying the storm at the bottom of a cold ocean. As I had long ago learned to do.

"You're welcome to live in the caravan while Leo's away," Wayshaw said. "He wasn't sure you'd want to, but he hoped you would."

Did he now. And how, Leo Takahashi, was I supposed to live here surrounded by relics of you and "be free" at the same time?

I said nothing. Finally I typed to Catarina, *Thank you. I appreciate that. I think I'll stay in Leo's caravan a while. Till I feel steadier, as you say.*

I sent it off and mumbled, "I'll stay for now."

My head was aching, my body weak. Remembering the partially prepared dinner I'd sprinted away from, I calculated I hadn't eaten anything since lunch, some eleven hours ago. Though I had little appetite, I would be no good without strength. I shuffled to the kitchen and got started with crackers and a glass of water.

"I'll ask Catarina to bring your possessions over," Wayshaw said, tapping at her phone.

"I'll get them."

"I'd rather you stayed here."

"The verge is five miles away and uphill, and it's dark. I'm not going to run for it."

"Reassuring. Please stay inside for the time being anyway."

I had never before harbored a wish to cross the verge. Just an occasional curiosity, like everyone. It turned out having someone you loved on the other side increased the temptation a great deal. But while the fae realm was perilous to humans at any hour, the night brought out especially fearsome types of fae. Goblins, ghoul-sylphs, fair feasters. I truly was not about to race up there in the dark.

I was also not going to just give in and resume my job.

I'll bring your things over, Catarina texted. *And will get anything else you need.*

I thanked her, finished eating, and prowled around the caravan, nosing into drawers and closets. Wayshaw cast a wary eye on me but left me to it. Catarina brought my packed bag, gave me a long hug, and proposed we meet for breakfast in the morning. I agreed, and she went home.

I hated lying to her. I'd never done that before.

Since all I appeared to be doing was pulling out possessions of Leo's and examining them, Wayshaw eventually eased her surveillance and resumed reading a book.

In the kitchen, I filled a water bottle and stashed it in the side pocket of my pack. Under the guise of snacking, I got out a few protein bars and a bag of trail mix and slipped those in too.

Sitting on the floor near Leo's bed, I injected a long-sleeved gray T-shirt and a pair of jeans with the strongest protection spell I could manage. I'd put the same one into his tattoos earlier. It wouldn't resist fae enchantment forever, but it was better than nothing. I found almost no iron in the caravan, despite having been sure I'd seen defense items in the closets before. I prayed Leo had taken those. It meant, though, that all I had was a thin iron chain, the kind of thing most Eidolonian humans own, which had been coiled at the bottom of my pack all these months. Now, with my hands inside the pack so Wayshaw wouldn't see if she happened to look, I streamed a spell of extra defense into that too.

I got into Leo's bed, shut the curtains, and turned out the bedside light. Wayshaw stayed up, reading under the Turkish lamp. Unable to sleep, I ended up staring at pictures and videos of Leo on my phone, while internally I screamed my soul raw.

Please survive the night. I'm coming for you.

I had the ride request placed via app by the time the dawn glowed through the window. Wayshaw was still reading. She nodded to me as I went into the bathroom. I nodded back, my pack casually in hand.

The bathroom window was too small for me to escape from. She knew that. Likely she was only concerned about keeping me from the caravan's doors. But months ago I had easily enough used my magic to slice open an interior wall to extend my bunk, and today I had no scruples about cutting into the exterior.

I locked the bathroom door, cleaned up, and changed into the enspelled clothes. Then I turned on the shower, for acoustic masking, and got to work removing the window and part of the surrounding wall. Within ten minutes I had an unlovely but adequately large rectangle of open air before me. The window—still unbroken—sat propped against the wall. Chunks of wallboard and metal lay in a heap. I shoved my pack outside, stepped onto the toilet, and jumped out, leaving the shower running.

I shouldered the pack and took off at a sprint. A surprised shout of my name followed me as I tore past the troupe vehicles. I didn't look back. I was panting by the time I got to the hired air surrey waiting by the road.

I flung myself into the passenger seat, crashed the door shut, and gasped to the driver, "Fly."

The driver, a woman around sixty, spared only a second to make sure I was settled safely, then swung us skyward. "Someone chasing you?" she asked.

I looked back at the caravans shrinking below us. A few people had run out to stand forlorn and watch me escape. So far, I hadn't spotted Uwila, the only member of the troupe who could fly. Duplicitous of me, to use her for quick transport last night, and now feel relief that she wasn't coming after me.

"Don't think so," I answered.

The driver navigated us, quiet as the wind, over the rising slope west of the Great Eidolonian Highway. Houses, gardens, and trails slipped past a hundred feet below. "I'm dropping you near the verge?" she verified. "Along the trail?"

"Yes." For my destination, in the app, I had picked a spot a quarter-mile south of the place where Leo had been last night. I wanted to be farther from the road, so no vehicles could easily catch up to me, plus the spot was far enough from the verge guard stations that the authorities would be less likely to detain me.

"I don't try to stop people from where they're determined to go," my driver said, "but if you're planning on walking into the fae realm, have to say I can't recommend it." She brought the surrey down, gliding nearer to the ground as we approached my landing spot.

"A person I love is in there." I stared into the trees.

"Sure, that's why most people go in." She landed the surrey with the lightest of bumps, in a patch of dirt between the hiking trail and the forest. "I'm just saying, these one-person rescues don't tend to go well."

"I have enough shielding." I opened the door and hopped out.

"No such thing as enough shielding, in there." She regarded me a few seconds. "Listen. In this area, dryads might be your best bet for help. I'd stay out of canyons, caves, and swamps."

"Have you been in there? In this region?"

She shook her head. "Only helped airlift out some folks who were rescued from it and were brought to the verge. What was left of them, anyway."

A chill immobilized me. But only for a moment. All the more reason, then, that I had to find Leo.

"Thank you," I told my driver sincerely, and I turned and walked to the trees.

I had to hike a couple of minutes uphill, threading through shrubs, before reaching the verge itself. An enspelled barbed-wire fence marked the line, complete with one of the signs every Eidolonian knows by heart: *WARNING! Crossing the verge poses grave dangers to humans. Emergency assistance cannot reliably be reached past this line. Respect the truce: do not enter!*

The forest beyond the fence was a dense, dark wilderness. Some tree trunks reached twenty feet in diameter, their canopies stretching more than a hundred feet above. In the shadows, things slithered, fluttered, and hopped. Eyes caught sunlight and blinked at me, low on the ground and high in the trees. The smell was a seduction all its own: sweet moss, rich earth, spicy leaves. Notes from the throat of some faery drifted out on the wind. Easy to see how humans could clamber in there in wonder and never come out again.

A black-and-white monkey leaped onto a branch and stared at me.

"Are you fae?" I asked. "Can you speak?"

Some animals were just animals, even in the fae realm, but some were fae in animal form. It was hard to tell the difference simply by looking.

The monkey curled their tail around the branch. "Of course I am, and of course I can." Their voice was high and nasal, not unlike a monkey's call.

I pulled out a small bag of chocolate chips, one of the gifts I'd brought. "I'm looking for a dryad to guide me. Can you introduce me to one?"

The monkey swung down, hanging by their tail, and reached out a long arm to grab the bag. They swung back to the branch and started eating the chocolate. "The dryads all went up the mountain. To have a meeting about moving their haunt, or some such matter."

"All of them?"

"The ones who can walk. These of course are still here." The monkey nodded toward one of the giant trees. "They never move anymore. Too ancient. Hardly speak either. Not much use as a guide."

As with animals, you couldn't always tell which plants were fae and which were just plants. I couldn't see any difference between the dryad tree and the others.

I looked up and down the fence. The verge guards could wander by on patrol any minute, and if they found me, they'd escort me away. "Do you know of the fair feaster named Nalibak?" I asked. "He was here last night."

The monkey faery tipped the rest of the chocolate chips into their mouth and tossed the paper bag aside. "He caused a stir, coming here, dragging his ugly shadow-sack of a lair."

"Do you know where the lair is? Can you show me?"

"I know where it was yesterday. Today I've not looked. Why look for something ugly?"

"You can have another gift if you take me to his lair."

"I can take you to where it *was*."

"That's fine. Then can you help me ask other fae if they know where he went?"

The monkey faery tilted their head at me, then turned. "In here."

Tail switching impatiently, they waited for me while I temporarily neutralized the spells on the fence, dulled the barbs, and pulled open a space between wires large enough to get myself and my pack through. Good thing humans, not fae, created the fence. I wouldn't have had much luck with fae spells.

The fae had little reason to keep humans out. They could easily enchant, maim, or kill us, whereas we couldn't do much to them. Most fae didn't mind the occasional human visitor: we made for good entertainment. The danger signage, verge guards, and witch-enspelled fence existed entirely as warnings to and from fellow humans. Up until today, I had heeded those warnings. In one impulsive step, I broke that record.

I ducked under the wires. Static electricity crackled across my skin, then vanished as I passed the fence. I stood in the fae realm. The air felt thick with magic. The rich forest scent enwrapped me.

The monkey faery bounded ahead, branch to branch. "Come!"

For what might have been half an hour—though of course I'd left measurable time behind—I followed the monkey through the forest. The trunks and roots were so massive, I quickly became unable to tell which direction we had come from, and I often had to crouch, climb, or crawl to follow the monkey faery.

"Here. You see?" they finally said, stopping at a clump of thorny bushes. It stood atop a ridge, a steep slope falling away beyond. Trees kept the whole area in shadow.

I stopped, panting, and peered at the thorn thicket. The only notable thing I could see was a tunnel within it, blackened and crushed, as if frost-burned. But the tunnel merely led into the bushes and ended, empty. "I don't see a lair," I said.

"It *was* here. It isn't anymore."

"So he moved it? Can we track where he went?"

"I do not track. I do not care where he went."

"Who can track him? Can you find a faery who would help me and not lead me into danger? I have gifts."

"Wild dogs can track. Bears can track… Oh! Yes?" The last exclamation was aimed at another monkey faery, who swung in, chattering in the fae tongue.

My guide chattered back, then bounded up to follow the other.

"Wait," I shouted. "Where are you going?"

"We must chase away an eagle," my guide—perhaps ex-guide—called down. "It threatens the babies."

With no further explanation, both monkeys took off, leaping through the branches.

"Babies?" I shouted after them, but they were gone.

I turned, seeking anyone who might help. Figures moved in the trees, but none approached. I ventured into the short tunnel. Many of the blackberry canes seemed to have been sheared off at the ground to create the space. Their stubs were hard under my shoes. The tunnel was just high enough for me to stand in without ducking.

"Does anyone know where Nalibak and his captive went?" I asked, to whomever might be listening. "Has anyone seen a human taken yesterday by a fair feaster?"

Something rustled near my shoulder. A blossom bud hopped to the end of a blackberry stem and blinked at me. Their whole body seemed to be a pale green eye wrapped in leaf. They were no more than an inch tall.

"The fair feaster ravaged our thicket." The voice was a high-pitched chirp, the way a grasshopper might sound. "If you are his friend, we will pierce you through with thorns."

"Not his friend," I hastily said. "I don't like him either. Here—I brought gifts."

I got out a few options. The blackberry faery picked a chantagram with a recording of my mother playing "Clair de Lune" on piano. After listening to it a few times, the tiny bud seemed content and told me, "Fair feasters move through the darkness. Their path is shadow to shadow."

"Yes?" I tried to understand. "They hate bright light."

"They move by making a path through bits of darkness. And when they wish to be still, they create a lair of darkness to dwell in."

"All right." I still didn't grasp what this meant for my purposes. "Can we tell where he went?"

"His lair was here, in our thicket, to shelter from the daylight. In the night, the darkness is all around. He could have gone any which way."

"Do you know which way he went?" My teeth were nearly clenched.

"Not I. I do not go traveling about. Some sniffing creature, that is what you need. A mountain cat. An alligator."

I rubbed my face. Wild dog, bear, mountain cat, alligator. Everyone had suggestions. "How far could he have gone in one night, bringing a human along?"

"As far as he wishes, as long as there is darkness."

Nalibak had seemed to move eerily fast, the few times I had seen him. "So he could be at the other end of the island already? Or the top of a mountain, or..."

"Any such place." The blackberry faery played the song again, the chantagram huge in their tiny green toes.

I sat on the ground and cradled my head in my hands. Leo was lost to me. I'd been a fool to come here alone, without preparing better. I needed help from someone reliable, not just the first alligator faery I happened to run into. I had to return to the human realm to get a proper fae guide before I sank myself any deeper into danger.

I lifted my head. "Can you tell me which way the verge is?"

"Down the slope," the little faery said.

I stepped out of the tunnel and studied the slope plunging beyond the thicket. "That isn't the way I came."

"Nevertheless, that way lies the verge."

I looked back in the direction I had come from. But nothing seemed familiar. Either the landscape had changed in the last few minutes, or I had been so hell-bent on finding Leo that I hadn't paid sufficient attention.

There were only a few types of fae who could lie, and everyone knew who they were. Goblins and fair feasters were the main dangers. Ordinary plant and animal fae told the truth.

"That's the nearest way to the verge? Straight that direction?" I pointed.

The blackberry faery hardly gave me a glance. "It is."

I dubiously examined the region at the base of the slope, but decided it didn't count as a canyon. A ravine perhaps. Was a ravine safer than a canyon? Perhaps the verge did lie on the other side—the verge wasn't a straight line; it had lots of curves and jags. Even so…

The ground crumbled under my feet. I slid down the slope, heels skidding, backpack scrunching behind my head. Scrabbling with both hands, I caught a root and came to a stop. But the root yanked itself out of my grasp, disappearing into the earth, and I slid again. This time a large rock stopped me, the soles of my feet slamming against it. While I paused there, catching my breath, the rock pivoted, as if purposely throwing me off. I fell and rolled.

The entire slope went like that—the earth tugging my footing out from under me, piece by piece, until I lay bruised and scratched at the bottom.

I stood, brushing myself off, and glared up at the ridge. "I'm *very sorry* my unwelcome human self touched you," I said, sarcastic.

The earth did not feel the need to respond. Unless the pebble that sailed down and bounced against my shoulder was an answer.

Trying to climb back up was obviously unwise. I turned to survey the terrain I had landed in. Trees made a feathery cover. Sunlight filtered through. Birdsong and the croaks of other animals drifted in the air. It was a pretty spot—or would have been if I hadn't known it was the fae realm. But I had no other direction to go.

I'd been walking no more than five minutes, the landscape carrying me gradually downward, when the ground became muddy. Then soupy. Ferns and cattails took over, among swamp oaks. I stopped. Swamps had been on my air surrey driver's list of things to avoid. I looked for a way around the wetland, first toward the right, then the left, but the swamp seemed to lie across the entire bottom of the ravine.

I finally found a fallen tree that created a bridge. Whether the ground would still be soup at the other end, I didn't know, but I had no other real options. Given how my deals with local fae had gone so far, I rejected the notion of asking a flying faery to carry me to the verge.

The log was higher than my head and required a slippery climb up its broken branches. On top, though, the bark was dry and easy enough to walk on. The trouble was the surrounding trees, whose limbs frequently lay in my way. I had to push aside or crawl under them, sweating at the prospect of losing my balance and falling into the muck. Fae hung all around, observing me. I would have taken some for ordinary birds, except they were chattering to each other in the fae language. The ground below had become a shimmering sheet of water with plants growing out of it. The long back of something slender surfaced. A line of little blue flames spouted along its spine. Then it went under again, the blue lights vanishing.

I never did find out if the other end of the tree touched dry ground.

Partway across, a vine slid down and splayed tendrils across my face, lightly, as if feeling out the shape of me. I panicked and swatted it. It retaliated by coiling around my arm and yanking me off the tree.

Falling, I braced for impact. Instead I snapped to a stop, dangling from the vine, my shoes a short distance above the murky water.

"Please put me back," I begged. "I'll—I'll give you gifts."

The vine lowered me and let go. I splashed into the swamp. The water came to my waist, and when I tried to climb onto a smaller log nearby, underwater vines—or underwater *something*—wrapped around my ankles and held me fast. I was breathing in quick jags, adrenaline spiking.

Gifts. I had promised gifts.

Off key and strangled by panic, I began singing "Nature Boy" from *Moulin Rouge*. Given how unattuned to nature I had proven to be today, the choice of this song might seem funny someday, if I survived.

The vine swung near my face as if listening, and the underwater things at least failed to hurt me any further. When the song ended, the vine reached for my face again, and whatever was underwater tightened its grip around my legs. I yelped straight into the next song in the musical, and both sets of vines relaxed again.

I was still singing, hoarse and wretched, when the sky began fading to a sunset peach.

CHAPTER 25

LEO

As soon as we stepped into the fae forest, Nalibak said, "We leave this lair behind," and reached for me.

I jumped back. "No touching skin!"

He made an irritated rattling noise. "I must pull you through the darkness. Humans are too slow."

I got out a pair of wool gloves, treated by matter-witches to protect against spells, and put them on. "There."

Ayda had said, and Melu Ros had confirmed, that with all my precautions in place, I couldn't fall under Nalibak's entrancement. At least, not by much. It took unprotected proximity, ideally skin contact, to be infected by a fair feaster's spell.

Also, the last person whose skin I had touched was Vai, and my suffering heart demanded I protect that record for as long as I could.

Nalibak grasped my hand—his fingers ice-cold even through the wool—then we shot forward into the dark. Wind howled. The ground skipped away under my shoes, making me teeter and flop in the air, dangling from Nalibak's grip. Land flashed by in a blur of shadows and noises. Leaves and twigs whipped my face, sometimes sharp enough to cut.

Then, with a slam, we stopped, and I crashed to my hands and knees on rocks. "Gods damn," I complained. "Did you have to make it painful?"

"Far, far away we fly, from all those curious sun-shining pests by the verge."

I kneaded my limbs and found bruises, but nothing broken. "Where are we?" My voice echoed, suggesting a cave. All I could see was the pale glow of Nalibak's figure, and several pinpricks of yellowish-green. Glow-worms.

"Two mountain-hops away from the great volcano, colder up the island, high and into the lava caves."

I parsed that and guessed, "Two peaks north of Pitchstone Mountain? In a cave made of cooled lava?"

"Ever so high and jagged. Humans are never here."

Feeling around in my pack, I found one of the glass spheres, the size of a grapefruit, and said to it, "Light, please."

It lit up bright white. Nalibak hissed, shielding his face.

"Lower light!" I said. "Moonlight, please."

The sphere cooled to a dim bluish glow, still enough to see by, but less offensive to Nalibak.

"The horrid thing shatters across the rocks," he said, "if it ever glares so bright again."

"Yes, fine, sorry." Anger made me want to flare it anew, maybe even concoct an attack plan using it. But Nalibak could best me in any fight, and then he'd make good on his threat and destroy my lights. I'd be lucky if that was all he did. Then how much more awful would the rest of my year be? Besides, I was apparently in the dead center of the fae realm, high on a mountain. Escaping alone was essentially impossible.

I set the sphere on the ground—it was enspelled to stay put and not roll away—and took a few steps. A lava-tube cave, as promised. No stalactites or stalagmites, just chunky gray rock with tiny bubble-holes in it, like pumice. Nalibak stood before me, in his not-really-Vai guise. Several paces past him was a glimmer of lighter air.

I nodded toward it. "Can we step out and see? If humans have never been here, I want to check it out."

"It is the fae realm, my tender moth-wing. I protect you in the lair. Things out there could rip you apart."

"What, you can't protect me a few steps that direction? I obviously can't escape, I just want to see where we are." Since Nalibak didn't answer, studying me with his head tilted at an eerily steep angle, I added, "I'll get depressed if you never let me look around outside. I won't be able to give you stories and songs and interesting arguments if I'm depressed."

It wasn't even a lie, though I had no compunction lying to him. He could lie to me. Our partnership was not built on a solid ground of trust, just a few essential stepping-stones of it.

"Come," he said.

The cave's mouth was a jagged opening in the ceiling. I was impressed, and grateful, he had swung us down into it without bashing me any harder against the rocks. Now he drew me out of it in a similarly swift movement—he took my gloved hand, and in one second I went from standing under the patch of sky to stumbling on a windswept mountainside.

When I had recovered my balance, I stared. A wild land stretched out, bathed in twilight blues and purples. Forested foothills rose and fell. We were above the timberline, only rock and patches of snow around us. The peak of our mountain loomed overhead, mantled in snow. To the north and south stood the colossal silhouettes of other peaks. Stars speckled the sky, thick as sugar. A gigantic winged shape soared past, emanating red light and blotting out the stars.

"A drake?" I said in awe. I'd seen them on occasion, at festivals, but they tended to shrink themselves to human size, and more or less human form, at such times. It had been years since I'd seen a full-size one in the wild.

"Fire bringer," Nalibak muttered. "They live near."

Drakes belonged to the fire element. Fair feasters hated fire, along with bright light. I watched the drake spiral down into the forest. *I have to stay alive*, I thought. *I have to tell Vai about this incredible place.*

Then Nalibak yanked my arm, and we were back down in the lair. "Ah." He sniffed me. I reared back. "Shall your first story be about the person who wished to come with you?"

I jerked my arm free. "No. I'm never talking about them with you."

"It's delicious, your longing. Grubs and pollen and birds in their shells all in one crushed handful."

Exhaling, I wandered toward the glowing glass ball on the cave floor. "No. Tonight's story…is by a human named Shakespeare. It's called *Much Ado About Nothing*. Are you ready to hear it?"

I often worked evenings, performing or writing or both. I'd told myself this part would be easy. And the performance part *was* simple enough, though the quality suffered, given my lack of props, lighting, effects, or other actors. Nalibak also had an irritating habit of interrupting with remarks or questions. Even that I didn't mind too much—it helped stretch out the hours. Shakespeare's antiquated phrases required frequent explanation, but Nalibak, prone to weird evocative phrasing himself, lapped it up.

I had no way to know what time it was. Clocks held no relevance here, and in any case I hadn't brought one. A night in the fae realm might last ten minutes, or ten nights, in the human realm, and to the person experiencing it, it might seem to race by, or creep along.

I was yawning after performing the entirety of *Much Ado About Nothing*, with dozens of pauses for explanation, and five encores to repeat parts Nalibak had especially liked. Those were the parts in which the characters were in the most anguish—such as Claudio grieving for Hero, and Beatrice raging that she would eat Claudio's heart in the marketplace. Nalibak asked whether she was a type of carnivore who particularly liked hearts, and I had to explain about metaphors, although also had to admit murder was on the table in that scenario.

After, I sat on the cold rocks and had a bite of a witch-made food bar—one quarter of a bar kept you alive and decently well for a whole day. After drinking the last of my human-realm water, I swung the empty bottle at him. The enchanted galangal root rattled inside, ready to purify its next batch. "I'll need a water source. Is there a stream around, or should I stuff this full of snow?"

"A great pool, it lies deep in the cave. I take you to it, then we come back and speak more of eating hearts."

"Fantastic." I got to my feet. "Over here, behind this section of rock, this is going to be the toilet area. We both stick to that. Work for you? Great."

Every Eidolonian human has asked with fascination by age five whether the fae realm has bathrooms and has learned that it doesn't, at least not by our standards of plumbing. But it also isn't overrun with filth, because there are such things as dung fae, along with other creatures, like bugs and possums, who eat waste. Besides that, the fae have scads of magic. They can transform organic matter easily, if they want.

The fae realm has no infrastructure as humans know it: no mail service, roads, central government, legal system. Each haunt structures its lifestyle as its denizens prefer. When with Nalibak, I was in his haunt, or more properly his lair, population of one. Two if you counted me.

The lack of plumbing, I had decided by the next day, was not even one of the top five things that bothered me most about his tiny dominion. After what seemed like more hours than a night could possibly hold, I had blearily asked when dawn would come, and Nalibak had said, "Oh, it is hateful daytime now. Continue! Speak to me of the Dark Lady and her crisp coral lips." For by now I had wandered into Shakespeare's sonnets.

That was when I realized the patch of sky behind him was not dark but concealed. He had waved darkness across it like a blackout shade, so I could not even see a hint of sunrise.

I glared. "I need *rest*. Do you know nothing about humans?"

"What am I to do during all the horrid bright day, while you sleep?"

"Should've thought of that before keeping me up all night. How about I entertain you during the horrid bright hours—some of them anyway—and during the night you can go out and..." I flapped my hand in his direction. "Feed on things. But for now, I'm sleeping."

After grumbling, he relented, then folded himself up like a gargoyle in a corner of the cave. I spread out my camping mattress and sleeping bag. Every time I glanced toward him, he was perfectly stationary but staring with a rapt expression at me from twenty feet away. Try sleeping soundly with that going on.

Yet I did succumb to exhaustion, and after waking, I found that even Nalibak wasn't my top complaint. My body insisted via a hundred aches that sleeping on the ground was the most horrible thing I'd done to it in years. The mattress, though enspelled for comfort, apparently could only do so much against the dramatically chunky rock floor.

My mouth tasted foul. My throat was hoarse from talking through the night. My feet, in the shoes I had kept on to stay warm, were nonetheless too cold and somehow also too sweaty. My skin felt coated with grime. My heart was in tatters.

After dragging myself upright, I stood rubbing my temples while tears seeped from my closed eyes. When I opened them, there was nothing to see but a cold cave in the glow of the glass ball, and the slime trails of glow-worms. I would also see Nalibak, should I decide to look toward his corner, which I did not.

I couldn't do this. Not for another day, let alone a year.

Some steadier part of my mind answered: *You survived the night. Nalibak left you alone as promised. It's natural you're tired and sore. Have something to eat.*

The voice hardly sounded like my own. It was smooth and tranquil. Perhaps Vai's.

If only I had let Vai come along.

"What lies did Shakespeare tell about the fae?"

I squinted in confusion at Nalibak. "Oh. I didn't say he lied, he just didn't know." We had gotten briefly onto that subject last night. "That was mostly…*A Midsummer Night's Dream*. I'll do that one today. But first, instant coffee. And you have absolutely got to hush until I'm done with it."

Chapter 26

VAI

I could barely sing songs or tell stories anymore. My voice was dying.

Morning had come at last, and I'd drunk all the water I had brought. I had also eaten a granola bar and broken apart a second one to share among the creatures who had gathered near. Their numbers had increased. Along with the vine fae and the underwater tentacles (they were almost certainly tentacles—I had ventured to feel down with a hand), my audience now included the serpent with the blue flames on its back, a water-lily faery floating around and treading water with its eight legs, and a pair of ducks. They might have been ordinary nonmagical ducks. I couldn't tell.

Given I was still submerged from the navel downward, in contact for hours with at least the tentacles and who knew what else, my panic had given way to fatalistic resignation. So this was how I'd die: either passing out and drowning right here, or, if I did get out, expiring from enchantment damage a short time in the future. I'd long since given in and peed where I stood, since I was trapped and drenched anyway. Now I was out of water and might never be hydrated again. I could try putting swamp water into the bottle to be purified, but I found it hard to trust that the galangal root's spell would be strong enough to handle it.

Then I heard foliage being thrashed. Splashes, snuffles. Birds flapping and shrieking. Before I could do more than turn in alarm, a screen of willow branches got knocked aside and a gigantic brown bear leaped at me.

Everything in me liquefied. My mouth fell open. I thought, *No, this is how I die*—but the bear splashed to a stop, stood on its hind legs, and sniffed me. Then it roared something in the fae tongue, causing all the other creatures to scatter. The tentacles withdrew from around my ankles. I gasped in relief and sloshed backward. But I was weak and dizzy, and would have fallen if the bear hadn't reached out its huge front limbs and gathered me up.

Draped over its furry shoulder, I saw Wayshaw's head emerge from the water.

"This was what we were trying to prevent you from doing, you know," Wayshaw said to me.

"I know," I croaked. "Sorry."

"This is Melu Ros," she added.

It took me a moment to remember. Ayda's father. The bear faery.

"Good trackers, bears," I mumbled. I let my eyes close as Melu Ros lumbered out of the water, carrying me and my pack as if I weighed no more than a wet leaf.

"Where were you trying to go, anyway?" Wayshaw asked.

"Back to the verge. A faery said it was this way. Is it this way? It didn't seem right."

"Well, yes. Technically." Wayshaw sounded annoyed. "From inside the fae realm, you reach the verge if you keep going far enough *any* direction. It's an *island*."

Which was the last thing I remember from that day.

I woke in an unfamiliar room. Sunny, clean, sparsely furnished. My bed had side rails, and a rolling cart nearby held medical monitoring devices, blinking quietly. Sensors were taped to me on nose, chest, wrist, groin.

I had gotten myself hospitalized. This should have alarmed me, but I was still fuzzy-headed, perhaps sedated. I didn't recall being injured. Enchantment damage, then.

My left side was unencumbered, in a light hospital gown, but my right was loosely wrapped with bandaging, even covering my fingers and toes. I felt a healing charm enspelling the material. Something lightweight plastered the right side of my neck and face. With my free hand I touched my cheek and found it damp and slimy.

I began unwinding the bandaging around the fingers of my right hand, just to see.

It fell away to reveal green. My hand was coated with a furry, slimy substance. The spell in the bandaging felt like it was at odds with the magic in the green slime—like the slime was what the healers were trying to rid me of.

I felt again at the right side of my face, pinched a bit of the stuff, and yanked. Thready wet green bits came off in my fingers, the same seaweed hue as the matter on my arm. Any sedation effects evaporated as horror surged through me.

The door opened. Someone entered, in the white coat of a healer. "You're awake. Good afternoon, Vai. How do you feel? Are you able to talk?" Her ID tag read Julia Ebisawa, Healer, She/Her.

I swallowed, finding my mouth sticky. "I think so. What day is it?"

"June twenty-first. Happy summer solstice."

"I've been here almost a month?"

Healer Ebisawa checked my right eye, then my left, and shone a light into my right ear. "Nope, they brought you in two days ago. Your time across the verge lasted something like three weeks. Open please."

I opened my mouth so she could look into my throat.

A month already gone. This was good, in a sense. Only eleven more months until Leo's sentence was up. Except—was he even still alive? My stomach twisted in panic.

"So," Healer Ebisawa said, "what you seem to have is a spell making you grow algae all over your skin on the right side of your body. Probably from one of the fae you encountered in the swamp."

I nodded, absorbing this diagnosis. "Why only the right side?"

"No idea. Fae spells are often pretty random." She peeled back the top of my gown and applied a stethoscope to my chest. "Deep breath in, please." After listening to my breathing and heartbeat, she added, "We want to make sure it stays on your skin and doesn't get any deeper. So far it's looking all right in that respect. What I'm hoping, and I'm sure you're hoping too, is that the spell caused an acute effect and not a chronic one."

"One that'll go away eventually, you mean, and not stay with me forever?"

"Exactly." She drew back my blankets to examine the rest of me. "I want to keep you here another two days to monitor any change. If it hasn't gotten worse, and you're stable, you can go home, but we'll still want you to come in regularly for treatments."

"Sorry—where am I? What city?"

She straightened up after having a look at my toes. "Tesoro. Your hometown, they tell me. You're at Catalano Hospital, on Mille Colori."

I looked toward the window, though all I could see from my bed was the sides of other buildings. So we were about half a mile down the street from Jin Troia Hall. I had walked right by this hospital on Rose Night, with Leo, in a gauzy cloud of bliss.

"Let's try getting you to the bathroom, see if everything's working all right," Healer Ebisawa said. "Then I want you to have something to eat and see how that goes too."

The tasks of bathroom and food did at least go all right. I didn't feel well, but given the circumstances, I could have felt worse. The most horrible moment was facing myself in the mirror. I looked like something the troupe would have devised for comedy, my face and body sprouting algae all over the right side, the left clean, a perfect vertical line demarcating the halves. The arbitrariness, and the slime, would have been hilariously absurd if it weren't for the possibility that the algae would spread into my internal organs and kill me.

Numb with disbelief, I sipped the soup Healer Ebisawa brought me and listened to her instructions about keeping the enspelled bandages on.

After that, I was left alone. I found my backpack in a closet and plugged in my phone, which had run out of power. I had just gotten back into bed when someone on staff poked their head in and said, "You have a visitor, if you're up for it."

I expected it to be Wayshaw, since she had helped rescue me. Instead a short woman with dark curly hair came in, carrying a basket covered with a cloth. "Hi, Vai."

I stared a moment, then realized her presence also made sense, given, for one thing, she lived in Tesoro, and for another, her father had been the one to carry me out of the fae realm. "Ayda. It's good of you to come."

"We're in this together. You and I are connected by wanting to throttle Leo." She set the basket down. "That's a club with a large membership, actually. I should say we're in the smaller group of those who love him dearly but want to throttle him."

"I think that's a fairly large club too."

Ayda sat on the chair beside my bed. "So. Now you know. I'm the reason you're miserable."

I looked away with a stab of guilt, for that thought had in fact crossed my mind in the hours since learning the whole story. But it wasn't fair, nor even true. "Leo made the choice. Without even consulting you, the way he told it."

"I was fucking furious. I've blamed myself ever since. I should've known he'd do that, if I complained to him."

"He does always want to fix things for people. Give them happiness."

We sat there with that poignant fact between us. Then she pulled the basket onto her lap. "I brought you some herbal concoctions. Healer Ebisawa says they're fine to use on top of the ones you're getting here. I'm going to make you a tea, and you have to drink it. No arguing."

That evening, Wayshaw also came to visit.

My conversation with Ayda had been comforting, the pair of us commiserating over our worry for Leo, and our exasperation with him. The sight of Wayshaw, however, made me defensive. After all, I had deceived her and caused her a great deal of trouble.

"I'm sorry for damaging the caravan," I said, my gaze on my lap.

She sat in the bedside chair. "We've repaired it. It will suffice."

"I'll do any additional fixes when they discharge me."

"No rush." Wayshaw didn't seem angry. But then, I'd never seen her angry, so I wasn't sure what it might look like. "Did Leo ever tell you why he invited me to join the troupe?" she asked.

"He said you were sad about a friend regenerating. And the troupe offered you something new to do."

"His offer saved me from regenerating as well. I was feeling as if I no longer had any reason to stay in this life. Leo showed me another path. One that has brought me happiness."

Wayshaw still sounded matter-of-fact, but sympathy squeezed my chest. With fae, regenerating is not suicide—they know they'll be reincarnated, and they even supposedly get to pick how. But starting over means leaving behind most of one's memories, they say. She must have felt desolate, or at least deeply weary, to have been contemplating that step.

"I didn't know that part," I said. "I'm sorry."

"I'm grateful to Leo. It's why I enjoy doing good for him, in the ways I can." The silvery green in Wayshaw's eyes caught the window light like fish scales. "Leo wants me to keep you safe. Will you continue to defy his wishes?"

I flexed my bandaged fingers. "I don't plan to endanger myself further. But…" My throat caught. My eyes filled with tears. "I don't want to spend a year without him. Or longer. He might not come back at all."

"We're doing whatever we can to ensure he'll come back. But nothing's certain. It isn't certain *you'll* survive the year, even if you stay in the human realm, is it?"

"Evidently not." We were quiet a minute. "He told me I shouldn't wait for him," I added. "I should be free."

"Did you agree to this deal?"

"No."

"Then does it matter what he said?"

I plucked a tissue and wiped my eyes, then sat up straighter. "No."

CHAPTER 27

LEO

Keeping track of how long I'd been in the fae realm proved maddeningly impossible. Days and nights passed with more or less the right number of hours, as far as I could tell, but I was usually not allowed to *see* the daylight, thus could only ask Nalibak whether it was dark or light. At first I tallied the days as closely as I could.

One evening, when I again wheedled Nalibak into stepping outside to see the stars, a small owl swooped up, perched on a rock, and asked in a flutelike tone, "What does this human do up here, in company of a fair feaster?"

Occasionally a faery ventured near with such a question. Nalibak usually chased them off, but he allowed a conversation now and then. I think he took pride in showing other fae his captive.

"I'm jester to this monarch," I explained, pointing a thumb toward Nalibak, who grimaced and spread a wider pool of shadow around himself. "Friend, have you been to the human realm recently? I'd love to know what day it is there."

The owl groomed a wing with their beak. "I flew above their celebrations today. It is Air Festival."

My breath caught. Summer solstice! By my calculations I'd only spent six days with Nalibak, but it had already been three weeks out there.

"My abundant gratitude to you. Hang on a sec." I dug into a pocket and drew out one of the carved shell beads I'd brought as gifts. This one was shaped like a bunny. The owl faery took it, black talons scraping my palm.

"You're welcome to stay and hear the next play," I added, "if—"

"Fie!" Nalibak hissed. "The plays are for me alone. Begone with your prize, bird."

This was the trouble with having started Nalibak on Shakespeare. He had already begun throwing around words like "fie" and "begone."

The owl hooted something in the fae tongue, then spread their wings and took off.

Still, the news boosted my spirits. "Summer solstice." I clapped my hands and rubbed them together. "Well well. Happy solstice to you, my despot."

I shouldn't have rejoiced so soon. Fifteen nights later, by my reckoning, during another brief outside stint, a firefly turned into a will-o'-the-wisp and hovered near us. Again I offered a bead and the question of what day it was.

"Air Festival is underway," the faery said. "I believe it's the third day."

I gaped, but my follow-up questions confirmed it: this time, fifteen days in the fae realm had only amounted to a day or two in the human realm.

I had to despond for a while after that, lying inside a blanket cocoon and playing a chantagram I had brought of Vai and other troupe friends rehearsing *Moulin Rouge* dances in the sun, in Serpentshore. Nalibak only managed to convince me to get on with the day's performance by offering to suck the unhappiness from me and replace it with "sweet thrall sap."

I tugged the blanket off my head, scowling, and told him that sounded like a carbonated beverage. But I hauled out my e-reader and picked the next story.

Nothing happening to me was funny. The habit of turning life into comedy died hard, however, so I kept making such remarks, though they now came out bitter rather than cheeky. More than once I called Nalibak the world's worst literary critic, or the most annoying college student ever.

The insults didn't faze him. He enjoyed my grumpy moods, in fact. But it was true that my roster of five hundred—yes, five hundred—plays, novels, films, and other stories, which I had curated as carefully as any teacher crafting a gargantuan syllabus, was not reaching its most appreciative possible audience here. Nalibak focused on the wrong details and asked unsettling questions. If the fairy godmother wanted to help Cinderella, why didn't she kill the stepsisters and stepmother, and give Cinderella their house and fine gowns? A pool of fresh tears, like that in *Alice's Adventures in Wonderland,* would have immense "delicious energy," so wouldn't it be delightful to find a way to keep Alice, or anyone really, crying forever? Peter Pan seemed to be the story's hero, and presumably this was because he kidnapped children and made them worship him?

I kept performing the stories anyway, because if I didn't, he would go back to threatening Ayda, or Vai, or someone else I loved.

Yes, I felt like Scheherazade. Yes, I told him the story of Scheherazade in those early weeks. He asked if the bloodthirsty sultan was a fair feaster. I guessed not, given the amount of people the sultan kept around, but I suggested he and Nalibak might get along well.

Every time I opened my eyes from sleep and found I was still alive, in a cave on a fae-realm mountain, I thought both *Thank the gods* and *Fuck, I have to get through another day*. I wondered if I'd ever achieve the enlightenment of a truly wise person and feel only the gratitude. Both I and everyone who knew me would probably vote no on that.

Staying clean was not difficult, at least, thanks to the witch-made goods I had brought. Papery wafers of laundry soap flashed a cleanliness spell through my clothes to expel sweat and dirt. Magic wipes or soap tablets did the same for my hair and skin, and dental mints permeated my mouth with magic to zap germs from my teeth.

I worried constantly about losing my supplies, though. Nalibak wove a magical protection around his lair, but I had no doubt there were other fae more powerful, or more cunning, who could filch my stuff while he was away, especially while I slept. It had already happened once. I had started with three glowing orb lights, and always left one on while I slept. But one day I awoke to darkness. My light had disappeared. Nalibak wasn't back yet, and when he did return he insisted he had not destroyed it.

"The bat fae could have taken it," he said. Which for all I knew was true.

I became paranoid and tried to keep all my possessions touching me at all times. This made it hard to sleep or relax. It was no way to live.

Melu Ros was scheduled to track me down and bring me more supplies after three months had passed in the human realm, but if each day out there took an average of, say, two weeks in here, I could run out of not only lights and laundry supplies but food. Then what?

In the glow of the orb, I recorded a few minutes of a chantagram to a loved one each day, smiling as bravely as I could and reassuring them I was totally fine, please don't anyone worry. Of course, it was possible those missives would get stolen, too, before I had a chance to send them.

I began to see how easy it was to go insane in the fae realm, even if an enchantment never touched you.

VAI

My phone had acquired a flood of anxious messages in the weeks I'd been away, mostly from the troupe, but some from Ayda and Javier and Charles. Evidently news had spread of Leo's deal with Nalibak. Everyone now knew. None of us could do anything about it.

The human government had no authority in the fae realm. They sometimes made deals allowing representatives to cross the verge, with a fae escort, to search for a missing person. If that person was an adult who had entered the fae realm of their own volition, however—for instance, in an agreement with a faery—then the authorities stood down. The fae held deals sacrosanct, and fae, on the whole, wielded far more power than humans, so respecting deals was the wise diplomatic choice.

Leo had made his decision. We all knew where he was, roughly speaking. But we could not rescue him.

I was discharged from the hospital after two days, as the algae was not advancing. Since healers needed to monitor me for at least another month, I stayed in Tesoro for the time being, taking a hotel room. I insisted that Wayshaw leave and drive down to rejoin the troupe, who were in Sevinee. I had Ayda here for company, as well as Javier.

I'd been surprised to get a short but solicitous text message from Leo's brother. *Thanks for trying to help Leo. I'm going to bring you some meals from the grocery.* I gratefully accepted his help and began the tentative process of getting to know him.

I had to ask, in one of the visits, how Leo's aunt and uncle were taking the news. Javier bowed his head. "Dad's worried. Mom's acting like it's Leo's own fault for being reckless."

"They have some processing to do," Ayda said diplomatically.

Then there was my own family. In about four months, Kwal's spell would end, and they would remember me and likely summon me. Plus I would need to be available for legal hearings. Between those considerations and my need to stay here another month for medical check-ins, I would need lodgings in Tesoro beyond just a hotel room.

I went apartment hunting. In the streets, people's glances lingered on my face an extra second, but nobody commented. Probably they thought I was half-fae and were just trying to guess what kind exactly.

Two blocks from the high rise containing Daphne's apartment, I encountered an Apartment For Rent sign. The lettering above the building's door said L'Andalusia. It had three stories, sand-yellow stucco walls with green trim, a Spanish-tiled roof, and a front garden with bottlebrush trees and white geraniums.

After touring the apartment, I signed a lease for it. It was a two-bedroom ground-floor unit accessible via the back garden, which held olive trees, lilies, and blue-flowering ceanothus around a colorfully tiled fountain. The whole apartment was smaller than the parlor where my mother's piano had resided, in our former house. But more spacious, of course, than the caravan.

I visited the storage unit where Kwal had stashed my possessions, chose some for the apartment, and made a list of what else I needed. At a furniture store, I picked some pieces and arranged for them to be delivered on my move-in day, the first of July. All the while, two jarringly different visions of the future a year from now overlapped in my thoughts. In one, Leo and I were alive, healed, and reconciled, perhaps having blissful sex on this bedding I was swiping a credit card for. In the other, he was dead of enchantment damage and I was sitting in the apartment, broken forever, staring numbly at the pretty fountain outside the window.

There was a third option: *I* would be dead of enchantment damage. But in that event I would probably not be around to see what followed.

People sometimes showed up and kept me company. Javier and Ayda were the most frequent visitors, and Catarina and Mathilde trekked up once to see me, taking a week off from the troupe. They arrived on the second of July, which they had somehow found out was my thirty-second birthday, and helped me set up the apartment. Catarina brought a bouquet of roses and delphiniums, and Mathilde picked up tapas for us.

We talked about Leo, a little. "He kept some things private. He didn't want us to worry," was what the troupe folk mainly came around to as an explanation.

Javier and Ayda had known him longer, and I trusted their interpretation, which boiled down to "He sacrifices himself too much. He blames himself for everything."

It made sense. I saw now why he'd been evasive. I more or less got why he had underestimated my feelings for him. Understanding made me less bewildered but not less shredded apart inside.

Catarina held my hands before she and Mathilde left to catch their train. "We want you to come back to the troupe," she said. Behind her, Mathilde nodded.

I said that once my enchantment was stable enough to allow me to travel, I would likely rejoin Quicksand. But in November I'd have to return to Tesoro to face my family, so…

"Come to us when you're ready," Catarina said. "Whether it be five days or five years from now."

Charles texted a few days later: *Hi Vai. Well, since Daphne can't tell you herself, I guess I will. She and Hazuki are officially a couple. They seem really happy.*

Hazuki was the kung fu sifu, our neighbor Heddy's niece. This news didn't surprise me, given the vibe between them when they'd attended *Moulin Rouge*. But I could guess how it affected Charles. He hadn't even appended any of his usual smiling emojis or hearts.

I thanked him and asked if he was doing okay. Which led to agreeing to meet him for tea.

At a café near my apartment, Charles set his elbows on the table, his fingers in his hair. "Vai," he lamented. "I'm so pathetic."

Charles unburdened himself, rambling about his feelings for Daphne, a torch he had carried since he first met her and followed her to Eidolonia ten years ago. Even now, he didn't cry—his eyes kept their usual wet look without any tears actually falling. But his voice was broken and his bearing more distraught than I'd ever seen.

He sighed after his monologue and swirled the ice in his coffee. "I clearly need to move on. It's just hard, you know?"

"It is."

"Is that how it is for you and Leonidas? I mean…" He gestured toward my half-green body. "You risked your life to rescue him."

I picked at the algae on my wrist. Merely wearing clothes presented challenges lately, as the algae dampened everything. Luckily it was summer, and in the dry warmth I could wear loose garments, like today's linen kaftan.

"Leo," I said quietly. "He goes by Leo. I knew I couldn't rescue him, exactly. I was just trying to…join him."

"He didn't want you to?"

I gazed at a dot of sunlight refracted through my clear mug of tea. "He didn't want me endangered."

"But you love him?"

"He loves me too." The words came out defiant. It felt important to say aloud what Leo had said, both in writing and in person. *I love you. I do. That will never change.* Of course, he had also said *Don't wait for me. Be free.* I didn't have to disclose that part. "But we couldn't change the deal," I added. "All I can do is wait."

"I'd wait too. If the person loved me back." Charles drank from his glass, ice chips clinking. "Have you heard anything about your family's case? Do they keep you informed, like if they find new leads or anything? Though I suppose you probably don't want to think about that either."

"I talked to the lawperson a couple weeks ago. The only update she had was that settling out of court is looking more like a possibility now."

Charles's brow smoothed. "Oh, whew, that'd be so much better for you. Way less stress." Then he squinted. "So, fair feasters. They sound *terrifying*. And you all have some way to track this particular one down? Like, summon him? How? Though I'd much rather know how to keep them away!"

I drank my cooled tea. "Well. To track them, you need something like a bear faery. An alligator or a mountain cat would also work."

***

Good news, Ayda texted me in early August. *My dad made some inquiries in the fae realm and has heard through the grapevine that Nalibak has Leo up in some mountain cave. The human is seen from time to time. He's still okay, sounds like.*

She added three heart emojis, which in my rush of emotion I had no reluctance in echoing immediately. I then typed, *Thank you so much. Thank Melu Ros for me too.*

Of course. He'll be taking Leo some supplies on August 27, so get any letters or gifts to me by the day before, okay?

I promised I would. Then I collapsed on my couch, on my back, breathing in shudders as tears ran down into my ears. I was so enormously grateful, and also, *I could not live like this*, month after month.

I collected things to send him. I bought an armload of shelf-stable, nutritious snacks and meals, baked him protein-rich peanut cookies, packed it all into a cotton bag that I enspelled to ward off fae and pests, and stuck a note in it: *Still better for you than a pack of ramen.*

Choosing what to write in a proper letter was harder. I didn't want him to know yet about my failed attempt to go after him, nor my enchantment damage. He would only worry. I sent another text to Ayda, then copied it to Javier, then the troupe, requesting they please not tell Leo either, in case they were sending any correspondence via Melu Ros.

But what *should* I say? If I were Leo, I would prefer a chantagram over a letter, so I could see and hear my loved one. But I wouldn't be able to show my face without revealing the algae.

I went to Ancona Beach on a scorching day and took a five-minute video as I walked along the shore. People surfed, swam, flew enchanted kites. Kids sculpted sand. Two soaked puppies played in the edge of the waves, at the feet of an elderly couple.

"I thought you might want to see some daylight and some other humans," I said, off camera. "I'm in Tesoro for a little while. Ancona Beach is much hotter today than last time we were here." I went on like that, mentioning everyday things. Finally I let the camera linger on a boat with a yellow sail, and said, "I'm not doing what you said, forgetting about you and moving on with my life. I refuse. I'm waiting for you. Our conversation is not over."

I ended the video and uploaded it onto a blank chantagram. Let him be frustrated that he couldn't see my face, and that I was refusing to move on. Maybe wanting to argue with me would boost his will to stay alive.

CHAPTER 28

LEO

"It was the right choice," I insisted, mouth mashed against my pillow. I was awake but kept my eyes shut and clung to the dream. I'd had it many times: Vai was following me around, furious, demanding I let them stay in the lair. "No," I kept saying. "I don't even have enough supplies for myself, let alone for us both. I won't let you suffer. That's why I stopped you." They wouldn't listen. They kept loathing me and refusing to leave, at the same time.

Finally a throb in my eye socket awoke me fully. I rolled onto my back. My spine had gotten stiffer every day from sitting and lying on nothing but rock, and the tension had spread through my shoulders and neck, giving me a chronic headache. My camping mattress provided some respite, but obviously not enough to heal me.

Lately my ankle and wrist ached too, from the other day when I had slipped while getting water from the cave pool. From the way other people's injuries had felt under my hands, I was pretty sure it was only a sprain. But as an exo-witch, I couldn't heal myself.

Then there were my feet. They were nearly always cold, and I had developed red sensitive patches on the tips of some toes, which I was pretty sure were chilblains.

I had medicines, from Ayda and the rest, but I resisted using them. A twisted ankle would get better over time. But what if I fell again and got a deep cut? I should save the powerful healing bandages, of which I had only four, for that kind of thing. They had also supplied me with antimicrobial meds, both topical and oral, but chilblains were a circulation problem, not a microbial one, as far as I knew.

A bigger problem was that I was running out of food. My count of days was now one hundred and fifty-two, far beyond the ninety or so that should have passed before Melu Ros showed up with supplies. But even if I'd counted accurately, which was unlikely, it meant nothing, since I didn't know how long it had been on the human side.

I was down to four nutrition bars, a handful of stale almonds, and three packets of electrolytes. I had to save the electrolytes. I might get sick and need them. A couple of days ago I'd had six bars, plus a bag of dried apples, but when I got everything out of my pack to inventory it, the apples and two of the bars had disappeared. Or maybe just one bar had disappeared and I had eaten one while checking my stash. Maybe I was remembering wrong. Was I losing my grasp on reality, or were creatures stealing my things?

All this poured into my mind before I even lifted my head from the pillow. "See, it's better you aren't here," I told Vai. "We'd both have starved by now."

A clatter of pebbles. A scrape of claws on rock. Fresh wind streamed in, along with light. I scrambled up. Nalibak's barrier was gone, and against a deep blue sky tinted with the peach of dawn was the silhouette of a bear.

"Leo," it said. "Are you well?"

I blinked. "Melu Ros?"

He swung down a duffel bag. "It's August twenty-seventh, or was when I crossed the verge. I've brought you supplies. Are you fae-struck yet?"

He shifted to human form and, bearded and burly and naked, came to examine my limbs, then sniffed me. "Not the best I've ever seen," he said, "but I don't think you're enspelled, at least." He whapped me on the shoulder. "Keep it up."

"I'm going insane. Stuff is disappearing—I never see anyone steal it, but I don't know what I could have done with it, but maybe I ate it? I mean when it's food. I don't think I could have eaten a globe light. Nalibak says it's bats. Could it be bats?" I was clinging to his arm. I had missed touching another warm, living creature.

Melu Ros sniffed the air. "I do smell bat fae. Monkey fae too. They've both been here, and they have a tendency to take things. But fair feasters like to put on glamour and cause hallucinations, so, if your protections fail, that could happen too."

Letting go of him to spread my hands around my own arms, I felt a tingle in the lines of my tattoos. Vai's protection, interwoven with the tattoo artist's. "I think the spells are still active. Unless I'm imagining that."

"They felt strong when I examined you." Melu Ros scooted the duffel bag in front of me. "New supplies, as well as missives. Everyone is fine."

I dropped to my knees to tear into the bag. "Thank you! Oh gods, thank you. Everyone's okay, really?"

He pointed to a baggie of greenish capsules I had just found. "Take one of those. Ayda's health-boost blend. You need it. Then eat something."

I shoved a capsule into my mouth, swallowed it, and kept digging. The next thing I found was a banana. I ripped straight in and bit off half of it. Sheer heaven.

"Sit," I implored with my mouth full. "Talk to me. I miss you all so much. Nalibak's out, devouring the souls of the innocent or whatever."

"I am not," an icy voice said. And there was Nalibak, looking less like some cheap Vai knockoff this morning and more like Nosferatu. "Out," he spat at Melu Ros. "You delivered trinkets, now you leave."

Melu Ros turned back into a bear—a wall of brown fur invaded my space. "As if you've ever honored agreements. You've let him grow unhealthy. I'm not pleased."

"Given I'm not to touch him, how am I to heal him?" Nalibak retorted.

"That's fair," I said, still chewing banana. "I do not want him touching me."

"This is a dreadful place to keep a human," Melu Ros said. "Cold and hard and isolated. He cannot be here in winter. He'll freeze."

"Excellent, for now that you've found us, we leave."

"Hold up," I protested, gathering my goods. "Let me pack."

"Go," Nalibak said to Melu Ros, "or I whisk him away this instant, with or without gifts."

I gave Melu Ros a pleading look. Though I ached to talk to him, the food, medicine, and letters ultimately mattered more.

"Here." I scrambled to get the stack of chantagrams I'd recorded, and handed them to Melu Ros. "Please deliver these."

Nalibak loomed over me. "Leave," he repeated to Melu Ros.

Melu Ros gave a full-throated roar, but pivoted and lumbered out, loping down the mountainside.

"The sun comes." Nalibak's frozen hand gripped my shoulder.

"Let me fucking pack and get hold of everything. You want quality entertainment or not?" I was shoving things into bags and zipping compartments as fast as I could.

"Hurry. You have it? Come."

With my backpack barely on my shoulder, and my arms and one leg wrapped around the duffel bag, I got yanked through the shadows, away from the cave I had loathed, on the mountain with the stunning view I had only briefly gotten to enjoy. I never even learned its name.

VAI

I had one awful phase, not long after handing off the chantagram and supplies to Ayda. While I anxiously waited for Melu Ros to come back with a report on Leo, the algae spread to the inside of my lip and nostril, and I began coughing up bits of green slime. I cannot convey how repulsive this was. The hospital readmitted me and fitted enspelled pads in my mouth and nose, as well as dosing me with medicines and having exo-witches give me hands-on healing. They confirmed that the bits I was coughing up were merely from the algae at my lips and nostril, of which I was accidentally inhaling or swallowing little shreds. Again, this was a nauseating thing to go through. But the healing did its work, and gradually the algae not only receded from my facial orifices but from the rest of me.

As if its growing season was simply over, it dried up and fell off in flakes. By the start of September, none remained. The healers detected no active magic anymore. It left my skin tinted green, though, as if my right side had been dipped in dye. The color might fade and vanish over time, they said, but might not. Side effects of enchantment damage often stuck forever.

There'd been a time in my life when this development would have dealt a hard hit to my vanity. It wasn't an attractive tint—the most generous thing I could compare it to was a pear. But it was far better than the algae itself, and it served as a visible reminder of what I had tried to do for love. I accepted it.

I would not go back in after Leo, much as I wanted to. My first attempt would have killed me if Melu Ros and Wayshaw had been any slower, or if the healers had been any less skilled. Those reminders were sobering enough to keep me on the human side. But forget Leo and move on? Absolutely not.

With magic, I dyed a streak in my hair the same green as my stained skin, made another streak in a teal that complemented it, then colored my nails teal on my right hand. Those touches helped it look better. My damage could be a fashion statement.

Melu Ros finally returned—his two days of travel in the fae realm had amounted to a week in ours. Ayda texted me. *Leo is okay. Not completely healthy or happy of course, but my dad says the protection spells are holding. He sent a chantagram for you. Bringing it to your place now.*

When she arrived, I stammered that she should come in for tea. She looked at my trembling hand holding the chantagram, smiled kindly, and told me she'd leave me to it for now. We could talk later.

Alone, I sat on my floor and unsealed the turquoise card.

My breath caught as Leo's face leaped up, illuminated with a soft lamp, everything dark behind him. He looked foggy and low-resolution, the way it looked if you used a chantagram's built-in image capture rather than uploading a video from your phone. Phones barely worked in the fae realm, and Wayshaw had said Leo didn't have his along. I didn't care about the quality. It was Leo and he was alive and he was talking to me.

"Hi, Vai," he said with a brilliant smile. "I just wanted to tell you everything's okay, and I'm so sorry for the sleeping spell. Are you furious? I don't blame you. But there was no way I was going to be the reason you ruined your life. Anyway, I'm sure by now you're relieved you didn't come. You're probably on to your next awesome adventure—as you should be."

While I drank him in, barely breathing, he told me about performing one-person comedies, dramas, fairy tales, and musicals for Nalibak, and how little Nalibak grasped the point of any story. He had recorded pieces of the chantagram's message on several different days, giving it the effect of a series of journal entries. It totaled some forty-five minutes, and more than once he apologized for how long it was and insisted I must be bored and probably wasn't even watching anymore.

Only toward the end, when his face was thinner, and the purple in his hair more faded, did he look into the camera with somber eyes. "I miss you," he said. "I keep dreaming about you, about how mad at me you must be, and I still would never wish this on you, for you to be in the lair. All the same, sometimes I want you here, so much." He looked down. "I got so used to being with you." Then he lifted his face again. "Anyway! By the next time I can send mail, your spell will be over, and you'll have talked to your family. I know that'll be rough. I'm thinking of you." He kissed his fingertips and touched them to an imaginary wall between us. The video ended.

For a long time I sat on my floor and stared unfocused at a reflected swatch of sunlight on the ceiling.

Then I composed an email to Wayshaw, Genevieve, and Catarina, asking if I could please return to Quicksand for the next two months, to do any menial work they needed. Also, I would like to stay in Leo's caravan, if that option was still available.

LEO

Where we next landed, it smelled like the cold remains of a bonfire. Black ash smudged my shoes.

Nalibak said, "Isn't it a sweet, dead place?" and let go of me.

I dropped my luggage, opened the duffel bag, and shooed him away. Though salivating at the food inside, I pushed past it until getting to the chantagrams. Soon I found Vai's and stared at it like it was made of diamonds. Should I give in to temptation and watch it immediately, or save it for last?

A glance at Nalibak, gliding around growling his ice-chip sounds and setting up his curtain of darkness, decided it for me. These days, I might not have a tomorrow.

I swiped my finger across the wax stripe. In a three-dimensional space no bigger than my hand, sunshine bloomed. Waves lapped. Humans played. The summer-blue ocean stretched to the horizon.

I pivoted so my back shielded the light from Nalibak, but it was only a faint replica of sunlight. I had shown him chantagrams containing daylight videos before, to display dances or plays, and they hadn't caused him pain. He had just grimaced and called the sunlight ugly.

All he did now was glance at me and say, "A new story, my hoarding squirrel?"

"Shut up. I'll tell you later."

Vai's voice spoke, off camera. "I thought you might want to see some daylight and some other humans..." Goose bumps flourished down my limbs. I felt electric, lucid for the first time in weeks, unaware I hadn't *been* lucid till now. I lowered the volume on the card and brought it closer to my face, not wishing Nalibak to steal Vai's voice to mimic later.

I laughed in surprise at Vai's defiance in their final lines, then huffed in dissatisfaction as the video ended. Not once had they shown their face or even so much as their foot.

Their missive stayed in my mind even as I opened everyone else's messages and learned with relief that all the people I knew were, seemingly, doing fine. Aunt Yubara and Uncle Luis hadn't sent anything, but Javier's chantagram explained that. "We haven't told them yet they can send things to you. I doubt they'd say anything helpful."

Ayda had sent herbal medicines. Catarina had sent another e-reader loaded up with books, most of which were new to me. And lots of people, including Vai, had sent food.

I went for the freshest first, devouring an apple and several mouthfuls of hard cheese. "Where are we?" I finally asked Nalibak.

As ever, I could barely see anything other than what was illuminated by a magical undying penlight, which I'd clipped to my coat zipper to make it less likely to get stolen. The air was warmer here, and the ground seemed mainly to be cold cinders and earth.

"Where the fire fae burn and abandon, above the seashores of the whales and the serpents."

I sucked cheese from my teeth while decoding that. "Near Port Baleia and Serpentshore, in some part of the forest the fire fae burned?"

"Yes, yes, so I told you."

"It's my daily word game, deciphering what the fuck you're talking about."

"This tree reached high, stretched wide. Its death was ages ago, but it still stood. Like the creatures in your stories. Zombies."

I crinkled my face at him. "A dead tree is not a zombie."

"Then time hollowed it, and the wildfire burned away its heart, and now it makes a precious lair, a place of longstanding death."

"Super." My sarcasm would usually have been harsher, but my bag of messages and supplies was buoying me up.

One-quarter done with my exile. Granted, if every quarter lasted as long as the first one had, the next three would be brutal. But I cupped the hope tenderly in my hands anyway, like sunlight in a chantagram.

When Nalibak left for the night, I opened a blank chantagram and began recording. "Vai! Thank you so much for the sunshine at Ancona Beach. It was exactly what I needed. Were you punishing me by not showing your face? I deserve that. I hope it's true what you said, that our conversation isn't over. I really hope we get to have that conversation. Even if all you want to do is yell at me."

CHAPTER 29

VAI

The creak of Leo's caravan door, as I opened it, shot deep into me and flung me into the past. Stepping inside, I shut my eyes, identifying the scents. Aged vinyl and metal and carpet, dried grass, faint stale coffee, dusty fabrics and powdery makeup, and—probably because only Wayshaw had been living in it lately—a hint of ocean. For a moment I felt it was that night in November, the first time I'd stepped through this door. Or any of the myriad days since, when I had come in to make dinner or change clothes. Nearly every time, Leo had either been arriving with me or already here, calling out a greeting. If I kept my eyes shut, maybe his voice would break the silence.

But it was Wayshaw, patiently standing behind me, who spoke. "You can have his bed if you like. Unless you prefer the bunk."

I opened my eyes and wandered to Leo's bed, where I picked up one of his pillows and smelled it. That was the sharpest needle yet. Eyes shut, pillow against my nose, I just breathed.

Either finding nothing unusual about my behavior or opting not to comment, Wayshaw said, "Have a seat. I'll drive us to the park."

She had picked me up at the train station in Kagami. It had been a long rail journey from Tesoro—around the north end of the island and down around Kikenna Bay to Kagami—but it had soothed me to be returning to a place I'd been happy. Now I remembered why I had initially resisted this idea.

I don't want to stay with the troupe, if you're not there.

But what would I do instead? Stay in Tesoro, having morose tea dates with Charles while waiting for my family to remember me?

The engine thrummed to life. Swaying as the vehicle lurched forward, I swung down into the seat near the bed and prepared to greet the rest of the troupe.

Immersing myself back into Quicksand's world occupied my time, and being around my troupe friends did often make me smile. In the three months I'd been away, they had acquired two new actors, and three of the previous members (not counting Leo) were absent. One dancer-tumbler and one actor had left to take other jobs, and Darius was taking a season off, to rejoin the troupe in winter. The changed roster, the new sketches and plays, and the silence of Leo's caravan gave life a surreal tilt. The longer I trudged along, though, constructing and cleaning sets and costumes, taking walks with Catarina, moving from town to town, theatre to theatre, the more it resolved into reality.

On a crisp day in October, in a cloud of caramel-popcorn scent at a Port Baleia park, I stood in the crowd and watched the sketches. The absurdity was irresistible, and soon laughter welled up from deep inside me too. I hadn't laughed, not properly, since before Leo was taken. Probably not since the first of May, in fact.

Leo would call that a sad existence.

I made it a point to laugh again, every day going forward, as authentically as I could. Whether to please him or spite him, I didn't know.

October plodded past. My right half stayed pale green, but no other enchantment damage surfaced. I helped with choreography. Learned about stage lighting from Uwila. Recorded videos for Leo, showing my face a little this time, black-and-white-filtered to camouflage the green. Stood lost in memories in the meadow above the sea where I had once laid hands on his body and pulled hairs away.

We arrived in Tesoro toward the end of the month, in time for Lord Festival. Kwal texted me, the first I'd heard from him in a while. I hadn't bothered telling him about my romantic troubles or my disastrous trip into the fae realm. He wasn't allowed to help, and I didn't want to make him fret.

Hello Vai, how are you? Kwal wrote. *At nine a.m. on the second of November, I'm to meet with Daphne. I'll remove the spell from her. After that I have an appointment with your mother, and then your father and uncle. By noon, the spell will have ended for all of them, and they will remember you.*

Why nine a.m.? I answered, of all responses.

It seemed a more convenient time than midnight. But I can change the time if you wish.

Nine is good. Thank you. I'm in Tesoro now. After seeing Daphne and Mom—if they want to see me—I'd like to see you too.

I look forward to it, Kwal said. *I've been sad not to see you this past year.*

I feel the same. Thank you for being there, I typed.

I didn't think I would care much anymore, after everything I'd been through. I envisioned myself composed, accepting whatever my family said. For those who were enraged, I'd understand. To those who welcomed me back, I'd be grateful. If they were *all* angry and none welcomed me, so be it. The day I'd blown the whistle, I'd accepted that possible outcome.

But the night of November first, I was too nervous to sleep. I'd returned to my Tesoro apartment for the time being, to be closer to Daphne just in case, and now the rooms felt huge and empty after the cozy clutter of Leo's caravan. On the morning of the second—awake in the dark, before dawn—I couldn't eat a bite. Sipping weak tea at the kitchen counter, I watched the minutes creep forward as the sun slowly rose.

At 9:05 a.m., a text from Daphne arrived with a chime. Hardly breathing, I opened it.

Vai!!! Oh gods, I can't imagine what you've been through. I feel like a full year of missing you has caught up with me all at once. I want to see you!!

I started breathing again, weightless with relief.

Kwal says you're in Tesoro, she added before I could respond. *Can you come over this morning? Or can I come to you?*

Hey sis. I've missed you too, I typed back. *I'll come to you.*

We made plans—her apartment in fifteen minutes. Kwal, when setting up their meeting, had wisely advised she clear her schedule for a couple of hours.

Mind swirling with all the things I wanted to tell her, I rushed out. Down the street. Into her building, across the lobby with the vintage chandelier, up the stairs, texting *I'm here* as I walked.

Her door swung open. Daphne's hair was damp and held back in a white headband. She wore lavender yoga pants and a plum hoodie. Her eyes were wide. "Oh, Vai," she said.

I stepped forward, and we hugged. I sank against her, smelling her familiar herbal shampoo. "Hi," I said.

She set me at arm's length, brows drawing together as she touched the green half of my face, with the expertise of a healer and the worry of a sister. "What happened to you?"

At that question, so simple yet so immense, my eyes filled with tears. My throat closed.

Seeing the change in my face, Daphne pulled me back into the hug. Collapsing in her arms, I sobbed on her shoulder, harder than I'd cried in ages. Though I tried to rein it in, I might as well have attempted to stand in the way of a tsunami.

She got me inside and seated us on her sofa, where she kept holding me and giving me handkerchiefs. By the time I could talk, there were six drenched, crumpled handkerchiefs on my lap. Wiping my eyes with the seventh, I started talking about Leo. I barely even mentioned the family debacle and Kwal's spell—that was just the opening incident that had flung me into the grand drama.

"And," I eventually said, "of course through it all I missed you, and Mom, and home, and I felt guilty, especially when I read about Mom and Dad splitting up. But that just made me lean on Leo more. He saved me from being lonely. He made the year so *good*. Then…it shattered."

I had already told her about Nalibak, and where Leo was now, to explain my enchantment damage.

Daphne leaned her head on my shoulder and propped her foot on the coffee table. "Gods, Vai. You have been through it."

I blew my nose. "So have you. Charles sometimes filled me in, to keep me updated. I'm so sorry. How bad was it?"

"Compared to you, I've had a *great* year. I mean, no, it was awful when the scandal hit, and everyone was asking me questions I didn't know the answers to. And the weird part? I kept feeling like there was someone I was supposed to reach out to, commiserate with. But I couldn't think who." She angled her head to look up at me. "I don't think I forgot you. Not completely."

"It must have driven you all crazy. Trying to figure out who the whistleblower was."

"Sometimes we'd wonder—but then, because of how the spell worked, we'd just *stop* wondering. And look!" She picked up her phone. "Before you got here, I was searching through past messages. Friends were saying your name and I didn't even register it. I didn't even ask who they meant."

"Kwal went to everyone he could. Explained about the spell."

"Good thing. Our friends would've started worrying about our mental faculties."

I gathered the handkerchiefs into a heap. "Do you remember you saw me? Twice in the past year." I hadn't mentioned that yet.

She lifted her head to stare at me, then I saw the revelation spread across her face.

I smiled. "Thanks for coming to the show."

She smacked both hands on my thigh. "Oh my gods. That was you! Vai, you were amazing. Please tell me you're staying in theatre."

"I'm back with Quicksand now, but...it's not the same." I rearranged the handkerchief pile. "I thought I'd see if you had any job openings. I could work at your clinic."

Daphne settled back, head resting on the cushions. "I can always find work for a matter-witch with your talents. But I question whether you'd be happy there. Even with your heart broken, you seem more content now, more yourself, than you ever did working for Airtight. Or than you would working for me. Try it if you like, but..."

I looked at the ceiling too, feeling drained, in a clean way, as if an infection had been lanced. "Well. You're usually right about things."

While I was with Daphne, my phone started buzzing. Video call from our mother.

When I answered it, giving the screen a shy wave, my mom covered her mouth with her hand. Her eyes looked red around the edges, but they crinkled now, as if she was laughing and crying at the same time.

Daphne leaned into the frame. "Hey, Mom. Look, I found a sibling. I forgot I had this."

"Mom, I'm so sorry," I said.

"Vai. No." She uncovered her mouth. Her silver hair was in a neat braid down one shoulder. "I love you. First I have to say that."

"I love you too."

"You have nothing to be sorry for. To have lost the knowledge of one of my children—it's always been one of my greatest fears, that someday that damned clause would be enacted, and this would happen. Knowing you were out there in the world, without any of us..."

"Vai joined the theatre," Daphne piped up. "They're a costumer and a dancer and all kinds of things."

Mom's expression brightened. "Did you really?"

I nodded. "I ran away with the Quicksand Theatre Company."

She tipped her head back with a laugh. "I only wish you'd done it sooner. Can you both come over?"

Daphne and I stayed with our mother a couple of hours, sitting at her dining room table with tea, then making sandwiches when we got hungry. Kwal arrived, and I rose to embrace him.

After telling me he was glad to see me, his smile faded and he adopted a straighter posture. "I've been to your father and uncle. The spell is lifted from them too."

This, a clench in my stomach reminded me, was the step I'd been dreading.

"They're shocked," Kwal continued. "Angry, for now. I took the liberty of bringing their lawyer, and he advises them not to communicate with you yet. They seem willing to abide by this suggestion."

The clench inside me caved inward, going cold. "No message for me, then?"

Kwal shook his head. "Keep in mind, Vai, the law protects you if anyone attempts to threaten or intimidate you for reporting what you found."

I sank back down into my chair.

"I don't think you should contact them," Daphne said quietly. "We haven't, Mom and I, very often."

We'd talked of this, of course, in the last few hours. Things were understandably ruptured between the wrongdoers and the innocents in my family. But I realized from the loneliness inside me that I'd been hoping anyway for a message from Dad and Uncle Joe. *Vai, we're so sorry. We're ashamed of what we did and the position we put you in.*

Instead, silence and anger.

"I have the three of you back," I said. "I'm grateful."

Which I was. But my family had been torn into pieces, and we could never be stitched back together into our old pattern again.

CHAPTER 30

LEO

I had unlocked a new level of torment.

At first I rather liked the burned-out tree lair. We were at low elevation, so it was warmer. The ground was reasonably level. The water source Nalibak whisked me to every night was a pool fed by groundwater, and with the fireflies and glowing sprites circling it, it was the most beautiful thing I'd seen since the mountaintop view. The fire-fae burn had been years ago, and the forest was recovering, shoots of trees and purple-blooming fireweed all around, beneath the giant trees that had survived the blaze. When the flower fae sang, I could hear them, faintly, from inside the lair.

But. In the lair, the ash got stirred up by us moving around, and I developed a cough from inhaling the particles. Coughing up black-streaked phlegm wasn't even the worst part—at least Ayda's herbs helped soothe my lungs. No, the splinters took the prize.

This had been a tree, thus the walls and floor were made of disintegrating wood. All you had to do was brush your skin against it to get a fresh batch of countless, tiny, hair-thin splinters. I could never get them all out. They worked their way inside my clothes. I lived with tingling stabs and rough, irritated patches of skin, all over me, every minute. I combated the condition with tweezers and salves, which did help, but I'd only get new splinters as soon as I began healing from the previous ones.

I contemplated asking Nalibak if we could move, but if he offered to go back to the mountaintop, I knew I would turn that down—I'd had my absolute fill of that place. And there was no guarantee the next place would be better. The fae realm held dangers much worse than splinters. I needed to tamp down my complaints and enjoy the singing flower fae and just hope my skin toughened up.

Meanwhile, would inhaling bits of fae-realm ash into my lungs and having splinters of fae-realm tree under my skin penetrate my defenses and expose me to enchantment damage? I didn't know. Worrying was useless. Still, my mind fixated on the idea, second-guessing every pain or mood, dreading that it might be an enchantment.

Ayda had sent mood-improving concoctions of enspelled herbs, capsules of mustard yellow. I put off taking them, because surely *this* didn't count as a serious enough malady to merit using my stash. I wasn't crying in my sleeping bag all day. I could still remember lines and act out plays for Nalibak. I just was never happy anymore, and I worried all the time. But wasn't that a normal way to feel, given where I was?

One rainy evening, a slim dryad at the pool told me Lord Festival had just ended. It was November, then. A year since I'd met Vai. Which meant their family's spell had ended.

I couldn't sleep that night, tormented—first—by picturing what Vai must be going through. If any of their relatives dared turn a cold shoulder to Vai, if anyone made Vai feel terrible…well, what I wanted to do was storm out there and deliver a blistering lecture to those people. But of course I couldn't even walk ten steps without hitting an impenetrable wall of darkness. Only Nalibak or a more powerful faery could take me away from the inside of this tree.

Then—second—I recollected that Vai was resourceful and resilient and probably already had people, maybe a particular someone, who cared for them. It had been six months since we last saw each other. It had taken less than six months for Vai and me to become mutually interested. By this point it was inevitable that Vai was attached to someone new.

Now I was depressed. I shouldn't have been. I had predicted this months ago, and I'd given Vai my blessing to move on. Nonetheless, my brain teemed with thoughts of Vai's rosy smile brought to life by someone else, their dark eyes drinking in someone's face from kissing distance. I hoped that person was good to them. If that person *wasn't*, I'd—

But I had no right to judge. As if I'd been so good for them. I'd made Vai miserable. Made them cry.

Even the fae realm couldn't come up with torture to top this.

In the morning, bleary and queasy, I had to admit I had no proof Vai was seeing anyone, and no power to do anything about it if they were. But if I ever wanted to find out, I had to survive till at least the next mail delivery.

I took one of Ayda's mood-improvement capsules. The thing was astonishing. The fog in my mind cleared, and I could see I obviously hadn't been eating enough—too paranoid about hoarding food—so I had two handfuls of trail mix alongside my daily bite of protein bar, and I treated myself to one of the three remaining peanut butter cookies Vai had sent. I still felt sad. Being away from everyone I loved, and acknowledging their lives were progressing without me, was a dagger in the soul that one pill couldn't remove. But at least the medicine helped me see that it was all right to be sad.

The pill wore off a day later, though. And I only had twenty-four of them. Sunk back in my emotional ravine, I didn't deem myself worthy of taking another one. I shouldn't use them up, because what if someday I *really* needed one and had none left?

The pills stayed in my hoard, alongside the hardening pieces of dark chocolate, wrapped up in parchment paper, that I was saving for some other day.

VAI

In the case against my father and uncle, the court finally assigned the hearing a date: the last day of November. Four days before that, I handed off another chantagram, along with a pack of food, warm clothing, and other gifts, to send to Leo via Ayda's father. November 27 was his quarterly check-in.

"I'm stressed. I'm downcast," I admitted in the chantagram, after telling the good news of being reunited with Daphne and Mom. "Not a word from my father or uncle. Avoiding contact is the wise thing to do, legally, but it feels like they both hate me now and we'll never speak again. That isn't what I wanted, though I don't know how I thought it would turn out differently."

I let my face show, sitting by a window in my apartment. I planned to apply a black-and-white filter to the video again to hide the green in my skin. Outside, the fountain burbled among evergreen shrubs.

"I haven't been back to Quicksand all month, and can't go back until I'm done with my legal obligations," I continued. "I've been helping at Daphne's clinic, but…I miss the troupe. I want to run away to it, like I did a year ago. But this year I can't, and this year you aren't there anyway. I shouldn't feel lonely, now that I'm back with Daphne and Mom. But I do. Lonely and guilty both. I wish you were here. Every day I wish that. Please stay well. Please come back whole."

I hoped Melu Ros would return before the hearing date, bearing news that

Leo was all right, but of course he didn't. I had to face that day without any knowledge of whether Leo still lived.

Daphne, Mom, Kwal, and I congregated at my mother's apartment on the thirtieth and sat together, waiting to be summoned by the court. Finally, at almost five p.m., one of the lawfolk phoned. Dad and Uncle Joe had pled guilty to the charges, in exchange for a lesser sentence than what they might have otherwise faced. The judge had given them a brutally high fine, a prohibition against founding another business for five years, and twelve months apiece of house arrest. Another one-year deal showing up in my life.

Their plea meant the case would not go to trial. I was grateful, and even thought for a moment that they'd chosen this route to spare me the stress and media exposure of public testimony. Then I realized it also spared them the same thing. They were protecting themselves, not me.

A few days passed. We still hadn't heard from Melu Ros. Warped by desperation, I emailed my father.

Dad,

The lawfolk say it's permissible for us to talk now. I wanted to tell you that while I still feel I did the right thing, it was an extremely hard choice, and I never wanted to break our family irreparably. I hope someday you do want to talk, and Joe as well.

Four days from now, I'm leaving Tesoro to rejoin the Quicksand Theatre Company, where I've been working for most of the past year. They're currently in Amanecer. Unless something comes up, I won't be back in Tesoro till around late April. So if you'd like to see me this month, it should be soon.

I wish you and Joe well.

Vai

That evening, an email from Marcello Delvecchio bloomed like an ink stain on my screen.

Vai,

Come tomorrow at ten a.m. Address is below. Joe says he's not ready yet, so it'll just be me.

Dad

Friendly? Surly? Dad's mood was always hard to read in his written correspondence. He'd never been an emoji user.

Kwal came to the meeting with me, at my request. Having a buffer along seemed prudent.

Dad and Uncle Joe now lived in two separate units in a building on the southern edge of the city. When he let us in, I gauged his apartment to be perhaps one-tenth the size of our former house.

We warily sized each other up. In our former life, we would have hugged, but he didn't offer, so I didn't either.

He looked weary, his short hair combed back with less shine than he used to imbue it with. He wore the vintage Dior sweater in white, with blue stripes at cuff and collar, that he'd been magically keeping in good repair for decades; navy trousers; socks; and the enspelled iron ankle cuff of a house-arrest prisoner.

"What happened to your face?" he asked coolly.

"Enchantment damage. I went into the fae realm to try to help a friend."

"Reckless. Not like you. At least, I wouldn't have said it was."

To give us privacy, Kwal stayed in the kitchen, having brought a book to read. I followed Dad to the living room, where I sat in an armchair and Dad sat on the sofa. He had a cup of espresso on the coffee table, but didn't offer us any.

The walls and most of the furnishings were gray. The place was probably pre-furnished, as it was not the color palette nor the styles Dad would have chosen. He saw me eyeing it and said he'd probably order some art. "Something cheap, since I can't be spending so freely anymore."

I asked if he had ideas about what he would do for a job now. His jaw tightened. He sipped his espresso. Maybe repairs and restoration, he said. Things like the vintage sweater.

I remarked I'd been doing similar at Quicksand, fixing and altering props, costumes.

"Probably what you always wanted to do anyway," he said. "Theatre, that kind of thing." His voice still sounded cool, even a bit derisive.

So all these years he'd guessed I would have preferred a different job. He hadn't said anything, had let me keep serving him and Uncle Joe instead.

"I do like it," I answered. Then my insolent mouth couldn't keep from adding, "It's an honest living."

Dad met my gaze, his eyes like black ice. "Did you come here expecting an apology?"

"Did you invite me here expecting one?"

He gave a sarcastic laugh. "I can't understand it. You didn't even come to us. Didn't even ask. Just went straight to the authorities."

Heat prickled under my collar. "I can't understand why you and Joe ever got involved with those horrible people."

"They aren't horrible. They—look. On this island, with magic everywhere, you literally don't know if what you're seeing or hearing or touching is real. You have to know who you can trust. You have to know who's loyal."

These were just Humanist Party talking points. My pulse sped up.

"I thought family could be trusted," Dad went on. "I never thought *you* would be disloyal. I can't believe it."

"I *was* loyal. Right up until you violated *my* trust."

"We were protecting you! You know it's better not to know our clients' details."

"You didn't tell me because you knew I wouldn't participate. You probably even knew I'd report you. That's why you went on using me and keeping me in the dark."

Dad's fingers tightened on his knees, his knuckles going white. "Don't you tell me why I did what I did, or what I thought. You are young and idealistic, and you haven't lived through all I've—"

"We're done." I got to my feet. "This was a bad idea."

"You're lucky I'm even talking to you. Joe might never talk to you again, you realize that?"

I didn't stop, going through the kitchen, giving Kwal a tense glance. Kwal got up, slipping his book into a pocket.

Dad appeared in the doorway as we put our shoes on and stepped into the building's corridor. His face was maroon, his lips drawn up to show teeth. "Word's spreading, Vai. Everyone knows you're a traitor. Someone who betrayed their family. Did you even think it through?" He lurched toward me.

I startled backward. Kwal moved between us and swept his fingers down toward Dad's ankle cuff. It lit up in a ring of orange lights and emitted a repeating chirp. Orange meant a warning, I knew from reading up on the house arrest arrangement. Kwal had activated it. If it went to red, law enforcement would arrive.

Dad stopped and clamped his lips shut. Breathing with flared nostrils, he stepped back into his apartment. The chirps stopped.

"I'm protecting your family," Kwal softly told him. "Including you."

Dad looked at me, then Kwal. "Not sure you can avoid taking sides anymore, friend. I think I see which one you're choosing."

"In this matter I'm free to choose, and have not made any deal," Kwal answered. "I'm fond of you all. And you would only feel worse if you hurt Vai any further."

Dad exhaled. He pulled back into his apartment, said, "Go," and shut his door.

That night a cold snap blew in. Frost sparkled on fallen leaves. The wind bit at my cheeks and numbed my fingers. The weather report said it was early in the season for such low temperatures, and the way the ocean currents looked, we were in for an especially cold winter. Sleeping outside in this was unfathomable. If the weather around Nalibak's lair was the same as here, then Leo might already be dead. Melu Ros still hadn't returned to tell us one way or the other.

I stood in a hilltop park, one of Tesoro's highest points, and looked west toward the fae realm. In a whisper, I begged all the powers to keep Leo warm. I set offerings on the frozen grass: reproductions of Japanese woodblock art, held down in the wind by chunks of driftwood an artisan had carved into dancing figures. I poked a stick of agarwood incense into a clump of weeds. The smoke whipped westward into the dark, as if the fae were hungry to breathe it in.

I stayed on my knees, shivering, numb, until the incense burned out. Not one word came to me on the rushing wind.

CHAPTER 31

VAI

The next day, I acquired the number of Leo's aunt Yubara from Javier and sent her a text.

Hello Yubara, my name is Vai, and I was Leo's caravan-mate at Quicksand. I was wondering if I could meet you sometime today or tomorrow, to talk briefly. I miss him and would like to speak to people who knew him better than I did. Thank you, and hope to hear from you.

She answered an hour later. *I can only imagine what he's told you about us. Yes, we can meet. You might as well judge for yourself.*

I thanked her, and we agreed to meet at her boutique at noon. Even though I had proposed this meeting in a spirit of something like challenge, I walked to the address with dread, given her answer. What type of dragon had I just invited out to battle with me?

The boutique was small, its storefront a few paces across, on a pleasant street in east downtown. Mannequins in jewel-tone formalwear and wool business-casual stood in the windows. As I paused to take in the fashions, finding I quite liked them, a woman in her sixties stepped out, wrapped in a golden-brown faux-fur coat. The royal blue of her long skirt matched her cloche; and her russet boots, with two-inch heels, set off the coat's color. Gold medallion earrings twinkled against her bobbed gray-and-black hair. She gave me a vaguely curious glance. "Vai, I assume?"

I nodded. "Pleasure to meet you."

"Do you mind if we walk? I prefer it these days, rather than chaining myself and others to some table."

We set off down the sidewalk. "I wanted to ask how you were doing, with Leo's situation," I said. Very nearly a lie. After my meeting with my father, I was belligerent and had come here to dig out the truth of why she and Luis had dealt so much damage to Leo's psyche over the years. I wanted to demand how they could have done such a thing to an orphaned child. But my nature wasn't *quite* that confrontational, so I started from a more innocuous angle.

"You must care about him." She glanced at shopfronts as we walked. "To come check on his family."

"Javier and Ayda have been kind to me. What he did for them was incredibly generous, and they're grateful. Yet…"

"Yet it was the most reckless, absurd gesture he's made in his life, which is saying something." Before I could decide on a riposte, she grimaced. "I've…not been perfect toward him, Vai. I'm sure he's told you."

"He insisted the fault was his," I said, which he had, though I didn't agree with that assessment.

"It frustrates me that I've not been perfect, because I'm a perfectionist. So were my parents, which is surely why I'm this way. Anything my sister or I did that was less than grand-prize-winning, they had critiques ready. Leo's tried to tell me this about myself, but I thought he was just talking back. He can be so infuriating. But now that he's gone and might not…return, I'm beginning to see he was also sometimes right."

I crossed a street with her, dazed at where this conversation had landed. "No parent does everything perfectly. No human does."

"I didn't realize until talking with Luis and Ayda and Javier lately how unloved I made Leo feel. I didn't know how to deal with him. He behaved so differently from Javier. I was trying to help. Bring him up to higher standards so his life would be better."

Some of my father's sentiments echoed in those words. But Yubara's shell seemed to have cracked, letting in gleams of understanding, a stage my father had not yet reached.

"It must have been hard," I said, "adopting him at such a sad time."

"He must hate us." She sounded bewildered. "I never wanted that. Now I don't know how to fix it." She glanced at me with a twist of her lips, the first smile she'd shown me. It lasted only half a second. "There are skills I excel at. Then there are some, such as being a loving parent, that it would seem I have no aptitude for."

"I expect you do love them. Javier and Leo both."

"Of course. But if either of them feels that I don't, then I've done a rotten job."

We wandered into a park, a square between city buildings, and slowed at a sculpture of three sprites standing in a stack. "Do you think I can learn?" she asked.

"Now that I've met you, I think so."

She looked me in the eyes. "Javier and Luis said the same. I still feel that if I can't do it perfectly, I might as well not try. But as you say, that isn't a logical conclusion. Humans aren't perfect."

"I'd be grateful if you did try. It'll make Leo happy. When he returns."

Yubara turned to the statue again. Neither of us pointed out the boldness of my saying "when," not "if."

"I wish my father could be half as understanding as you're being," I added.

"Oh? What's he like?"

"His name is Marcello Delvecchio, and he—"

"Oh." She looked at me with a blink. "Yes, I know of him. Then you're—"

"The whistleblower. Who betrayed him."

"Well, that's what he and his brother should have expected, getting involved with that viper Walda Portnoff."

"I'm glad we agree."

"Tell me more, if you feel like it. My turn to lend an ear."

I gave her the outline as we walked back to her shop. I made sure to stress that Leo had been my salvation in that dark time, the most wonderful choice I could have made in someone to run to.

"I wish he'd told us more about you," she said. "I expect he was guarding your privacy. But having met you, I think more highly of him now. And not nearly so highly of myself."

"You'll do all right." We reached the boutique, and I looked again at the mannequins. "Did you design any of these clothes?"

"All of them." Yubara lifted her chin as if ready to take an insult.

"I love them. You've managed to walk the line between classic chic and bold innovation. That's not easy to do."

She beamed, then gave a nod to my outfit—overcoat, shoes, and hat. "Thank you. From you, that's a worthy compliment."

LEO

As before, a minute after Melu Ros arrived to exchange the season's supplies for my outgoing mail, Nalibak snarled and spat and insisted we move lairs at once. Melu Ros had time only to lay his paws on me in a burst of healing, urge me to take a *lot more* of Ayda's medicines, *Leo you idiot.* Then, in my shocked-awake state, I shoved my messages into his grasp, grabbed my belongings, and got hauled through the darkness in Nalibak's frozen talons.

Something stabbed my lungs with every cough. My body felt alternately too hot and too cold, and I'd been convinced Melu Ros was a dream up till the moment he hit me with healing magic. I now also saw, as I crashed to a slick ground, that the edges of my backpack were crusted with frost, and my fingernails had a blue tint to them.

"Something in that burned-out tree," I rasped, on my knees, "was not good for me."

"Your suffering was a succulent meal," Nalibak said. "But I grow bored of you, the weaker you get. You've half a year yet of stories and agonies with which to entertain me."

"I fucking hate you," I said, with no real energy.

"Humans are such buttercups, wilting in a bit of frost. Hadn't you garments to keep you warm?"

I tucked my fingers inside the opposite cuff, finding the silk undershirt. "Yeah, but the spell wears off after a while."

"Which of these clumps of moss will revive you?" He fluttered his fingers toward the bag Melu Ros had brought. "Take them, and become interesting again."

I bit into a medicine-laced fruit-leather strip. Chewing, I finally looked around and nearly choked.

The light clipped to my coat reflected back at me in a thousand gleaming ripples. The surface overhead and all around was deep black with such a sheen that I was convinced Nalibak had somehow ensconced us in a bubble of air at the bottom of the ocean.

"Where are we?" My hand shot out to the wall, but instead of water, it met something so hard and sharp it sliced my fingertips. With a hiss, I yanked my arm back.

"A chunk of pitchstone," he said. "As new as a baby's teeth. With immense lingering anguish."

My fingers had three fine cuts across them, welling blood. I pressed them to my shirt to stanch it, looking at Nalibak cautiously. But the times I'd injured myself, he had never done the movie-vampire thing and turned ravenous at the sight of my blood. He'd told me dismissively that he could always smell it anyway, injuries or no, and he'd only swoop in to drink if I was losing so much blood that it'd be a waste not to.

"Pitchstone?" I asked.

"The flank of the volcano. Ula Kana flung it about as she battled the fae and witches. One of them the prince with the lava-flower hair."

My groggy mind caught up. "Pitchstone Mountain? Ula Kana—" My gaze shot to the wall again. "Ula Kana's prison is on the other side of this? She's *right there?*"

"Isn't it delicious? Ghosts of humans roamed, and living mortals too, dangling in cages not far from here. They were freed, such a pity, but their blood and bones flavored the earth. Their misery, I taste it still."

"Ula Kana hates humans. And can make other fae do whatever she wants. For you and me both, isn't this a little *too* dangerous?"

"Her prison is secure. She cannot touch us."

The ground shook. Heat bloomed from the wall, and someone screeched something in the fae tongue, the roar of fire curling around their voice.

The hairs on the back of my neck stood on end. I'd never seen the volcano faery Ula Kana in person, in the months she was zooming about the island and wreaking destruction, a couple of years ago. I was lucky. Seemed like half the country had glimpsed her before the mission to trap her on Pitchstone Mountain had finally succeeded. She had led the forces that had destroyed my hometown, Miryoku. I would never again see my parents' graves, thanks to her. Not unless I went wading deep into the fae forest and somehow found them in the overgrown foliage.

Maybe Nalibak would be willing to take me there next. Unlikely.

I had to admit the geothermal heat was welcome, though. My joints began to soften, and I leaned against the wall in relief. The scream and the earthquake had already faded.

Nalibak chuckled—always a chillingly weird sound, like someone rattling carved-bone runes to decide your fate. "She was uttering choice words for some faery who declined to enter her prison and keep her company," he said.

"If only you could feast upon the suffering of fae and didn't need mortals for that." Settling against the obsidian wall, I ate the rest of the fruit leather. The healing magic brought my brain closer to fully-online, and I remembered with a zap of excitement that I had new messages from my friends. I hauled the bag over.

The messages came across as unreal, though—the voices, faces, and words of my loved ones popping into this enclosure of warped black glass adjoining a fae prison. I couldn't make sense of it.

How could it be that, somewhere in the wider world, maple tree leaves were still turning brilliant red and spiraling down to carpet the park outside Catarina's caravan? How was Javier grousing about this year's low supply of pears? How was Ayda still tramping the human realm, picking mushrooms and mosses in autumn daylight, wearing that same hairy orange scarf she'd had for a decade?

All these things were a dream. At the same time I somehow knew they did exist, and that they were the very reason I had put myself in Nalibak's clutches—so that, in Ayda and Javier's case at least, those everyday activities could go on existing.

I found the package from Vai. Cookies, a bottle of protein shake, homemade whole-grain bread, a small container of real butter, and various other foods that struck me as treasures from another dimension. Warm clothes—arriving now that I'd finally gotten a volcanically warm lair and didn't need them. A string of multicolored lights with long-lasting witch-made batteries. And a chantagram.

I released my breath in a rush as Vai's face appeared in black and white. *This* felt real. I hadn't seen Vai since leaving them asleep in that field at the end of May—except for in videos recorded before that, of which I'd brought a few.

Now their hair was longer, the ends brushing their shoulders. In the first few clips, they said they were with Quicksand on the west coast, and told me about it. Then, toward the end, they were in their new apartment in Tesoro, showing me the courtyard. They'd reunited with Daphne and their mother, but couldn't go back to Quicksand yet, and felt low about their father's and uncle's silence. Vai's gaze slipped aside, and they said they felt guilty and lonely. They wished me well, and the video ended.

Troubled, I cupped my hands around the card. I watched it again. They never said they were dating anyone. They also never said they weren't. Well—if Vai felt lonely, then whoever they were with was not doing a good enough job. This wasn't how things were supposed to go. Vai was supposed to be *happy*.

A fluttering hiss came from Nalibak, from across the funhouse hall of rippling black. "A sharp passion. Your returning strength brings such treats."

"*Shut up*," I shouted. The words bounced in the glass walls.

I grabbed the light string Vai had sent and clicked the switch. The bulbs came on in a rainbow of colors. I laid the string along the uneven base of the obsidian wall, then stretched out on my back. The walls curved and met overhead to make a ceiling, which became a murky, nonreflective black farther behind me, presumably where Nalibak's lair-veil took over, shrouding us in. But in this obsidian hollow surrounding me, the rainbow lights reflected in a thousand overlapping streaks.

How like Vai, to give me not merely something I needed—light—but something especially beautiful.

"Come, thou day in night," I whispered.

"Day in night?" Nalibak retorted. "Who would make such a wish? What a ruinous thing to do to the beauteous night."

I said nothing else, only grunted. I had not performed *Romeo and Juliet* for Nalibak and never would. Nor *Moulin Rouge*. Tragic love stories were one thing I refused to face.

CHAPTER 32

VAI

It was December, and I was back with Quicksand, helping prepare for Fire Festival, when Ayda texted to let me know Leo was still all right—more or less—and that a chantagram was headed to me by air-fae courier. Kneeling in Mathilde's bus beside a trunk of costumes, I sank back on my heels, weak with gratitude. Half the year gone. If we could both get through the remaining half with our minds intact, I swore I wouldn't care if my father and uncle never spoke to me again.

His chantagram arrived that evening. I sat on his bed, drew the curtains shut, and opened the message.

Leo's face lit up the bed-cave, smiling but thinner and paler than last time. A few days of beard shaded his jaw. "Vai! Thank you so much for the sunshine at Ancona Beach. It was exactly what I needed. Were you punishing me by not showing your face? I deserve that. I hope it's true what you say, that our conversation isn't over. I really hope we get to have that conversation. Even if all you want to do is yell at me." He lowered his gaze. "But it's been half a year by the time you get this, and I really *hope* you've stopped giving me much thought. You deserve to be out there, loving people and beaches and animals, and being loved. If you do send another message, I'd better hear that's what you're up to."

While I cringed, thinking of the message of loneliness I'd sent him, which by now was in his hands, he changed the subject, describing the burned-out tree somewhere in the northwest, where he'd spent the last three months. He surmised Nalibak was going to change their location every time Melu Ros showed up, because Nalibak hated having people know where he was. Melu Ros could track him regardless, but "I wish to make him work for it" was apparently how Nalibak put it. Leo's impression of the fair feaster was chillingly—and hilariously—on point. I grinned for a moment. If Leo hadn't lost his acting skills, maybe…just maybe…he was okay.

But. Then came the next several installments, recorded onto the same chantagram over the weeks. With each, he seemed more listless. He paused, groped for words, looked off into the darkness. And he was coughing, a cough that sounded thick and painful. His beard grew in fuller, and bruise-colored circles lay under his eyes.

In his last entry, with a blanket wrapped around him so that only his face showed, he spoke without segues or much coherence.

"It's freezing, I don't know why I'm freezing. It's still autumn, not winter, right? Maybe I'm wrong. Sometimes I'm hot. I wish this place had heated floors. You noticed the heated floors in my caravan the first day. I keep remembering that. Nalibak's asked me a few times if I'll do *Moulin Rouge*, but I won't. I could do it from memory, of course, but I can't go back there. Just thinking of it, when one of the songs gets stuck in my head, this…feeling eats me alive. The feeling of falling in love with you, getting to be together. Knowing I'd have to leave you. It was the worst and the best time. I can't go there again. I'm glad it was you I fell in love with for the last time. You deserve love, Vai, please don't forget that. I hope you're loved and happy right now, and I…I'm just glad I was there. For a while. I…should go to sleep. Goodnight. I love you."

The chantagram ended. Fear lodged like a stone in my throat.

Melu Ros had said Leo was alive and "more or less" well *after* this was recorded. I shouldn't worry. But…

I grabbed my phone and texted Ayda. *He was coughing and seemed sick in the chantagram. Do you know if Melu Ros healed him?*

Sorry yes! My dad did say he gave him healing and made him take my meds. The idiot better follow all my instructions and take every damn one on the regular.

I breathed a bit easier. *Thank you. That reassures me.* But, knowing Leo's shabby level of care for himself, it didn't truly reassure me.

What could I do, though? Nothing, except drag my legs off the bed, make dinner, and go on helping the troupe.

⁂

Toward the end of December, Daphne, Mom, and Hazuki came to Dasdemir. They stayed in a hotel near the palace, planning to take in Quicksand's performances as well as some tourist sights. I met up with them at a restaurant on their first evening.

"Daphne and I went out of town together last year for Fire Festival too," Mom said. "We chose Port Baleia. Too cold. So this year, the south."

I glanced out at the chilly rain. "Sorry that didn't work out."

She laughed. "But this time we're with you." She beamed across the table at Hazuki. "And you!"

Hazuki smiled. She'd gotten a short haircut lately. The black locks spiraled out in spikes with gold glitter ends, matching her black-and-gold blazer. "Happy to take a break from all my work in Tesoro."

"Has the kung fu academy been busy lately?" I asked.

"Oh, sure, but I mostly meant Speak Up Witch. Our grassroots group."

I'd seen the group in the news. They'd been one of the sources exposing the crimes of Walda Portnoff and other Humanist Party folk.

"Hazuki was one of its founders," Mom told me.

"When everything came out about Airtight," Daphne said, "I remembered the group and got in touch with Hazuki. I felt lost and wanted to talk to someone who saw these situations all the time. We hadn't talked in years, but she seemed honestly delighted to hear from me."

"I *was* honestly delighted." On the table, Hazuki laced her fingers into Daphne's.

"We met for coffee," Daphne went on. "She said the first thing I should know was I'm not alone. This was happening all over the country, families being split along political lines. She made me feel better." She smiled at Hazuki. "And we started talking a lot more."

One of the sharp edges of tension residing in my chest relaxed a little. Something good had come of my actions after all.

"Shoot, that reminds me." Hazuki got out her phone. "I need to ask London if she'll write up our event."

It took me a minute to place the name. "The London who came to *Moulin Rouge?*"

Daphne nodded. "She writes for a lot of publications, and sometimes does posts for Speak Up. Charles knows her, too, so we all made a group of it for the play."

"We have a New Year's event coming up," Hazuki said, typing. "One post from London, and we'll get twice as many people as we would've."

"She wrote about Airtight," Mom said. "When the news first broke. She was extremely fair, I thought."

"And she didn't name Vai." Daphne glanced at me. "Even though she figured out early on who the whistleblower was."

I nodded. "I guessed as much, when we met at the show. And she somehow knows Charles?"

"She met him when she was researching Airtight," Daphne said. "Mom and I declined to be interviewed, but London found friends of the family—including Charles—and talked to them. Then later they ran into each other at a Speak Up event, and I guess they stayed in touch."

Hazuki's phone lit up with a message. "Sweet. London's on it. She'll do a post."

"What's she working on lately?" Mom sipped her wine.

"She's been untangling Portnoff's accomplices," Daphne said. "Airtight's part in it was easy. The info *in* all those documents, though—all the money transfers, the contacts—that stuff has been taking investigators a year and a half to dig through."

The swallows of wine in my stomach turned sour. I'd held those documents in my hands, flipped with incredulity through the pages, my brain jamming with the influx of evidence.

"There was more than I could take in, when I saw them," I said quietly. "I remember payments to the election commission board. Large transfers to and from accounts in America. Background info on people—I hadn't heard of most of them. But looked like the kinds of things you'd blackmail someone for."

Hazuki's mouth flattened. "Matter-witches who helped tamper with the ballots. That'd be some of them. Or who can hack into accounts, conceal records. The whole thing's a fucking mess." She glanced with a flinch at Mom. "Sorry."

Mom tilted her wine glass toward Hazuki. "No, you speak the truth."

"London's been trying to find out who they are," Daphne said. "It's harder than you'd think, given the concealment skills these folks had."

I used to imagine it, in my quiet days as an Airtight Spells security specialist. How I would pull off, say, an embezzlement, and cover all traces of it. I would never have done it, but it was a minor thrill to envision. With my skill set, I was well positioned for such a scheme.

So were my father and uncle.

"Got grim last summer," Hazuki said. "London tracked down a source, a witch who'd worked for Portnoff and was willing to talk, as long as London helped him get legal immunity. But before they could meet up for the interview, he disappeared. A month later, turned up dead along the verge. Fair feaster got him."

Silence for a few seconds. Then everyone's gazes flicked, in a panic, to me.

"Sorry," Hazuki said, mortified.

I shook my head. Cleared my throat. "Suspicious timing," I contributed.

"Right?" Daphne said. "But no one's been able to prove a connection. It's not like fair feasters care about human politics."

"No. I suppose not."

The waiter brought our dinners. I dragged my fork tines across my bucatini, wondering what Leo was eating tonight. If he was well enough to eat. If he was even alive. If I had done a sufficient job protecting him, with my spells and gifts, or if, once again, I had not been enough.

"I've had three glasses of wine," I said, recording myself on video that night. I was alone, sitting on the caravan floor. "I normally have, um, zero. I do not feel great. But I need to tell you some things. See how I'm green here?" I turned my face toward the camera, touched my cheek. "Enchantment damage. From the fae realm. I went in after you, the day after Nalibak took you. Got stuck in a swamp for a whole night, fae surrounding me, tentacles around my ankles. Melu Ros and Wayshaw found me. Woke up in the hospital, algae growing on my skin. I told everyone not to tell you. But now I'm telling you.

"See, I'm not good enough. I couldn't save you. I want to come rescue you—every day I want to. But if I cross the verge again, I'll probably just die this time. Then how will I ever know what happened to you.

"You say you love me. You also say I should move on. Leo. Listen. *I love you too.* I have not moved on. If you honestly love me but don't want to be with me, then just say that. Tell me clearly. But if you're just being…*you,* and thinking you're not good enough, and that I'm just taking pity on you, then *you're wrong.*

I love you. I'm waiting for you. I want another chance with you. I don't know how to be any clearer."

I stopped to breathe for a minute, slumping back against the bed, my eyes shut. "I should get some of the headache meds Catarina has. The enspelled ones. Before bed, I should really do that. Um. Stay alive. Take care of yourself. I don't know how to get to May fucking twenty-seventh. Even when I just see the number twenty-seven, I freeze, I… But. Let's just. Both try to do that. Get to May twenty-seventh. Deal?"

I stopped the video. I'd delete that tomorrow, probably.

Then I did text Catarina and acquire the meds, and took them before going to bed. Because I might as well take care of myself and thereby not be a complete hypocrite.

CHAPTER 33

LEO

I soon learned that the region surrounding Ula Kana's magical prison on Pitchstone Mountain could not be called a desirable place to live. It might, in fact, have been one of the most dangerous neighborhoods in Eidolonia.

Our lair had a mostly-level floor, geothermal heat, shiny walls that reflected lights, no splinters or mold, and not nearly as much ash as you might expect on the side of a volcano. But it was also utterly lawless, even by fae standards.

No particular group of fae had wanted to take up residence here, what with Ula Kana's constant, furious presence. Our chunk of obsidian was a short distance outside her imprisonment barrier, which in turn was a dome of invisible magic, encircling a few miles of hardened lava, inside which she was free to fly about and rant at whoever got close. Which, I could soon assert, she did on the regular. We could hear her through all the barriers.

The undesirability of the location was partly why Nalibak had set up a haunt there. No one was likely to protest our presence, if they even noticed it, any more than you'd protest a rat dwelling at the foot of an evil fortress. The only fae who showed up were individuals or small groups curious to get a look at Ula Kana and maybe stir up trouble by infuriating her. Some came to offer their allegiance—an offer that never amounted to much, as none had the power to free her. Hunters from a nearby haunt—earth fae with antlers and armored bodies—helped maintain the magical barrier and swept through now and then to chase off troublemakers. The result, all told, was continual violence and cacophony just outside our lair.

When I'd been ill, in the tree-trunk lair, I hadn't cared much about going out. Nalibak, I dimly recalled, had brought back water for me a few times, grousing about the smell of the enchanted galangal root in my water bottle.

None of the maladies and injuries I had sustained had entirely gone away since then. The ankle and wrist I'd sprained in the first lair still twinged. The splinters from the second lair were gone, but my skin stayed rough and scaly in places. The chilblains on my toes hung on. My respiratory infection improved, but lingered as a throat tickle that kept me coughing. I was always either starving (but strictly rationing my food and never eating to fullness) or disgusted by the mere idea of eating. Given my ongoing stress and lack of proper exercise, my whole body was stiffer, weaker, thinner, and in more pain than it used to be. The purple extensions in my hair had fallen out, and my natural hair felt thinner between my fingers. Some of it had turned gray. I'd given up on counting the days, but these signs of aging probably weren't a result of the natural passage of time. It couldn't have been *years* I'd spent in here. Could it?

But—feeling somewhat better after the healing Melu Ros had given me and the herbs Ayda had sent, I did beg leave to breathe the fresh air and view the stars. That would be good for me, surely. I should have known by Nalibak's low chuckle that the world outside was not going to be quite as enchanting this time.

When I first stepped out into the chilly moonlight and turned toward the mountain, the sight struck me motionless with awe. The obsidian wall in Ula Kana's prison was easily a hundred feet high, glinting and jagged and alien. Our piece, where Nalibak had tucked the lair, looked like a broken hunk of coal next to it. Above the wall, Pitchstone Mountain's gigantic scoop-topped peak stood against the night sky, emitting a wavering red glow: the firelight of lava seething in the caldera.

"Very Mount Doom," I commented.

"Doom, yes, for so many," Nalibak said.

"No, it's—never mind. We haven't gotten to Tolkien yet."

As we approached a pine forest, where apparently our water source lay, a howl keened through the air. Another answered it, the two voices twining eerily together.

"The wolves stink," Nalibak said, "but I do savor their song."

"There are *wolves* here too? You know, fuck it, I'll take the wolves over the rest of you. Happy to hear about the wolves."

The stream for my fresh water, running through a channel of slimy rocks, was warm, smelled of sulfur, and tasted like salt and metal, even after being shaken around with my enchanted bit of root. But the water didn't seem to do me any harm, and in a strange way I appreciated the novelty of the taste. The trouble, really, was getting there and back each time.

On another night, a band of harpy-goblins came flying through the forest, careening a few feet off the ground. They were like giant slugs with eagle wings, pink eyes, and jawless lamprey mouths ringed with teeth. Nalibak flung a cloak of darkness around us, and they whipped past, chittering. "So those would've attacked me," I said. To check.

"They pick up squishy living things," he said, "fling them to each other in the air. How they play! They hold on with their teeth, which makes an amusing sprinkling rain of blood while they toss their plaything about. Then it inevitably falls and breaks."

So I'd heard, regarding harpy-goblins, but hearing it as a tale in the comfy human realm was a different experience from hearing it at night in the fae realm after several of them flew straight at you.

Yet another night, we altered our route to avoid a convocation of alligator fae arrayed on the rocks. Our new path took us through the forest, where I spotted three slender trees glowing silver, their winter-bare limbs splayed across the stars. They stood out among the dark pines like a lovely vision.

Since we were walking, rather than speeding through Nalibak's shadowpath, Nalibak wasn't holding on to me, and I was free to veer aside. I crunched through pine needles, ignoring Nalibak's rather casual, "Not that way, unless you wish to go mad." Soon I stood under the trees, staring up at their cold grace in the starlight. Something nagged at my mind about trees with white bark, but these days my mind was fuzzy. I dreamed, and told a lot of stories, and did little else. Maybe the white trees were from a fairy tale?

Only when one of them swung a skinny branch down and swept it toward my face did I remember. I yelled, fell to the ground, and scrambled away.

"Go mad if not die," Nalibak continued, sounding bored. But he came closer and flapped a ripple of darkness at me to chivy me farther away from the trees.

"Birches," I said, breathless with horror. "Whitefingers."

Every human kid knew the rhyme. People sang it to be fun and spooky on Hunter's Night and Halloween.

Walking through the birch grove, keep your head,

Or the whitefingers touch you and then you're dead!

"Nearby," Nalibak said, "there is a whole forest of them. Such dense darkness, even in the day. So many bones. Delicious pain, but I would not put my lair in it. The shrieks of the ghosts are tiresome, and the whitefingers keep tapping, tapping, all the night and day."

It was then I truly understood how easy it would be to die out here. All I would have to do was approach one of those birch trees. The whitefinger, the faery possessing it, would stroke me with a long white limb, and that would be it. I'd either die or lose my grasp on reality, and in the latter case, some other faery or animal would find me and finish me off in no time.

The scariest thing about that realization was the soft, cool acceptance I felt. *So that's how I could do it,* a part of my mind said. *My suffering would end. The suffering I'm undergoing now, the suffering I drag along from the past, the suffering still ahead of me—because even if I get home, I'll still suffer there. It never ends. This way, it would.*

I had watched and performed enough theatrical tragedies to recognize this as a red flag. *This Leo, this character in the play,* another part of my mind commented, *I hope he doesn't give up. I'm worried about him.*

I lay that night in the obsidian curve reflecting the rainbow of lights Vai had sent, while these two aspects of myself debated each other on a stage in my head.

Why do I feel this deep wish to help you?, the calm one said to the distraught one. *Who exactly* are *you? How can you let me know you better?*

It was a confusing, enigmatic play. I couldn't guess how it ended.

VAI

Daphne, Hazuki, and my mother came to Quicksand's Friday night performance. I was in one of the sketches, in another nonspeaking role, this time as the front end of a moose. (The sketch was "Eidolonians in Canada.") Afterward, Catarina, Fred, and Kornelia went to a café with us. I invited Wayshaw, too, but she declined, opting to go dive into the bay for the night as per usual.

Fred and Kornelia got immersed in a political conversation with Hazuki, Daphne, and me, which veered sometimes into C-dramas we had all watched. Meanwhile Catarina and my mother drew their chairs together at the other end of the table, talking in low voices.

The café had an upright piano, which we cajoled my mother into playing. She asked permission from the barista first. The guy shrugged and waved her over, then a minute later stood stunned, pastry plates forgotten in both hands, as her fingers struck the keys in a high-paced, major-key allegro. A Haydn sonata, I believed. Five flawless minutes later, she twirled it to its end. The room broke into applause.

She moved into something moodier—Chopin. Catarina, who had been standing mesmerized at the end of the keyboard, moved closer to murmur to her, and my mother responded, flashing a grin. The next time I looked, Mom had scooted over on the bench and Catarina was sitting beside her as she played. They stayed that way for the rest of the hour.

They had lunch together the next day—I found out via a texted photo from Catarina, showing the two of them at a window with a bay view. They found time a couple of days later, despite Quicksand's hectic festival schedule, to go to the Royal Opera House for a matinee of *The Magic Flute*. They invited me, but I encouraged them to go without me. Daphne, Hazuki, and I already planned to explore the waterfront district that afternoon, and besides, it warmed me to see my Quicksand mother and my biological mother forming a friendship.

I recorded several short videos for Leo over the weeks, to compile onto a chantagram for the next delivery, which would be at the end of February. I did not expect, but was pleased, to record a message in late January saying, "My mom texted me and told me she's been in touch a great deal with Catarina, since going back to Tesoro. According to her, *We think it's becoming something more than friendship. I know she's your friend and I hope this is not strange for you.* I answered that I think it's wonderful. Then I went to Catarina's caravan and teased her. I don't think I've ever seen Catarina blush before. She covered her face and said, 'Vai, I've been knocked clean off my feet.'"

I smiled, my gaze drifting out the window. We were on the Southwest Peninsula, and fog shrouded everything. "My approaching you, and joining Quicksand…it led to them meeting. Even if I…" *Never see you again. At least it brought them together.* I couldn't say it. "Even if it doesn't work out for them in the long run," I revised, "it's lovely for now."

LEO

I felt afraid lately. Probably because of all the lethal fae roaming outside our lair. Some of them, I had to figure, had enough power to rip open Nalibak's darkness veil and grab me out of it like an eagle seizing a duckling. I worried especially in the hours when Nalibak was gone, because he at least could protect me to some degree.

"I better not end up with Stockholm syndrome for Nalibak, of all fucking people," I told Vai, in a chantagram message. I lay back on my mattress and let the camera take in the colorful lights and the streaky obsidian reflections. "I've heard wolves howling. I keep having this fantasy. A wolf gets separated from her pack, or she just leaves. Maybe she's young, or small, or not as fast as the rest. She wanders to the lair and somehow gets in. We make friends, the wolf and I. She can't be around when Nalibak's here, of course, because he's an asshead and wouldn't allow it. But every time he clears out, she comes to see me. She curls up beside me, and I can finally sleep easy."

The loyal wolf lying beside me was one of the only images that allowed me to fall asleep anymore, in fact. Of course I often thought of Vai—holding them, kissing them—but that wasn't an image of pure comfort. It was desire and longing as well as guilt and torment.

Because I had never hurt this theoretical wolf. Never lied to her.

"What do you think, Vai?" I said on the video. "Does this mean I should adopt a dog, if I get back? *If*. Lately it all seems much more dangerous. I don't know if I've gotten more paranoid or if I'm actually seeing things more clearly. It does a number on anyone's brain, being in the dark all the time, being locked up. How did humans ever survive those early years, when they first landed on Eidolonia? When the whole place was fae territory. Do you ever wonder? How many lost their minds and disappeared into the wild? And people still do. We still do.

"If I didn't have the plays and songs to perform, and didn't have Nalibak to talk to, even though he's the worst…I'd be insane by now. More than I already am. I might not even be alive. I tell stories and become other people, and that's the only thing, other than messages from you all, that staves off the depression. The loneliness. Fuck. Maybe that's what I've always been doing, with theatre." I fell silent. I'd lost track of what I'd been talking about.

"I'm not sure who I even am. Maybe I never knew. Anyway. Apparently this person wants a wolf. Or a dog. Proof I'm losing it, right?"

The difficulty all this time, I was starting to see, wasn't surviving. It was understanding why I should want to survive.

Chapter 34

VAI

I had bad days sometimes, that February. Unable to sleep or concentrate, one day I begged Wayshaw for help, and we went to the verge. It involved climbing a hill above Kikenna Bay, on a trail of slippery mud, in even denser fog than the layer lurking over the water.

At the verge, a sylph approached and spoke to Wayshaw. I presented a gift—a tin of candies, enchanted to enable the eater to blow colored bubbles that floated around and lasted an hour each. In exchange, the sylph promised to seek news of a human named Leo taken captive by a fair feaster named Nalibak. She swept off into the fae realm. She had instructions on how to find us, even if it were weeks later and we were in the next town.

Having sent off this inquiry still didn't make me sleep well. And no one came from the fae realm with news, not the next day, nor the next week.

We reached the day in late February when it was time to deliver messages and gifts to Ayda, to send to Leo. The sylph still hadn't come. Heartsick, I sifted through the videos I'd sent, applying the black-and-white filter to each before collating them on a chantagram.

I found the one I'd recorded while drunk and watched it.

Leo needs to hear this, I thought. *He should know how things stand.*

I left it in color, because in the video I spoke of my green skin. I left in the love declarations. I left in my inebriated pauses. All of it. Though I'd recorded this video before the others, I uploaded it last. Let it be the final word.

LEO

It caught me unawares when Melu Ros next thundered into the lair. I hadn't prepared outgoing messages in a while. I'd been lost in my own abyss.

Also, I had almost certainly broken my right foot. I can't even claim it was in some valiant fight with a harpy-goblin. I slipped on the rocks at the stream one night and tumbled, twisting and snapping some bones in the process.

I hated that I hoped, for a little while, that a dreadful infection might take hold, sweep through my blood, and kill me in my sleep.

The concerned Leo from the improv sessions in my head stepped forward and sternly instructed me to get the healing bandages and wrap that foot up. I complied. If only because my friends would think me the stupidest person they'd ever known if they found it unused in my pack, after I'd died of an untreated injury, and they would wonder why they had even tried to help me by sending such goods.

The break did begin to heal, but such things took a couple of weeks. Thus Melu Ros found me sitting with my bandaged foot propped on a pile of clothes.

I stared at the bear, my mind in a fuzzy cocoon. Was this the wolf I had wanted? Or one of the fae intruders I had feared? Or a fever dream (did I have a fever again)?

He sighed, morphing into human form. "It's getting old, my arriving and your not recognizing me."

Then I understood he was Melu Ros, and I scooted over to grab my stash of messages, firing questions at him. So it was February twenty-seventh? How was everyone? Did he have trouble getting here, with all the hostile fae prowling around?

He waved off the questions, focusing on my foot. Then he sniffed in surprise and admitted I'd done the right thing, using the bandages and keeping weight off it. He scooped up the duffel bag from last visit, which now contained my outgoing messages; deposited the new bag of supplies at my side; and regarded me for a few seconds. When he reached out, I flinched back.

"Sorry," I said. "Instinct. I…trust you." But I still felt afraid, having grown accustomed to not letting any fae touch me—and fae were the only people I saw anymore.

Melu Ros didn't reach out again. "Everyone just wants you to keep hold of your mind and your health," he said. "We're all thinking of you. Next time I see you, it'll be to bring you home. So please be alive and sane on that day, will you?"

This promise of my rescue was just another story, one of my library of five hundred fictions. But the responsible Leo of my two-person play honestly believed in hope, and he took the job of answering.

"I'll try," I said.

Then—as before, in another development that was getting old—Nalibak blew in and snarled at me to get my "seashells and storybooks," we were leaving.

My broken foot hindered me. I scooped everything into my pack. Shoes—e-reader—new duffel bag—collapsible cup with tea in it, spilling all over my wrist—

Off we launched. The obsidian lair vanished behind me in a twinkle of moonlight and little colored lights—

I hadn't grabbed the string of lights Vai sent me. The pang this dealt me was profound. Losing them seemed a terrible omen, and Nalibak was never going to take me back there for them, so no use asking. All I could do was mourn in silence.

This time, as our flight was at night, we didn't have to wend a path through shadows at ground level, nor keep a darkness veil around ourselves. Nalibak swept me through the night air like a supersonic bat, whipping around trees and over hills. Without his cloak of darkness, I could see more, and my eyes grabbed at each scrap of novelty. A river shimmering under the moon. A ring of fire sprites twirling in a ravine. A thousand will-o'-the-wisps lighting up the branches of a redwood. A car's headlights—

A car's headlights.

The rectangular lights of a house's windows.

The flash of a lighthouse beam.

I twisted in Nalibak's grasp to look back, the precious lights already fast disappearing behind us. "Those—that's the human realm, right?"

"A sliver," Nalibak said. "Must cross it to get here."

Here, I learned with a thud against sharp barnacles, was somewhere near the sea. Waves sloshed. The smell of the ocean saturated my lungs, thick enough to taste salt. The rock beneath me was wet, and deeply cold after our volcanic enclosure. Nalibak had already wrapped us in our fair-feaster darkness dome. I got up, hopping on my good foot. "Can I see?"

From Nalibak came the tongue-flickering sound he made when he enjoyed the taste of something. "How you long. How you ache! The sight of your people's paltry lights did that? I should dangle you above them and then snatch you away more often."

"Fuck you, I just want to see where we are," I snapped.

He made a pleased trill. "Your anger! You have not flung it at me like a handful of moth wings in such a long time."

That was true. I'd done it often in the first months, then less and less. My fire had dwindled.

"So we're in the fucking ocean," I retorted, as irritated as he could ever hope for.

"Thousands of rocks, all sizes, off the shore. All fae territory. A thousand places to put a lair. So many interesting dead or wounded things washing up." He stepped aside, and the darkness lightened.

I limped forward, one hand on the barnacled wall.

Icy wind blasted my face. Moonlight quivered in shards on the ocean. A wave shattered perhaps ten feet in front of me and just a few feet below, spraying across my body. A droplet of salt flew between my lips and sparked on my tongue.

Our island was no more than a sea stack, a hollow rock jutting above into a spike, and extending at least a hundred feet behind us. Across a churning expanse of water, two other stacks stood above the surface. I could no longer see any lights to signal where the mainland might be. Sailors said there was an eerie zone like that. The ocean surrounding Eidolonia was all fae territory, and once you got far enough out, the sea fae made it so you couldn't see the mainland unless they wished you to. Which, as a general rule, they did not.

I eventually got from Nalibak that we were off the east coast, probably near Punta Rosa. Honestly, it didn't matter. I was exactly as unreachable here as on any other sea stack. What mattered was that I had new messages and supplies.

I found Vai's chantagram and held on to it for an agonizing few minutes until Nalibak finally left to explore and terrorize the nearest coast. Then I opened it.

At first, good news. Catarina getting together with Vai's mom! And Vai was still living in my caravan, working with Quicksand. It heartened me to hear.

Then. The last clip.

Vai was tipsy, disconsolate. With…pale green down half their skin. Enchantment damage, from trying to find me, months ago. What? No one had told me. And the feelings Vai confessed…

I watched the clip again and again, terror and dismay bounding inside me. Also something akin to excitement. Hope. Joy?

None of these positive emotions were acceptable. Vai was telling me they were miserable and damaged, all because of me. I was not allowed to feel anything but guilt. Vai insisting they loved me and were waiting for me...all right, some people would be justified in feeling excitement and joy about that. Not me. I hadn't earned it.

Stop feeling those things. *Stop.*

There was one other surprising chantagram: from my aunt Yubara and uncle Luis.

In the first clip, Yubara sat alone at the kitchen table, wearing a pink blazer and purple scarf. "Hello, Leo," she said. "Javier and Ayda finally allowed us to know we could send you messages this way. Rude of them to withhold the information so long. But here we are."

She talked about a new employee at the boutique, a festival project involving making scarves, the removal of a rockrose bush in the garden. Then she folded her hands on the table and looked down.

"I see why you chose this," she said, to her knuckles. "This sacrifice. You believed it mattered less for you to be taken away than if it had been Ayda or anyone else. You believed we all wouldn't care as much, on the whole." Her fingers tightened. "I'm sorry you believed that. I'm sorry for my part in your believing that, because I expect my part was rather large. This is your home. You're one of my children. I know our family doesn't say it enough, but...I love you. I want us to both feel like proper family to each other, someday, if that's possible. I'm going to work on it." Her gaze lifted back to the camera. "Please look after yourself. I want you safe, and I want to see you again." She smiled—awkwardly, but sincerely. And the clip ended.

While I huffed out a stunned breath, the next clip started. Uncle Luis sat alone at his home office desk, reading glasses on.

"Leo, hi, kiddo. Heck of an adventure you're having, huh?" He grimaced. "Listen, I want to get right to it. I'm real sorry. For not standing up for you, when you were young. Not stepping in. You were just a kid, you needed someone to do that, and that should've been me and Yubara. We dropped the ball." He looked aside. "The truth is...you remind me so much of Cesar."

That was my father.

"Even back then, you did," he said. "I was missing him, and feeling bad I hadn't spent more time with him. I think it made me scared of getting close to you. I wasn't sure how to do it without it hurting—not just me but maybe you too. I kept telling myself it didn't matter that I wasn't speaking up. Kept thinking things would work themselves out. I'm just so sorry."

He smacked his hands on his lap and looked into the camera. "Anyway! Don't eat any food from that side of the verge. You know that, right? Guess if you've made it this long, you already know that. Apparently you're reading lots of books to this fair feaster, performing stories and things. Have you done *The Three Musketeers* yet? It was one of my favorites as a kid. I'm sending a copy along to you."

He continued, talking of things he had read or watched lately, then said goodbye. True to his word, he had included an old paperback copy of *The Three Musketeers*. I had not in fact performed this one for Nalibak yet, so that made me smile.

I lay back then, pondering age-old hurts. Was I able to become part of a loving family? Would we succeed, after all the habits that had ossified for each of us? My relationship with my aunt and uncle felt like something already past, which perhaps I could mend. But even if I didn't, I would be all right. Javier and Ayda, and Ayda's parents, were still my family, and so were my Quicksand folk, if they welcomed me back.

The biggest question revolved around Vai.

The central activity I did in my spare time for the next several days was rewatch Vai's chantagram and ruminate on it. Because what had *I* sent in my message to them? Rambling about wolves, and then, one more time for good measure, a sentiment like "Anyway, go live your life, don't worry about me." I hadn't said "I love you," though I did love them, *so much*. I hadn't wanted to burden them by saying so. Yet maybe I'd done more harm by withholding the words.

One day, after my fifteenth or so viewing, Nalibak purred from a corner of our barnacle cave, making me jolt and fall over on my mattress.

"This is what has given you such flavor recently? It pours off you when you hear this story. A monsoon of sour and sweet and musk."

I slid the chantagram inside my shirt, where I'd been keeping it. "I *hate* when you appear like that. Humans in general hate it. Have you not figured that out?"

Of course he had. We probably gave off a special spice when we were jump-scared.

Nalibak glided closer. "What gives you such despair? Do you not wish to hear that this person loves you?"

I lay on my side, gazing across the rock floor with its seaweed layer. At least it had dried. Nalibak's darkness spell kept the waves out. "I'm not talking about it with you."

"You don't think it true? That this person loves you?"

"They don't love me anymore, if they ever did," I insisted. "Vai's too smart for that."

"You feel you aren't worthy."

"I *know* I'm not."

"They say they love you. Why do you not believe?"

"People say things like that to console others," I tried to explain.

"Ah. They lie. I lie! Vai is like me, you are saying."

"No!" I said. "Vai is nothing like you."

"But if Vai says they love you, and you believe Vai is smart and does not lie, why do you not believe? The convoluted tortures of your desires, such a twisted snail shell."

I sputtered that Vai was just *mistaken*, that was all, and Nalibak wandered into one of his nonsense rambles and eventually left the lair again.

I curled up and kept arguing in my head. But none of my arguments stuck. In fact, they ended up taking me back and back in time, each of my behaviors and beliefs explained by something that had happened earlier, until I was looking at myself as the six-year-old learning his parents had died.

Tears bathed my eyes, clean and bitter. That child hadn't done anything to deserve this calamity. I wanted to hug him, pick him up and promise he could live with me forever. He did deserve love. But of course that was a long time ago. I'd changed since then.

I followed him to Tesoro, where his aunt and uncle, overburdened and grieving, failed to provide him adequate therapy, and failed also to recognize the needs and quirks of his hyperactive, inattentive brain. Small Leo was confused at the exasperation of his teachers and relatives, but he didn't know any other way to be. I wanted to step in and hide him behind my legs, then turn to those adults and lecture them about what this kid needed from the grown-ups in his life, and how you could not blame *him* for the problems he was having. Naturally that child should have been loved, and deserved the love he did get.

Then teenage Leo, beset with surging hormones: I observed him gravitating to Ayda and defending her, seeing past the disturbing parts of her, recognizing her brilliance, her value. He was completely right that anyone who was rude to Ayda deserved to be punched or at least yelled at. I had always believed that. But that had been because I recognized that *Ayda* deserved love. Only now did I see that teen Leo, with his loyalty and compassion and undauntable laughter, deserved exactly as much love.

Even Leo of less than a year ago, doing all he had done for Vai—sheltering them, cheering them up, helping establish them as a valued member of the troupe, loving them with his whole heart and body—that Leo was someone I mostly appreciated. If he had been someone other than me, I would have understood his actions and even forgiven him.

Was it therefore all right for someone to love him, despite his flaws and mistakes? Could I believe that anyone did?

Yes.

That simple affirmative shook my world, though I still had trouble accepting it.

I was worthy of being loved, and furthermore, it was a cruelty to Vai if I acted like their love was not real, not something I believed in.

The tears were all over my face now. Ever since meeting Vai, I had operated under the assumption that we could never be together for the long run, that obstacles would always stand in our way. Those obstacles had mainly amounted to my inferiority, which I figured would always be present, even if I survived the lair. But if I had been wrong…

I had to survive. I needed to see Vai, open all the honesty valves, find out if we truly wanted to be together.

For possibly the first time in my whole imprisonment, I felt a shining desire to get through this and *thrive*. With it came a pure, cold fear. My mortal life out here on this sea stack, surrounded by fae, was so precarious, and I'd been injured so much already. Everyone's best efforts, including my own—even including Nalibak's—might not see me to the finish line alive.

CHAPTER 35

VAI

It was a week into March, and not only had Melu Ros failed to return yet with the latest on Leo, but the sylph I had charged with finding news on him still hadn't come back either.

Adding to the tension, Daphne phoned and told me she and Hazuki were worried about their friend London. "Charles texted me this morning to ask if I knew where she was," she said. "She hasn't been answering texts."

I wandered down the caravan's corridor. "Is she working undercover for an article, maybe?"

"We wondered. But Hazuki asked someone at the *Mirror* if they'd heard from her, and they said, 'No, and she was supposed to turn in an article this morning. It's not like her.'"

"Who's she investigating lately? Are you thinking someone interfered with her?"

"We feel alarmist to worry about that. She knows what she's doing."

"But," I prompted.

"Last we heard, she was 'following the money' on Walda Portnoff's case."

"And people commit violence over money every day."

"Or over secrets involving money."

Two days later, I saw a brief article about it: "Award-winning journalist missing," with a photo of London. I gazed at her savvy grin, imagining the ache her parents and loved ones must be feeling. Who would know that emotion better than I?

I texted Charles. *I'm troubled to hear about London. I know you two are friends. I'm sorry, you must be worried.*

He didn't answer. I decided if he did respond, and if he was amenable, I'd take the train to Tesoro on my next resting day and treat him to lunch and condolences.

LEO

One day Nalibak returned to the lair with a visitor in tow.

Nalibak *never* invited other visitors. Fair feasters only ever voluntarily spent time with their solitary captives or, occasionally, with another fair feaster. By the slippery, jerky way this person moved, and the uncanny sheen of their faux-human appearance, I knew they belonged to that second category: another fair feaster.

The moment I realized it, I am not ashamed—much—to admit I pissed myself a little. I flung myself backward, slamming against barnacles. My throat went rigid and I could only wheeze.

So this was it. Nalibak was bored of me and was ending it. He didn't dare feast on me himself, in dread of Melu Ros's retaliation, but he'd brought a colleague to do it so he could at least enjoy my slow death at a close distance.

"No," I forced my tongue to say. "Don't. If you..."

Then I saw what the gloom of the lair had initially hidden. The other fair feaster had already brought along a human.

"My friend Tagasath," Nalibak introduced. "She heard of the human I kept, and wished to show me hers. This one also came from your city. It would be so savory if you two suffering ones knew each other!"

"From Tesoro?" I said. "What?"

Tagasath dumped her captive on the ground. The person feebly moved one arm.

I crawled nearer, dragging my injured foot, my heart pounding a racket. Did I actually *hope* this was someone I knew and cared about? Was I wishing so desperately to see a loved one again that I'd welcome them even in these circumstances?

The person had dark shoulder-length curls obscuring their face and neck, and was of short stature. From the unwashed smell, dirt-smeared clothes, and pallidness of what I could see of their skin, they were in even worse shape than me.

"Who is this?" I asked, too fearful to touch them.

"Another human brought her to me." Tagasath had a lower, raspier voice than Nalibak's. "We make deals, from time to time. Her name is London. Her terror and righteous anger, such a robust flavor."

London.

London stirred, whimpering, and waved a hand at me as if to ward me off.

"It's all right," I said. "I won't hurt you. We met once, at Jin Troia Hall. I'm Leo Takahashi. Leonidas."

She rolled onto her back. Her hair tumbled out of her face, revealing bluish lips, fluttering eyelids, and several thin cuts on her neck. Her wrist bore some too. Fair feasters didn't leave fang-puncture marks like vampires in stories. They behaved more like vampire bats, making neat incisions with their sharp teeth or nails and then drinking from them.

I longed to offer healing, but the fair feasters were watching with such palpable delight, chirruping to each other in the fae tongue. What if this was some illusion they had concocted, to ensnare me in a spell?

I had never heard of a fair feaster setting a trap quite like this—with a separate victim as bait. Usually they just cloaked themselves in the appearance of someone appealing. And if they had wanted to torment me with a false image, they surely would have chosen a person I knew well, not someone I had only met once. Nalibak likely didn't even *know* I had met London. The pair of them were possibly just pleased about how horrified I was to see the damage done to another human.

Leo, chastised the responsible piece of my mind. *If you don't believe she's truly a wounded human, you do not have to care about her supposed suffering. If you do believe she's human, you have to help her. Decide.*

Drenched in cold sweat, I laid my hand on London's neck and infused her with as much healing as I could. But my energy was nowhere near full strength, and her enchantment damage was severe. I wasn't as good at detecting maladies as some exo-witches, but I could tell, from how my spell seemed to be falling into a void, that she was unlikely to survive without a whole team of expert healers.

"How hard he tries," Tagasath said, reverting to English. "How desperate. It smells of sweet blood."

"Humans are inconsistent," Nalibak remarked. "Giving their own life to save each other one day, killing each other the next."

"Come on," I murmured to London, channeling energy into her. The sea stack seemed to wobble as I grew dizzy. "Wake up." I transferred one hand from her chest to her head and shifted my magic, aiming to sharpen her mental state.

This was a journalist. Wrote about politics and local events. Much too smart to wander into a fair feaster's clutches. *Another human brought her to me,* Tagasath had said. "Who tricked you?" I asked.

London twisted like she was in a bad dream. "What did you do?" she mumbled. Her eyes were still closed. I doubted she was talking to me. "The others…"

White sparks started flashing in my vision. I would pass out if I kept giving her magic. Panting, I stopped.

"It's my favorite flavor, when they betray one another," Tagasath said.

"The most exquisite," Nalibak agreed. "They do it more than any other creature. More even than the rabbits, who let the predator catch the slowest so the rest may run free."

I looked up at the fair feasters. "Who did this?" It was attempted murder, by someone who didn't want blood on their own hands. Intended to look like a random, tragic fae attack. Like those other deaths by fair feasters in recent years. "Why did they give her to you?"

"One human wants another to stop existing," Tagasath said. "They bring the person to me. I feast. Why must I know more?"

"Who?" I repeated. I tapped London's cheek. "London. Who brought you to the fair feaster?"

"I did not ask his name," Tagasath said. "It does not matter."

I shook London's shoulders gently. "London! Who was the last person you saw? Please. I want to help you. Who betrayed you?"

"Sh…" she began. Worked her dry mouth. Opened her eyes, squinted, then moved her unsteady gaze until finding mine. Her focus sharpened. She gripped my sleeve. "Charles," she said.

VAI

A few days passed. No one had found London. No one had come with any news on Leo. The troupe was in Port Baleia, and I was in the March sun helping the props manager put together movable stair units, when a sylph soared overhead in a violet streak. She dropped to stand near Leo's caravan and peered into a window.

It was the sylph Wayshaw and I had spoken to at the verge, weeks ago. I ran over. My hands were trembling.

"It took some tracking," she told me. I couldn't read from her neutral tone whether the news was good or dreadful. "I had to find a mountain cat faery who would help. Then when we did find the trail, it ended with no one there, and we had to start over. We found another report of a fair feaster with a human captive."

"And?" I was shaking all over now.

"The human has died. We are sorry."

My legs collapsed. I fell to my knees in the grass, gasping.

Maybe it's a different human, my brain screamed. But I walled off that thought. First, I shouldn't wish that on anyone. Second, I had to prepare myself in case it *was* Leo. This always could have been the ending. I knew it from the first night I had seen Leo talking to Nalibak.

"Where is he?" I asked. "The human."

"A friend is bringing the body to the verge," she said. "I came ahead to tell you."

My stomach threatened to revolt. Or I might burst into tears. I couldn't do any of that, not yet. First I had to go there. Reunite with him, in this most terrible of all possible ways.

The sylph offered to carry me to the verge. I didn't have the presence of mind to tell anyone where I was going. I just let her gather me up and fly with me, swift as a falcon, up the forested hill. Third time in a year I was being flown in a rush to the verge. Probably the last, because I'd have no reason to seek news of Leo after this.

Then the time difference. Hours I waited, shaking, blank, nauseated, heartbroken. The sylph stayed above me, resting horizontally between two tree branches, as if doing nothing but feeling the breeze.

I ached for someone to bring me Leo's body. Get it over with. See it, know it as truth, begin to move on with my grieving and then the rest of my hollow life.

The stench walloped me before I even heard the rustle of the other sylph landing near. She lowered a stiff, dirtied corpse to the forest floor. I rose, numb.

I'd only seen a dead person once before. My grandfather, five years ago, after a swift decline following a heart attack. He had passed away in his bed at home. My mother—his daughter—had already called an undertaker to come, and they had prepared him before the rest of us arrived to say goodbye. The visit had been sad but not horrifying. He looked more or less like himself, asleep.

It didn't compare, didn't come anywhere close, to seeing a murdered human on the ground in the woods.

Somehow I stepped closer to look, though my limbs had turned to heavy clay. The person was short, with curly hair. The lifeless hands resting on the ground were small, not the strong-fingered hands I knew so well.

This was a woman. This wasn't Leo at all.

My mind in a complete shambles, I leaned over to see the face turned away from me.

London.

The breath gushed out of me. I staggered backward. Life swept into my soul, the sweetest rush of hope, and immediately I felt like the worst person in the nation—to be *relieved* that a human who had died was not Leo.

"Oh," I choked out. "This is a different person. I know who she is. Not...who I was looking for, but...thank you. For bringing her. People will want to know."

People would want to know. Right. I shuffled into fresher air and sunlight and fumbled out my phone, which I had been resolutely ignoring. I hadn't been able to say anything to anyone until I had proof that Leo was dead.

A few worried messages from troupe friends already waited on my screen. I quickly sent *Sorry, I'm all right, back soon* to each of them. Then I called emergency services and told them what I had found. After that, I called Daphne and told her too.

"Oh," she said. "London...oh no. Vai, are you all right? You're not used to this." As a healer, Daphne had seen her share of gruesome tragedy. "Please drink some water and get yourself to friends who'll look after you, okay? That's a horrible thing to go through." For I had also told her about the dark span of hours there, where I had thought it was Leo.

I promised I would do all that. Then I returned to the sylphs and asked some questions.

What had happened, it seemed, was that the first trail they followed, which dead-ended, probably *was* Nalibak and Leo. That had led up to Pitchstone Mountain, and the mountain-cat faery had learned from some alligator fae in the vicinity that they had regularly seen the pair together. But that pair had recently fled through the night sky, leaving no easy trail to follow. The next lead they found regarding a fair feaster with a captive must have been, upon closer inspection, a different fair feaster and a different human. The human's name had been lost in the rumor mill, and one name starting with L had been close enough to another, in the ears of the inattentive local fae. Fae didn't generally remember things *wrong*, but they could *forget* things they had heard.

It did not, of course, guarantee Leo was still alive. But at least I had no evidence to the contrary.

It all caught up to me then. Death. London. Fair feasters. Leo. The lair. My whole miserable year and a half.

The world spun. Thinking I was surely about to throw up this time, I dropped to my hands and knees. Then everything went into whiteout, and I forgot where I was or what I had been so concerned about.

I opened my eyes to Catarina's kind smile. Trees flickered above her. Voices murmured. "Hello. You fainted," she said. "No wonder, poor darling. Can you take a little water? Wayshaw's managed to get some into you through your skin, but I'd feel better if I saw you drink it."

Piece by piece, in an accelerating deluge, everything came back to me. I sat up, ignoring the mug she pressed toward me. "Is there any news? Leo?"

Maybe they'd found out Leo was *also* dead. Maybe victims of fair feasters were dropping out of the forest like withered plums.

"No," Catarina said. "Nothing. Just poor London. Please drink. I don't want the lawfolk to descend upon you until you've recovered a little. They'd like to take down your statement."

I took the mug and sipped. I was sitting on a towel outside her caravan. Several people in the uniform of the law watched us from across the grass, next to their patrol car. With a sweep of sorrow for those who loved London, I finished the water and handed the mug back to Catarina. "Thanks. I can talk to them now."

CHAPTER 36

LEO

I couldn't eat for at least a day, after seeing London. Before Tagasath scooped her up and left again, I crawled to the two fair feasters and begged.

"Save her. Return her to the verge where she can get help. Please don't let her die. Can I make a deal?"

A reckless offer. I was already spread thin, thanks to the deal I was currently serving out. Still, this was a life-or-death emergency.

They lapped up my pain but waved their limbs apathetically regarding the actual request. "Tempting. But she won't live, not now," Tagasath said. "Likely will die before the next burning dawn."

That seemed true. I had felt London's ebbing life myself. "Then...tell someone, a human, about Charles. You have to. Charles the crosswater from America—go back to the verge, find a human, and tell them..." I babbled a minute or two, stressing all the pertinent details, the reasons it was important to report Charles to the law.

They grew bored. This story was entertaining, yes, but it would provide more delicious angst if Charles were free to keep skulking around and having fellow humans murdered. Fair feasters could not grasp the urgency I felt, any more than Nalibak could ever grasp the ethical or sympathetic points of a play.

I tried to hold on bodily to London, not let her be taken. As if I were strong enough. They took advantage of my dread of their touch—they advanced, and I flinched, and Tagasath easily got her out of my grasp. Then she and London were gone. I sat breathing in shaky sips.

"Tagasath never does leave them alive," Nalibak told me. "Most of my kind don't. I sometimes do. I am an oddity. Isn't that a delight?"

I hunched against the wall, dried mussel shells stabbing my shoulder. "Charles. The little fucker. Why would he do it? How many people has he done this to? *How* did he do it?"

"He summoned Tagasath and made an arrangement with her. She said as much. Why are you shocked? Do your stories not constantly include human betrayers and killers? You call them 'juicy parts.'"

"Roles—those are roles, it's different. How did he trick London into coming along? She'd carry St. John's wort. She's too smart not to."

"He lied to her and overpowered her. Like any worthy predator. Surely he took the dreadful yellow flower off her, after weakening her, so Tagasath could touch her."

That did seem the likeliest scenario. But that meant we were in premeditated, serial-killer territory. Did he use one of the illegal, but available on the black market, charms to knock people unconscious—magical versions of chloroform? Then smuggled her to the verge in the night, and…

It was like with the harpy-goblins, or the whitefingers, but worse. Human murderers existed; we all knew that. Watched movies about it. Ate popcorn during it. But learning you'd met one of them, and having one of their victims dropped at your feet—that flung you into entirely another league of horrified understanding.

"He's out there. With them," I whispered. My loved ones. Who thought him sweet and sort of clueless and essentially trustworthy. He and Vai *texted regularly*. "Please. Let me send word to them, *please*."

But Nalibak had no interest in cooperating. Why should he betray another predator? He was already staying away from my friends as agreed. Our deal said nothing about stopping anyone else from hurting them. I begged and argued for what might have been a whole day, and he ate up my agony but didn't budge.

Eventually it was dusk, or so he reported, and time for him to leave. "Sweet sleep," he sing-songed before flickering out of the lair.

But sleep was no more a possibility for me than food was.

VAI

URGENT. Have you heard from Charles?

The text was from Daphne. Eight days had passed since London had turned up dead. Daphne, Hazuki, and the rest of London's friends—as well as surely her family—were heartbroken. I assumed Charles was, too, but he still hadn't said a word.

No, I typed back, my heartbeat picking up in alarm. *He hasn't answered my messages. Is he missing too?*

Could say that. As of a couple days ago, his number seems to be disconnected. And today the lawfolk called me to ask what I knew about him, because he's wanted for questioning in London's death.

Cold sheeted through me. *What??*

A security camera a few streets from her apartment showed him driving past, with London in his car, the night she was last seen. They just found the footage today.

Fuck, I texted.

I didn't know the man intimately, but...he couldn't have, wouldn't have, didn't have any motive to. Unless we were all very wrong about the kind of person he was.

The lawfolk soon got court permission to use a summoning spell on Charles. It would give him an irresistible urge to bring himself to the downtown law station in Tesoro. After seventy-two hours, which was more than enough time for anyone to catch a train from anywhere on Eidolonia to anywhere else on the island, he still hadn't shown up. They concluded he either had fled the country, had entered the fae realm, was hiding out on Eidolonia with a resistance charm on (enabling him to resist the summoning spell), or was dead.

By now these reports were in the national news, updated daily.

They searched his apartment. It appeared he had packed a few things and left, probably several days prior. His car was still there, the interior scrubbed clean. They found no DNA traces of London nor of much else.

Hacking into his accounts turned up correspondence with Humanist Party members. Also with the two previous victims of fair feasters, from the past couple of years. He had said he knew them a little, I now recalled, and he'd seemed upset about their deaths.

Daphne and I exchanged messages and calls, stammering our unsettled feelings. How had we been so unsuspecting? So arrogant? We'd been sure he posed no threat—we were locals, with magical powers, while Charles was the meek, starry-eyed newcomer. He had acted the part so well.

It was likeliest he had fled back to the United States. There was no record of him leaving Eidolonia, but it wasn't hard to find pilots or boat captains willing to transport you off the island unofficially. The fae, as well as the Eidolonian government, paid far more attention to who *entered* the country, not who left it. If Charles had exiled himself, good riddance. If he'd left without a memory charm, he would never even remember Eidolonia. Already Hazuki was making furious plans to go over there anyway, track him down, and drag him back to face punishment. Just in case the law decided not to bother.

These plans for vigilante justice were interrupted, to my great relief, by Melu Ros's return. Ayda's text said only, *My dad didn't have long to see Leo before Nalibak whisked him off. Said he seemed not too bad, considering. Just "confused."* She added an emoji that I thought was a concerned face.

Were they on Pitchstone Mountain? I asked.

They were. Your sylph's first lead was correct. Now, though, who knows where.

The air-fae courier arrived with Leo's chantagram.

My heart lifted when Leo showed the light string I had sent, sparkling in the obsidian. Decorating his space seemed a sign he might be all right. My worry grew, though, as he embarked on further rambling messages. They were less disjointed than the previous chantagram's but still didn't exactly make sense.

He didn't know who he even was? And he wanted to adopt a wolf?

Other pieces did make sense, but in a way that chilled me. He spoke of loneliness and depression, and how his career as an actor—becoming other people—was the only thing that had kept him alive.

Oh Leo. Please stay alive. I know who you are, even if you don't.

This time he didn't say "I love you." When he'd said it in the previous chantagram, he'd been delirious with illness. Maybe it meant no more than a drunk acquaintance saying it. In this missive, he just smiled and said, "Anyway, Vai—you're amazing. You said you were lonely last time, and I really hope that's not the case anymore. Everyone who meets you should want to make you happy. I want you to be living your life and flourishing. Okay? Please don't worry about me! Take good care." And he kissed his fingertips at the camera, and that was all.

Well. If he did still live, by now he had seen my final chantagram, complete with green skin and wretched love confession. Frustration burned hard inside my chest. Did he really not feel the same anymore? Or was this all acting—telling me what he thought Brave-Captive Leo should say?

"I swear, if he does die, and I never get to find out," I told Catarina at our next teatime, "I will hunt down his ghost and scream at him until he tells me."

"If I were a gambling woman, dear, I'd put a truckload of money on his still loving you. But let's not talk ghosts." She steepled her fingertips, touching them to her chin, a pose she had often taken when directing us in *Moulin Rouge*. "Let's assume he's coming back, alive and sane. What will you want? What will you say to him?"

I almost hated the effervescent hope that burst to life inside me at the notion. But it wasn't like I hadn't thought about it.

I puffed out my cheeks. "If he comes back in sound mind, then I still want to be with him. If that's what he wants. I want him to be truthful about it, I don't want him to say yes out of pity. But we'll also have to talk about how he lied to me—concealed the truth. It wouldn't be healthy to shove that behind us and say, 'It doesn't matter now.'"

"Perfect. Say exactly that. Except, one word: I would suggest *and*, not *but*. 'I want to be with you if you're interested, *and* we need to talk about how you lied to me.'"

My storm of hope and fear settled into a steadier heartbeat. I nodded and picked up my tea again. Then, my mind wandering to Leo's daydreams of a canine friend, I asked, "Do you think I should adopt a puppy?"

She didn't even hesitate. "Only if I can come with you and cuddle all the contenders."

CHAPTER 37

LEO

What went wrong for me next, to the best of my knowledge, happened this way.

Unable to eat, sleep, or shake my terror surrounding Charles and fair feasters, I had an atrocious night. Vomiting isn't pleasant at any time, but it turns out it's even more miserable when you're alone, you're terrified, you can barely walk because your foot is injured, and your latrine is a jagged, narrow hole in a rock, opening over a wet ledge that the high tide washes twice a day.

I had threatened Charles, at Jin Troia Hall. I had fucking *threatened a serial killer*. He undoubtedly was looking to take vengeance. He would stalk Vai or somebody else I cared about. Any night now, Tagasath would return and dump someone I loved into my arms, dead.

I blearily got out the herbs Ayda had sent and chose one: not a drug for nausea, but for inducing calm, since the root of my problem was anxiety. Nausea was just a symptom. These herbs came in the form of sticky little chewable bars. I ate one. But it's possible I actually ate two, stuck together, which I mistook as one. It's definitely true that the directions said to eat them with food, not on an empty stomach. Well—I would have food in a bit, when I felt calmer.

Then time stretched out like taffy, and my pains melted. I lay on my back, staring in wonder at my emotions, which were colors bouncing and rippling around the inside of the cave like the aurora borealis.

Light. That was what I needed. Now I understood. Seasonal affective disorder had been destroying me. The darkness had already killed London. It was going to kill all of us.

At some point I likely started mumbling, or yelling, these revelations. Because then a new light glimmered, aqua-green with flickers of white. Someone crawled into view. A human, naked and shining wet, with curly hair and shimmering eyes.

"London?" I whispered.

Couldn't be sure. I'd only seen London once when she was in good health, and that was nearly a year ago. She probably hadn't looked like herself anymore after Tagasath captured her. But if it turned out she had gotten healed and had come back to reassure me…

"Hello." Her melodious voice echoed in the sea cave. "Are you well?"

I sat up, planting my hands at my sides. We were rocking back and forth in the ocean. Our sea stack was a ship, plowing through waves. "I've been worried sick about you," I told her. "Are *you* all right?"

"Of course. Spring is in the wind, in the seaweed. Why were you calling out?"

"Oh, I… Light. All this dark is making me crazy. We're humans, we need light, you know? We need to be with each other, in the sun."

"Is that all you'd like? To be in the sun?"

"Gods, yes. Nalibak never lets me out in daylight." I stretched a hand toward the gorgeous water-shimmer surrounding her. I could smell it, the warmth of sunlight on the ocean. Nalibak's barrier never let in this much fresh air. Thank the gods London had been able to crack through it.

"I'll help you," she said. "Take my hand."

I'd touched her before, and it hadn't hurt me. When I took her hand I laughed, because it felt like Wayshaw's: smooth and cool, with webbed skin between her fingers. London must be part fae. Lots of people were. Crawling awkwardly, I let her guide me through the stinging edge of the lair. Then—

Sunlight. So much light I had to squeeze my eyes shut, and they still welled with tears that trickled down my face. The golden-red glow permeated through my eyelids. Life-giving air wrapped around me, full of daylight. Nighttime air had a different texture, and it was all I'd felt for almost a year.

London patted my hand. "Better! Yes?"

My tears were flowing from happiness now, not only from light-sensitivity. I opened my eyes a sliver and got bombarded with so much brightness I still couldn't see a thing. I blinked and blinked, opening them farther.

"Yes," she encouraged. "Look, look!"

Finally there was the world. In daylight. The brilliant sun hung above the horizon, scattering gold across the rippling ocean. Seals poked their heads out of the water. Fish jumped. Gulls swirled and shrieked.

I was laughing and sobbing. I stretched out my arms to let my cave-pale skin soak in the light.

She tugged on my elbow. "Do you want to swim? Swim with us."

Something about the "us" clanged a warning bell in my head. I looked at her again.

This person had silvery, reflective eyes—like Wayshaw's—and her curls went halfway down her back. London's hair had only reached her shoulders. Hadn't it? And wasn't this person leaner and more angular than London? Also...how *had* she cracked Nalibak's veil and gotten in? Or gotten me out?

My emotion auroras stained the sky with neon violet. I scooted back, almost toppling into the water. "Don't touch me!"

"As you wish." She pulled her hand away.

But the harm had been done. She might have already enspelled me. Was she a fair feaster? Was all of this a hallucination?

"What are you?" I demanded. "Where are we?"

"We're in the sun, as you insisted. I'm of the merfolk. What else would I be?"

Not London. London was probably dead after all.

"Don't touch me," I repeated. "Stay back."

"Staying back." She sounded amused. "Not going to swim with us, then?"

"No! Get away." I should be with Nalibak. Where was he? Now I knew I was insane—wanting Nalibak's company rather than an unknown merperson's. I *lived* with a merperson, back home. Granted, as Wayshaw herself had told me, not all merfolk could be trusted.

"Call for me if you wish. Enjoy the sun." With a graceful flip, she was off the rock and into the ocean, legs becoming tail in a ripple of sunbeams.

Breathing hard, I stared at my hands, then the bouncing waves, then the sea stacks. Was any of it real? I wanted the sun so badly to be real.

I stared it down, heartbeat after heartbeat, watching my emotions warp around it in a searing kaleidoscope. If I stared long enough, I would see through the spell, as I'd seen through the fake London. My eyes were stinging, watering. I kept my gaze fastened on the sun's glare. Its colors were shifting, flashing from red to black and sometimes electric blue. When would I know if it was real?

Blackness swooped over me. Icy claws gripped me under the arms and yanked me backward. I landed on my bed, the breath shocked out of me.

"Sunstruck mortal brain," Nalibak snarled. "To trust a meddling, slimy merperson. Every place I take you, you seek to die."

I couldn't see a thing except smeary colors like paint splotches. "Where's my light?"

"Collect your things. If the merfolk are getting in, we do not stay."

Pawing at my jacket, I found the penlight but still only saw splotches. "Is it on?" I lifted my face toward the sounds of Nalibak's movements. "Are you glowing? Please glow or something. I can't see."

"Your light glows, I glow, you are mad, collect your things."

Now a new glow: but only the yellow-white of my panic, shuddering across my vision. "I can't see."

"Then take your possessions without seeing, for we leave."

Hyperventilating, I felt around, grabbing things. "Wait! It's—is it daytime? Was that actually daylight?"

"Yes, day, you were sunstruck."

"But how can we travel in the day?"

"The shadows. The way I returned here just now. They go beneath this rock in caves, under the sea, all the way to the shore." Then he paused and added, "I cannot take *you* that way, though. Too narrow, the passages, and full of water."

As if I needed something new to panic about. "Then—"

"Come," he snapped. "We leave."

"I can't see," I repeated helplessly, even as I groped around and stuffed things into my pack. My mind was still reeling. London—intruder in the lair—Charles—Ayda's herbs—enchantment damage—

Nalibak grabbed me, declaring I'd collected "enough." Then it felt like I was being wrapped in a cold silk bag, and off we flew. A few breaths of ocean air, then it warmed and turned earthier, branches scratched my hands, and we landed abruptly.

A circular patch of darkness stayed at the center of my focus. Around it was muddled color. Something unsettling tugged at my mind about Nalibak saying the sunlight had been real.

But my eyes were too tired to keep open. All of me was wilting like a cut wildflower. Nalibak was grumbling, asking how was I going to entertain him when I had taken leave of my mind and my health. I had no energy to answer. There was nothing in the world but sleep.

When I crawled back into consciousness, I was so hungry I felt feral. Blinking and cleaning my eyes with my knuckles didn't clear the haze of washed-out colors that covered everything. I patted my hands around. Packed dirt. Stubbly vegetation. The smell of earth and greenery.

"Awake finally?" Nalibak inquired.

My hands met my pack. The compartment where I kept food was already open. Likely I hadn't zipped it all the way shut before being hauled off. It occurred to me that creatures might have crawled into it and stolen things, as I wasn't sure the pack's protective enchantments worked if the compartments were open—and the enchantments didn't seem to work on all creatures. But, ravenous enough to take the chance, I plunged a hand in and found, to my relief, no nest of rodents, but instead a protein bar. My water bottle was still with me as well, thank all the gods. I did nothing but scarf down the bar and guzzle water for a minute.

"So," I said, feeling steadier, "tell me if this sounds accurate. I had anxiety about Charles and London, which made me sick. I took too much of one of Ayda's medicines, which made me hallucinate. Then a merperson got in and put a spell on me that got me truly fucked up."

"A temporary spell." He sounded bored. "To make you obsessed with your interest of choice. You chose the sun. Unfathomably."

"Then I stared at the sun because I had to know if it was real. Which it was. Which is why I'm now functionally blind."

"Accurate, yes. Is it a tragedy, this story?"

I spread my hands over my eyes. "No, I actually think it'd be hilarious, if Quicksand told it." If it weren't happening to me in real life. I dug into my pack again and found some of the packets and bottles Ayda had sent. I held them out toward Nalibak. "Can you see what each of these says, please?"

"I cannot read. Is your mind so gouged that you forgot?"

Of course, Nalibak couldn't read. I started laughing hopelessly. "We were so stupid. Planning for my coming here. We knew it'd be dark, so we made sure I had *lights*. Undying lights. But we never thought about what I'd do if I couldn't *see*. Should've marked everything with enchanted audio tags. Or braille. Should've learned braille ahead of time. Oh, yeah, this is a comedy. No question."

"You will perform a comedy tonight?"

"Friend, all I can perform now is stuff from memory. Because *I* cannot read anymore either. This light is on? Really?"

We verified I indeed could not see anything, except a bit of extra glow where my clip-on light was. Hilarious. I was such an idiot.

I also asked how the merperson got in, and Nalibak grumped that the ocean contained so many types of "horrid fae" with unpredictable powers that one could never really be safe there. The fae realm on the land side didn't seem much safer from my perspective, but that was immaterial.

I learned we were quite close to where Nalibak had taken me away last year. A lair amid blackberry bushes, which he'd used at that time. "Where your beloved friend searched for you and failed to find you," he added. "A blackberry faery screeched this information at me while you slept."

So Vai had been right here, looking for me. They'd gotten their enchantment damage from some faery close by, most likely. I desperately hoped they were still safe and well.

After further groping around, demanding that Nalibak help me, I determined I was missing lots of items. Fallen out on the journey across the sea, probably. Nalibak had wrapped us in a shadow to fly us through the sunlight—something fair feasters could do if they had to, but hated doing.

What I had lost, as far as I could tell, going by memory:

All the lights except the penlight I wore.

My two ebook readers full of stories.

My shoes.

All the clothes I wasn't already wearing, except one set of long underwear.

My blank chantagrams.

My pillow and sleeping bag.

My hairbrush.

My skin-cleaning products.

The magic-enhanced charger to keep my tech alive.

A lot of my food and nearly all my first aid supplies.

The chantagrams I'd preloaded with videos, as well as the chantagrams from my friends. All of them. *All of them.* I retained only the one from Vai that I had tucked inside my shirt, for which I was grateful, but tears filled my eyes at the realization that all the others were gone, probably forever.

In fact, it would be shorter to list what I did still have.

My mouth-cleaning dental mints.

My mattress.

The clothes I was wearing: socks, jeans, sweater, jacket, and underclothes of thin silk.

My laundry-soap wafers.

Several packets of Ayda's herbs, which, after recent events, I did not dare consume, since I couldn't read the instructions.

My items of iron—two thin chains and the velvet-over-iron choker, which I was already wearing.

My water bottle with the enchanted galangal root.

One tin of pecans and dried cranberries, two packets of freeze-dried meals, one paper-wrapped chunk of chocolate that had been wedged deep in a corner of my pack, and two protein bars.

My hands were tingling with numb panic. "I need to know what day it is. How much longer I'll be here."

"Always you ask this. It's so uninteresting."

"I could starve," I shouted. "I dropped most of my food, or something stole it—"

"Raccoon fae, I surmise. I smell them about. Don't you smell them? With their crafty little hands—"

"I can't eat fae-realm food," I cut in, still yelling. "Look what happens when I just get *touched* by a faery. And that's with all my protective spells." I flapped my fingers toward my tattoos and clothing.

"That is true. Without those, the merfolk spell might still be upon you. You might be composing poems of love about the awful sun."

I cradled my face in my hands. To have only just found my desire to live—to warn everyone about Charles, to tell Vai I loved them, to promise all my friends I was going to do better for myself and for them—and now to have the very means of life stripped away…

Going by traditional story beats, we had once again veered out of comedy and into tragedy.

"Please." I spoke into my hands. "Nalibak, please help me." I uncovered my face and sat up on my knees, though all I could see was a patchwork of fuzzy tints. "You agreed to keep me alive, and you've honored your word. You've been the main reason I've stayed safe all this time. You could have hurt or killed me, but you haven't. I'm grateful—sincerely. And I need your help if I'm going to survive to the end of this deal."

All was quiet except for the dry sliding noises, like windchimes made of bone, that usually indicated Nalibak was thinking.

"You do need me." His tone was bemused. "You *are* grateful. You, I think, do not lie. You are like a victim when I enthrall them, and they stay and cling to me. It is…new, for you. You have never tasted like this. But I have not enthralled you."

"I believe you. But I truly might not live unless you help me."

"It isn't as interesting as I hoped." Now he sounded grumpy. "We like it, yes, having our victims cling and need. But we do it only because they would run away if they did not wear the thrall. On you…I have liked your contrariness better. Your sours and bitters, oh so many of them."

Even in my panic, I could recognize this connection between us as a remarkable moment. I acknowledged it with a pause. "Well. I'll have a lot more contrary moods, in all the flavors, if I get to live longer."

More clicks. A rustle of dry leaves. "We will ask what the day is."

According to a fox faery in the forest, Lady Festival had just ended. It was therefore early May. I only had to make it to the twenty-seventh. My food might stretch me that far, but only if one night here equaled one or more nights in the human realm. Never a calculus you could rely on.

Nalibak, grouchy, told me he would allow an unprecedented deal with another faery to go out and fetch me human-realm food, but only once I was about to run out of my current supply.

In blindness, I told, sang, or invented stories. Though it kept me in a constant state of worry, to reach out without knowing what I might touch, I learned to move around by feel and sound and smell. Still, I often stumbled and hurt myself. Wary of using up my food, I frequently skipped eating rather than erring on the side of eating too much. I grew weak, dizzy. One of my worse injuries from falling, a cut on my knee, began to feel hot. Nalibak complained my stories were suffering in quality, but he still went out and refilled my water bottle for me.

Why was Charles killing people?, I asked him repeatedly. Had he killed anyone else? Did my aunt and uncle ever really love me? Did Vai still love me?

What will you tell people my last words were? Can you say they were something clever, please? No, something peaceful. No, something loving. Tell them I'm sorry, and I love them, and do you think I'll be a ghost? Do you think I'll be able to tell them myself?

Ghosts do sometimes narrate stories, you know.

I don't want water. No. I don't need food. Don't touch me. Do not. I just need to rest. If I'm gone when they come to get me, you'll tell them?

CHAPTER 38

VAI

I kept as busy as I could to avoid losing my mind during the last quarter of Leo's absence.

Charles was all over the news. Lawfolk arrested Humanist Party members, who chose to give damning testimony of Charles's activities in exchange for a gentler sentence in their own crimes.

Money and power. From what these people said, those had been Charles's motives, unoriginal though they were. While playing the newcomer naïve about Eidolonian politics, Charles had gotten in deep with the Humanist Party. He might even have met them via my father and uncle.

That led to one scrap of comfort: the law questioned Dad and Uncle Joe as part of their investigation, and found they'd had no knowledge of Charles's deals with the fair feaster, nor that he'd had any connection at all with those deaths. Uncle Joe sent Daphne a message expressing his horror and condemning Charles for deceiving our family. *He seemed such a nice kid.*

Joe and Dad still didn't send me any messages. But it was somewhat reassuring to know we were on the same page regarding Charles.

The Humanist Party had charmed Charles with its promises to do right by ordinary nonmagical humans, and made use of his knowledge of the United States and its banking system to help acquire bribes—such as property in, and money stolen from, America. He of course had been allowed to take a cut.

The killings, the deals with the fair feaster, didn't start till later.

The first victim worked in finance and had begun to notice a strange pattern of transactions, in accounts Charles could access via his job. She called him to ask about it. He played clueless, then hung up and, in a panic, asked his Humanist Party contact what to do. He would be caught, they would all be caught, the whole scheme would unravel—

Unless this finance worker happened to disappear. Taken by fae, for instance. Tragic thing, but always a risk.

"What really horrifies me," Daphne said in one of our calls, "is that I think I gave him the idea. Of using fair feasters. Once, when I was out with him, we ran into Leo and Ayda. I was treating Ayda at the time for her enchantment damage. Charles was terrified at the idea of fair feasters. He asked so many questions. We told him everything we knew. Trying to *soothe* him."

"He would have learned about them before long anyway," I assured. "Everyone does, living here."

"Still." After a moment, she huffed a laugh. "He must also have taken interest in Leo that day, at least a little. Or in any case used him as an excuse to ask me out. Because Charles was the one who first suggested we go see a Quicksand show. Remember? All those years ago. You came along."

The first time I'd been to see the troupe. Starting a tradition of seeing them every time they came to town, because whether or not Charles had been riveted by Leo, I definitely and instantly had been.

"I suppose I have to be grateful for that," I said.

Her voice hardened. "No, you don't. He was just making dates to keep hanging around our family."

Then the same with the second victim—the one London had been scheduled to interview, who had disappeared before she could talk to him. That person, too, had been on the cusp of uncovering the money trail that incriminated Charles. The difference with London's own murder was that Charles must have realized, perhaps after abducting her, that he was going to get caught anyway. More of Portnoff's accomplices were getting arrested. Any day now, they'd find one of the few who knew about Charles's crimes. A single truth spell, administered by the law, would be all it'd take. The noose was tightening.

So he had fled. Most people figured he'd gone crosswater, with second-likeliest scenario being "dead in the fae realm." Lawfolk had sent out wild-dog fae to track him, in case he was still on the island, but none had picked up a trail. There were of course charms one could use to cloak oneself against that kind of tracking, and he had probably used them, if he *was* still in the country. But I didn't want to give him any more thought than necessary.

Much more pleasant to focus on was my new puppy. Her name was Truffle. She was five months old and fifteen pounds, so wasn't likely to weigh more than twenty-five or thirty by the time she finished growing—a manageable size for caravan living. Gods only knew what her mix of breeds was. She was black; with white feet, belly, and nose blaze; tall ears; long snout and legs; and a skinny tail that looped off to the left. She adored playing tug with an old sock or anything else I allowed her to bite, and sleeping like a furry log against my side. I adored her and stoutly believed that no animal in the world had ever been cuter. And now at least I had someone keeping me company on my haunted nights.

April crept by. Blossoms bloomed so exuberantly that I was sure the flower fae were mocking me. May finally arrived, and each day slogged even slower.

We reached Tesoro. I visited my mother and sister, and Ayda and Javier. I trained the puppy. I fixed costumes and props. In the eyes and tense lips of the troupe members, I saw the same preoccupation I felt. We drove onward, as scheduled, from Tesoro to Punta Rosa, then Punta Rosa to Sevinee.

Finally it was the twenty-seventh—a midnight and then a dawn I saw with my own sleepless eyes, sitting in the caravan with the dog in my lap. Melu Ros loped off into the fae realm to find and bring back Leo.

Then, of course, *more* waiting. Each day, I exchanged texts with Javier and Ayda, and remarks with troupe friends. Nearly all the exchanges were lighthearted—jokes, memes, puppy pictures, self-deprecating anecdotes about how scatterbrained we felt. Wayshaw declared that if ten days went by without news, she would go into the fae realm to learn what she could.

If we had gone those ten days or longer, I would have stormed into the fae realm myself, despite how terribly it had gone last time. But after six days, a phone buzz early in the morning woke me. As I grabbed it, it buzzed again, then again. Three messages from Ayda:

HE IS BACK. He is alive.

Not sure yet in what condition. He's unconscious and seems malnourished and probably with injuries/infections. My dad healed him the best he could, but he needs more care. He's at the hospital. J and I are on our way there now. Come when you can!

Sorry which hospital!! Useful to know right? Gladheart in Bahía Rosa.

I was out of bed so fast, feet on the floor, that Truffle was startled into a spate of barking. It was 5:50 a.m., a June morning already bright with sun.

The next fifteen minutes were pandemonium. Wayshaw was just returning to the caravan—thank the Lady, as I didn't dare leave without her, but also would have gone mad if I had to wait. The rest of the troupe, hearing the news, clustered around in excitement. They made plans as to who could come to Bahía Rosa today and who would stay in Sevinee to keep performances running. The show must go on. Leo would agree.

Catarina grabbed an overnight bag and jumped into our caravan to ride with us. I didn't even register who else was coming in other vehicles. Wayshaw started the caravan and we were off.

It was only about an hour to Bahía Rosa. The three of us (four, counting Truffle on her leash) reached the hospital at the same time as Javier and Ayda, who had come south from Tesoro. Melu Ros was already there, having been the one to bring Leo in.

The hospital staff told us they needed more time assessing Leo, without the distraction of visitors, but as soon as they had him in stabler condition, they would let us in. "We've gotten him conscious again," one healer told us, "but he's still experiencing a lot of confusion. That's normal for what he's been through."

This didn't slow my racing heart. I had feared, all the way here, that I might find a Leo whose mind, as we had known it, was gone forever. I was about to crawl out of my skin, knowing he was in the next room and I wasn't allowed to go to him yet. The others surely felt the same. But all we could do was sit in waiting room chairs and look to Melu Ros for more details.

In his beard, threadbare T-shirt, and lumberjack jeans, he set his elbows on his knees and told us, in his oddly lovely voice, how the mission had gone.

Entering the lair, Melu Ros had been met with an alarming sight: Leo unconscious and ashen, and Nalibak lying with his body curled around Leo's torso. Roaring, Melu Ros had bounded forward. He had Nalibak flattened to the ground in seconds, huge paw clutching his throat and chest.

"I was not feeding on him!" Nalibak snarled. "I was healing him."

"You lie. Always. You were killing him!"

"He would not wake for three nights and days. I sent a monkey faery to get human-realm food, but still they have not returned. I did not wish *you* to torment me for endless years because he died in my lair. Therefore I touched him. Only to give energy, not to drink it—yes, I can do that. Only to keep him alive. See for yourself."

Since Leo did appear to be alive and, in Melu Ros's examination, apparently neither enthralled nor injured by Nalibak, Melu Ros huffed an uncertain thanks and picked Leo up. Leo still wore the velvet-wrapped iron choker, so Nalibak couldn't have drunk from his neck even if he'd intended to. But the rest of Leo was unmarked too, free of cuts from Nalibak's teeth or nails.

Nalibak approached as Melu Ros shouldered Leo's bags. "He entertained me well," Nalibak said softly. "He fulfilled the deal. He thanked me. I could have let him die, the year was over anyway. But…I did not want that."

According to Melu Ros, Nalibak sounded puzzled. The fair feaster shuffled closer to peer at Leo's face. "I do not want you to die," he told Leo. "Isn't that strange?"

That had been their goodbye. Leo surely didn't hear the words. Then Melu Ros whisked him away, leaving Nalibak to roam the island through paths of shadows, to lure and feed upon living beings for countless years to come.

Just not any of us.

After a span of silence, Ayda said, "We're free of him. We really, finally are." Her voice caught, and she wiped her eyes. Javier leaned over to hug her.

Then a healer emerged. "We could use the help of people he knows, after all, it appears."

Our whole group got up and crowded into the room.

It would have taken me half a minute or more to recognize Leo, if I hadn't known he was the one in the hospital bed. Beard to his neck. Thinning, graying hair. Sunken eyes that darted around, paranoid. Gangly limbs, too skinny, drawn up so he was huddled in a ball amid rumpled sheets. One knee had a thick white bandage around it.

They'd gotten him into a hospital gown and bathed him, from the look of it, but that was presumably while he'd been unconscious. Now four members of hospital staff stood just out of striking distance, hands out as if ready to stop him from bolting or fighting. Things lay scattered on the floor: pillow, blanket, bandages, tipped-over bottles, tray.

"Leo?" Ayda said. "Hey. It's us. You're back in the human realm. In the hospital, to get healed up."

Leo's gaze flicked toward her but didn't seem to focus. "I don't know what's real."

His voice. I breathed silent thanks to the gods. Despite all that had ravaged him, his voice was still his. Unsteady, panicked, but without a doubt Leo's, resonant and expressive.

"I know," Ayda said. "It's confusing, when you first get back."

"I can't see," Leo said. "There's no way I can see who you are, and even if I could..."

"You can't see?" Javier demanded. "Why not?"

Leo blinked. "Javier?"

"Obviously. Are you gonna let us near you to heal your eyes or what?"

"We have some enspelled bandages we'd like to try," one of the healers put in. "But he, ah...hasn't quite been ready to let us put them on."

I couldn't speak. A thousand questions jammed my throat. As if sensing my turmoil, Truffle whined, by my feet.

"The hell was that?" Leo asked.

"Vai's dog," Catarina said. "They got an adorable puppy. Hi, Leo. It's Catarina. Vai and Wayshaw and I are here too."

"Vai didn't have a dog," Leo said. "See, this isn't real."

I recovered my voice. "I just got her. She...likes living in your caravan. I'm sorry about the dog hair. I'm doing my best to keep it cleaned up."

Everyone else chuckled—nervously—but Leo just mumbled, "There's no way to know what's real. I got blinded when I thought the sun *wasn't* real, and..."

"You got blinded from staring at the sun?" Javier said. "Seriously?"

A tiny smile flitted across Leo's face. "That *is* the tone Javi would use."

"Fine, say we all walk out of here and leave you," Javier retorted. "Free to do what you want. Where you gonna go? When you can't even see."

For a second Leo didn't answer, only hugged his knees tighter. "Fair question."

"I promise you're safe," Wayshaw said. "You know I can't lie."

"All of your voices sound real." Leo's toes, bruised and scratched, curled in the disarrayed bedsheet. "But my chantagrams. They got all of them. They could have stolen your voices from those."

"We're really here," I said. "How about this. We'll put the bandage near you, and you can put it on your eyes yourself. When you're ready."

"At worst," the healer added, "the bandage won't do anything. This is just our first attempt. If it doesn't fix your vision, we'll try something else. But your friends are right. You're safe."

"I just don't want to get it wrong again," Leo said.

"Leo," Melu Ros said. "You trusted me all these months. I've healed you several times, I brought you out of the lair, and I won't let anything happen to you. If you trust anyone, you trust me, right?"

Leo rocked backward and forward. "How do I know it's really over?"

Melu Ros walked up, took the bandage, and set it on Leo's bed. "There. The bandage is by your ankle. Put it on your eyes."

It felt like a full minute passed, all of us doing our best to be unthreatening presences. Leo finally crept a hand out and touched it. Then, with a sigh, he pulled it toward himself and placed it over his eyes. "I just hold it here?"

"You can tie it," the nearest healer said. "They have strips of gauze attached for that."

Leo felt along the strips, then tied them around his head like a blindfold.

Only then did hope blossom in me. His behavior hadn't been that of someone who had permanently lost their sanity. He had moved, in a few minutes, through the natural human progression from panicking to wary questioning to grouchy resignation.

I had hardly behaved any better after returning from merely one night in the fae realm. For someone who'd spent roughly a year there, in near-complete darkness and with a maddening fae companion, Leo was faring remarkably well.

Tears blurred my vision. Even if I never again got to be closer to him than this, even if he decided against a relationship, he was alive, he was home, and he would recover. For today, that was enough.

"This is probably another dream of mine," Leo said, sounding almost petulant, "but just in case any of you can receive messages in *your* dreams, I need to tell you to have Charles the crosswater arrested. He's killed people. Handed them over to fair feasters."

"Oh, we know." Spite sharpened Ayda's voice. "Evil fucker."

"The whole country knows," one of the healers said. "We tried to tell you, when you were talking about him earlier."

"He's in hiding," Wayshaw said. "Probably fled the island. Hasn't hurt anyone since, as far as we know."

"I saw London," Leo insisted. "The fair feaster, the one Charles gives them to, she brought her. Just to—to traumatize me. London was barely alive, but… she told me it was Charles who betrayed her."

"Eyewitness account," Catarina said. "That will be extremely helpful, Leo."

"I didn't save her, though." Leo's voice fell in sadness. "I couldn't. Nalibak said she'd die. I suppose she must have."

I kept my mouth shut. This wasn't the time to describe the day I'd seen London's body brought out of the woods. Some of the others glanced at me. But Ayda only said, gently, "Yeah. She did."

"Charles and Vai texted each other." Leo ran his fingers along the gauze above his ear. "I'm so scared he'll go after Vai next. Or someone else I know."

"He hasn't," I assured. "I'm fine. But Daphne and I are horrified that we were friends with him."

"Lord and Lady. Why was he killing people?"

"Oh, that's easy," Javier said. "Money. Influence. Power. Why else?"

"He got in with the Humanist Party," Wayshaw said. "They made use of him. Including his willingness to dispose of people who found out about their illegal activities."

"That's such a stupid reason. But I guess no stupider than most villains." Leo gingerly touched the bandages on his eyes. "These feel nice. Soothing."

"See?" a healer said cheerfully. "Not making things any worse."

Ayda knelt to pick up the knocked-over items. "You really went berserk, didn't you. I'm just tidying up. I won't touch you if you're not ready."

"Ah, Ayda. It was worth it, to do this for you. Even with all the damage I took. I have no regrets."

Drawing a shaky sigh, she set the items on the bedside table, then cleared her throat. "I still wish you hadn't. And at the same time I'm so grateful, and relieved it's all over. *And* you can't do anything like that ever again, all right? Not for anyone."

"Agreed," I said, as did several others.

Truffle wandered forward to investigate what was under Leo's bed. I moved forward, knelt, and pulled her back. "Truffle. We're not getting under there."

"Vai?" Leo said. "Did you say 'Truffle'?"

"It's my puppy's name." I stayed in a crouch, within touching distance of his foot, my heart pounding.

"Of course Vai would choose a fancy food name," he mused.

"I do like both the mushroom and the chocolate variety of truffle," I said. Why? Why were we discussing this, now?

He turned his face toward me and breathed in. "You smell like Vai." He sounded softly amazed. "Their perfume. I haven't smelled that in…such a long time. I loved it. It was imported from France, I saw the bottle. Expensive stuff. Vai's rich."

"Used to be rich," I corrected. "I still have a couple of accounts, and the Mercedes, but these days I'm just living in a caravan and doing manual labor for an obnoxious theatre troupe."

He gave a startled laugh. "A joke? Nalibak never jokes. He doesn't know how."

"We are not Nalibak," Melu Ros grumbled. "I'm insulted you could even consider the idea."

"A hallucination or a dream is likelier," Leo conceded. "Though…those didn't include smells. Not smells from home, like this."

"Here, wait." I handed Truffle's leash to Catarina, then retrieved the cloth shopping bag I had left by the door. "I brought you some things from the caravan. Here, dark-roast coffee, your favorite. Smell."

Leo slowly reached out. I set the foil bag in his palm, my hand still not touching his.

He felt to the top of the bag, unrolled it, and sniffed. "Coffee! I've missed coffee so much. I lost most of my food…weeks ago, maybe more. This smells incredible."

Encouraged, I pulled out a small jar. "This is your moisturizer, the kind you used after taking off makeup. It doesn't have much scent, but…"

He set the coffee down, accepted the container, unscrewed the lid, and sniffed. "Ahh." He dipped a fingertip into the moisturizer and rubbed it on the back of his hand. "I should have brought some of this along. My skin got so irritated. Remind me to tell you about the splinters."

"I can live without hearing about the splinters," Javier contributed.

"And, here." I set a rolled-up sweater next to his foot, where he'd feel it. "It's your red-and-black sweater. It's been in your closet, so it probably smells like the caravan."

Leo gathered up the sweater, pressing it to his nose. "It does," he said in wonder. "Oh my gods. It does." Tenderness cracked his voice. He shook the sweater loose and felt along each arm. "It has the little hole in the left arm and everything. This really is my sweater. This all really…" Suddenly he reached out, patting the edge of the mattress. "Where's your hand? Vai, give me your hand."

I sat up on my knees and placed my hand in his.

His palm was damp with sweat, his grip tight. He felt between my knuckles. "No webbed fingers," he said. "You're not a merperson, at least. You're warm. You feel like Vai."

"So you've decided we're real?"

"I've decided," he said, that tenderness now pouring strong through the crack in his voice, "that if this is a dream or a hallucination, I want to stay in it."

We twined our fingers together. "Good," I said, my voice unsteady. "Welcome back."

Everything returned to my mind in a rush then: how the last message he'd seen from me was my drunken ramble, revealing my fae-realm enchantment, confessing I loved him. And how the last time we'd seen each other in person, I'd clung to him in tears and insisted he bring me into the lair with him.

"Um," I began.

Leo had perhaps just put all that together too. "Vai." He spoke my name sweetly, at least, and kept his fingers tangled in mine.

"Everyone else wants to greet you," I hastened to say, my ears hot. I refused to have this conversation—however it turned out—with an audience of some nine other people.

Leo lifted his face, startled, then beamed. "Right! Oh my gods, you're all actually here?"

"Yeah," Javier said, annoyed. "Do we get to hug you now or what?"

I gave Leo's hand a squeeze—he squeezed back—then I let go and moved aside to let his loved ones crowd in.

CHAPTER 39

LEO

When I had meandered out of unconsciousness and found I was being touched by multiple sets of hands or paws, yeah, I freaked right out. What fae haunt had snatched me away? How had Nalibak allowed it to happen? Or maybe he *had* allowed it because my year had expired while I was asleep, and I was no longer his responsibility.

Thus the flailing. The yelling. The crashing and chaos. The refusal to let anyone near. I was taking it *seriously*, people, this new ethos of treating myself with love and care.

But the intriguing details trickled in and piled up. My reasonable self pointed to them, eyebrows raised, waiting for me to notice. Eventually my despairing self grew exhausted from freaking out, leaned on the reasonable one's shoulder, and fell quiet. And paid attention.

The mattress beneath me was soft and clean. The sheets, and the garment someone had put on me, felt and smelled like crisp human-realm cotton, not the cave-air-drenched wool or denim or silk I had worn all the time lately. What I heard wasn't fae songs or dripping rain, but voices speaking English, backed by the beeps and buzzes of technology. Nothing smelled like dirt or moss or blackberry vines. Whatever had been used to wash me had left a lemony scent. The air smelled scrubbed clean in a way that was familiar and domestic.

Only within the last minute had I stopped fending everyone off with dedicated violence. Listening, taking in the words, I realized new people had entered. And if they really were who they sounded like they were…

I did *not* want to make another "staring at the sun" mistake. So I stalled. But the details stacked up, and my senses grew clearer—all but my vision, swathed in bandages.

Those bandages took a dampening of tears as I finally, fully realized I was holding Vai's hand. Surrounded by friends. In the human realm. It wasn't a dream, or at least was about ninety-eight percent certain not to be.

Thank gods they had washed me with lemony stuff. I didn't wish to know how my clothing and skin had looked and smelled when Melu Ros first brought me in, and I definitely didn't wish Vai to know.

Vai and I then stuttered to a halt. What to say? If this were a play, a romantic comedy, it would take just a few lines each.

I've missed you! I'm so sorry for everything. I still love you, if you'll have me.

I love you too. Of course, all is forgiven. Come to my arms.

First, however, we weren't about to act that out in front of everyone. Second, our past hurts could not be swept away that easily. We required a long, private conversation, probably several of them. And today there just wasn't time.

The human world had *so much* going on. I'd forgotten how many details needed attention, in civilization.

I was deluged with visitors. Besides the original group, several more troupe members had peeled themselves away from the Sevinee performances and dashed up for a visit. Healers kept cutting in to monitor, poke, or salve some part of my body, or to feed me. Wayshaw gave me my phone back, having switched on the voice-assist options, and I almost passed out at the backlog of messages. I talked and texted, catching up. It was wonderful and exhausting.

I opined I'd rather not have a beard anymore, and one of the healers gave me a clean shave via magic. My medical team had me get out of bed and hobble around to see how my legs and feet were doing, and to show me where everything was: sink, toilet, call button, water bottles, table of gifts. Learning these locations by touch was necessary, as I still essentially couldn't see. The eye bandage gave me a tiny improvement in perceiving hazy patches of light or color, but not much else. They removed the bandage and brought in an optometrist witch, who did tests and measurements, then left to make me a pair of enspelled glasses that were to be ready tomorrow.

Though everyone could tell I was falling asleep where I sat by seven o'clock that evening, I begged them not to leave. Someone had to stay with me all night. Javier and Ayda jumped in as volunteers.

While I lay drowsy and cozy, tucked in, everyone else filed by to say goodnight. Vai ran their knuckles lightly across mine and promised, "I'll come back first thing in the morning."

"Bring my favorite doggie," I murmured. Truffle had snoozed on my lap for some of the afternoon, snuggled in a furry heap against me, and I was completely smitten.

"I will." Vai flicked back a lock of my hair from my temple. "I may also give you a haircut, if you'll let me."

"I will let no one else."

Then everyone left except Ayda, who took the first watch. She settled onto a rolling cot the hospital had brought in, beside my bed.

"I recall a couple nights like this," I said. "You in the hospital, back from the lair. Me staying next to you all night."

"I was so grateful." Her voice sounded choked, but I could hear a smile in it too. "You could've gone home those times."

"I didn't want to be home. Your house was more like home than mine was. You, your folks, the hundred guitars and drums."

"Whichever friendly musicians were living there that year."

"That was the life I wanted. You all made me feel welcome. Which..."

Ayda was quiet a few seconds. "Your aunt and uncle are worried sick about you. I think you've finally managed to make them feel guilty. Make them realize they love you."

"That wasn't why I did it."

"I know. But, handy side effect."

"It'll be nice to talk to them again. I mean that." I settled deeper into my bed. "Do you think...Vai will still want to be with me?"

Her scoff suggested it was a stupid question. "You two need to work that out yourselves. But if you'd seen how much they suffered, *pined...*"

My heart twisted into a poignant knot. I smiled, Fred's words from Rose Night returning to me. *About time! You could cut the pining with a chainsaw.* "We've both done a lot of pining."

"You're recovering," Ayda said. "Vai doesn't expect you to rush into anything."

"I want to do it right. Be in good shape for them." I traced my finger in a circle on the bedsheet. "I'm not used to thinking it's something I might actually be allowed to have. Vai. A proper relationship."

"Couldn't be a weirder prospect than Javi and me in a relationship. And check it out, we're still together."

"If you'd broken up while I was in there, after all I did so you two could stay together, I'd have to kick you both in the ass."

She laughed, full-throated.

"Tell me more about your year," I mumbled. "All the boring details. Lull me to sleep."

"Okay. For starters, we built some herb-growing boxes, for the courtyard behind the shop. It's a spot that gets shade a lot of the day, so I couldn't grow things that love sun, but luckily things like mint, dill, parsley, catnip all grow fine in the shade. Funny about the catnip, though, there are a couple of cats that roam around, and they sometimes get into the courtyard and start eating it..."

I wandered into a mellow dream somewhere around there.

Splendid—having someone else tell me a story, for a change.

VAI

The next morning, Truffle and I arrived at the hospital at 8:05 a.m. Javier waved to me from a waiting room chair and informed me his parents—Leo's aunt and uncle—were in with Leo at the moment.

"They got into town last night," Javier said. "Leo had already gone to sleep, so they came back this morning. Truffle, come here! Come here, sweet baby." His voice transformed into high-pitched affection as he addressed the dog.

I let go of her leash so she could trot over to him. "How is he?"

"He slept most of the night. I had the second shift." Pulling Truffle onto his lap, Javier yawned. "This morning he had *two* bowls of oatmeal and strawberries. And only one cup of coffee. Healthiest damn breakfast I've ever seen him eat."

That reassured me. I fixed myself a cup of green tea at the drink station.

I'd already learned that Leo's aunt and uncle had finally sent him a chantagram, with a message of amends, so I didn't yet worry how their conversation might be going. If we started to hear shouting, Javier and I could intervene.

But before I'd even finished my tea, Yubara and Luis emerged from Leo's room. Yubara beamed. "Vai! Lovely to see you."

I rose. "You too."

"Can't say I adore visiting Bahía Rosa—nothing much to *do* here—but for Leo we came."

I introduced myself to Luis, who shook my hand. "Happy occasion, huh?" he said. "Whew!"

They needed to be off, to check out of their hotel. "I expect we'll see you back in Tesoro," Yubara told me.

They ambled out, and Javier handed me Truffle's leash. "Go on in." He nodded toward Leo's room. "I'm going to take a nap." He and Ayda had a hotel room nearby too.

When I entered, Leo was standing by the window, wearing some of the clothes I'd brought him: soccer shorts and a turquoise T-shirt advertising a show Quicksand had put on seven years ago.

"You're up," I said.

"Hello." He smiled. "Yeah. They said it's good for my bones and muscles, to get walking around again." He ran his fingers along the windowsill. "When I stand here, I can see a little more light."

"It's a bright morning." He was bathed in sun. I wandered over with Truffle. "That was quick. The visit from your aunt and uncle."

His hands explored the window frames. "My family's not one for long-drawn-out heart-to-hearts. I bet they wouldn't even have mentioned their chantagram, if I hadn't brought it up."

I swallowed and looked down, my pulse thumping. "So you did get our last batch of messages."

"Yeah." He lifted his face into the sun. "Saw them all. Then lost them all, when I went blind and Nalibak hauled me across the ocean. Except this one." He stepped to the table containing his jumble of stuff. From inside his beat-up backpack, he drew out a chantagram—creased, flattened, and stained. When he held it up, I could just make out my own writing on it. "Kept it inside my shirt," he said. "Thank goodness. Or it would've gotten lost too."

"Oh."

He'd kept it close. Good sign—probably?

"I want to thank you for being honest." He came back to the windowsill and leaned his rear against it, turning the chantagram between his hands. "I want that between us, from now on. Honesty."

"So do I."

"When you said you were lonely…all I wanted was to escape and come fix it. Not that my being there would have necessarily fixed it—"

"It would have."

"Oh." The syllable carried surprised encouragement, and he paused. "I'm sorry, though. For not saying more. In my messages—and before that, when I was keeping things from you. I'm also sorry for using magical force against you. It's illegal, I know. I'll understand if you want to press charges."

It took me a couple of seconds to realize he meant putting me to sleep in the field, so I wouldn't interfere with Nalibak taking him. I puffed out a laugh. "No, you were right to stop me. Considering how it went when I did cross the verge."

"I'm glad you're all right. Or, more or less all right."

"I'm glad you are too." We were both leaning on the windowsill now, our shoulders almost touching.

Leo closed the distance, tipping aside. Our arms pressed together, and he rested his head on my shoulder. I leaned my temple against his sun-warmed hair. Truffle lay across one of my feet and one of Leo's, relaxing with a pleased snort.

There was too much to say. We needed more than a few stolen minutes between hospital visitors. If there was anything I'd learned from hanging out here yesterday, it was that a healer or a friend would be entering this room an average of once every six minutes.

"So you spoke to your aunt and uncle about their message?" I asked, retreating to a safer topic.

"Mm," he confirmed. "I thanked them. Said yes, I'm interested in becoming a happier family. I'll do my part, or at least try. Also..." He crouched to pet Truffle. She rolled onto her back, feet in the air. "They want me to come to their house in Tesoro when I'm discharged. Recuperate there for a bit. I agreed to."

I gazed down at the appealing scene of Leo scratching my puppy's belly. "That's good. Accepting the olive branch."

"Will you be going onward with the troupe? They're heading south now, I gather."

I gave it a few nonchalant seconds, as if I hadn't already decided to be wherever Leo was, for as long as he'd let me. "I have my place in Tesoro. I could go there. To be around, help with things. Only if you want."

"I'd love that." He took one of Truffle's forepaws, which she was waving in the air, and swung it lightly. "If it's what *you* want. Remember, we're being honest now."

"I want to be there."

Though he kept his face turned toward Truffle, I could see the curve of his cheek as he smiled. "Good."

Someone knocked on the open door. "Hey there. Got your glasses for you, Leo. Are you ready?"

The person's hospital ID tag read Marty Diniz, Optometry, They/Them. They were short, with dark hair in a topknot, and wore glasses with aqua frames. Marty got Leo seated, took out a pair of brown-framed glasses, and with a "Heeeere we go," slid them onto his face.

Leo cringed, blinked, then said, "Oh. *Whoa.*" Then he started laughing, the fragile laughter of someone possibly about to cry. He looked at his hand, at Marty, at the window, at Truffle—he squeaked in joy as she wagged her tail.

He looked at me.

"Oh," he repeated, smiling so wide he almost looked like his old self.

We just stared at each other, mesmerized, for several seconds.

"I love this part of my job," Marty remarked.

Leo pulled his gaze away and examined the rest of the room. "Am I forgetting what colors and lights look like? Or are they a little weird?"

"Remember I *am* half green," I said. "You're not seeing that wrong."

"No, I know." Leo laughed. "But the weirdness is everywhere."

"It's going to look a little weird," Marty confirmed. "The spell on the glasses is basically creating a picture for your optic nerve to send to your brain. It can look kind of like an image on a screen."

They discussed technical details, and Marty made adjustments to the lenses based on what Leo was seeing. Overall Marty declared the glasses a success, and told him to wear them "whenever you want to, you know, be able to see stuff." After promising to check in tomorrow, Marty congratulated Leo and strolled out.

Leo got up and approached the mirror over the sink. He and his reflection regarded each other. I joined him and met his gaze in the mirror.

"I haven't seen myself in a year," he said. "Not in proper daylight, in an actual mirror." He touched his clean-shaven, emaciated cheek, then threaded his fingers through his graying hair. "Oh, Leo, sweetheart. You've really taken a beating." His gaze moved to me. "I've, uh, had some conversations with myself in recent months. My mind might not be all there anymore."

"Nothing wrong with that. I imagine it's more pleasant to have a conversation with yourself than with Nalibak."

But it did darken my mood, the reminder that Leo was not simply going to spring back to the playful, vibrant person he'd been before. This past year would require processing, and its effects on his mental health might never entirely leave him.

Then again, couldn't I say the same? And: honesty between us, from now on. That would be the strongest tool we had against any of our ills.

Joyful noise in the corridor. A crowd burst into Leo's room. Squealing, Kornelia hugged Leo. Fred, Darius, and Mathilde dove in for their turns. Catarina stood near, beaming. They all babbled, explaining they had to return to Sevinee tonight, but had stolen the morning to come see him. He catalogued, upon their demand, all the things he was currently being treated for. Broken foot, almost healed now; infected knee and some other spots, doing better today; malnutrition, being battled with healthy food; blindness, hence the glasses; widespread joint inflammation and muscle loss, which was going to improve if he eased back into an active life rather than living cramped in a dark cave.

They wanted to talk more, but Leo held up his hands, spine straight, as if he were on stage insisting that an audience hush and listen.

"I have eaten this morning, but I have not yet showered," he said. "And I've been looking forward *avidly* to showering. Sit and make yourselves comfortable, or go get coffee and then come back, while I get clean. Then Vai will give me a haircut. *Then* we will speak further."

CHAPTER 40

LEO

A shower. In warm, running water. This was heaven. I'd kept reasonably clean during my year in the lair, but only via products that pulled away grime by magic. I hadn't properly washed my whole self, with warm, clean water, in a whole year.

I should have been thinking more about how my aunt and uncle were actually attempting to mend their relationship with me. And how the glasses restored enough vision that I could almost function the way I used to, though it would take lifestyle adjustments and regular witch-optometrist visits. And how the unanimous message from Quicksand had been, "Come back whenever you're ready," so work was sorted, but still something to decide on, regarding timing. And how the healers had recommended I see a medical professional every month for the first year, sooner if I developed any weird symptoms, and once every six months for the following year and maybe the rest of my life. Ideally a mental health counselor too.

And I should think about Vai.

How Vai's green half had taken only a minute to get used to when I got my vision back, because their breathtaking beauty was still one hundred percent intact. How they'd kept their hair longer, in a low ponytail, with strands of dark brown and teal swinging around their jawline. How they looked at me the way they always had, with that quiet, level gaze, but how their face now also held a fragile hope and happiness. How we needed to talk, and decode in plain language what all our shared silences meant.

But. All of that was deeply stressful to think about. So: running water! Showers! The most blissful invention. How had I ever taken them for granted?

My old self—my despairing self—was all set to take over. He said, *Just show everyone what they want to see. Don't ask for things, don't be a burden, help wherever you can, and for gods' sake, be funny and charming. Smile!*

My mature self, though, who had stepped up to tell people that I aimed to be honest going forward, had a different message. *Yes, there's a lot to deal with. Some of it's going to be uncomfortable. But if you take it one step at a time, and bring love and honesty with you, you'll end up at the best possible outcome that was ever on offer for you anyway.*

So that was how I did it. The next two days consisted of talking to healers and loved ones, and bringing myself bit by bit back into the human realm. Vai cut my hair, using magic to enact a cool choppy style with an undercut. I also took Vai up on their suggestion to change my glasses frames from brown to purplish-black. The color suited me better.

The hospital discharged me after three days. Javier and Ayda gave Vai, Truffle, and me a ride back to Tesoro. Wayshaw bade farewell to us for the season and took the caravan south to rejoin Quicksand. In Tesoro, Yubara and Luis set me up in my old bedroom, with clean sheets and trays of coffee and food, and the window open to let in the fresh air.

Vai's sister Daphne was my new primary healer. I liked this arrangement not only because Daphne's skills were top-notch, but because Vai volunteered to give me rides to my appointments in their Mercedes. The main draw, of course, was spending time with Vai, but I admitted out loud the Mercedes made me feel like a swanky celebrity.

"Which is good for your healing," Vai agreed.

My healing did have to take center stage. Not wrecking myself was my new priority in life. Ayda often came by to hang out with me, bringing herbal remedies, all of which were vetted by Daphne.

When she brought the first batch, Yubara said, "Please email me your detailed instructions for these, and I will make sure he follows them. I trust you implicitly. You do excellent work." She paused, then added, "That shade of green is attractive on you. Quite becoming."

Ayda and I waited for the additional remark, the one that would spin the compliment backhanded. It didn't come. Ayda stammered a thanks. Yubara smiled and left us alone in the living room.

Ayda turned wide eyes to me. "Whoa."

"Am I hallucinating or did I just hear that?" I asked in a whisper.

"We both heard it," she whispered back.

Healing magic was a marvelous thing. After just a week, I had regained some weight, had more color in my face, and felt stronger, less achy, and more focused. One of the main directives Daphne gave me was to get my body moving again. Vai, to my pleasure, was quick to accept my invitation to go for daily walks, during which we often paused at some scenic spot to do yoga stretches.

On those outings, taken all over the Tesoro area during that beautiful June, we laid the groundwork of honesty. We started by talking about the "cursed year" we'd each undergone—more than a year in total really, encompassing the magical amnesia of Vai's family, then their friction with each other later; and my taking on Ayda's deal, then serving out the sentence in the lair.

Vai told me about their day and night in the fae realm, and the algae spell. It would be funny if Quicksand did it as a sketch, Vai insisted. Though I ached at the wild grief that must have propelled them into such danger, I said I'd had the same thoughts about my sun-blindness episode, and about nearly every conversation between Nalibak and me. So much nonsense it was actually comedic. Or could be played that way.

"But not all of it was funny," I admitted. We were walking a trail that led from Tesoro toward the sea, winding between meadows and houses. "I felt... low, a lot of the time. Depressed. With no real options except waiting it out, knowing I might not survive. Sometimes my anxiety went full Godzilla mode—worrying about my health, or whether you all were okay. The worst was when I saw London. She was dying, and Charles was out there with the rest of you, and there was nothing I could do. That was how I ended up accidentally taking too much of Ayda's happy trippy bars and staring at the sun. That plus a merperson spell. Got confusing around there, I'm not sure."

Our trail was descending a hillside dotted with wildflowers, and Vai stopped to wind the vine of a white sweet pea around their finger. "That was the worst for me too. The day they found London."

"It had to be horrible. I'm so sorry you saw that."

I'd heard the short version. London had gone missing, and one day a sylph had shown up, bearing news. They'd led Vai to the verge, where another faery brought out London's body, drained of life by Tagasath. I had not asked for further details. I hadn't wanted them, and I suspected nobody who'd been there that day was eager to relive them.

"I thought it was you who had died," Vai said, face lowered. "For a few hours there. The message the faery brought was...not clear. I don't know if anyone told you that part."

Chills shocked through me. "No. I didn't hear. Oh, fuck, Vai."

They were still winding the stem around their finger. A white blossom fell off. The aloof, sweet smell of crushed flowers flickered through the breeze. "We were originally looking for news of you. The sylph heard about a human killed by a fair feaster, and the identities got mixed up somehow. I sat by the verge for almost four hours, waiting for them to bring the body. Thinking the whole time it was you." Drawing a shaky breath, they dropped the flowers. "I still feel awful. For being so *relieved* when I realized it was London instead."

"Vai." I moved forward and hugged them from the side, my breath tripping on a sob.

Vai turned and wrapped their arms around me, fitting us closer. "Missing you was hard enough." I'd never heard their voice so strained. "But thinking you were dead..."

I held them tighter, fiercely, as if to convince them of my vitality. "I'm sorry."

"I know I was...petulant...in the last chantagram. But that was before they brought London out. You can forget I said any of it, if you like. I'm just glad you're alive." They pulled away and wiped their eyes on their sleeve.

I wiped mine too, sniffling. "How could I forget? No, listen." I looked out to the hazy blue line of the sea, my heartbeat erratic. Were we doing this now? "I do want to talk. I just didn't want to dive in first thing, put you on the spot. I want to be considerate of you this time."

Vai took a tissue from their pocket and blew their nose. "I'm going to be more careful with you too. After everything you've been through."

"No, don't worry about—" I stopped and shook my head. "I need to learn not to reject it, when people want to treat me kindly." I straightened up, meeting their gaze. "Thank you. That would be nice."

We walked on. The sun grew hot as the morning advanced, and when we reached an oak with wide green branches, I wandered into its shade, sat on the ground between its mossy roots, and patted the spot next to me. Vai sat.

Lady, send me confidence and luck. I inhaled a deep breath and began.

"To answer what you said in your chantagram: I still love you too. I wanted to say it the minute I realized you were really there next to me, in the hospital, but...everyone was around, and...I didn't know if you felt the same anymore."

"I do." Vai spoke without hesitation, gaze on the ground.

"There were two things I needed to stay alive for. Two things to come back and communicate. That was the main one. The other was warning people about Charles. But it turns out everyone already knew about him. So."

"So you *finally* told me the main one." Now they sounded wry.

"I'm sorry. I didn't mean to leave you in suspense. I wanted to get my feet under me, see who we both are, now that our curses are behind us."

"And..."

I leaned into Vai's side. "And I'd like to date you properly, if the offer still stands. If it doesn't, it's all right." My pounding heart informed me I was breaking our agreement of honesty with that statement. It would not be all right even a little.

Vai looked at me, eyes still red around the edges. "After everything, you really think I might say no?"

My nerves began giving way to bedazzlement. "Guess I still have to work on valuing myself more highly."

"You do." They pulled my hand onto their knee, encasing it between their palms. "I'm sorry too. I used spring equinox and Rose Night as excuses to be intimate with you, letting you think it was casual, without telling you my feelings until later. That was dishonest."

"But I did the same. And worse. The dishonesty on my part was *vast*." I locked my fingers between Vai's. "I did so many things wrong."

"The main thing you did wrong was not telling me the whole story. You didn't let me know you fully."

"Well, of course not, because if you knew me fully..." I felt the sting at the bridge of my nose again. "You wouldn't have loved me."

Vai stroked their thumb along mine. "I know you fully now. And I love you more than ever."

That was the kind of statement upon which you had to sway over and lean your forehead on your beloved's temple. So I did. "I love you," I whispered. "I'm so glad I'm not saying that as part of a goodbye this time."

Vai turned their face and kissed me, light and lingering, on the lips. "Hello."

I kissed them back, savoring it. The smell of mossy oak and sweet pea flowers would render me dreamy for the rest of my life, I already knew it.

Vai cleared their throat. "That is, if I do know you fully. Is there anything else you should tell me?"

"Hmm." I pulled free and straightened my glasses. "Okay. It's time I come clean. I lead a band of highly trained top-secret assassins."

"Oh. Do you."

"We've been responsible for coups d'état in five different countries. Hundreds have died by our blades. We are swift, brutal, and merciless."

"I see."

"Foreign agencies such as the CIA and MI6 know me only as the Blue-Ringed Octopus. Because I am one of Earth's deadliest creatures."

"Mm-hm."

"They've never caught any of us. There's a price on my head of—"

Vai planted a hand on my face and pushed me back into the dirt.

Their mouth smothered my grin. The warm weight of their body settled onto mine. Kisses, and kisses, and kisses.

They stroked my flushed cheek. "Do you believe it now? That I care about you. That we all do. That was the other central thing you did wrong—not believing."

"I'm trying," I said. "I'm...closer to it."

"Will it help if I remind you every day?" Vai brushed my lips with another kiss.

"Wouldn't hurt."

"Will it help if I show you?"

"Oh. *That* sounds illicit. I love that."

They pinned me down for another half a minute, kissing me, then helped me up. "We're in public. And you need to recover."

I took their hand as we ambled back to the path. "You're planning activities that are strenuous enough to damage my recovery? Goodness. I feel faint."

"No—I just mean there's no rush." Their face was flushed, but they were smiling.

"You should text your sister, to check. 'Hey Daphne, medical question: is it okay for Leo to have sex?' I don't think she'll suspect why you're asking."

"Stop," Vai laughed.

They drove me home. We lingered at the curb in the Mercedes, kissing for a few minutes, before I dragged myself away and walked to the house.

When I entered, Yubara looked up from her seat by the breakfast nook window. Clothing design sketches were strewn across the table. "Glad you finally snapped up Vai," she said. "I would've had a stern talk with you if you'd neglected to act on that."

Voyeurs, honestly. Around me my whole life.

In the old days I might have given a smart-ass retort. A few lines did occur to me. But we were at peace now, Aunt Yubara and I; and besides, in this matter we were also in full agreement. So I swept her a stage bow, with the grateful smile I gave every audience, and sauntered away.

CHAPTER 41

VAI

I had Leo back. My life was suffused with joy. Also I was rediscovering how impatient I could be: I wanted him with me all the time, and even while treating him delicately, I was finding every excuse to touch him, pull him close, steal kisses. To be fair, he was doing the same right back.

"Dancing counts as good exercise," he suggested on a walk. Which led, within sixty seconds, to us drawing up tight together so we could move through tango steps, in Ninfea Park, as "El Tango de Roxanne" from *Moulin Rouge* played from my phone.

After that, we bought ice cream from a cart, relaxed in the shade, and dissected our family dynamics.

"I don't know if we'll ever heal," I said, of the relationship between me, my father, and my uncle. "That might be all right. I can learn to be without them. But it feels like having led two lives, one before all this, and one after."

Leo felt the same, with pre- and post-lair, and not just because of what the lair conditions themselves had done to him. "Things are definitely better now with Yubara and Luis," he said, lying on his back, his head on my thigh. His empty ice cream cup sat beside him. "But we've said the important things, and I worry if we hang out together too long under the same roof, we'll lapse back into our old ways."

I scooped up some of my chai-coconut ice cream and offered it to him. He leaned up and ate it. "Too early to return to Quicksand, though?" I asked.

"Daphne wants me to stick around for appointments for another few weeks at least. I'd prefer it—keeping her as my healer while I can."

I pushed ice cream into my mouth to make sure I wasn't overly impulsive with my next words. After I swallowed, I said, "If you want…I do have a spare bedroom in my apartment. No pressure, though."

Leo bounded upright, beaming. "Yes! I do want. I was angling for that, to be honest. But I didn't think I should just invite myself into living with you."

"I invited myself into living with you during our first conversation. We then lived together for six months, in much tighter quarters than my apartment."

"Well, when you put it like that." Leo leaned in and kissed me, sweet and chai-spiced.

So he moved into my apartment. He got his own bedroom, so as to have autonomy and not feel like he was under any relationship-based obligations. We were roommates, as before. Yet we were also in a delicious new limbo, because this time we were dating. We got to kiss, hold hands, and reminisce about flirtatious episodes from the months we'd shared the caravan. And Rose Night loomed in our history, something neither of us could possibly forget.

Four days after he'd moved in, we were squished together on the sofa, popcorn and afternoon tea on the coffee table. A streaming service waited on the screen, its menu hanging neglected while, instead of picking something to watch, we kept up our latest conversation.

"Not even a slow dance with a fada?" I asked. "For Nalibak's entertainment? I'd forgive you."

"No," he laughed. "Nothing. Nalibak hardly let anyone near, and anyway, it's not like I wanted to get *more* enchantment damage. I was a proper celibate monk the whole year. But you—really, you didn't even go to coffee with anyone?"

"Charles," I said dryly. "And Catarina. Troupe folk. But no, never as a date. I was holding out for you."

"I hope you weren't miserable the entire time." Leo set his hand on my thigh and kneaded it. "Were there ever, at least, moments where you remembered Rose Night and got just a bit turned on?"

We hadn't spoken much about that yet, and a tingle sparked to life, low in my belly.

"No." I let the word hang in the air a second before adding, "There were *lots* of moments when I remembered Rose Night and got *deeply* turned on."

The worry cleared from Leo's eyes in a starburst of delight. "*Were* there."

"And you? I suppose, in the lair, it's not likely..."

"The lair is an unsexy place. But..." He uncurled a sideways smile at me. "Dreams can be evocative things. So can daydreams, even. There were a few times." He squeezed my leg again. "And lately I'm finding it's hard to think of anything else."

I casually set the remote on the coffee table and slanted across him to apply my mouth to his neck.

We lost the afternoon in one of those mesmerizing conversations where we confessed things we found hot, about each other or about intimacy in general. We weren't even doing much besides talking, squashed together on the sofa, kissing and trailing our hands up and down each other. Sometimes pouncing and grinding a little.

I was feral with need after a time, my hands and legs locking Leo where I wanted him. Leo's mouth had become hot, his body supple and clinging, beneath me on the sofa.

Truffle snoozed, oblivious, lying like a pile of rags against the wall.

Leo's glasses had been relegated to the coffee table—lately his vision had recovered enough to discern more gradations of light and movement, so at home he felt safe without them.

"If there's one image that turned me on the fastest," he murmured, "it's being on my knees for you, in the stockings and sequins, on the hard floor, with you pulling my hair. *Gods*." He laughed. "Why am I like this?"

Everything in me ratcheted up to a sizzling level, but I kissed him softly. "I liked it too. But things like that, making you hurt, now that you've been through so much pain…I don't know if I could do it."

"I did wonder, at the start, if having a masochism kink would be a benefit in the lair. But, no, the fair feaster variety of suffering turned out not to be sexy." He wriggled his spine, moving against me in an imploring way. "Circumstances are different now, though. When it's you, and we're here, and you're gonna give me cookies afterward…then I do want it."

I laced my fingers into his. "You'd stop me? If there's anything that's not appealing. Say the word 'unsexy.'"

"Good safeword. I will." He sounded breathless, his gaze fixed on my face. As if awaiting instructions.

My heart was beating in my throat. I took his wrists, secured them in one hand, and pressed them above his head, into the sofa cushion. He swallowed, a visible bob in his throat. "You only get cookies afterward," I said, "if you're good."

He grinned, but tamped it down a second later and nodded. "I know I haven't been good. But I will be."

I ran a fingertip down his side, from shoulder to thigh. "You think there's something I should punish you for? What's that?"

"For how I treated you. How this whole past year and a half went. For the way I am."

"The way you *were*. You're going to be better now."

"Yes. I'll be better."

"Hmm." I made sure to sound skeptical. Then I pulled back, stood, and said, "Get up."

Leo stood too, moving carefully in his near-blindness.

"Take your clothes off," I said.

His inhale was ragged. "All of them?"

"All."

He smiled again, but kept quiet. His shirt, socks, trousers, and underwear slid to the floor. He stood before me naked, his many tattoos linked up, a familiar work of art. Compared to the last time I'd seen him fully unclothed, more than a year ago, he was still much too thin, but it only filled me with fondness and the determination to keep taking care of him and feeding him. He was also already hard. As was I—which he must have known, given our close position a minute ago.

Still dressed, I walked around to his back and drew his arms behind him to hold his wrists together. Lightly enough he could yank free if he disliked it. I waited a moment, but he stayed like that. "Walk forward," I said. "I'll guide you."

I hadn't had time to script this, nor even come up with a scenario. This was only a bit of improv. Whatever I ended up choosing, it wouldn't take long for either of us.

Steering him slowly, I guided him into my bedroom. After whisking back the blankets, I hopped onto the bed, sat with my back against the headboard, and told him, "Come here. Sit against me, between my legs."

Leo felt his way to the bed, climbed on, and scooted back, nude against my clothed body. I could feel him trembling. "Is that good?" he asked.

"Very." I slid my arms around his chest, circled his nipple with my thumb, then pinched it. He tipped his head back, panting. "You turned my life upside down," I said in his ear. "How dare you? From the first time I saw you on stage,

I became obsessed. I had to know you. Get inside your caravan."

"I let you stay. Wasn't that nice of me?"

I moved to the other nipple to play with that one, and he groaned. "It only pulled my life apart more. You flirted. Teased. Touched me. You were *trying* to drive me crazy."

"I wasn't," he begged, lifting his hips, but I wouldn't touch there yet. "I didn't think you cared. I wanted you. I…couldn't resist, when you let me get close."

"You let me close, all right." I slid both hands down to his hipbones, fingers curling into the soft insides of his thighs. "Took me to bed. Made me love you. How was I ever going to be the same after that?"

"I'm sorry." He shut his eyes, brows pulling together. "You can have anything you want." He strained his hips up again.

"You'll treat yourself better from now on?" I said, stern. "You'll be whole, and healthy, and open?"

"*So* open," he said, a laugh in his voice, unable to resist a double entendre even now.

I smiled. "We'll look into that next time. I'm too impatient today. As are you." I finally closed a hand around him, and the breath rushed out of his mouth. With the other hand, I snagged the lube I'd placed nearby, smeared it on both palms, and began massaging him in long strokes.

He dropped his head back on my shoulder, breathing hard, draping an arm up around me. "But," he tried to protest, "I want to take care of you first."

I was throbbing, my jeans confining me tight, but I kept caressing him. "Too bad," I said. "This is how I want you."

"I can't…" He was moving up into my strokes, in a rhythm. "It's too…"

"Yes." I bit his ear, just hard enough to sting.

That was all it took. Heat flooded my hands, and he arched up in my arms, shuddering over and over. Then he draped down against me, catching his breath. "Oh. I have *missed* you."

I nuzzled the ear I had bitten, soothing it with kisses. "I love what you've done to my life. Thank you."

After letting me wipe him down with tissues, he twisted around to face me and spread his hands across my middle. "What shall I do for you?"

"Anything." I undid my jeans, shoved them down. "Just…"

He slid lower and mercilessly got to work with mouth and hand both.

The urgency after waiting so long, and the illicitness of it—being barely undressed, while he was completely nude and servicing me—were no match for me. He brought me off in no time, while I clutched at the sheets, panting.

Then he rested his cheek on my bare hip, petting my skin. "I should get my glasses," he mused. "Want to see you like this."

"I can get them," I mumbled.

"No, no. I'm able. Don't move." Feeling down to the floor with bare feet, then with hands outstretched to the door frame, he made his way into the hall.

I heard the flapping sound of the dog shaking herself. Leo chirped, "Hi Truffle! You're up from your nap. Yes, I'm naked, I know, very strange. Oh no, are we going to traumatize you?"

"She's a dog, Leo," I called. "They stick their faces in each other's rears upon first acquaintance."

"True. Vai's always right. Aren't they, Truffle?"

Leo returned, wearing glasses, underwear, and T-shirt, which he apparently considered being sufficiently dressed to not scandalize the dog. I blushed when he paused beside the bed to regard me. In line with his request, I was still bare from lower ribs to mid-thighs, and disheveled all over.

He breathed a blissful sigh and crawled into bed. We lay there in a drowsy embrace.

"Did you ever figure it out?" he asked. "What drew you to me, all those years ago."

"I think…it was partly that I could've been you, if I'd been braver. If I'd pursued dancing, costuming, theatre, having fun. Instead of knuckling under to what I thought my family wanted."

"That makes sense," he said. "But that could apply to anyone in the troupe. Not just me."

"I suppose I can admit now that I found you extremely cute. Of the whole troupe."

"Nooo." He paused. "Or. Okay. I'll try to accept that possibility."

"Also…maybe I'm just projecting this thought backward, now that I know you. But there was something about your expressions, and the way you acted, in drama versus comedy…I got the impression you might be troubled. Sad.

Like maybe you needed someone like me. A friend who cared and understood. But again I could be projecting, because I also wanted to be cared about and understood, and I wanted it to be you doing that—this popular, vibrant actor. Because that would prove I was more than what people saw. Different than the role I played in my family. Or something." I rubbed my forehead. "Help. I'm monologuing."

"You are. You never monologue! I'm fascinated." Leo resettled his ear on my shoulder. "You were right. We did need each other."

"We did." I tightened my embrace.

"And you say *Charles* first brought you to a Quicksand show? I hate to owe him anything, but—"

"It was quite the silver lining. In the 'having to know Charles' situation."

Leo hummed a pensive sound.

After a few minutes he popped up on his elbows. "Okay. Topic change. Since you seem down to try it, I have several role-play scenarios in my head. Can we go over them?"

CHAPTER 42

LEO

One could say we owed our getting together not only to Charles but to Walda Portnoff, former Member of Parliament, whose corruption, through a twisted path, sent Vai fleeing to my caravan. She, we were vindictively happy to hear, was convicted for her crimes and given a prison sentence. The fair and magical nation of Eidolonia would be unlikely to see her run for office ever again.

The investigations related to her crimes continued. Unsavory rocks were overturned, and Humanist Party creatures lurking beneath them were dragged out. These investigations led to two developments of particular interest to us.

One: elections were approaching to replace Portnoff's seat, which had been temporarily held by a subordinate of hers, and the current frontrunner for the office was Hazuki Baluyot—grassroots activist, black belt in kung fu, and Daphne's lover.

Two: the lawfolk located and arrested Charles Christopher.

He had never left the island. He'd been staying near Dasdemir with an exo-witch in the Humanist Party, who was changing Charles's appearance. This exo-witch was one of the recipients of Charles's cash-from-America scheme, and was also tied into the bribes that facilitated Portnoff's election fraud. Once the law finally tracked him down, it wasn't long before they learned he was sheltering Charles.

Why hadn't Charles just left? Gone back to the U.S.?

"I love Eidolonia too much to leave," Charles said, in the one brief statement he gave the press after his arrest. "Everything I've done has stemmed from my love of this island."

Which of course sounded like unmitigated nonsense, and Quicksand took all of about three and a half hours to incorporate his quote into their next round of sketches. (Vai and I hadn't returned to the troupe yet, but we gleefully watched their shows via livestream or recordings whenever possible.)

"But in a way," I told Vai, "he's like Nalibak. I don't know if Nalibak can love, but he *likes* humans so much that he wants to keep one of us near whenever he can. Even though it means torturing us. They're both insane, by our standards, but..."

"Not by their own," Vai finished.

Charles was being held in Tesoro until his trial. It was almost inevitable he'd be convicted and imprisoned.

About a week after his arrest, Daphne got a call. He had requested to talk to her. In person, if she consented.

Hazuki, Vai, and I came with her. I'd never visited anyone in prison before. Charles sat in a little room at a table, waiting. The jail officials only let Daphne into the room, which was fine with the rest of us. We didn't particularly wish to speak to him. But we were allowed to stand in an adjoining room that looked in on the interview room through a window. It wasn't even one-way glass—he could see us, the official told us, but he couldn't hear us. We, however, could hear him, thanks to a speaker that the official switched on in our space.

Charles glanced at us, then lowered his eyes. He looked tired, hair limp, mouth sagging. He wore a checked shirt and soft trousers. Unlike in his native country, Eidolonia let prisoners wear their own clothes, but that was because our lawfolk also had them wear enspelled metal cuffs to keep them from acting out. He folded his hands on the table, and I spotted the dark line of the cuffs peeking from his sleeves.

Daphne entered and sat opposite him. They exchanged stilted greetings.

Then Charles told her, his gaze turned down to his interlaced fingers, "I wanted you to know it was always true, that I loved you. I still do. I was never, ever going to hurt you, or anyone in your family." His gaze flicked to us, in the window. "Not even Vai. Who made things public that were a problem for me. Because I knew you would be devastated if anything happened to your sibling."

"Hazuki, though?" Daphne asked after a moment.

He looked down again. "You can't expect me to be happy that you love someone else."

She waited, we all waited, for further reassurance that he had never considered having Hazuki killed, but it didn't come. All he said was, "Anyway, you can rest easy. There's nothing I can do now. I want you to be happy."

"I wanted that for you too." She sounded sad. "When I met you, in the States, you seemed...kind, and forlorn. And you were willing to trust me and come to Eidolonia. I thought I was giving you a better life."

"Of course you were! I was telling the truth when I said I loved Eidolonia. The day you brought me here, I was so in love I couldn't breathe. With you and with this island. All I wanted from that moment on was to live here forever. Yes, with you, but—even if you didn't feel the same, being here was *far* better than my life in America." He spat a bitter laugh. "You met my family. I wasn't loved or respected. I had no real friends, just—people who lived near me. Everyone was shallow, judgmental. You were this goddess arriving out of nowhere, whisking me away to the enchanted land."

"Then why betray so many of us?"

"Because it didn't work out here, either, did it? I wanted to be treated as an equal, but I was only ever a nonmagical crosswater. A pet who was supposed to be dazzled by everyone's powers. Which I was, but...I was never going to belong. Only the Humanist Party valued ordinary people like me. They were the only ones who took me seriously."

"They were using you," Daphne reminded him. "For your ability to get money from America."

"Well. At least I had value to *someone*. To the rest of you, I didn't matter. No matter how long I lived here, I was always going to be on the outside, looking in. You can't understand what that's like." He raked his glance across us in the window again. "Golden native children. Born into magic, loved and cared for. You all think you've been so isolated and powerless. You have no idea."

Vai growled, and I laid a hand on their back to soothe them. My sweetheart probably wanted to storm in there and remind Charles exactly what the rest of us had been through, especially me.

But I honestly wasn't even thinking of myself, nor my friends. I was too morbidly fascinated with Charles's performance. How much of this villain speech did he truly believe? Or was it all manipulation?

"I'm sorry it went this way," Daphne said. "I'm sorry I didn't understand."

Hazuki snorted. "Meaning, sorry I didn't see earlier what you're really like, or I would never have brought you here," she said, and Vai grunted in agreement.

Charles didn't seem to pick up on that interpretation. "I knew early on I wasn't worthy of you," he said. "I just held on to hope regardless."

At that, I did think of myself—a twist in my belly reminding me of all the times I had dodged the hard relationship work by just declaring I wasn't worthy of Vai. In penitence, I leaned against them. Vai wrapped an arm around me.

Daphne and Charles didn't have much else to say. They concluded their visit, and Daphne came out, pale but resigned. We embraced her and took her away.

That was the last time any of us saw him.

After getting Daphne's go-ahead regarding my health in late August, Vai and I sublet the Tesoro apartment and, Truffle in tow, rejoined the Quicksand Theatre Company. We took the train to Kikenna Bay to meet the troupe. Not only was Wayshaw waiting for us with the caravan, but so were as many troupe members as could fit in Kornelia's caravan, greeting us at the station with garish hats, glowing bubbles, and noisemakers. It was embarrassing and ridiculous, and made me laugh harder than anything had in ages. Gods, I loved my co-workers.

I worked only part-time hours at first, easing back into the performing-arts life. A couple of my hospital visitors had been journalists, originally there to gather my account of seeing London in the fae realm, but they then asked further questions about what I was doing in a fair feaster lair in the first place, and recorded my saga. An uplifting human-interest piece, after the tragedy of Charles and London. I'd declined further interviews, but the scattering of emails I'd gotten from Quicksand fans told me they would welcome my return.

I made my debut that year in September, in Port Baleia, in a sketch in which I played myself, and Genevieve played an eccentric news host interviewing me about my ordeal, with questions as pointless and absurd as any Nalibak himself might have asked. ("When you were cruelly isolated in the lair, what heinously disgusting personal habit were you finally able to indulge?" "Locked away from humankind, what did you miss more: fondue or blowjobs?") The audience howled with laughter. The troupe made plans to keep this character of Genevieve's and think up other people they could interview.

I collaborated in creating humor, with people who understood human comedy. I watched in pleasure as Vai was given the job of choreographing a sketch involving ballroom dancing and pulled it off beautifully. I wandered, sat, and lay outdoors in the daylight whenever I could, even when it rained. I went to weekly therapy via video call. So did Vai, after a while, finally admitting they weren't perfect, and maybe needing to be perfect was in fact something to talk to a therapist about. I tried to make a point of enjoying every omelet and cup of coffee and fresh bunch of grapes. Everyone I talked to, I looked into their eyes, through my wonderful glasses, and reminded myself to be grateful for their presence.

Despite the occasional panic attack in the dark, or anxiety deluge out of nowhere, and despite Vai going through a few of those too, we were mostly all right. Any low mood I had on a gray afternoon got lifted to the sunniest heights merely by a troupe friend saying, "Where's your darling lover? I'm supposed to learn some dance steps." Vai was *my lover*. How could I continue to have a bad day after remembering that?

Catarina and June were still mutually enamored too. Whenever possible, June arranged her piano performances to take place near the city Quicksand would be in, and joined us for a week or two. And Catarina frequently took days off to go to wherever June was.

Charles's trial date was set for spring. Until then, he remained in prison. Tagasath may have done the actual killing, but given the amount of premeditation involved on Charles's part, he was being charged with murder. Three counts, one for each victim.

Then one day he disappeared.

The prisoners at his facility were kept busy with various jobs, one such job being to tend vegetables and nursery plants. Just after sunset one evening in October, as the prisoners were finishing their shift, Charles walked alone to the back wall of the garden to put away an armload of plant pots. Those who witnessed it said he lingered there a minute. Then a silent darkness swept down the wall from above, pouring over Charles and outward. Within seconds, it retreated again, pulling back up, leaving the gardens undamaged. Charles was gone.

Given the darkness veil, and Charles's history, it was almost a guarantee that a fair feaster had taken him. He may even have been expecting it. No one could say.

The lawfolk did their due diligence in searching for him but found nothing. Inquiries in the fae realm confirmed that some had seen a fair feaster fly past with a human, though no one seemed to know where they had ended up.

A couple of weeks later, Charles's body was found outside the verge, at the north of the island. He'd been drained of life, and of a fair amount of blood too.

Vai and I looked uneasily at each other for a long span after learning the news.

"Would Nalibak..." Vai asked, trailing off as if not daring to voice the question.

"I'm not sure," I answered, in honesty.

Did it disturb me, if he had? Taking into consideration everything I knew about Charles, and about Nalibak?

I wasn't sure about that either.

VAI

On a December evening in Amanecer, Nalibak emerged one last time.

It was a resting day. Leo and I were walking a seaside trail after dinner, braving the cold wind. The lights of houses twinkled a short distance away, enough to see by. But there was sufficient darkness, apparently, for a fair feaster to appear.

"Friends." His voice was too near for comfort, a drawn-out word, eager and cold.

Leo flinched and sucked in a breath.

I saw him then, in the shadows beside a pile of driftwood: white skin, spiky dark hair, glamoured outfit of light shirt and black trousers.

While I grabbed my phone, ready to flick the light on, Nalibak said, "I'll go away if you wish! It was our deal. I am aware."

"Yes, it was our deal," Leo snapped. He was shaking. "You can't be here."

"I come only to tell you a story. The tale of what happened to the betrayer, Charles. I, this time, can perform a story for you, my tart stinging nettle."

I paused, thumb ready to hit the light button.

Leo's hand tightened on my arm. "You killed him?" he asked Nalibak.

"Not I. Tagasath. She craved him from the beginning. Such dark, sticky longing ran in his veins. She invited me, when he sent word to her."

"How did he send word?" I demanded. "He was in prison."

"Raccoon fae. They crawl into the space where the locked-up humans care for plants. One spoke to Charles. A message, he sent to Tagasath, through this creature. 'Come, take me away, we can make another deal.'"

"Who did he offer? As the deal." My voice was shaking now too.

"He did not say. Perhaps he had not yet chosen. Tagasath fetched him, as he asked. But *she* had already chosen. As soon as she embraced him, she put him under thrall."

"He didn't carry the..." Leo's sentence trailed off. "No, I suppose if he knew she'd be taking him, he'd have ditched the St. John's wort beforehand."

A massive risk to take, for a chance at freedom. Or did Charles know it would be the end?

"He came willingly," Nalibak crooned. "How he smiled. How he held her. 'A magical Eidolonian loves me and desires me,' he said. 'This is all I wanted.' I can lie, you know, but he did say this. He did taste of joy. Of comfort. As people under the thrall often do."

Leo and I exchanged a glance. Likely we were both remembering Charles's bitter confession. How he only wanted his love for the island and its people to be reciprocated.

"She did not make him suffer long," Nalibak continued. "She kept his adoration running juicy and fresh for as many a day as she could. Then, when he waned, she finished it quickly. His reward. You see? For bringing treats to her. She gave him a happy death."

The waves crashed. The winter wind whistled in my ears.

"Thank you," Leo said. "For telling us. Also...thank you for keeping me alive, those last days in the lair."

"I thank you for that too," I said. "Truly." It felt absurd, to be thanking the fair feaster who had made our lives a nightmare for so long. Yet without Nalibak's final contribution of healing, Leo probably wouldn't be here.

Nalibak made a dry purring sound in response, his unblinking eyes fixed on us.

"And now," Leo added, "yeah, please do leave us alone and never come back, for the rest of our lives."

"This deal I respect," Nalibak answered, apparently taking no offense.

A breath later, there was nothing but the driftwood and the ocean and the winter darkness.

~

"*Yes,* it's too soon." Leo laughed as he said it, squinting in incredulity at Fred.

"Too soon," Kornelia piped up in agreement.

It was almost spring, and Quicksand was holding a planning meeting, all of us sitting in a Port Baleia community center auditorium. Genevieve led the meeting, standing before us with glasses on their nose and tablet in hand.

"Oh, come on," Fred defended. "We could call it *Thanks for the Serial Killer, America*!"

"We cannot do a 'quickest ever' version of the Charles Christopher story," Leo said. "We can't make that funny. No one can. Because it's too soon."

"Probably someone could in fifty years," Darius said, as if to console Fred for his idea.

"Definitely in a hundred," Shelini put in.

Fred sighed and flopped back in his chair. "Fine. Idea retracted."

"But what about the 'Leo in the lair' story?" Uwila asked. Everyone's eyes returned to Leo, sitting beside me. She added, to him, "You keep saying it'd be funny if we did it."

Resting his cheek on his knuckles, he flicked his gaze across all his friends. Then he shrugged, smiling. "If you think it's worth doing. I don't mind."

"Not too soon?" I asked him. I didn't want him sacrificing himself again, even just for comedy.

He shook his head. "I think it could help me heal. Besides, I didn't murder anyone, so that does make the humor easier."

I nudged his leg, gratified he was agreeing for the right reasons.

"I think it could be a full-length play," Kornelia remarked. "Not just a sketch."

"Yeah, it's a lot of material," Mathilde said.

"One rule, though," Leo added. "I do not play myself."

Genevieve scoffed. "Course not. Wouldn't be half as funny."

The group went on to debate whether Leo should play Nalibak instead, but he had no interest in that either. "I don't have to be in it," he said. "I'll be providing the facts. Collaborating on the writing."

"Directing, even?" Catarina suggested.

Leo looked at her, and after a moment he smiled. "Yeah, maybe."

"You'll really make it a comedy?" I asked him in an undertone, while the others buzzed with conversation.

"I'm definitely not going to write it as a tragedy. Nor even a drama." He wrinkled his nose at me, teasing.

I refused to be baited. "Maybe one of those comedies that has moments of genuine drama? That catch our emotions unexpectedly, between laughs?"

His gaze held mine. "Those are the best, aren't they?"

I twined our fingers together, brought up his hand and kissed it, then leaned against his shoulder as our friends went on planning the season.

Other stories of Eidolonia, available now:

Lava Red Feather Blue: the story of Ula Kana's dangerous return, and a reckless witch awakening Prince Larkin from his enchanted sleep.

Ballad for Jasmine Town: the story of the destruction of the town of Miryoku, and a summer romance that sprawls beyond the seasons and defies the borders of the verge.

Acknowledgments

Considering I handed over this book to my beta-reader team right before the 2024 US elections, an exceedingly distracting time in human history, I am more honored than ever that so many of you actually read the whole thing and sent me your notes. From the nothing-but-raves to the lots-of-critique, and everything in between (I recommend getting the whole spectrum of feedback styles on your beta team if possible), I needed and loved all the input on this wild story. Heather, Tracey, Jess, Kevin, Aaron, Rebecca, Remy, Jackye, Marcie, Jennifer, Melanie, Kit—I thank every one of you with sincerity and exuberant hugs! Also a shout-out to Addie for reading an early chapter, and for friendly texts and garden pictures along the way.

Michelle and Beau at Central Avenue Publishing, thank you so much for once again giving me a tremendous amount of your expert time and attention, and for making the process fun and friendly. I count myself lucky to be in this corner of the publishing industry! Coral, thank you for the gorgeous cover art, with which I am in love. And Annie, thank you so much for bringing to life the first official map of Eidolonia!

Jamie, Bianca, Jasmine, and Felicia, so many thanks for coming through with blurbs for this book! Writer friends who know what it's like in the marketing trenches are priceless. Can't wait to read more stories from all of you!

Many thanks to my husband and kids for accommodating my freelance writer/editor lifestyle, and for letting me drag us to several musicals and theatre shows—including of course *Moulin Rouge* when we were in NYC. I love you, and it is genuinely fun to live with you all.

Molly Ringle was one of the quiet, weird kids in school and is now one of the quiet, weird writers of the world. Though she made up occasional imaginary realms in her Oregon backyard while growing up, Eidolonia is her first full-fledged fictional country. Her previous novels are predominantly set in the Pacific Northwest and feature fae, goblins, ghosts, and Greek gods alongside regular humans. She lives in Seattle with her family, corgi, fragrance collection, and a lot of moss.

She is the author of *Persephone's Orchard, Underworld's Daughter, Immortal's Spring, The Goblins of Bellwater, Lava Red Feather Blue, Ballad for Jasmine Town, The Ghost Downstairs, Sage and King,* and *All the Better Part of Me.*